Before becoming a full-time writer, Simon Scarrow worked as a teacher, and for a while ran a Roman History programme taking parties of students to a number of ruins and museums across Britain. Having enjoyed the novels of Forester, Cornwell and O'Brian, and fired by the knowledge gleaned from his exploration of Roman sites, he decided to write what he wanted to read – military page-turners about the Roman army in the first century AD. His seven other action-packed novels featuring Macro and Cato, including *The Eagle in the Sand* and *Centurion*, are all available from Headline (for a full list of titles, see inside). He has also published with Headline the first two volumes of a quartet based on the lives of the Duke of Wellington and the Emperor Napoleon, *Young Bloods* and *The Generals*; the third volume, *Fire and Sword*, will be published in early 2009.

Simon Scarrow lives in Norfolk with his family.

For more information on Simon Scarrow and his novels, visit his website at: www.scarrow.co.uk

By Simon Scarrow and available from Headline

The *Roman* Series

Under the Eagle
The Eagle's Conquest
When the Eagle Hunts
The Eagle and the Wolves
The Eagle's Prey
The Eagle's Prophecy
The Eagle in the Sand
Centurion

The *Wellington and Napoleon* Quartet

Young Bloods
The Generals

THE EAGLE'S PROPHECY

SIMON SCARROW

headline

First published in 2005
by HEADLINE BOOK PUBLISHING

First published in paperback in 2006
by HEADLINE BOOK PUBLISHING

This paperback edition published in 2008
by HEADLINE PUBLISHING GROUP

8

ISBN 978 0 7553 5000 1

Typeset in Bembo by Avon DataSet Ltd,
Bidford-on-Avon, Warwickshire

Printed in the UK by CPI Mackays, Chatham, ME5 8TD

Headline's policy is to use papers that are natural, renewable and recyclable products and made from wood grown in sustainable forests. The logging and manufacturing processes are expected to conform to the environmental regulations of the country of origin.

HEADLINE PUBLISHING GROUP
An Hachette Livre UK Company
338 Euston Road
London NW1 3BH

www.headline.co.uk
www.hachettelivre.co.uk

This book is dedicated to my friend and neighbour Lawrence Coulton, who was killed in an accident while flying for the RAF as I was completing this novel.

Lawrence was one of those rare individuals with a wholly infectious sense of enjoyment. His company was a huge pleasure for everyone who had the privilege of knowing him.

A brief introduction to the Roman Navy

The Romans took to naval warfare reluctantly and it was not until the reign of Augustus (27 BC–AD 14) that they established a standing navy. The main strength was divided into two fleets, based at Misenum and Ravenna (where much of this novel is set).

Each fleet was commanded by a prefect. Previous naval experience was not a requirement and the post was largely administrative in nature.

Below the rank of prefect the huge influence of Greek naval practice on the imperial fleets is evident. The squadron commanders were called navarchs and had command of ten ships. Navarchs, like the centurions of the legions, were the senior officers on permanent tenure. If they wished, they could apply for transfer into a legion at the rank of centurion. The senior navarch in the fleet was known as the Navarchus Princeps, who functioned like the senior centurion of a legion, offering technical advice to the prefect when required.

The ships were commanded by trierarchs. Like the navarchs, they were promoted from the ranks and were responsible for the running of individual ships. However, their role did not correspond to that of a modern sea captain. They were in charge of the sailing of the ship, but in battle the senior officer was actually the centurion in charge of the ship's complement of marines. This is why I have used the Greek ranks in the novel, rather than offering a misleading equivalent in English.

As far as the ships go, the workhorse of the fleets was the trireme. Triremes measured about 35 metres in length and 6 metres across the beam, and each had a crew of 150 rowers and sailors as well as a century of marines. There were other classes of vessel that were correspondingly larger (quinquiremes), or smaller (biremes and liburnians) but all shared similar features and were designed primarily for swift manoeuvre in battle. As a result they were light in the water, not very seaworthy and horribly uncomfortable for journeys any longer than a couple of days.

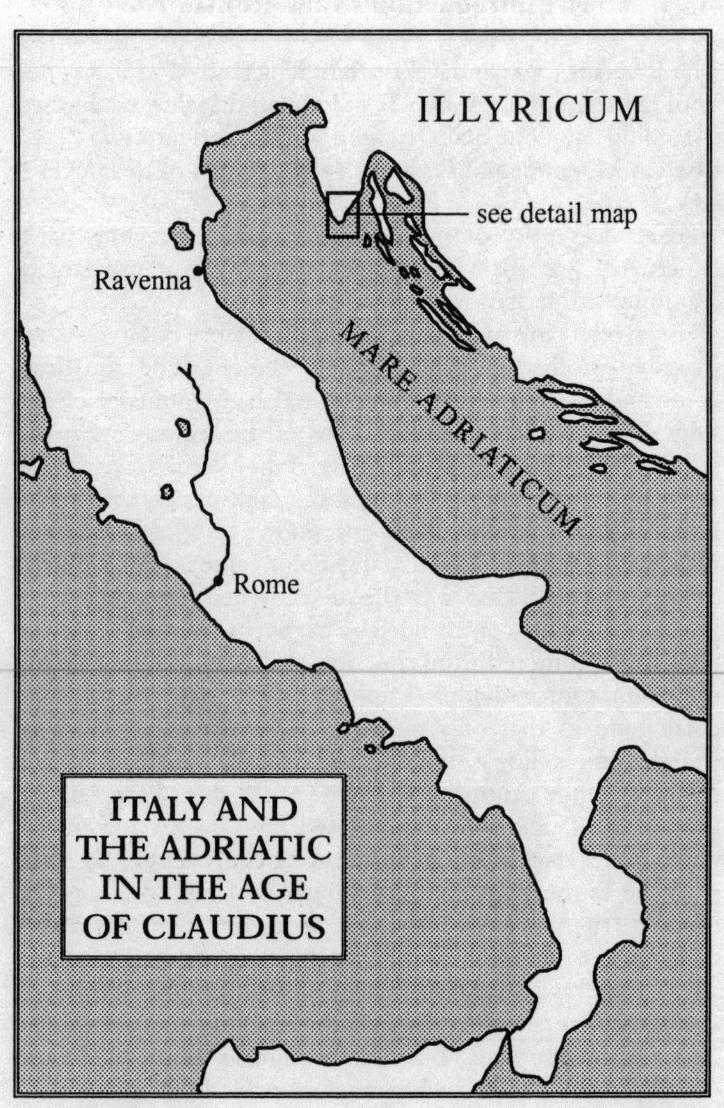
ILLYRICUM
see detail map
Ravenna
MARE ADRIATICUM
Rome
ITALY AND
THE ADRIATIC
IN THE AGE
OF CLAUDIUS

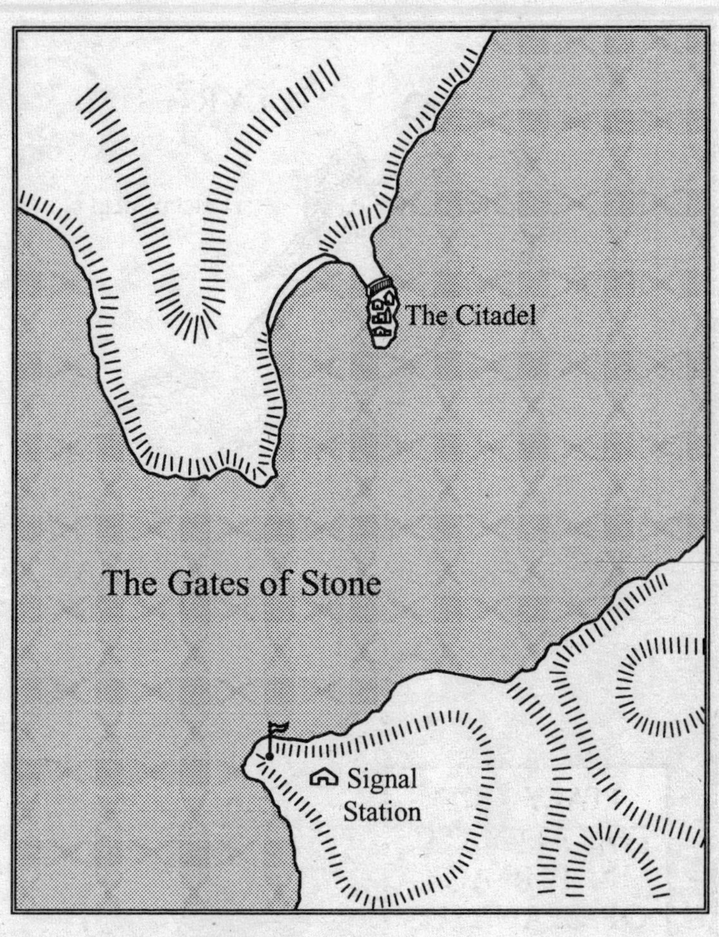
The Citadel
The Gates of Stone
Signal
Station

CHAPTER ONE

The three ships lifted as the gentle swell passed beneath their keels. From the high steering deck of the merchantman, the port of Ravenna was visible for a moment before the vessels slumped down into the trough. The merchantman was caught between two sleek liburnians, secured in place by several boarding hooks tethered to stout posts on the ships on either side. The pirates aboard the liburnians had shipped their oars and hastily dropped their mainsails before swarming aboard the merchantman. The assault had been hard-fought and bloody.

Proof of the fury of the attackers lay scattered upon the deck: the broken bodies of sailors, sprawled across dark smears of blood on the smooth, well-worn planking. In amongst them lay the corpses of over twenty of the pirates, and from the steering deck the captain of the larger liburnian frowned as he looked down on the scene. They had lost too many men taking the ship. Usually, the howling wave of armed men pouring over the side unnerved their victims so much that they dropped their weapons and surrendered at once. Not this time.

The crew of the merchant ship, together with a handful of passengers, had met the pirates right at the ship's rail and held them off with a gritty determination that the pirate captain could not recall seeing before – certainly not in the steady run of trading vessels he and his men had been preying on for the last few months. Armed with pikes, boathooks, belaying pins and a few swords, the defenders had held their ground as long as possible before they were forced back by superior numbers of better armed men.

Four of them in particular had drawn the pirate captain's eye: big, solid men in plain brown tunics, armed with short swords. They had fought to the end, back to back, around the base of the mast, and had killed a dozen pirates before they had been overwhelmed and cut down. The captain himself had killed the last of them, but not before the man had slashed open his thigh – a flesh wound, now tightly bound up, but still throbbing with a painful intensity.

The pirate captain made his way down on to the main deck. He stopped by the mast and prodded one of the four men with his boot, rolling the body on to its back. The man had a soldier's build and bore several scars. Like the others. Perhaps that explained their skill with the sword. He rose to his feet, still looking down at the dead Roman. A legionary then, as were the man's companions.

The captain frowned. What were legionaries doing on the merchantman? And not just any legionaries: these were hand-picked men – the best. Hardly casual passengers returning on leave from the east. No doubt they had organised and led the defence of the merchantman. And they had fought to the last drop of blood, with no thought of surrender. A shame, that, the captain reflected. He would have liked to offer them the chance to join his crews. Some men did. The rest were sold to slave-traders who asked no questions about the provenance of their property, and who were wise enough to ensure that the slaves were taken to market at the opposite end of the Empire. The legionaries would have been equally valuable as recruits or slaves, once their tongues had been cut out; a man would find it hard to complain about the injustice of his enslavement if he lacked a voice . . . But the soldiers were dead. They had died purposelessly, the captain decided. Unless they had been sworn to protect something, or somebody . . .

So what *were* they doing on the ship?

The pirate captain rubbed the dressing on his thigh and glanced round the deck. His men had thrown open the hatches of the cargo hold and were passing the more precious-looking pieces of cargo up on to the deck, where their comrades tore open the boxes and chests, scrabbling through the contents in search of valuables. More men were below decks, going through the possessions of the passengers, and dull thuds and splintering crashes sounded from beneath the planking.

The captain stepped over the bodies at the base of the mast and picked his way forward. Pressed into the bows were the survivors of the attack: a handful of sailors, mostly injured, and several passengers. They watched him warily as he approached. He nearly smiled as he saw one of the sailors trembling as he tried to edge away. The captain forced himself to keep his face devoid of expression. Below the dark, matted locks of his hair, piercing black eyes looked out from beneath a strong brow. His nose was broken and twisted, and knotted white scar tissue curved up across his chin, over his lips and up his cheek. His appearance had a wonderful effect on those that beheld him, but the injuries were not the marks of experience borne by a life-long pirate. Rather, they had been with him since childhood when his parents had dumped him as an infant in the slums of Piraeus, and he had long since forgotten the cause of his hideous scarring. The passengers and crew of the merchantman wilted before him as the pirate halted a sword's length away and ran his dark eyes over them.

'I am Telemachus, the leader of these pirates,' he said in Greek to the terrified sailors. 'Where is your captain?'

There came no reply, just the nervous breathing of men facing a cruel and imminent fate. The pirate captain's eyes never left them as his hand reached down and slowly drew his falcata.

'I asked for the captain—'

'Please, sir!' a voice interrupted. The pirate's gaze slid to the man who had been so desperate to back away from him. Now the sailor raised his arm and pointed a wavering finger along the deck. 'The captain's over there . . . He's dead . . . I saw you kill him, sir.'

'Did you?' The pirate's thick lips curled into a smile. 'Which one?'

'There, sir. By the aft hatch. The fat one.'

The pirate captain looked over his shoulder and his eyes sought out the rotund body of a small man spread-eagled on the deck. Smaller by a head now. The latter was nowhere in sight, and Telemachus frowned a moment until he recalled an instant after he had jumped down on to the deck. Ahead of him a man, the merchantman's captain, had screamed and turned to run away. The glittering edge of the falcata had arced through the air, through the fleshy neck with barely a jolt, and the captain's head had leaped up and over the side.

'Yes . . . I remember.' The pirate's smile broadened into a contented grin. 'So who is the first mate?'

The sailor who had done all the speaking so far, half turned and nodded faintly at a large Nubian standing beside him.

'You?' The pirate gestured with the point of his blade.

The Nubian gave his shipmate a withering, contemptuous glance, before he nodded.

'Step forward.'

The first mate reluctantly advanced and looked warily at his captor. Telemachus was glad to see that the Nubian had the guts to meet his gaze. There was one man, at least, amongst the survivors. The pirate pointed back to the bodies around the foot of the mast.

'Those men – the tough bastards who killed so many of my lads – who were they?'

'Bodyguards, sir.'

'Bodyguards?'

The Nubian nodded. 'Came aboard in Rhodes.'

'I see. And who were they guarding?'

'A Roman, sir.'

Telemachus glanced over the shoulder of the Nubian at the other prisoners. 'Where is he?'

The Nubian shrugged. 'Don't know, sir. Haven't seen him since you boarded us. Might be dead. Might have gone over the side, sir.'

'Nubian . . .' the captain leaned closer and spoke in an icy, menacing tone, 'I wasn't born yesterday. Show me this Roman, now, or I'll show you what your heart looks like . . . Where is he?'

'Here,' a voice called out from the rear of the huddle of prisoners. A figure pushed himself forward, a tall lean man with the unmistakable features of his race: dark hair, olive skin and the long nose with which the Romans were prone to look down at the rest of the world. He wore a plain tunic, no doubt trying to pass himself off as one of the cheap fares who spent the entire journey on deck. But the man's vanity was irrepressible and an expensive ring still adorned the first finger on his right hand. The large ruby set into a gold band caught the captain's eye immediately.

'You'd better pray that comes off easily . . .'

The Roman glanced down. 'This? It's been in my family for generations. My father wore it before me, and my son will wear it after me.'

'Don't be too sure.' The captain's amusement flickered across his scarred features. 'Now then, who are you? Any man who travels with four brick shit-houses for company has got to be someone with influence . . . and wealth.'

Now it was the Roman's turn to smile. 'More than you can imagine.'

'I doubt it. I have quite an imagination when it comes to wealth. Now, much as I'd like the rare opportunity of sharing some talk with a man of culture I'm afraid we haven't the time. There's a chance that one of the lookouts at Ravenna witnessed our little naval action and has passed the word on to the local navy commander. Good as my ships are, I doubt they'd outfight an imperial squadron. So who are you, Roman? I'm asking for the last time.'

'Very well. Caius Caelius Secundus, at your service.' He bowed his head.

'Now that's a nice, noble-sounding name. I imagine your family might be able to stump up a decent ransom?'

'Of course. Name a price – a reasonable price. It'll be paid, then you can set me and my baggage ashore.'

'As easy as that?' The captain smiled. 'I'll have to consider . . .'

'Captain! Captain!'

There was a commotion from aft as a pirate burst from the hatch leading down into the passengers' quarters. He was carrying something bundled in a plain cotton sheet. He held it up as he scurried forward.

'Captain, look! Look at this!'

All faces turned towards the man as he ran to the bows,

and then dropped to his knees as he carefully laid the bundle down and swept the folds of cloth back to reveal a small chest, constructed from a dark smooth wood, almost black. It had a glassy gleam that spoke of age and many hands caressing its surface. The wood was reinforced by bands of gold. Where the bands intersected, small onyx cameos were set into the gold, likenesses of the most powerful of the Greek gods. A small silver plate on the lid bore the legend '*M. Antonius hic fecit*'.

'Mark Antony?' For a moment the pirate captain was lost in admiration for the beauty of the thing, and then his professional mind began calculating its worth, and he looked up at the Roman.

'Yours?'

The face of Caius Caelius Secundus was blank.

'All right then, not yours . . . but in your possession. Quite a piece of work. Must be worth a fortune.'

'It is,' the Roman conceded. 'And you may have it.'

'Oh . . . may I?' Telemachus replied with elaborate irony. 'Most kind of you. I think I will.'

The Roman bowed his head graciously. 'Just permit me to keep the contents.'

The captain looked at him sharply. 'Contents?'

'A few books. Something for me to read, while the ransom is arranged.'

'Books? What kind of books would be kept in a box like that, I wonder?'

'Just histories,' the Roman explained quickly. 'Nothing that would interest you.'

'Let me be the judge of that,' the captain replied, and bent down to examine the chest more closely.

There was a small keyhole in the front and the chest had been so finely constructed that only the faintest of lines showed where the lid met the bottom half of the chest. The captain glanced up.

'Give me the key.'

'I-I haven't got it.'

'No games, Roman. I want the key, now. Or you'll be feeding the fish, in small pieces.'

For a moment the Roman did not reply, or make any move. Then there was a glittering flash as the captain's arm swung up and the point of his sword stopped a finger's breadth from the Roman's throat, steady as a rock, as if it had never moved. The Roman flinched, and now at last he revealed his fear.

'The key . . .' Telemachus said softly.

Secundus grasped the ring with the fingers of his other hand and struggled to get it off. It fitted his finger snugly, and his manicured fingernails tore at the skin as he tried to free it. At last, lubricated by smears of blood, the ring came free with a grunt of effort and pain. He hesitated a moment and then offered it to the pirate captain, his fingers slowly uncurling to reveal the gold band resting in the palm of his hand. Only it wasn't just a ring. On the underside, running parallel to the finger, a small, elegantly crafted shaft protruded, with an ornate device at the end.

'There.' The Roman's shoulders sagged in defeat as the pirate captain grasped the ring and fitted the key to the lock. It was designed to be inserted one way only, and he struggled a while before he managed to find the correct orientation. Meanwhile, the rest of his crew crowded forward to see what was happening. The key slotted home, the captain eased it round. There was a soft click and the lid eased up a fraction. With eager fingers Telemachus raised the lid, swinging it back on its hinges to reveal the contents.

He frowned. 'Scrolls?'

In the small chest lay three large scrolls, fastened to ivory pins and covered with soft leather sleeves. The covers were so faded and stained that the captain guessed the books must be antique. He stared at them in disappointment. A chest like this should have contained a fortune in jewels or coins. Not books. Why the hell would a man travel with such a wondrous chest, only to use it to carry a few weathered scrolls in?

'Like I said,' the Roman forced a smile, 'just scrolls.'

The pirate captain flashed him a shrewd look. 'Just scrolls? I don't think so.'

He stood up and turned towards his crew. 'Get this chest and the rest of the loot on to our ships! Get moving!'

The pirates bent to their task at once, hurriedly transferring the most valuable items of the cargo on to the decks of the two liburnians tied alongside. The bulk of the cargo was marble; valuable but too heavy to load on to the pirate vessels. It did have one immediate use, the pirate captain thought, smiling. It would take the ship straight to the bottom when the time came.

'What are you going to do with us?' Secundus asked.

The pirate captain turned from supervising his men, and saw the sailors watching him closely, making little effort to hide their fear.

Telemachus scratched the stubble on his chin. 'I've lost some good men today. Too many good men. I'll make do with some of yours.'

The Roman sneered. 'What if we won't join you?'

'We?' The captain smiled slowly at him. 'I have no use for a pampered Roman aristocrat. You'll be joining the rest of them, the ones who won't be coming with us.'

'I see.' The Roman squinted towards the horizon and the distant lighthouse at Ravenna, calculating the distance.

The captain suddenly laughed, and shook his head. 'No, you don't see. There'll be no help from your navy. You and the others will be dead long before they could send a ship out here. Besides, there won't be anything left for them to find. You and this ship will be going down together.'

Telemachus didn't wait for a response, but swiftly turned away, striding back across the deck and swinging himself down on to the deck of his vessel with well-practised ease. The chest was already waiting for him at the foot of the mast, but he spared it only a brief greedy glance as he stopped to give his orders.

'Hector!'

The grizzled head of a stocky giant loomed over the rail of the merchantman. 'Yes, chief?'

'Prepare to fire the vessel. But not before you pick the best of the prisoners. I want them taken on board your ship. You can kill the rest. Leave that arrogant prick of a Roman till last. I want him to sweat a little before you deal with him.'

Hector grinned, and disappeared from sight. Shortly afterwards there was a series of splintering crashes as the pirates cut some timber to build a pyre in the hold of the merchantman. The captain turned his attention back to the chest, squatting down in front of it again. Looking closely, he became aware of just how fine a piece of craftsmanship this was. His fingers stroked the rich sheen of the surface and bumped lightly over the gold and onyx cameos. Telemachus shook his head again. 'Scrolls . . .'

Using both hands, the captain eased the catch open and gently raised the lid. He paused for a moment, and then reached in and lifted out one of the scrolls. It was far heavier than he had thought it would be, and for a moment he wondered if there might be some gold hidden inside. His fingers worked away at the thong, and he raised the scroll up to see the knot better, and was aware of a faint citron odour emanating from the book. With a little effort the knot came undone and he shook the thong to one side, holding the end of the parchment in one hand as he unspooled the first few pages of the scroll with the other.

It was written in Greek. The script was old-fashioned, but legible enough, and Telemachus began to read. At first his features registered a sense of confusion and frustration, as his eyes steadily scanned each line of text.

There was a sudden scream of terror from the deck of the merchantman, cut short abruptly. A brief pause and then another scream, followed by a shrill voice babbling for mercy, before it too was cut off. The captain smiled. There would be no mercy. He knew his subordinate, Hector, well enough to realise the man thoroughly enjoyed killing other men. Inflicting pain was an art he excelled in, even more so than the skill of commanding a sleek pirate vessel, manned by some of the most bloodthirsty men he had ever met. The captain turned back to the scroll and read on, even as more screams split the air.

A moment later, he found a phrase that made it all come clear. With a chilling flood of realisation he understood what he was holding in his hands. He knew where it had been written, who it had been written by and, more importantly, he knew how much these scrolls might be worth. Then it occurred to him: he could not ask any price for these, once he approached the right customers.

Abruptly, he dropped the scroll back into the chest and snapped upright.

'Hector! Hector!'

Once again the man's head reared over the side of the captured ship. He rested his hands on the rail, one still holding a long curved dagger, from which blood dripped in to the sea between the two vessels.

'That Roman –' Telemachus began – 'have you killed him yet?'

'Not yet. He's next.' Hector grinned. 'You want to watch?'

'No. I want him alive.'

'Alive?' Hector frowned. 'He's too soft for us. No fucking use at all.'

'Oh, he's going to be useful, all right! He's going to help make us richer than Croesus. Bring him to me at once!'

Moments later the Roman was kneeling on the deck beside the mast. His chest was heaving as he stared up at the pirate captain and his murderous henchman. There was still defiance in his manner, the captain noted. The man was Roman to the core of his being, and behind his cold expression no doubt contempt for his captors outweighed even the terror he must be feeling as he waited for his death. The captain tapped the chest with the toe of his boot.

'I know about the scrolls. I know what they are, and I can guess where you are taking them.'

'Guess then!' The Roman spat on to the deck at his captor's feet. 'I'll tell you nothing!'

Hector raised his dagger and lurched forward with a snarl. 'Why you—'

'Leave him!' the captain snapped, thrusting his hand out. 'I said I want him alive.'

Hector paused, looking from his captain to the Roman and back again with murderous eyes. 'Alive?'

'Yes . . . He's going to answer some questions. I want to know who he's working for.'

The Roman sneered. 'I'll say nothing.'

'Oh yes you will.' The captain leaned over him. 'You think you're a brave man. I can see that. But I've known plenty of brave men in my time, and none of them has held out for long against Hector here. He knows how to inflict more pain, and make it last longer, than any man I have ever known. It's a kind of genius. An art, if you like. He's extremely passionate about his art . . .'

The captain stared into the face of his prisoner for a moment, and finally the man flinched. Telemachus smiled as he straightened up and turned to his subordinate.

'Kill the rest of them, quick as you can. Then fire the ship. Once that's done I want you on board here. We'll spend the time it takes to get back home with our friend here . . .'

As the afternoon light slanted across the rolling surface of the sea, a thick swirling cloud of smoke engulfed the ravaged merchantman. Flames licked amid the smoke as the fire below the deck took hold and spread throughout the vessel. Soon it flared up and the rigging caught light, a fiery tracery of ropes, like infernal decorations. The crack and pop of burning wood and the roar of flames was clearly audible to the men on the decks of the two pirate vessels as they bore away in the opposite direction to the shores of Italy. Far over the eastern horizon lay the coast of Illyricum, with its maze of deserted and remote inlets and islands. The sounds of the dying ship slowly faded behind them.

Soon the only noise that cut across the serenity of the ships sliding through the sea was the demented screaming of a man being subjected to the kind of torture he had never conceived of in the most hellish of his nightmares.

CHAPTER TWO

'Rome . . . bollocks . . .' Centurion Macro grunted as he eased himself up from his bed roll, wincing at the terrible pain in his skull. 'I'm still in Rome.'

Through the broken shutter a feeble shaft of light cut across the dingy room, and fell fully upon his face. He closed his eyes, clenching the eyelids shut, and slowly drew a deep breath. The previous evening he had drunk himself insensible and, as usual, he silently swore an oath never to touch cheap wine again. The previous three months were littered with such oaths. Indeed, their frequency had increased disturbingly in recent days as Macro had begun to doubt that he and his friend Cato would ever find a new posting. It seemed as if an age had passed since they had been forced to quit the Second Legion in Britain and returned to Rome. Macro was desperate to return to military life. Surely there must be some vacancies in one of the legions spread along the vast frontier of the Empire? But, it seemed, every centurion on active service was in distastefully good health. Either that, Macro frowned, or there was some conspiracy to keep him and Centurion Cato off the active service list and still waiting for their back pay. A complete waste of his many years of experience, he fumed. And a poor start for Cato, who had been promoted to centurion not even a year ago.

Macro cracked open one eye and glanced across the bare boards to the other side of the small room. Cato's dark, unkempt curls poked out from under several layers of cloaks and blankets that overflowed the cheap bed rolls. Stuffed with straw and stinking of mildew, the threadbare bedding had been almost the only item on the inventory when they first rented the room.

'Cato . . .' Macro called softly, but there was no reply. No movement at all. The lad must still be asleep, Macro decided. Well then, let him sleep. It was late January and the mornings were cold and there was no sense in getting up before the sun had risen enough to bring some warmth to the densely packed city. At least it wasn't like that mind-numbing cold they had endured last winter in Britain. The endless misery of the damp and chilly climate had worked its way into the very hearts of the legionaries and set them to melancholy thoughts of home. Now Macro was home, and the terrible frustration of eking out his life on dwindling savings was driving him mad.

Raising a hand to his head, Macro scratched at his scalp, cursing the lice that seemed to breed in every corner of the crumbling tenement block.

'Bloody lice are in on the act as well,' he muttered. 'Has everyone got it in for me these days?'

There was some justice to his complaint. For the best part of two years he and Cato had fought their way through the savage tribes of Britain and had played their part in defeating Caratacus and his Celtic horde. And their reward for all the dangers they had faced? A damp room in a crumbling tenement block in the slum district of the Subura as they waited to be recalled to duty. Worse still, due to some bureaucratic nicety, they had not been paid since arriving in Rome and now Macro and Cato had all but run through the money they had brought back with them from Britain.

A distant hubbub of voices and cries carried across from the forum as the city shuffled to life in the bleak glow of a winter dawn. Macro shivered, and pulled his thick army cloak about his broad shoulders. Grimacing at the rhythmic pounding in his skull, he eased himself to his feet and shuffled across the room to the shutters. He lifted the cord off the bent nail that secured the two wooden panels and then pushed the broken one out. More light spilled into the room as the worn hinges grated in protest and Macro narrowed his eyes against the sudden glare. But only for a moment. Once again the now-too-familiar vista of Rome opened up before him and he could not help being awed by the spectacle of the world's greatest city. Built on to the unfashionable side of the Esquiline hill, the topmost rooms of the tenement block looked out over the insanely crowded squalor of the Subura, towards the towering temples and palaces that surrounded the Forum, and beyond to the warehouses that were packed along the banks of the Tiber.

He had been told that nearly a million people were crowded within the walls of Rome. From where Macro stood that was all too easy to believe. A geometric chaos of rooftiles dropped down the slope in front of him, and the narrow alleyways that ran between them could only be divined where the grimy brickwork of the upper levels of the apartments were visible. A shroud of woodsmoke hung over the city and its acrid stench even overwhelmed the sharp tang from the tannery at the end of the street. Even now, after more than three months in the city, Macro had not grown used to the raw stench of the place. Nor the filth that lay in the streets: a dark mixture of shit and rotting scraps of food that not even the meanest beggar would pick through. And everywhere the dense press of bodies that flowed through the streets: slaves, traders, merchants and artisans. Drawn from across the Empire, they still bore the trappings of their civilisations in an exotic medley of colours and styles. Around them swirled the listless mass of freeborn citizens looking for some form of entertainment to keep them amused when they were not queuing for the grain dole. Here and there the litters of the rich were carried above and apart from the rest of Rome, their owners clutching pomades to their noses to catch a more fragrant breath in the ripe atmosphere that embraced the city.

That was the reality of life in Rome and it overwhelmed Macro. He wondered at the mass of humanity that could tolerate such an affront to the senses and not yearn for the freedom and freshness of a life far removed from the city. He felt sure that Rome would soon drive him mad.

Macro leaned his elbows on the worn sill and peered down into the shadowy street that ran along the side of the tenement block. His eyes slid down the grimy brickwork of the wall stretching below his window in a dizzy drop that foreshortened the people passing below into four-limbed insects; distant and just as easily dismissible, as they scuttled along the dim street. This room on the fifth floor of the tenement was the highest Macro had ever been in anything made by man, and the elevation made him feel a little dizzy.

'Shit . . .'

'What's shit?'

Macro turned and saw that Cato was awake and rubbing his eyes as his jaw stretched in a yawn.

'Me. I feel like shit.'

Cato examined his friend with a disapproving shake of his head. 'You look like shit.'

'Thanks.'

'Better get yourself cleaned up.'

'Why? What's the point? No need to make an effort when there's nothing to do for the rest of the day.'

'We're soldiers. We let it go now and we'll never get the edge back. Besides, once a legionary always a legionary. You told me that.'

'I did?' Macro raised an eyebrow, and then shrugged. 'I must have been drunk.'

'How can you tell?'

'That's enough of your lip,' Macro grumbled as he felt his head begin to spin gently. 'I need some more rest.'

'You can't rest. We have to get ready.' Cato reached for his boots, put them on and began to fasten the leather ties.

'Ready?' Macro turned to him. 'Ready for what?'

'You've forgotten?'

'Forgotten? What have I forgotten?'

'Our appointment at the palace. I told you about it last night, when I found you in that tavern.'

Macro frowned as he strained his mind to recover the details of the previous evening's binge. 'Which one?'

'The Grove of Dionysus.' Cato spoke patiently. 'You were drinking with some veterans of the Tenth and I came up and told you I had got us an interview with the procurator in charge of legionary postings. At the third hour. So we haven't got much time to get ourselves breakfasted, washed and kitted up before we head to the palace. There's racing today at the Great Circus; we have to get out early if we're going to beat the crowds. You could do with something to eat. Something to settle your stomach.'

'Sleep,' Macro replied quietly, as he slumped on to his bed roll and curled up under his cloak. 'Sleep'll settle my stomach nicely.'

Cato finished tying his boots and stood up, ducking his head to avoid banging it against the beam that crossed the room; one of the few instances where being a head taller than Macro was a disadvantage. Cato reached for the leather bag of ground barley that stood beside the rest of their kit, propped up against the wall next to the door. He untied it and poured a measure into each of their mess tins, before carefully twisting the bag and knotting the ties once again, to keep the mice out. 'I'll go and get the porridge made up. You can start polishing the armour while I'm gone.'

When the door had closed behind his friend, Macro closed his eyes again and tried to ignore the pain in his skull. His stomach felt knotted and empty. A meal would do him good. The sun had risen higher and he opened his eyes again. He groaned, threw the cloak to one side and went over towards the piles of armour and equipment leaning beside the door. Despite sharing the rank of centurion, Macro had more than a dozen years of experience over Cato. Sometimes it felt strange to find himself obeying one of the lad's instructions. But, Macro bitterly reminded himself, they were no longer on active duty. Rank was largely irrelevant. Instead they were two friends struggling to survive until they finally received their back pay from the miserly clerks at the imperial treasury. Hence the need to watch every sestertian as they waited for a new posting. Not an easy task when Macro was inclined to spend what little savings he had on drink.

The narrow stairwell was lit by openings in the wall on every second landing and Cato, with his hands full, had to pick his way down the ancient creaking boards with care. Around him he could hear the sounds of other tenants rising: the bawling of young children, the intemperate shouts of their parents and the low sullen murmurs of those who faced a long day's employment somewhere in the city. Although he had been born in Rome and raised in the palace until he was old enough to be sent to the legions, Cato had never had cause to visit the slum areas, let alone enter one of the towering tenement blocks packed with the capital's poor. It had shocked him to realise that freeborn citizens could live like this. He had not imagined such squalor. Even the slaves in the palace lived better than this. Far better than this.

At the bottom of the stairs Cato turned into the heart of the building and emerged into the gloomy yard where the block had its communal cooking hearth. A wizened old man was stirring a large blackened pot on the griddle and the air was thick with the smell of gruel. Even at this early hour there was someone ahead of Cato in the queue, a thin pasty woman who lived with a large family in one room on the floor immediately below Macro and Cato. Her husband worked in the warehouses; a huge surly man whose drunken shouting and beating of his wife and children could be heard clearly enough in the room above. At the sound of Cato's nailed boots tramping across the flagstones she turned and looked over her shoulder. Her nose had been broken some time ago and today her cheek and eye were heavily bruised. Still a smile flickered across her lips and Cato made himself smile back, out of pity. She could have been any age between twenty and forty but the back-breaking labour of raising a family and the strain of tiptoeing round her brutish husband had reduced her to a wasted streak of despair as she stood barefoot in a ragged tunic, bronze pail in one hand and a sleeping infant clutched against her hip in the other.

Cato glanced away, not wanting to make further eye contact, and sat down at the far end of the bench to wait his turn at the hearth. In the arches on the far side of the yard the slaves of a bakery were already at work, heating the ovens for the first loaves of the day.

'Hello, Centurion.'

Cato looked up and saw that the baker's wife had emerged from her premises and was grinning at him. She was younger than Cato, and had already been married to the ageing owner of the business for three years. It had been a good marriage for the pretty, but coarse girl from the Subura, and she had plans for the business once her husband had passed on. Of course she might need a partner to share her ambitions when the time came. She had freely imparted this information to Cato as soon as he had moved into the tenement, and the implication was clear enough.

'Morning, Velina.' Cato nodded. 'Good to see you.'

From the other end of the bench came a clearly audible sniff of contempt.

'Ignore her.' Velina smiled. 'Mrs Gabinius thinks she's better than the rest of us. How's that brat Gaius coming on? Still poking his nose where it's not wanted?'

The thin woman turned away from the baker's wife and clutched her child close to her chest without making any reply. Velina placed her hands on her hips and raised her head with a triumphant sneer before her attention returned to Cato.

'How's my centurion today? Any news?'

Cato shook his head. 'Still no postings for either of us. But we're going to see someone at the palace this morning. Might have some good news later on.'

'Oh . . .' Velina frowned. 'I suppose I should wish you good luck.'

'That would be nice.'

She shrugged. 'Can't see why you bother, though. How long has it been now? Five months?'

'Three.'

'What if there's nothing for you? You should think about doing something else with your life. Something more rewarding.' She arched an eyebrow and pouted quickly. 'Young man like yourself could go a long way, in the right company.'

'Maybe.' Cato felt himself blushing and glanced round towards the hearth. The open attention he was getting from Velina embarrassed him and he desperately wanted to quit the yard before she developed her plans for him any further.

The old man who had been stirring his gruel was heaving the steaming pot from the iron griddle and headed carefully towards the stairs. The wife of Gabinius reached for her pots.

'Excuse me.' Cato stood up. 'Would you mind if I went first?'

She looked up, sunken eyes fixing him with a cold stare for an instant.

'We're in a rush this morning,' Cato explained quickly. 'Have to get up and out as quick as we can.' He made a pleading face and tilted his head slightly in the direction of the baker's wife. The thin woman pursed her lips in a smile, glanced at Velina with a barely concealed delight as she saw the other's look of frustration.

'Of course, sir. Since you're so desperate to get away.'

'Thank you.' Cato nodded his gratitude and placed the mess tins on the hot griddle. He ladled some water in from the water trough, mixed it into the ground barley and started stirring as it heated up.

Velina sniffed, turned and strode back towards the bakery.

* * *

'She's still giving you the eye then?' Macro grinned as he scraped the bottom of his mess tin with a scrap of bread.

'Afraid so.' Cato had finished his meal and was rubbing wax into his leather harness with an old rag. The silvered medals he had won in battle shone like freshly minted coins from their fastenings on the harness. He already wore his thick military tunic and scale armour, and had fastened polished greaves to his lower legs. He dabbed some more wax on to the cloth and rubbed away at the gleaming leather.

'Going to do anything about it?' Macro continued, trying not to smile.

'Not on your life. I've got enough to worry about as it is. If we don't get out of here soon, I'm going to go mad.'

Macro shook his head. 'You're young. You must have twenty or twenty-five good years of service ahead of you. There's time enough. It's different for me. Fifteen more years at the most. The next posting will probably be my last chance to get my hands on enough money to see me through retirement.'

The concern in his voice was clear and Cato paused and looked up. 'Then we'd better make sure that we make the most of this morning. I staked out the secretary's office for days to get this appointment. So let's not be late.'

'All right, lad. Point taken. I'll get ready.'

A little later Cato stepped back from Macro and examined him with a critical eye.

'How do I look?'

Cato ran his eyes over his friend and pursed his lips. 'You'll do. Now let's go.'

When the two officers emerged from the dark staircase and on to the street in front of the tenement, heads turned to take in the spectacle of the gleaming armour and the brilliant red cloaks. Each officer wore his helmet and the neat horsehair crests fanned out across the gleaming metal. With vine cane gripped in one hand while the other rested on his sword pommel, Cato drew himself up and stiffened his back.

Someone wolf-whistled and Cato turned to see Velina leaning against the doorpost at the street entrance to her husband's business.

'Well then, just look at the two of you! I could really go for someone in uniform . . .'

Macro grinned at her. 'I'm sure something could be arranged. I'll drop by when we get back from the palace.'

Velina smiled weakly. 'That would be nice . . . to see both of you.'

'Me first,' said Macro.

Cato gripped his arm. 'We'll be late. Come on.'

Macro winked at Velina and stepped out with Cato. Side by side they marched boldly down the slope towards the Forum and the gleaming pillars of the vast imperial palace rising up on the Capitoline Hill.

CHAPTER THREE

'Centurions Macro and Cato?' The Praetorian Guardsman frowned as he scanned the slate lying on the desk in front of him. 'You're not on the list.'

Macro smiled at him. 'Have another look. A good look, if you know what I mean.'

The guardsman heaved his shoulders in a weary sigh, to make it quite clear that he had been down this route many times before. He leaned back from the desk and shook his head. 'Sorry, sir. I've got my orders. No admittance to the palace unless your names are on the list.'

'But we are on the list,' Cato insisted. 'We have an appointment at the army bureau. With the procurator in charge of legion postings. Right now, so let us through.'

The guardsman raised an eyebrow. 'You know how many times someone's tried that one on me, sir?'

'It's true.'

'It's only true if you're on the list, sir. You ain't on the list so you don't have an appointment.'

'Wait a moment.' Cato concentrated his attention on the guardsman. 'Look here, there's obviously been some kind of mistake. I assure you that we have an appointment. I arranged it with the procurator's clerk yesterday. Demetrius was his name. Send word to him that we're here. He'll confirm the story.'

The guardsman turned towards a small group of slave boys squatting in a niche to one side of the columned entrance to the palace. 'You! Go to the army bureau. Find Demetrius and tell him these officers here say they have an appointment to see the procurator.'

'Thank you,' Cato muttered, and pulled Macro away from the guardsman's desk, steering his friend towards the benches that lined the walls each side of the entrance.

As they sat down Macro grumbled, 'Officious little prick. Gods! I'd love to have him on a parade ground for a few hours of hard drill. Soon see how tough he is. Bloody Praetorians! Think the world owes them a living. And the palace guard are the idlest bastards of 'em all.'

They waited in silence for the messenger to return and Cato looked up at the vast edifice of the palace looming above them. Built on to the side of the Palatine Hill, there were several tiers of accommodation rising high over the Forum. He had been raised within those walls. They had been almost the whole world to him – until his father died and Cato had been sent to join the legions over two years ago. Now, the once-familiar walls and columns felt like strangers, and seemed smaller, somehow. Of course, he reasoned, he had left the palace as little more than a boy, and had travelled across the Empire, across the sea, and had seen the horrors of battle. It was bound to have changed him, and made him see the world differently. But to feel like a stranger before the colossal walls that held so many memories for him made Cato's heart heavy. He suddenly felt far older than his years and shivered, clutching his military cloak tighter about his shoulders.

When the messenger boy returned there was a quiet exchange of words with the Praetorian Guardsman before he turned round and beckoned to the two centurions.

He nodded at Cato. 'Seems you were right, sir. Demetrius will see you now.'

'Oh, he will, will he?' Macro sniffed. 'That's bloody good of him.'

The Praetorian made a wry smile. 'You can't imagine. Anyway, follow this boy.'

They marched through the entrance portico, across a small yard and into the main body of the palace. Inside, the iron nails on the bottom of their thick leather boots echoed sharply off the high walls on each side of the passage. They passed wide doorways through which they could see the scribes and the clerks working at the endless record-keeping that kept the wheels of the Empire turning. The walls of the offices were lined with racks of scrolls and slates, every pigeonhole neatly marked with a numeral. Light poured into each room through latticed windows high up on the wall and Macro wondered what it must be like to spend long years working in such a confined space, with no view of the outside world.

They reached a narrow staircase at the end of the passage and climbed four flights before taking another corridor. The rooms leading off this corridor were bright and spacious, and most had windows that must provide fine views across the city. The slave boy drew up outside a wide doorway and rapped on the wooden frame.

'Enter!' a high-pitched voice called out.

Before they passed through the door Cato quickly whispered to his friend, 'Let me do the talking. I know my way round these palace types.'

The slave boy led the two centurions inside and they found they were in an ante-room. Two benches were arranged along the wall opposite three windows that let in plenty of light and air. Too much, thought Cato, as he felt the chill. At the far end of the room was a closed door. To one side of it was a large desk made of some dark wood, and behind it sat the clerk Cato had met briefly the day before. Demetrius was a slight man in a plain but freshly laundered tunic. He had the classic Greek profile and his thinning hair was carefully arranged in dark oiled curls. His whole bearing spoke of the power and influence he thought he wielded. Beside him stood a brazier, glowing warmly. Three other officers were sitting on the bench nearest to the heat.

Demetrius glanced up from a scroll and beckoned to them. 'Centurions Macro and Cato? You're late.'

Macro puffed out his cheeks, but Cato responded before his friend could protest. 'We were held up at the entrance. The guard had no record of our meeting.' Cato smiled. 'You know what they're like. I hope we're not too late for our meeting with the procurator.'

'You've missed it,' Demetrius said tonelessly.

'Missed it?' Macro jabbed a finger at him. 'Now, just you look here—'

'Come back tomorrow.'

'Not on your life.'

Demetrius shrugged. 'Your loss.' He glanced at the messenger boy. 'Please show these two gentlemen the way out of the palace.'

'We're staying!' Macro growled. 'And we will see the procurator. You'd better make sure of that.'

'The procurator's a busy man. You should have been here at the appointed time.'

Macro leaned over the desk and glared at the clerk. 'And you should have made sure our names were on that list.'

'Not my problem.'

'Then I'll make it your problem.' Macro reached for his sword, and Demetrius glanced down at the pommel as the first length of blade emerged from the scabbard. He flinched and his eyes flickered back to meet Macro's cold, determined expression.

'You wouldn't dare.'

'Try me.'

For a moment Demetrius wavered, and glanced to the other officers in a silent appeal for help, but they just smiled back and didn't move. 'I'll call the guards.'

'You can,' Macro nodded. 'But long before they get here, I'd have lobbed your scrawny arse out of the window. Must be a long way down . . .' He smiled at the clerk. 'Now can we *please* have our meeting with the procurator?'

Demetrius swallowed and fumbled for a waxed slate on his desk. 'Yes, er, let me see. He could spare you a few moments at the end of his current meeting, I suppose.' He looked up desperately. 'If you'll just take a seat . . .'

Macro straightened up and nodded with satisfaction. 'Thank you.'

As he and Cato joined the other officers on the bench he glanced at Cato and winked. 'I'll do the talking from now on. Think I've got the measure of these palace types.'

The other officers craned round to introduce themselves. Two of them were veterans; grizzled and scarred beneath coarse hair that was going grey. They each had a chest full of medallions on their harnesses and one wore a gold torque on his wrist. The third officer was a young man, recently kitted out and with not one decoration on his harness. He looked awkward and uneasy in the company of the vastly more experienced men.

One of the veterans nodded over towards Demetrius. 'Nice job, Centurion . . . is it Macro or Cato?'

'Macro. Lately of the Second Legion Augusta. Same as Cato here.'

'I'm Lollius Asinius. This here's Hosidius Mutilus. Waiting for travel warrants to join the Tenth Legion. The youngster's Flaccus Sosius. Looking for his first appointment.'

The young officer smiled quickly as he fixed his attention on the new arrivals. 'The Augusta? You've been in Britain then? What's it like?'

Macro concentrated for a moment before he replied, remembering the two years of the most intense fighting he had ever witnessed. So many men had died – good men he had known for years, and some he had barely had a chance to know before they were killed. Then there was the enemy: brutal and brave, and led by those deranged druid devils. What was it like? 'Cold.'

'Cold?' Sosius looked confused.

Macro nodded. 'Yes, cold. Don't ever go there. Get yourself a posting somewhere comfortable. Like Syria.'

Cato shook his head in despair. As long as he had known Macro he had had to put up with the constant refrain that Syria was the best posting in the Empire. It was Macro's lifelong ambition to wallow in the fleshpots of the east.

'Syria?' Asinius laughed. 'We've just come back from there. Been training some auxiliary units at Damascus.'

Macro leaned closer to Asinius, eyes bright with intense concentration. 'Tell me about it – Syria. Is it as good as they say?'

'Well, I don't know about that, but—'

The door to the procurator's office swung open and a man strode out into the ante-room. At once Cato and Macro rose up and stood stiffly to attention, quickly followed by the others. Demetrius rose last of all, taking just long enough to register his lack of obeisance. The man was wearing the full ceremonial toga of a senator, with a broad purple stripe running along the hem. He nodded briefly to the centurions and strode out of the ante-room as Demetrius stepped into his master's office.

'Centurions Licinius Cato and Cornelius Macro to see you, sir.'

'Are they on my list?'

'An oversight, sir. I'll punish the scribe responsible.'

'Oh, very well. Send 'em in.'

Demetrius stood by the door and closed it behind them the moment the two centurions had entered the procurator's office.

They found themselves standing on a thick rug, one of several that filled the large room. It was situated on the corner of the palace and had windows on two sides. Glazed windows, Macro noted with scarcely hidden astonishment at the luxurious furnishing of the procurator's office. On the far side, behind a marble-topped desk, sat the procurator, a fat man with a thick head of dark hair and a fistful of gold rings on the pudgy fingers of each hand. He glanced up with an irritable expression.

'Well, get over here, then! Smartly now!'

Macro and Cato marched over and stood to attention in front of the desk. The procurator snorted, and leaned back in his chair, revealing a rolling belly that stretched the wool fabric of his tunic. 'What are you here for?'

'We're looking for reappointment to the legions, sir,' said Cato.

The procurator tapped a pile of waxed tablets on his desk. 'So I understand. You must be Centurion Licinius Cato. You've been pushing for a new legion for several months now.'

'Three months, sir,' Cato replied.

'Well, from the quantity of your correspondence and the endless haranguing of my clerks it feels like several months.

Truth is, I cannot make any decision until I'm clear about your position.'

'Our position?' Macro cut in. 'What do you mean, sir?'

The procurator crossed his fingers and rested the folds of his chin on his knuckles. 'A few days ago I received information that Centurion Cato was sentenced to death by General Plautius, the commander of the army in Britain. Is that true?'

Cato felt a chilling sensation in the pit of his stomach. He nodded. 'Yes, sir. But I can explain.'

'I think you'd better.'

Cato swallowed. 'Our cohort was condemned to decimation for failing to carry out orders. As a result, the enemy general escaped with some of his men. Centurion Macro and I managed to capture him, and the death sentence was lifted by the legate of the Second Legion.'

'So I understand. As it happens, Legate Vespasian exceeded his authority when he rescinded your sentence. I might add that there's some concern, in higher circles, about the extent of your complicity in the death of your cohort commander. Both of you, that is.'

He fell silent as the two officers standing in front of him froze and tried to keep their faces composed. They dared not look at each other and stared straight ahead instead. The procurator continued, 'I understand that following the decimation there was considerable bad feeling towards your commanding officer.'

'Are you surprised, sir?' Macro shrugged. 'Most of the men blamed him for the cohort's punishment.'

'Most of the men?' The procurator looked at him closely. 'And the officers?'

Macro nodded.

'Then you will understand that the death of Centurion

Maximius has provoked considerable suspicion. Naturally, in the face of such grave accusations, the army bureau is investigating the matter fully. I've sent a letter to General Plautius requesting a full report on the matter. I'm still waiting for his reply. We should know the full facts soon enough. At which point you will either be in the clear, and I can consider you for some new postings, or you will be taken into custody and disposed of at the Emperor's convenience . . . In the meantime, I'd be grateful if you didn't try to leave the city.'

He looked up and noticed the despair in their faces and for a moment his hard bureaucratic mask slipped and he shook his head sadly. 'I'm sorry, there's nothing more I can do or say. I only permitted this meeting because I thought that you should know about the situation. In view of your records I felt that Rome owed you that much at least.'

Macro gave a thin smile. 'That much and far more, I'd say.'

'Maybe.' The procurator shrugged. 'That's not for me to judge. Now I think you'd better leave.'

Macro and Cato stared back a moment, until the procurator reached for a blank wax tablet and took up a stylus. They were dismissed.

Outside the office, Cato turned slowly to Macro, who could see that he was still stunned by the procurator's words. His thin shoulders slumped forwards.

'Come on, Cato . . .' Macro took his arm and steered him towards the street.

CHAPTER FOUR

They left the palace and fought their way through the crowds streaming across the Forum. Families clustered together amid bands of loud young men clutching jars of wine as they all made for the Great Circus to find good seats for the day's racing. Cutting across this tide of excited humanity, the two centurions made for a corner tavern. The usual morning trade of wagon drivers and night porters was just beginning to dry up as the exhausted, and now inebriated, men began to stagger home to their beds.

Macro waved the barman over.

'What'll it be, gents?' the weasily-looking youth asked politely as he eyed up their uniforms and estimated the tip he might expect from two centurions.

'A jar of your cheapest wine. Two cups,' Macro replied curtly. 'Quick as you can.'

'Quick is the order, swift is the service.' The barman smiled. 'That's our motto.'

'Nice.' Macro glanced up at him. 'But it would be even swifter if you just cut out the motto.'

'Right . . . yes. I suppose so.' The barman scurried off, leaving Macro to turn his attention back to his friend. Cato was staring across the heaving crowd that filled the Forum and up at the austere heights of the palace on the Palatine. Cato had not said a word since leaving the procurator's office and now he just sat in silence. Macro patted him on the arm.

'Cheer up, lad. The wine's ordered.'

Cato turned his head to stare at Macro. 'I have no legionary posting, almost no money left and now, it seems, I'm to be executed in the near future. You really think a cup of cheap wine is going to help me?'

Macro shrugged. 'Well, it ain't going to hurt you. In fact, it has a funny way of making things seem better.'

'You'd know,' Cato muttered. 'Had enough of it over the last three months to lay out an army.'

The barman came back, clunked a pair of Samian-ware cups on the rough wooden table between the two centurions, and filled the cups from a jug before setting that down with a cheap flourish.

'Heard the news?'

Macro and Cato turned towards him with annoyed expressions that clearly invited him to shut his mouth and beat a hasty retreat to behind the counter. The barman was not prepared to give up working for his tip that easily, and leaned against a stout wooden post that held up the three floors above the tavern.

'Porcius is back in town.'

'Porcius?' Macro raised an eyebrow. 'Who the bloody hell is Porcius and why should I be remotely interested in him?'

The barman shook his head in wonder at the ignorance of the two army officers. 'Why, he's only the best charioteer ever to have driven for the blues! He's top of the bill this afternoon. Runs his horses like he was born with reins in his hands. Tell you what,' he leaned closer, 'you got anything to spare for a bet, and I could get you good odds.'

'Leave 'em be,' a voice growled from the next table, and Macro saw the face of the guardsman from the palace as he turned towards the two centurions. 'Porcius is a jumped-up little tosser. Only thinks he's good. If the man had any talent at all he'd be racing for the greens. Sir, save your money. Place it on Nepos. He's racing for the greens.'

'Nepos!' The barman spat on the ground. He looked at the guardsman with contempt and the usual unthinking hostility that ardent supporters of racing teams reserved for each other. Then he strode back to the bar, muttering one last parting shot to the two centurions. 'Might as well piss your money down the Great Sewer as bet on that twat Nepos.'

'I heard that!' shouted the guardsman.

'Racing,' Cato said quietly. 'If anything destroys the Empire, it'll be racing.'

Macro wasn't listening. His eyes were fixed on the guardsman. He turned towards him and tapped the man on the shoulder.

'Hello, friend,' Macro smiled. 'These races – any good tips you might be willing to share with a comrade in arms?'

'Tips?' The man glanced round at the other customers, but no one seemed to be listening. 'Yes, I've got one tip for you. Don't bet on that bastard Porcius.' He tapped his nose. 'I know what's what, and I'm telling you, sir, Nepos is your man. Bung a few denarians on him and you'll be laughing. Now, if you'll excuse me, sir, I have to go.' He grated his stool back on the flagstone, rose rather unsteadily to his feet, steered a course out of the tavern and was immediately lost from sight in the flow of people in the Forum.

'Doubt he'll get back to the palace in one go,' Cato muttered. 'All the same, I wish I had his problems.'

Macro turned back to his friend, desperately searching for some crumb of comfort he could offer Cato, but he had never been good at that sort of thing.

'It's rough luck, lad.'

'Rough luck?' Cato laughed bitterly. 'Oh, it's better than that. I mean, after all that we've been through, after all we've done for General Plautius, you can be certain that patrician bastard'll make sure I get the chop. There's something you can safely bet on. Just to make sure that his shining reputation as a harsh disciplinarian doesn't get a mark on it. And the Imperial Secretary will back him up.'

'He might recommend a pardon,' Macro suggested.

Cato stared at him. 'He might not. Anyway, aren't you forgetting something?'

'Am I?'

'You're also under threat. What if the general decides he wants to put you in the frame over the death of Centurion Maximius?'

'I don't think he will. There's no evidence linking me to his murder, just a few rumours put around by a handful of idiots who won't accept that he was killed by the enemy. I'm not worried about that, not really. It's you I'm worried about.' He looked away in embarrassment and his eyes fell on his purse, tied securely to his belt. 'But most of all I'm worried about the fact that we're broke, and we're going to be very hungry in a few days' time unless some back pay comes through. If it doesn't, then we'll be on the bloody streets once the next month's rent is due. All in all, it's not looking too healthy, Cato my lad.'

'No.'

'So we'd better do something about it.'

'Like what?'

Macro smiled, and leaned closer across the table. 'Like taking advantage of that tip, and getting ourselves down to the Great Circus.'

'Are you mad? We're down to our last few coins and you want to throw them away on the races?'

'Throwing 'em away is what mugs do. What we've got is a sure thing.'

'No. What you've got is incurable optimism. Me? I'm a realist. If we place that money on a race we might as well just give it away.'

Macro slapped his hand down on the table, making the cups jump. 'Oh, come on, Cato! What little we've got is as good as gone anyway. If the tip's any use we should get reasonable odds, and, who knows, if the bet comes good we'll be able to keep the lupine pest from the door for a while yet. What have we got to lose?'

'Apart from our senses?'

Macro glared at him. 'Just for once, trust to fate and see what happens.'

Cato thought it over for a moment. Macro was right, he had pretty much lost everything else in his life, and even the latter was almost certainly forfeit. So why worry about a few coins? The general's response would arrive from Britain before the landlord's heavies could pin him to the wall for any arrears. He might as well live a little, while he could.

'All right then, let's go.'

By the time they had pushed their way inside the huge arch of one of the public entrances to the Great Circus there were only a few places left in the section reserved for the army. Most of the stone benches had been taken by Praetorian Guardsmen who were busy drinking from wineskins and making bets. Here and there were small clusters of legionaries – men on leave or, like Cato and Macro, waiting for a new posting. Quite a few were ex-soldiers, pensioned off or invalided out of the legions and taking advantage of their veterans' rights.

Emperor Claudius, in a shrewd move, had changed the seating plan so that the guardsmen were arranged either side of, and behind the grand imperial box. The senators had been shifted further off, much to their chagrin, and spilled out over their benches where they were waited on by their slaves, who served them heated wine in small goblets. Glancing beyond them, Cato saw the enclosure for the vestal virgins, the less spacious seating reserved for lesser nobles, and then the packed ranks of the common citizens, and above them, on the rearmost benches, the freedmen, foreigners and unattached women, many of whom were obviously plying their trade. Macro followed the direction of his gaze.

'Forget them. You can't afford it. Not unless Nepos does his stuff.'

Cato swung his gaze back towards the huge expanse of the track stretching out in front of them. Several race officials were crossing to the central island, while around them scores of slaves raked the sand into a smooth, even surface in final preparation for the first race. The assistants to the priests wheeled a cage of unblemished white goats towards the sacrificial altar in the middle of the island, directly opposite the imperial box.

All around the arena the usual hawkers sold snacks, cushions and brightly coloured scarves for each team's supporters. Amongst them prowled the bet-takers, accompanied by a heavy or two to make sure that the money was kept safe. Macro swallowed nervously, stood up, and made for the nearest; a swarthy-looking Hispanic, clutching a bundle of waxed slates tied together. Behind him lurked two huge men, powerfully built and horribly scarred, as most ex-gladiators tended to be. Each man carried a money box on a strap across his shoulders, and had a thick wooden stave to hand.

'Let me guess,' smiled the bet-taker as he sized Macro up and calculated his worth. 'You'll have a gold piece on Porcius, to win.'

'Er, no.' Macro felt embarrassment burning in his cheeks. He glanced round and continued in a low voice, 'Five denarians on Nepos, to win.'

'Five denarians?' The bet-taker looked disappointed. He quickly reappraised the centurion, and continued sarcastically, 'Sure you can afford it?'

Macro stiffened. 'Yes, of course I can. Five on Nepos, like I said.'

'Nepos? You know the odds are ten to one?'

'That's what I'm counting on.'

'Well, it's your money. If you're sure . . .?'

Macro frowned. 'Do you want to take the bet, or not?'

'I'm happy to take your money. Just a moment, please . . . sir.' The bet-taker opened his tablets and prepared to make a new entry with his stylus. He began to press some tiny notation into the wax, muttering as he wrote. 'Five den. on Nepos to win . . . Your name?'

'Centurion Macro.'

'Macro. Fine, now if I can just have your payment.' Macro handed him the silver coins from his purse and the bet-taker dropped them into one of the boxes carried by his heavies. The coins fell through the slot with a dull chink on to the money already taken in. The bet-taker nodded to the man carrying the chest. 'That's tally one hundred and forty-three.'

The ex-gladiator raised a large metal hoop from his side and fumbled amongst the small wooden pegs until he reached the right number and then worked it free and handed it over to Macro. The bet-taker smiled at him. 'Pleasure doing business with you, though I doubt we'll meet again. Now, if you'll excuse me . . .'

Macro tucked the wooden tally into his purse and hurried back to Cato.

'How much did you place on Nepos?'

'Enough,' Macro replied easily, then pointed across the heads of the spectators towards the imperial box. 'Look, there's Claudius' flunkies. He must be on his way.'

'How much?' Cato persisted.

'Oh, five denarians, or something.'

'Five den— Macro, that's pretty much all we have.'

'Actually, it is all we have.' Macro shrugged an apology. 'It's a risk, but I got odds of ten to one.'

'Really?' Cato responded sourly. 'And why do you think that's good news? He's got nine chances in ten of losing.'

'Look here,' Macro lowered his voice, 'our man said it was a sure thing. We stand to win fifty silver pieces when it's over.'

'I can do the maths, thank you. Fifty pieces, *if* Nepos wins.'

'He will, trust me. I have a feeling for these things.'

Cato shook his head and glanced away, letting his gaze turn to the imperial box. The household slaves were busy setting up a table of snacks and wines to the side of the Emperor's seat. Even at a distance of fifty paces, Cato could make out a platter of ornately arranged fowl glazed in what looked like honey. His mouth began to water at the sight and he felt his stomach churn with hunger.

The imperial household began to emerge from their private entrance to take their seats. A handful of favoured senators eased themselves down on to plump cushions set on the stools each side of the imperial dais. They were followed by some of the Emperor's freedmen and scribes, who stood at the back of the box. At last the white tufts of hair and the gilded wreath on top of Claudius' head came into view and a great roar of greeting swelled up from the crowd and echoed around the Great Circus. Louder than a battle, Cato thought. Far louder.

The Emperor stood still for a moment, basking in the popular acclaim. Only his head moved, in the characteristic twitch that no amount of self-control could prevent. At length Claudius slowly raised an arm and turned to greet his people, who responded to the gesture with an even greater roar. The Emperor's arm sank back to his side and he climbed on to the dais and slumped clumsily into his seat. As the Emperor's wife, Messalina, stepped up beside him, the cheering reached a new frenzy.

Macro leaned close to Cato and shouted into his ear, 'From what I've heard, I bet there's quite a few amongst them who know her almost as well as her husband.'

He grinned and Cato looked round anxiously to make sure that no one had overheard the comment. That was the kind of public comment that informers picked up and passed on to palace agents for a small reward. Then, one night, a squad of Praetorians would kick your door in and bundle you off, never to be seen or heard from again. Fortunately, Macro's foolish words were lost in the deafening roar of the crowd and Cato began to relax.

Then he saw another man entering the imperial box: thin, with dark hair and a plain white toga. Claudius beckoned to the newcomer with a smile, and indicated a seat just below the dais. Cato felt Macro cup a hand to his ear as he pointed towards the box with the other.

'Did you see who just arrived?'

Cato nodded. 'Our friend, the Imperial Secretary.'

'Do you think Narcissus knows we're back in Rome?'

'If he doesn't already know, he will soon.'

'Then we're in trouble. That bastard talked General Plautius into decimating our cohort.'

'I remember. He won't be happy that I'm still alive.'

Cato felt a surge of fear as he looked over the heads of the crowd at Narcissus. Not much escaped the notice of the man who controlled the Emperor's secret police, disposed of any threats and dispensed much of Claudius' patronage. And if he *did* know that Cato was in the city then he would be sure to tie up any loose ends as soon as possible, preferably by discreet strangulation in some dark, forgotten cell of the Mammertine prison. But there was a chance, an outside chance, that Macro and he had evaded the ever watchful eye of Narcissus, even now.

At that precise moment Narcissus turned in his seat and cast his gaze over the crowd and, before Cato could react, his eyes fixed in the direction of the two centurions. Cato felt his guts turn to ice. It was only an instant, then Cato slumped down on his bench, out of Narcissus' line of sight.

'Shit!' Cato muttered. 'Shit . . . shit . . . shit.'

Macro dropped down beside him, alarmed by the sudden change in his friend's expression. 'What's the matter?'

'He saw us. Narcissus saw me.'

'Bollocks. How could he? We're just a pair of faces amongst thousands. There's no way—'

'I'm telling you, he saw me!' Cato could almost feel the rough hands of the Praetorian Guardsmen Narcissus would be sure to send out to arrest him. It would all be over in a moment.

Macro stood up slowly and glanced towards the imperial box, before ducking back down beside his friend. 'He's not even looking this way. Just chatting with the Emperor. Nothing else. He can't have seen you. Relax!'

The cheering quickly died away as the priests prepared for the sacrifice to open the day's racing. Two assistants dragged one of the white kid goats out from the cage and, holding the struggling animal by its legs, they carried it up the steps to the altar and held it down on the gleaming marble surface. The chanting of the high priest could just be heard across the track, as he intoned the blessing of Jupiter, best and greatest, on the Emperor Claudius, his family, the senate and people of Rome, and the charioteers. Then, he raised a curved dagger above the bleating goat, paused a moment, the blade glinting in the sunlight, before he slashed it down. The distant bleating was abruptly cut off. For a moment the priest bent over the twitching body of the goat and worked at its stomach with the dagger. Then, he eased out the liver, glistening in purple and red as it steamed slightly in the cool air. He bent over the organ to examine it closely, then called over a colleague, who also looked at the liver before they discussed their readings. The priest suddenly lifted the organ aloft to signify that Jupiter had accepted the sacrifice and the races could proceed. A huge roar of relieved tension swept round the stadium. Macro slapped his hands down on his knees and grinned like a boy.

The pious speeches by the senate fathers were kept as brief as possible. It was the usual flowery offer of thanks to the sponsor of the races, in this case Claudius himself. The Emperor tapped his feet impatiently as he tried to catch the eye of the speakers and then made a quick waving gesture with his hand to get them to move on swiftly. The crowd cheered each speech politely, and then, as the last speaker climbed down from the podium on the island, they craned their necks expectantly, all eyes riveted to the line of gates at the far end of the Great Circus.

There was a moment of hushed expectancy. Then a great fanfare of trumpets shrilled out and the gates swung inwards to reveal the dark tunnels leading back to the marshalling area. There was movement in the shadows, then the chariot teams burst out of the tunnels and on to the sand of the Great Circus. The crowd jumped up and screamed with excitement, and slowly the cheers resolved into rival chants in support of each team, or of vulgar denigration of the opposition. Most of the Praetorians, clearly, were supporters of the blues and bellowed out the name of Porcius as he drove his team past the imperial box and saluted Emperor Claudius.

'Bastard better lose,' Macro said softly. Then he glanced around nervously and drew a deep breath. 'Come on, Porcius!'

Cato raised an eyebrow as he caught his friend's gaze. Macro shrugged. 'Just keeping on side. No point in starting a fight.'

The chariot teams completed a circuit of the track and then drew up in a line abreast, just in front of the Emperor. The crews clustered round, making final adjustments to the horses' harnesses and applying a last handful of grease to the chariot axles. The charioteers checked their reins and made sure that the razor-sharp safety knives were secure in their scabbards. Each charioteer wore a short, sleeveless tunic in his team's colours, and the light screens that folded around their legs were also painted in the team colours.

Macro focused his attention on Nepos, a wiry man with a dark complexion. Nepos stood erect and still in his green tunic. Too still for Macro's liking, almost as if he was too terrified to move. Or maybe he simply had nerves of steel. He'd better had.

Once the preparations were complete the crews withdrew from the track and the charioteers took the strain on their reins, holding back their horse teams. The animals had been raised to run flat out and jostled each other nervously, muzzles flaring as their powerful flanks heaved.

For a moment Cato forgot everything that troubled him as he sat forward on the edge of his bench and stared at the four chariot teams, tensed up and ready to explode into action. The Emperor nodded to the race marshal and the latter stepped up on to the podium at the front of the imperial box. He carried a small flag, which he carefully unfurled and slowly raised up until his arm was erect. Every eye of the tens of thousands of people in the Circus was on him and there was not a sound except for the snorting of the horses. The marshal waited until the teams were as level as they could be. Then he snatched his hand down and the flag dropped with a rippling flutter. Instantly the crowd roared. The charioteers cracked their reins and the horses kicked up plumes of sand as they yanked the chariots forward and the race began.

Porcius, true to his reputation, somehow managed to coax an extra burst of strength from his team and they had nosed ahead in the first length. The blues were just clear of the other teams as the chariots swerved round the end of the island, throwing up sheets of sand as the body of each chariot skidded round, and passed temporarily out of sight. The cheering of the spectators around Cato subsided as they turned their eyes to the other end of the island, waiting in tense anticipation for the chariots to reappear. Sand sprayed up an instant before the first chariot swung into view and the Praetorians leaped up in delight, screaming out their support for Porcius. Right behind him was Nepos, and Macro only just managed to restrain his cry of delight that Nepos was still in close contention. With desperate flicks of the reins Nepos steered his team to the outside as they raced down the track towards the imperial box. Gradually he closed on Porcius, then began to edge up alongside the blues. Porcius saw the danger and, with a quick tug on the reins, moved out to head off his rival.

A howl of outrage burst out from the supporters of the greens and Macro balled his hands into tight fists, but kept his lips clamped tightly together. Beside him, Cato just felt sick as he saw the man carrying the fate of their last few coins desperately rein in, then abruptly swerve left, closer to the island. Porcius had misjudged his manoeuvre and now his horses missed a pace as their charioteer urged them back on course. But it was too late. Nepos, leaning over the front rail of his chariot, was cracking his reins furiously and crying out encouragement to his team. They surged forward, inside the blues, past them and into the lead. Cato felt a surge of joy burst through his veins, and fought not to let it show.

'Yessss!' Macro punched his fist into the air, then looked round anxiously. Some of the guardsmen were looking at him in surprise, but quickly turned their attention back to the race.

'Watch it,' Cato muttered. 'I get the feeling we're not amongst friends.'

Back on the track, Nepos raced ahead, and rounded the island, disappearing from view. An instant later the blues swerved round after him and were gone. Already a sizeable gap had opened up between the leaders and the other two teams, the reds and the yellows, who were battling it out, neck and neck, trying to close up on the leaders. Once more the cheering on this side of the Circus died down as the race continued on the far side of the island. Heads swivelled to the far end of the central island, everyone watching intently.

Not everyone.

Cato glanced down into the imperial box and saw that Narcissus was staring back in his direction. Their eyes met. Cato was sure of it. The Imperial Secretary was staring directly at him, and there was nothing Cato could do but pretend it wasn't happening, as if he was just some face in the crowd. Then Narcissus raised a hand and pointed his finger at Cato, then waved slowly, before turning back towards the track. Cato felt the cold chill of terror trickle down his spine. He had been seen and recognised and there would be no avoiding the Imperial Secretary now. Cato knew he was as good as dead. Narcissus had beckoned to one of the guards officers and was speaking animatedly into his ear. It could be about anything, Cato hoped desperately; they could be talking about somebody or something else. Then Narcissus turned and pointed towards him and the officer nodded, and moved towards the entrance of the imperial box.

Cato grabbed his friend's arm. 'We have to go! Now!'

'Are you mad?' Macro shook his hand off. 'What's left of our money's out there. We're not going anywhere. Not until the race is over.'

'But . . .' Cato's mind raced. There was no time to explain it to Macro. And Macro wouldn't budge. 'All right! I'm heading back to that tavern. Find me there, afterwards.' He rose, snatched up his helmet and hurried up the steps towards the exit.

Behind him, Macro stretched out a hand. 'Cato! Wait! Oh, sod you, then!'

Cato scrambled down the steep steps into the arched gallery that ran around the Circus, under the banked seating. From there a wider flight of steps led down into the street, and his nailed boots echoed sharply off the columns and curved ceiling of the gallery. Above the dulled noise of the crowd he thought he could hear more footsteps, more nailed boots and a shout. He ran down the steps, three at a time, risking an injury in his bid to escape the Circus before Narcissus' men could stop him. At the bottom of the stairs he emerged from the shadows of the building and saw that there were still plenty of people ambling along the wide thoroughfare that ran beside the Great Circus. Cato knew if he ran he was sure to stand out from the crowd. He drew a breath and then moved in amongst the passers-by, filtering diagonally away from the steps towards an opening in the line of shops opposite, where a small side street ran down towards the Forum. Behind him he heard the clattering of boots on the steps, but, with iron will, he forced himself not to turn and look, but to keep walking steadily towards the side street. As people crossed his path, or barged into him, Cato refused to meet their gaze and moved on, all the while waiting for a shout from behind that would mean his doom. At last he reached the street corner, and ducked down the narrow alley, pausing only briefly to glance back towards the Great Circus. Four guardsmen were standing a few steps above the street, scrutinising the crowd, but none of them was looking in his direction.

Cato hurried down the alley, which was one of the older streets in the city, winding its way down the slope, becoming evermore narrow until the sky was only visible as a jagged line overhead, crowded by the eaves of the tightly packed tenement blocks rearing up on either side. Behind him the roars of the vast crowd in the Circus were gradually muffled. The atmosphere of the alley was thick with the rank odour of rotting food and sewage. He passed few people as he walked quickly along. A few surly-looking women watched him from open doorways and he had to squeeze past a small band of drunken youths, heading uphill towards the Great Circus. In the gloomy alley there were no landmarks for Cato to steer by, only where the slope led, and the broad sense of the direction in which he needed to move. Then, at last, he turned a corner, and the alley ran into a wider street, filled with people. To the left lay the Forum and, with a deep breath, Cato turned towards it and walked on at a steadier pace, trying not to look like the wretched fugitive he had become.

He found the tavern easily enough, and took a seat inside, close to a wall so that he could keep watch on the crowds outside and lean back into the shadows if he needed to avoid anyone's searching gaze. The young barman came over, drying his hands on a filthy rag. A flicker of recognition crossed his face and he grinned.

'Didn't go to the races then?'

'We did,' Cato replied quickly before he realised that his quitting the Circus so soon would look suspicious unless he could explain it. 'But I remembered I was supposed to meet someone here. My friend will join me later.'

'I see.' The barman shrugged. 'Well, that's a shame. What'll you drink?'

'Drink?'

'This is a tavern, friend, not a clients' waiting room.'

'A cup of wine. Heated wine.'

'Just a cup?'

'That's all I want, for now.'

'Right.' The barman threw the rag over his shoulder and headed back to the large wine jars set into the counter. He returned and placed a steaming cup down at Cato's table.

'That's one sestertian.'

With a sick feeling Cato realised that Macro had charge

of all their money, and he was back at the Circus. He glanced up at the barman. 'Keep a tab. I'll pay when my friend arrives.'

The barman shook his head. 'No tabs. House policy. You pay now.'

Cato cleared his throat and stared hard at the young barman. He lowered his voice to a rough growl. 'I said I'll pay later. Now leave me.'

The barman opened his mouth to protest. Cato leaned back against the wall, crossed his arms and nodded back towards the rear of the tavern. The barman eyed him coldly, then moved away and settled behind the bar to rinse some cups, and keep an eye on his difficult customer.

Cato turned his gaze back on to the crowd in the Forum and waited. Hopefully Macro would come to him once the first race was over, if Nepos had won. Then he'd collect his winnings and head for the Forum. An hour passed and the cup in front of Cato had been empty for a long while. He did not dare order another in case Macro did not turn up, and began to worry about how he would talk his way out of the tavern.

Then, a short distance away, the crowd parted as a patrician woman shrank back with a small cry of disgust. A figure in a centurion's armour shambled past her. His face was battered and bloody and for a moment Cato did not recognise Macro. Then, as his friend turned towards the tavern, Cato jumped up.

'Macro! Macro, what the hell's happened to you?'

CHAPTER FIVE

'Out of my way!' Macro shouted. He brushed Cato to one side and threw himself at the barman, swinging a punch to the young man's head. The barman had been working the Forum taverns for long enough to know how to react to such attacks. He ducked beneath the blow and stepped to one side, giving the centurion a firm thrust in the back as he swept past. With a splintering crash Macro sent a table and stools flying before he struck the unyielding bar counter with sufficient force to drive the wind from his lungs. He lay there for a moment, shaking his head, and the barman scurried back round the bar to snatch up a heavy club. The other drinkers in the tavern scrambled up from their seats and pushed towards the street, from where they turned back to watch the spectacle.

'Call the watch!' one of the customers shouted. The call was taken up by some other voices in the crowd that was rapidly gathering outside the tavern.

The last thing Cato wanted was any attention from the men of the urban cohort that policed the streets. He picked his way round the bar and grabbed Macro's shoulder.

'Someone's gone for the watch. Macro, we have to get out of here.'

Macro glared at Cato. 'Once I've finished with him.'

'Not now.' Cato glanced round and saw that the barman

was staring at them wildly as he raised his club. 'What do I owe you for the drink?'

'Drink?' The barman frowned. 'Just fuck off. Get him out of here.'

'Right.' Cato cautiously approached Macro and helped him up, keeping a firm grip on his arm. 'Come on. We have to go.'

Macro caught the note of urgency in Cato's voice and nodded. Then the two centurions picked their way through the splintered wreckage of the table and stools and out into the street. The crowd instinctively pulled back and gave them some space. Not far off, over the heads of the onlookers, four red horse-hair crests edged towards the tavern.

'This way.' Cato shoved Macro along the line of stalls on the edge of the Forum and they threaded their way into the bustling crowd of shoppers and sightseers. When Cato felt they had gone far enough he pulled Macro into a narrow alley behind the Forum and the two of them leaned up against the grimy plaster walls of an ancient shrine and caught their breath.

'What the hell was that all about?' Cato snapped.

'Eh?'

'That fight at the tavern. What the hell do you think you were doing?'

'That bastard was one of Porcius' supporters.'

'I know. So what?'

'Porcius won.'

'Is that any reason . . .? Oh, shit.' Cato's head drooped. 'The bet. You lost all our money.'

'What d'you mean I've lost it?' Macro responded angrily. 'It was *our* money. *Our* bet. You'd have had fair shares if we'd won.'

'But we didn't.'

'I know!' Macro smacked his fist against his chest. 'I was bloody well there when that twat Nepos drove his fucking chariot straight into the wall. Only a hundred feet short of the line. The Praetorians were pissing themselves laughing . . .'

'And?'

'Well,' Macro lowered his eyes, 'that's when I hit one of them.'

'You hit one of them?'

'Two, actually. Perhaps a few more as well. Can't quite remember. One of them didn't get up.'

'I see.' Cato spoke through clenched teeth. 'So not only did you lose our money, you've managed to get the Praetorian Guards on our backs. And now, thanks to your little rumpus in the tavern, the urban cohort are after us as well.' Cato rubbed his forehead to ease the torrent of tormenting thoughts cascading through his mind. 'On top of that, Narcissus knows we're in Rome.'

Macro looked up. 'Oh?'

'He saw me. Back at the Great Circus.'

'You're sure?'

'Of course I'm bloody sure. He looked right at me. He even waved. Before he sent some men after me. Why did you think I had to get out so fast?'

Macro shrugged. 'I had wondered about that. So what do we do now?'

'That's the question. Trouble is, there's no answer. We can't run for it. They're bound to have men watching for us at the city gates. We can't lie low in Rome, not without money.'

Both men were silent for a moment, before Macro reached a hand up to his face and winced as it came in contact with a huge bruise on his cheek. 'Ouch! That smarts!'

Cato glared at him. 'Well, you deserve it.'

'Thanks for your sympathy . . .' Macro looked up at his friend. 'We need to get off the streets.'

That night Cato lay on his side and stared at the wall, close enough to see his breath glistening on the cracked plaster, thanks to a shaft of moonlight probing through the broken shutter. He was more tired than he had been for months, yet his mind would not stop running over the day's events. The uncertainty over his future that had plagued him since returning to Rome now seemed quite trivial compared to the despair he felt at his present situation. Only a miracle could save him now. Tormented by such thoughts he lay still and stared at the wall for what felt like hours. Macro, as usual, had fallen into a deep sleep almost as soon as he had laid his head down on his mattress, and his snoring threatened to shake the tenement block down. For a while Cato entertained the notion of crossing the room and rolling Macro over on to his side, but that would mean leaving the snug warmth he had managed to build up under his tunic, army cloak and blanket. So he suffered the din, grew accustomed to it, and eventually drifted off to sleep.

A shattering crash snapped him into wakefulness. It was just after dawn, and the room was readily visible in the thin grey light. Cato sat up, turning towards the doorway just as the old iron latch sprang from its fixings and the weathered timbers of the door flew inwards and cracked sharply against the wall, dislodging a shower of loose plaster.

'What the hell . . .?' Macro raised his head just as four

heavily armoured soldiers burst into the room with swords drawn.

'Stay where you are!' one of the men shouted, raising his blade just enough to make the threat unmistakable. Cato and Macro froze, and the man lowered his sword as he addressed them in a more official tone.

'Centurions Macro and Cato?'

Cato nodded.

'Narcissus wants to see you.'

CHAPTER SIX

'Bollocks!' Macro shouted, and shot out an arm to where his sword lay against the wall. The Praetorian reacted at once and stamped his boot down on Macro's wrist. Macro gasped as the iron studs stabbed into his flesh, but before he could say another word he felt the point of a sword at his throat.

'I really wouldn't do that, sir,' the Praetorian said reasonably. 'You're outnumbered, you're on the ground and you'd be dead before you could even draw your sword. So don't give us any trouble.' He let the words sink in, and when Macro nodded, he slowly raised his boot, but kept the point of his sword poised over Macro's throat. Keeping his eyes fixed on the centurion he gave an order. 'Frontinus, get their weapons.'

One of his men sheathed his blade and took charge of the swords and daggers of the two officers. Only when the man had retreated out of the room did the leader of the squad withdraw the point of his weapon and step away from Macro.

'Get dressed. And get your kit together.'

Cato frowned. 'Our kit?'

'Yes, sir. I'm afraid you won't be coming back here again.'

Cato felt his blood chill. He was numb. So this was what it was like to be led to your execution. A cordial visit from the Imperial Secretary's henchmen and two more names were erased from history. He almost laughed out loud at the pretentiousness of the thought. He and Macro were not even worthy of a footnote. Two minor characters with walk-on parts in some provincial drama was nearer the mark. They were doomed to be forgotten, even within the living memory of the very men who took them to their deaths. That was how it was, and Cato felt the bitter anger of one whose life was fated to end meaninglessly almost before it had even begun. He looked up at the leader of the squad.

'Where are you taking us?'

'Told you, sir. Narcissus wants to see you.'

Cato smiled. No doubt the Imperial Secretary wanted a chance to bid them farewell so that they would be in no doubt who had crafted their doom. That was typical of Narcissus. No matter how small the triumph, he needed to witness it in person. Under more detached circumstances Cato would have been curious to reflect on the flaws of such an insecure personality, but with death seemingly imminent he had nothing but hatred and despair in his heart.

'Now then, on your feet, please, sir. I've got a busy morning; quite a few other appointments to fit in. So, if you wouldn't mind . . .?'

Cato rose up from his mattress warily, his mind racing with thoughts of fight and escape. He wondered if the Praetorians would finish him and Macro off there and then. But then, he supposed, they would have to carry the bodies away for disposal. They wouldn't like that. Much easier to make their victims take themselves away before being disposed of. Being careful not to turn his back on the Praetorians, Cato put on his boots and laced them up, before packing his clothes and equipment into his blanket. On the other side of the room Macro did the same. There was not much to leave behind: a few scraps of food, and odd items of clothing that had been awaiting repair. It puzzled Cato that the Praetorians were prepared to let them pack their possessions, until it struck him that the worldly goods of the two centurions might fetch a reasonable price back at the guards' barracks.

Cato folded his blanket over his belongings, tied the ends together, and looped the knot over the end of the marching yoke. When Macro had finished, he joined Cato a short distance away from the waiting Praetorians.

He looked down at his boot, as if checking his laces, and whispered, 'Think we should try and make a break for it?'

'No.'

The Praetorian smiled, anticipating the remark even though he had not heard it. 'Please, don't either of you do anything foolish. Me and the lads have had plenty of experience escorting people.'

'Prisoners, you mean,' Macro growled.

The Praetorian shrugged. 'People, prisoners, it's all the same to us, sir. We just collect and deliver. There's others who handle the messy stuff. I'm just warning you not to try and escape. It'd be an unpleasant business for both of us, if you get my meaning.'

Macro glared at him. 'I'd get it a lot quicker if you didn't dress it up so much. In the legions we call a spade a spade. We have to deal with the real messy stuff.'

'But we're not in the legions, are we, sir? In Rome things are done with more style.'

'Death's death, lad. There ain't no hiding that.'

'You'd be surprised what we keep hidden.' The Praetorian

smiled coldly, then stood aside and gestured towards the door. 'Now, sirs, if you wouldn't mind . . .?'

With two guards in front and two behind, their swords drawn, the centurions made their way down the narrow staircase and emerged into the stairwell at the bottom of the tenement block. The guardsmen had been seen entering the building and a small crowd of curious onlookers had gathered outside. As the prisoners and escort clattered on to the paved street, Velina emerged from the bakery. Her eyes widened in surprise as she saw Cato and Macro carrying their packs. She stepped out in front of the leading Praetorians.

'Cato! What's happening?'

'Out of the way, lady!' snapped one of the guards.

Velina looked round his shoulder. 'Cato?'

She tried to push past but the guard grabbed her arm and thrust her back against the wall of the tenement and then the Praetorians marched off with their prisoners.

They entered the palace through one of the servants' entrances that opened on to a narrow side street away from well-used thoroughfares. Cato recalled using the narrow gateway a few times as a child, when he had lived in the servants' quarters of the palace. There were few people around to see them taken inside, and Cato realised how easy this made it for people simply to disappear in the city. Once past the guards stationed at the entrance, the Praetorians took them along a corridor until they reached a stairwell, and then they climbed up through the heart of the imperial palace.

Cato turned to the leader. 'You're not taking us to the cells, then?'

The man raised his eyebrows. 'Evidently.' Then he relented and relaxed his stern expression for a moment. 'Look, sir, we were told to take you to Narcissus. That's all the orders we have, as far as you two are concerned.'

'You weren't sent to take us to be executed, then?'

'No, sir. Just to take you to Narcissus. That's all. If he decides you're for the chop, well then, that's different, and we might have to take you to the lads who get that job done.'

'Oh . . .' Cato looked at the man more closely, wondering how he could be so sanguine about his duties. Maybe the Praetorian had simply become used to it. Cato remembered that under Emperor Caligula the Praetorian Guards had been kept busy arresting and executing people throughout the three years of his reign.

After four flights of stairs they emerged on to a wide corridor with an ornate mosaic pattern flowing across the floor. Large windows, high up, admitted broad shafts of light. Cato had never seen the corridor before and as he felt a warm current of air rise up his legs he realised that the floor must be heated.

Macro pursed his lips. 'Our man Narcissus knows how to live well.'

The escorted party marched down the corridor towards an imposing door, almost twice the height of a man. The door was flanked by a pair of Praetorian Guardsmen, and in a niche to the left a clerk sat at a large walnut desk. He was neatly turned out in a soft wool tunic and looked up at the sound of echoing footsteps. The leader of the squad nodded to him.

'Centurions Macro and Cato, as requested by the Imperial Secretary.'

'He's in a meeting with the Emperor. You'll have to wait. Over there.' He pointed across the corridor with his stylus, to where padded benches lined another niche. The party crossed over and the two centurions gratefully lowered their packs, and took a seat. Two guardsmen stood either side of them. In the austere surroundings of the Imperial Secretary's suite of offices, Macro felt self-conscious about his unshaven and battered face. Glancing over at Cato, he saw his friend staring dejectedly at the mosaic floor, wholly absorbed in his misery.

The Imperial Secretary's meeting with Emperor Claudius went on, and on. As the sun rose above the sprawling city, the shafts of light slowly glided down the walls of the corridor and finally bathed the prisoners and their escort in a warm golden glow. Macro eased himself back and shut his eyes, and, despite their predicament, he began to enjoy the soothing sensation of the warmth and the hazy orange glow of the sunlight through his eyelids. So it was that he missed the faint creak of the doors as they swung open. As the guardsmen stiffened to attention, the clerk jumped to his feet and bowed. Cato rose quickly, but before he could stir Macro, the Emperor of Rome and his most faithful and trusted servant, Narcissus, emerged into the corridor.

'S-s-so, you really think it's that important?'

'Yes, Caesar.' Narcissus nodded to emphasise his agreement. 'It is a vital component of the work. Without it, posterity will be forever impoverished.'

Emperor Claudius looked at him wide-eyed, and there was a violent twitch of his head. 'Really? You r-really think so?'

'Yes, Caesar. Without question.'

'Well, put like that, w-w-what can I say? I had thought that my ch-ch-ch-childhood poetry might not be quite the ticket for an autobiography.' He smiled, twitched, and squeezed Narcissus' arm. 'But you've convinced me. As ever, your good t-t-taste and sound judgement are a perfect complement to my genius.'

'Caesar.' Narcissus bowed low. 'Your praise is undeserved. Any mortal with any literary sensibility at all could not mistake the divine brilliance of your powers of perception and description.'

Claudius beamed and clasped Narcissus' arm in gratitude, then froze as he spied Macro, nodding off on his bench. 'I somehow doubt that f-fellow shares your point of view.'

Narcissus glared into the niche and snapped an order. 'Get that fool on his feet!'

Two guardsmen took an arm each and hauled Macro up. He opened his eyes blearily. 'What? What? Oh . . .'

At the sight of the Emperor he was instantly awake and stood straight as a marble pillar. Claudius limped over towards him and looked the centurion over.

'Is this one of the men you were telling me about, Narcissus?'

'Yes, Caesar.'

'Hardly an impressive sp-sp-sp-specimen, I must say. But he looks like the sort of man we might sacrifice without losing much s-sleep.'

'Yes, Caesar. Once again you anticipate my thoughts.'

Claudius turned to Cato, with a look of surprise. 'And this other one, this boy? Surely he's not the other officer you mentioned. Why, h-h-he doesn't look old enough to even shave!'

Narcissus forced a laugh, and when his clerk followed his cue the Emperor turned round with a frown. 'No one asked you to join in!'

The clerk froze, and blanched, dropping his eyes at once.

'That's better.' The Emperor turned back to continue his examination of the two centurions. 'I suppose you know what you're d-d-doing, Narcissus. That other business we talked about will need careful handling. Are you sure the-the-these men are up to the job?'

'If they aren't, then no one is, Caesar.'

'Very well . . . I'll see you at dinner.'

'Caesar.' Narcissus bowed again, as did the Praetorians, his secretary and the two centurions. They kept their heads down as Claudius shuffled away down the corridor and disappeared into a side gallery. The moment the Emperor was out of sight there was a collective sigh of released tension. Macro felt as if he had escaped instant execution by a hair's breadth and the blood pounded through his heart.

Narcissus glanced at the two centurions and snapped an order. 'Bring them in!'

He turned on his heel and strode back into his office as Cato and Macro grabbed their yokes and, flanked by the guardsmen, they were escorted through the high doorway into the office of the Imperial Secretary.

The room was vast. Above, the ceiling rose to the same height as the corridor, and the floor was covered with animal skins, through which the heat of the hypocaust could still be felt. To the right stretched a wall made up of a honeycomb of shelving for scrolls and books. To the left, the wall was covered with a finely detailed painting of a huge bay that stretched out into the distance where it was lost in a faint haze. Looming over the coastal strip was a vast mountain, dwarfing the towns that lined the shores at its feet. On the far wall were four large windows, with spectacular views over the Forum and the sprawling slopes of the Subura beyond. Narcissus had crossed the room and settled himself behind an oak desk whose size was proportionate to the room, if not to the amount of paperwork upon it, which struggled to look burdensome. The Imperial Secretary noticed the admiring looks on the faces of the two centurions as they gazed out over the city, fascinated to see so much of it at once.

'Impressive, isn't it?' he smiled. 'It is the first thing that people who visit this office remark on. I find it inspiring and, at the same time, frightening. Terrifying even.'

He twisted away from Cato and Macro to stare out of the window, and continued in the same reflective tone, 'The Empire is ruled from here. From this palace. The palace is the mind that directs the muscles and sinews of empire. Down there, in the Forum, is the public expression of that power. The fine temples to scores of Gods. The basilicas where the fortunes of men are made and traded, and regulated by law. People from all over the world come to the Forum to marvel at the scale of our achievement. Together, the palace and Forum constitute a shrine to power and order.' He paused and raised a hand, pointing across to the rising slope of the Subura, a filthy mass of tile and plaster, poised like a wave about to crash down upon the Forum.

'That slum, on the other hand, is a chaos of poverty and depravity forever threatening to engulf and destroy the order we have created. The Subura is a daily reminder of what we might become if the Emperor and all who further his aims are swept away. The plebs are the barbarians within the gate. As long as they are fed and entertained we have them in our grasp. But let them get an inkling of their own power, or worse, let another person prey upon their baser motivations . . . and their superstitions,' Narcissus added with heavy emphasis, 'and they'll cut our throats.'

The Imperial Secretary turned back towards the two centurions with a weary expression. 'So, it is my task, my purpose in this life, to make sure that order is maintained and that Claudius remains in power. That means I have to identify and contain any and all possible threats to the Emperor. And it is your job, as soldiers sworn to obey his will, to aid me in any way I determine. Do I make myself clear?'

'Yes, sir,' Cato and Macro replied. Cato hadn't a clue what the Imperial Secretary was alluding to. But the hint that their services were needed, and no mention of execution, filled his heart with hope.

Narcissus nodded at their ready obedience, and leaned forward to rest his arms on his desk. 'Then listen closely. I have a task for you. Of course it's dangerous and entails great personal risk. But then you have nothing to lose. Isn't that right, Centurion Cato?'

'Sir?'

'Don't play me for a fool, young man. Your life is forfeit. I have but to raise my voice and call in the guards and have them put you to death on the spot. You, and even your friend here. And no one would even ask me the reason. As it happens, I have reason enough. See here.' He picked up a scroll on his desk. 'This arrived yesterday. From Britain. You know who it's from?'

Cato's heart sank. 'General Plautius?'

'That's right. And you can guess what he says.' Narcissus smiled faintly. 'The death sentence is upheld. In addition, the general states that there is enough circumstantial evidence to warrant the execution of Centurion Macro on charges of mutiny and murder. You are both dead already.'

He let the words sink in, staring at the centurions intently with his dark brown eyes, sunk deep beneath his plucked brow. Cato stared back, angry and afraid, as he knew that he and Macro were being thrust into new perils by the Imperial Secretary. Cato swallowed nervously before he replied.

'Unless we do your bidding.'

'That's right.' Narcissus nodded. 'You'll do my bidding, or be fodder for the carrion before this day is done.'

Macro sneered at him. 'And what is it you'd have us do for you? An assassination? Make someone disappear? What?'

'Nothing so easy,' Narcissus laughed. 'I have plenty of men for such menial tasks. No, for what I have in mind, I need two resourceful officers. Ruthless men who are also desperate enough to succeed at all costs. Men who know their lives are forfeit unless they carry out their orders. In short, men like you two. I won't demean your intelligence by offering the job to you. You'll do it, or you'll die here and now. All that remains is to tell you the details. Understand me?'

'Oh, we understand all right . . . sir.'

'Very well.' Narcissus leaned back in his chair and drew his thoughts together. 'A month ago a merchant ship was captured not far from the coast, off Ravenna. It happens from time to time. Someone fancies his chances as a pirate and starts preying on shipping. We can afford to overlook the loss of the odd vessel here and there, but if they get too greedy we send a squadron after them to scare them off. Only this time, the pirates captured a ship which happened to be carrying one of my most trusted agents. He was on a mission of the utmost sensitivity. He was taken prisoner, and tortured. They sent word that they want a ransom for him. Together with his ring finger. I assume that's some kind of pirate tradition to show they mean business.'

'You want him back?' Cato asked. 'Is that it? Is that all?'

'Not quite all. My agent carried within his baggage some items of great value to the Emperor.'

'Treasure?' Macro frowned. 'You want to send us on a treasure hunt?'

'Treasure? Yes,' Narcissus replied. 'But treasure that has far more worth than all the gold and jewels of Egypt.'

'Really?' Macro sniffed. 'I somehow doubt that.'

'What kind of treasure are we talking about?' Cato interrupted his friend.

'Scrolls.' Narcissus smiled. 'Three of them. The pirates want ten million sestertians for the return of the scrolls.'

'Ten million? Just for three scrolls?' Macro laughed and shook his head. 'You're not serious, sir.'

'I've never been more serious in my life.'

Macro's laughter died in his thoat as he beheld the intent expression on the Imperial Secretary's face. 'These scrolls – what's so special about them?'

Narcissus stared at him. 'You don't need to know. You will be told more, if the situation requires it. Suffice to say that if I gain possession of them then a great danger to the Emperor will be averted. For now, all that need concern you is your mission. You will find and recover the scrolls and bring them to me here. If you can manage it, I also want the rest of my agent returned. But if that should jeopardise the safety of the scrolls the agent must be regarded as expendable.'

'Who else knows about this?' asked Cato.

Narcissus thought for a moment. 'The Emperor. My clerk and one other.'

'Who is he, sir?'

Narcissus smiled and shook his head. 'You don't need to know. For now. In the meantime I have arranged for you both to be posted to the naval base at Ravenna. We're sending a column of marine reinforcements for operations against this new pirate threat. You can join them. The prefect has been told to find and destroy the pirates' lair. Your job is to make sure that you recover the scrolls, and my agent, once the pirates are defeated. You are also to make sure that any of the pirates who have read, or been in contact with the scrolls, are not taken alive. One last thing.' Narcissus leaned towards them again. 'It is possible that the pirates may have approached other parties with a view to selling the scrolls. If that's the case, my enemies will stop at nothing to get hold of them. You must trust no one. Understand?'

The two centurions nodded.

'When do we leave?' Macro asked.

'You already have. The reinforcements left Rome at dawn. You'll have to catch up with them once I've finished with you.'

Cato's mind reeled. 'What about all the paperwork? Our orders?'

Narcissus waved away the questions. 'My clerk has it all in hand. He'll give you the required documents as soon as you leave my office. Now, if you don't want to get any unnecessary blisters, I suggest you get moving, gentlemen.'

'Just one thing, sir,' said Macro.

'Yes?'

'Money. We'll need some to cover our expenses as far as Ravenna, sir.'

'I see. Very well. You can draw some petty cash from my clerk.'

'Thank you, sir.'

'That's all right.' Narcissus smiled. 'You can settle up, if you survive. Now, on your way.'

Narcissus leaned back and crossed his arms, clearly indicating that the meeting was over. Cato and Macro turned towards the doors. Before they could reach them the doors were swung open by a Praetorian on each side. Narcissus' clerk was waiting at his table, a wax tablet in each hand. As the centurions marched into the corridor, he held out the tablets. Cato took his and was busy tucking it into his knapsack when he glanced across the corridor and froze. Macro noticed his reaction and glanced round. Seated in the niche opposite was a heavily built man, running to fat. He wore the toga of a senator, and smiled slowly as he recognised the two centurions.

'Why, if I'm not mistaken,' he chuckled, 'it's my old comrades in arms, Centurion Macro and his little pet optio.' He paused as his eyes fell on the transverse crest of the helmet hanging from Cato's yoke. 'Centurion Cato? I don't believe it.'

Cato dipped his head in formal acknowledgement of the other man's rank, and he replied in an unusually cool voice, 'Tribune Vitellius, I wondered if we would meet again.'

CHAPTER SEVEN

'What the hell was that bastard Vitellius doing there?' Macro grumbled as he shifted his pack and adjusted his stride. 'I hoped I'd never lay eyes on him ever again, after that business back in Britain. Just goes to show. When you've really fallen in the shit, you can always count on someone to pile on another load.'

Cato grunted his assent at his friend's quirky fatalism. Life was like that. He'd already seen enough of it to know. Macro was right to be worried. The fact that the man had been waiting to see Narcissus immediately after them implied some kind of connection with the mission they had been forced to undertake. It might be a coincidence, Cato reflected. After all, Narcissus must be overseeing many operations. Even so, Cato could not shake off the feeling that their presence and that of the treacherous former tribune of the Second Legion were somehow linked. They had foiled a plot by Vitellius to assassinate Emperor Claudius, but after the event the wily tribune had left them with no evidence to bring against him, and so compelled their silence. Cato was certain that Vitellius was merely biding his time before he arranged for fatal accidents to befall Macro and himself.

The revival of this danger added to his existing fears, and Cato could not shake Vitellius from his mind as he and Macro trudged along the Flaminian Way. Even though it was a cold day, and a chilly breeze cut through the air, there were only patches of cloud in the crisp blue sky. After the first mile on the road, the exercise had warmed their muscles and Cato no longer shivered. They had left Rome at noon, pausing at the Sanqualian Gate to fill their canteens, and only with the walls of the city falling behind them had Macro felt safe enough to speak his mind. On either side of the broad paved road, tombs and mausoleums jostled with more modest memorials to the generations of the dead who had been buried outside the walls of the city.

The traffic on the Flaminian Way was heavy, with a constant stream of wagons and carts loaded down with farm produce, goods and luxuries heading for the great markets of the capital. Trundling in the opposite direction were empty vehicles. The two centurions marched past as swiftly as possible to catch up with the reinforcement column that had left the city hours before and was well on the way to Ocriculum. The column would make good time as traffic would clear the way for them as they passed, whereas the two centurions, being far less conspicuous, would have to weave their way through the other road users.

'We're not going to catch them before nightfall,' Cato grumbled. 'Not at this rate.'

'We might,' Macro replied, glancing over his shoulder at Cato. 'If we can keep the pace up. Come on, lad, no dawdling.'

Cato gritted his teeth and lengthened his stride, until he drew alongside his friend. 'You ever had any dealings with the marines before?'

'Marines?' Macro spat on the ground. 'Yes, I've come across a few. On the Rhine squadron. They used to take leave in Argentorate, same as us legionaries. Idle wankers, the lot of them. Spent all their time dossing about on the decks of their ships while we got on with the real soldiering.'

Cato smiled. 'I take it there's no love lost between legionaries and marines.'

'None,' Macro replied emphatically. 'We were at each other's throats from the off.'

'You do surprise me. Still, now we've got a posting to the marines, we'd better forgive and forget, eh?'

'Forgive and forget?' Macro raised his eyebrows. 'Fuck that! I just hate the bastards. Every legionary does. Mark my words, there's no such thing as a good marine. Idlers, wasters and the scrapings of the street. Anyone with any worth has upped and joined the legions. We'll have to cope with the leavings.'

'Not looking forward to a bit of drilling then?'

'Cato, my lad, there's drilling and then there's the kind of chaotic scrabbling about that is the specialism of your average marine.'

'So, when it comes to soldiering, they're all at sea?'

Macro closed his eyes briefly. 'Cato, that's the kind of crack that ruins friendships.'

'Sorry. Just trying to lighten the mood.'

'Well, don't. All right? Things are hard enough for the pair of us without you trying to joke about it.'

'Fair enough.' Cato glanced up as a column of wagons ground by on the other side of the road. Each wagon carried several men, well-muscled and looking at the peak of physical fitness. He nudged Macro. 'Could do with a few more like them in the legions.'

Macro looked round. 'Them? Gladiators. No, they're the last thing you want in the army. They think they know all that there is to know about fighting. That it's all down to fancy footwork and a nimble blade. Your bog-standard barbarian would knock 'em flat while they were still out to win points for style. Gladiators . . .' Macro shook his head wearily. 'So far up their own arses they hardly see the light of day from one month to the next. If you want someone at your shoulder that you can rely on, pick a legionary every time. And, if you can't find a legionary, then an auxiliary will do.'

Cato stared at him. 'You've really got it in for the marines, haven't you? Any particular reason? One of them run off with your sister, or something?'

Macro shot a look at his friend. 'Sister? No. Much closer than that. My mother.'

'Your mother?'

Macro nodded. 'A trireme turned up at Ostia for refitting. Crew came ashore for a few days. One of the smooth bastards chats my mum up and she drops the rest of us in the shit and sails off into the bloody sunset with her marine and is never seen again. I was not much more than a kid at the time. That was twenty years ago.'

Cato was stunned. In the two years that he had known Macro, his friend had rarely mentioned his background. And now this. Having grown used to the tales of old soldiers he could not help being suspicious. 'Is that true?'

'Have I ever lied to you?'

Cato shrugged helplessly. 'Well, yes. Frequently, as it happens. Soldiers' stories and all that. "The barbarian that got away", that kind of thing.'

'Oh.' Macro pursed his lips. 'This one's true. So I hate marines,' he concluded simply.

Cato felt a heavy weight settle on his heart. If Macro carried such prejudices with him all the way to Ravenna then life with the marines was going to be very difficult. The inter-service rivalry was bad enough without Macro adding his personal crusade against marine-kind to the situation.

Cato tried to reason with his friend. 'Don't you think it's a bit harsh to judge them all by the conduct of one?'

'No.'

Cato hissed with frustration. 'That's hardly fair.'

'What's fairness got to do with it? One of the bastards ran off with my mum. Now the boot's on the other foot and I'm going to stick it to them. And I'll have none of your nonsense about fairness.'

'Prejudice never solved anything,' Cato replied calmly.

'Bollocks! Which one of your fancy philosophers came up with that? Prejudice solves everything, and quickly too. As long as you've got the balls to see it through. How else do you think we got ourselves an empire? Through playing fair with a bunch of hairy-arsed barbarians? Think we talked 'em into throwing down their weapons and surrendering their lands? No. We regarded them as ignorant and uncivilised. All of them. And rightly so, in my opinion. Made kicking their heads in a lot easier at the end of the day. You start arguing with yourself about the pros and cons of their point of view and you'll be dead in a flash. Act as you find and life becomes simpler, and longer, probably. So, Cato, spare me your feelings about fairness, eh? If I want to hate marines, that's up to me. Makes my life easy. You want to cosy up to them, then that's up to you. But leave me out of it.'

'Well, if you insist.'

'I do. All right? Now let's change the subject.'

Cato could see that his friend would not budge on the issue. Not right now, at least. Perhaps Macro could be persuaded to be more reasonable over time; a few carefully chosen words here and there and their posting to the marines might be less of an unpleasant experience. If Narcissus was right, then this mission was going to be dangerous enough for Cato and Macro without having to worry about the loyalty of the men around them.

Cato leaned forward, adjusted the weight of the yoke on his shoulder, and marched on in silence. The Flaminian Way began to incline as it met a low ridge to the north of the capital. As the road evened out, Cato stepped off the road into the shade of a copse of tall cypress trees and set his pack down for a moment. Macro strode on a few paces, then paused, and reluctantly trudged off the paved surface and joined his friend.

'Not tired already?'

'A bit,' Cato admitted. 'I'm out of training for route marches.'

'Really?' Macro smirked. 'I'll make a marine of you yet.'

'Very funny.' Cato took a sip from his canteen and stared back down the road towards Rome, sprawling across its seven hills and spilling out on to the surrounding landscape. Having lived in the tight confines of the city for some months, it felt strange to Cato to encompass the city of a million souls in one glance. The vast edifice of the imperial palace complex was clearly visible, even at a distance of several miles, but now it looked tiny, like some construction of a child's set of building blocks. For a moment Cato wondered at the smallness of human achievement in a wider context. All the grand politics of the palace, all the petty prejudices and aspirations of the densely packed streets of the capital – all seemed futile and insignificant viewed from a distance.

Cato looked at his friend. For Macro it was different. He survived in the gritty world of immediate details and focused on the challenges right in front of him. It was an enviable perspective, Cato felt – one that he wished he could develop for himself. He spent far too much time thinking about abstract issues. In the legions that could cost lives, he reflected, and the abyss of self-doubt that plagued him yawned once more. Now that he was a centurion he was more conscious than ever about his failings, and yearned for the verities of the life that he assumed Macro enjoyed.

'If you've had enough of the scenery,' Macro broke into his thoughts, 'would you mind if we got on?'

'Right.' Cato pushed the stopper back into his canteen, took a deep breath and heaved the pack back on to his shoulders. 'I'm ready. Let's go.'

As the afternoon wore on, the scattered clouds thickened and blotted out the sky, eventually concealing the sun itself behind a miserable curtain of a dirty grey haze. As the centurions marched further from Rome and left the immediate belt of farms and factories that fed their wares into the capital, the traffic began to thin out. The slopes of the surrounding hills were more forested and there were fewer farms and other buildings. As dusk began to gather it started to rain; icy drops that stung the skin and quickly soaked the two centurions. Macro and Cato stopped at a small roadside tavern and bought two cups of heated wine while they got out their waterproofed capes and draped them over their shoulders.

Cato looked out through the curtain of drips that splattered down from the thatched shelter that gave out on to the road. 'This isn't going to pass quickly. How much further to Ocriculum?'

Macro thought a moment. 'Three hours.'

'It'll be dark in three hours.'

'Sooner than that with this weather.'

Cato glanced back at the inn. 'We could stay here for the night; catch up with the column tomorrow.'

Macro shook his head. 'I'm not paying to stay here when there's decent barracks just down the road. Besides, if we stay we'll have to push it to catch up with the column in the morning. No point in that. Drink up, and let's go.'

Cato shot him an angry look, then relented. It would be easier to endure a wet and discomforted Macro for the next few hours than put up with his grumbling for the rest of the night and the following morning. With a sigh of resignation he downed the rest of his cup, savouring the warm glow in his belly, and then shouldered his pack and trudged out of the inn. The rain was falling harder than ever, like silver rods, and veiled the surrounding landscape as it hissed on the paved surface of the road. They were alone on the road, Cato realised, and with a last longing look at the warm glow of the hearth at the inn, he turned and followed the dark shape of Macro.

A mile down the road, the air momentarily turned a blinding white, and almost at once their ears were deafened by a crashing roll of thunder.

Cato winced and called out to Macro, 'We should find shelter!'

His words were drowned out by a fresh detonation in the heavens and Cato trotted forward a few steps and grabbed Macro's shoulder. 'Let's find shelter!'

'What?' Macro grinned. 'Shelter? What for? Just a bit of rain, that's all.'

'A bit of rain?'

'Sure. What's the matter? You gone soft from too much city living or something?'

'No.'

'Well, come on then!' Macro shouted back above the din, and turned round and strode away.

Cato stared at him a moment, then with a shrug of resignation he set off in his friend's footsteps. The thunder grumbled above and echoed off the slopes of the surrounding hills. And so they never heard the clatter of horses' hoofs and the grind of the carriage wheels until the small mounted party was almost upon them. They came out of the dusk at speed, right behind the two centurions, and Cato just had time to turn, see the danger and throw himself to one side with a shouted warning to Macro as the cloaked horsemen swerved their mounts at the last instant. Macro leaped off the road and crashed into the drainage ditch a short distance from Cato. Above them flitted the shapes of two horsemen, a team of horses, drawing a light covered coach, and then two more horsemen. They ignored the two travellers they had driven from the road and clattered on without stopping.

'Oi!' Macro raised himself up on one arm. 'You bastards!'

His words were lost in the storm and moments later the gloom had swallowed up the coach and its escort, as Macro continued to hurl abuse after them. Cato raised himself up from the mud and retrieved his pack before going to help Macro. Once both men were back on the road, soaked and filthy, Macro calmed down a little.

'You all right, Cato?'

'Fine.'

'If we catch up with those bastards I'll give them a hiding they won't forget in a hurry.'

'We won't catch them. Not at the rate they're going.'

Macro glared down the road. 'Maybe they'll shelter for the night at Ocriculum. Then we'll see what's what.'

'Come on then, or we'll never get there.'

They raised their drenched packs and continued along the road, glistening in the teeming downpour.

Night came, swallowing up the last vestiges of daylight almost without them being aware of it, so dark had the storm become. They did not reach Ocriculum for nearly another two hours, and emerged into the wavering glow of covered torches at the town gate looking like beggars, drenched and streaked with mud from their tumble into the drainage ditch.

The gatekeeper slowly rose from a sheltered bench inside the lofty arch and stuck his thumbs into the top of his belt.

'Well, well, well,' he grinned. 'What have we got here? I assume you two vagrants can pay the entrance fee?'

'Get stuffed.' Macro growled. 'And let us through.'

'Now then.' The gatekeeper frowned and slid his right hand round towards the pommel of his sword. 'No need for that. You pay your dues and you can enter the town. Otherwise . . .' He nodded back down the road.

'Nothing doing, friend,' Macro replied. 'We're centurions, on active service. Let us through.'

'Centurions?' The gatekeeper looked doubtful, and Macro drew back his cape to show his army-issue sword and the unmistakable shape of his marching yoke. The gatekeeper glanced at Cato, who, in his soaked state, looked even younger than his years. 'Him too?'

'Him too. Now let us in.'

'Very well.' The gatekeeper nodded to a pair of men at the far end of the arch, and they pushed one of the gates in just enough to admit the two travellers. Macro nodded his thanks and trudged past the gatekeeper.

The marching barracks were a short distance from the town gate. A small arch led into an open yard lined with stables on one side and barrack blocks along the other three walls. Light glowed through cracks in the window shutter and spilled on to the flagstones in dull slants. A handful of covered torches provided enough illumination to show where they were going as Macro and Cato gave their details to the clerk at the gate and were given directions to one of the officers' rooms. As they crossed the yard Macro glanced at the vehicles in the wagon park: a neat line of supply wagons and there at the far end, a smaller more refined shape. He drew up so suddenly that Cato walked straight into his back.

'Shit! What did you do that for?'

'Quiet!' Macro snapped. He raised his hand and pointed. 'Look!'

Cato glanced round. 'Oh . . .'

There stood the carriage. Its lines were unmistakable. It was the same one that had sent them sprawling into the ditch a few miles down the road to Rome.

CHAPTER EIGHT

Cato hurried after Macro as his friend crashed through the door of the barrack block and strode into the mess. It was a large room, lit and heated by wall-mounted iron braziers. There was a bar and several tables at which a score of officers were sitting. Every one of them had turned to look at the man who had made such a dramatic entrance. A flash of lightning silhouetted Macro's stocky shape in the door frame, while Cato's bleached image stood out behind him. Then the lightning was gone and Macro's expression was lit by the rosy glow of the braziers. He smiled.

'Evening, gents! Centurion Lucius Cornelius Macro at your service. Now, can one of you tell me which cunt owns the fancy carriage parked outside?'

For a moment no one moved or spoke, until Cato caught up with his friend and pushed his way into the mess and out of the rain. The young centurion dumped his pack and sneezed so hard he bent double, and broke the spell. Macro nodded at him.

'This is Centurion Marcus Licinius Cato. He can't help it. Now then, as I was saying . . .'

The barman waved Macro towards the counter. 'Take a seat and have a drink, sir, and close the door.'

Once the filthy weather had been shut out, the two

newcomers stood dripping on the threshold, under the silent gaze of the other officers. Out of the corner of his eye Cato noticed a man rise from one of the tables against the far wall. He hurried over to a side door and disappeared down an unlit corridor. The barman set up two cups and filled them carefully from a large jug. 'There you go. Come and drink, and we can talk without spoiling the evening for my other customers.'

As the two centurions leaned up against the counter the barman shouted for one of his slaves and a thin child with a pinched face scurried out of the storeroom, rubbing the sleep from his eyes.

'Take these officers' packs to one of the rooms. When you've done that, come back for their cloaks. They'll need drying. Now go.'

The slave boy nodded meekly, scurried round the bar and headed for the two packs by the door. As Cato watched, the boy hefted his pack with a strained expression and staggered from the room under the weight.

'Now then, sir,' the barman was saying to Macro, 'if you want to drink in my establishment, then you'll behave, understand? Otherwise, I'll have to ask you to leave.'

'What makes you think I'd leave?' Macro smiled sweetly.

Without taking his eyes off Macro the barman called out, 'Ursa. Out here, now.'

A huge shadow filled the entrance to the storeroom and then a great blond head ducked into the bar. When the man stood up, his straw locks seemed to brush against the rafters. His arms were thick and hard, and his tunic stretched tightly around his huge chest and over his broad shoulders.

'Master?'

'Stick around while I talk to these gentlemen.'

Ursa nodded, and switched his gaze to the two centurions

at the counter, narrowing his eyes suspiciously. The barman turned back to Macro.

'If I say leave, you leave. Got that?'

'Oh, absolutely,' Cato nodded.

Macro shot him a look of disgust before he turned his attention back to the barman. 'Well? The carriage?'

'Belongs to a senior officer. On his way north. If you want to know anything more you'll have to speak to those men over there.' He pointed towards the table from which Cato had seen the man depart moments earlier. The remaining three customers watched the two centurions closely.

'Speak to them, by all means,' continued the barman, 'but keep it civil or I'll have Ursa sort you out.'

'Fair enough,' Macro replied. 'And thanks for the drink, friend. Come on, Cato.'

They eased their way through the room as the other officers started to talk again, low voices swiftly rising to the former level of drunken good humour. Macro drew up in front of the table and nodded at the men seated on the far bench. 'Evening.'

They nodded back.

'Chatty lot, aren't you? Mind telling me who you are? Who you work for?'

They exchanged glances before one of them cleared his throat. 'We're not at liberty to discuss that, sir.'

'Let me guess.' Macro cocked his head to one side as he appraised the men. 'Too well dressed to be common legionaries. And too afraid of a fight to be anything other than Praetorian Guards. Am I right?'

The man nodded, then spoke quickly. 'Yes, sir. And you know the regulations. We raise a fist against a superior, even one from the legions, and we're dead men.'

Macro smiled. 'What do you say we go outside and settle this without any question of rank? Just us and you three.'

'Settle what exactly, sir?'

'This.' Macro indicated the mud plastered to his tunic. 'A little souvenir from the ditch you madmen forced us into back on the Flaminian Way a couple of hours ago.'

The guardsman's eyes widened as he recalled the incident. 'That was you? I thought you two must be tramps. Please accept my apologies, sir. No harm done.'

'Not yet. Now then, are you going to settle this like a man?'

'Settle what, Centurion?' a voice called from the doorway leading into the dark corridor. Macro and Cato turned round and saw a dim figure emerging from the shadows. The man paused.

'Well, well. It is a small world indeed. Wouldn't you agree, Centurion Macro?'

'Vitellius . . .' Macro whispered.

'That's right.' Vitellius chuckled lightly as he emerged into the full glow of the mess room. The guardsmen leaped to their feet, the bench grating across the floor beneath them as it was forced away from the table. 'But I would prefer it if you addressed me by my proper rank. I take a dim view of insubordination. You'd do well to remember that.'

'Oh, really . . . sir?'

'Yes. Really.' Vitellius fixed him with a cold stare for an instant, before the calculating smile returned to his lips. 'I gather you wanted a word with me. Something to do with my carriage, I understand.'

'Your carriage?' Cato's eyebrows rose in surprise.

'Yes, mine. Good evening to you too, Centurion Cato. Good to see you here. Both of you. Just like old times. We must have a drink. Barman!'

'Yes, sir?'

'A jar of your best wine and three goblets. Goblets, mind.'

'Yes, sir.'

Vitellius waved a hand at his bodyguards. 'Get up and leave us alone. Make sure my friends and I are not disturbed.'

The guards saluted and hurriedly made for another table nearby, yet not so near as to permit them to overhear what was said between Vitellius and the two centurions.

'Sit down please, gentlemen.' Vitellius waved at the vacant bench.

Macro shook his head. 'No thank you, sir.'

'That wasn't a request, Centurion. Now sit down. Both of you.'

With a pause just long enough to mark their distaste and a measure of defiance, Macro and Cato took their seats. Vitellius smiled at them and then eased himself down on the bench opposite. The barman arrived with the drinks and poured the wine into three silvered goblets, before setting the jar down on the table and leaving them to their discussion.

Macro spoke first. 'What are you doing here, sir?'

'I'm on my way to take up my next appointment.'

'Appointment?' Macro frowned. 'You're returning to active service? Which legion is going to be cursed by your treachery this time, Tribune?'

'Tribune?' Vitellius put on a shocked expression. 'What makes you think I'm resuming that rank? I've moved on to bigger and better things now that Claudius himself is my patron.'

Macro leaned forward and lowered his voice. 'If he knew how far you had conspired against him . . .'

'Well, he doesn't. And he's never going to find out, gentlemen. He has complete trust in me, and so does

Narcissus. So don't start getting any ideas about telling them any stories. You'd never be believed, and I assure you the consequences would be far worse for you than for me. Do we understand each other, gentlemen?'

Macro nodded slowly. 'Fair enough, sir. So tell me, what are you doing here?'

'Like I said, I'm on my way to take up a new appointment.'

'Where's that then?'

'Really, Centurion, we're going to have to work a little harder at formalities. Especially as I am about to become the new prefect in command of the fleet at Ravenna . . .'

'You?' Cato stared back, open-mouthed. 'It can't be true.'

'It is. I assure you. Granted, I have no experience of naval operations, but I can rely on others for that. My real mission is far more vital, and I'll need every measure of cooperation from you two to see it through. I want that understood.'

Cato rubbed his brow. 'You're the one Narcissus told us about.'

'I am. From now on, you two are under my command. Both as officers attached to the fleet, and also as agents acting for Narcissus. I'll be watching you closely. If you give me any cause to doubt your loyalty to the Emperor, and to me, I'll have to report back to Narcissus. And we know what that means, don't we? A short interview with the palace interrogators and a nasty, obscure death. You won't be missed, I can assure you. Meanwhile, your lives are in my hands, gentlemen. Serve me well and you'll live. I'll come out of it something of a hero. You'll have your lives. You can't have everything. But I can, and one day I will. On that day, you had better be on my side.'

'I can't believe this,' Macro muttered to Cato.

'We'd better,' Cato replied, struggling to hide his anxiety. 'He's quite serious.'

Vitellius smiled. 'Your little friend has it right, Macro. Now that we understand the situation, and each other, I think it's time for a little toast.' Vitellius picked up the jug and filled each of their goblets to the brim. Then he raised his and smiled at them across the glimmering surface. 'Gentlemen, I give you partnership! At last, it seems, we are on the same side.'

He raised the goblet and drained it steadily, his eyes fixed on the two centurions. When he had finished he set the cup down and gazed at the two goblets standing untouched on the table in front of Macro and Cato. He smiled.

'As you wish, gentlemen. I'll indulge your insolence on this occasion. But mark my words well. The next time you give me one shred of defiance or discourtesy, you'll pay for it.'

CHAPTER NINE

The column assembled in the yard at dawn. A centurion, assisted by a team of optios, had been appointed to lead the marines across to Ravenna. These officers stormed into the general barracks and began turfing the men off their sleeping mats and screaming abuse into their faces. Amongst the marines terrified recruits hastened out into the cold dawn air, many half dressed and shivering. Dazed by their rough handling, the men stumbled into line, some still struggling into their clothes. As they readied their packs for the march, Macro cast a critical eye over them.

'Not exactly an impressive bunch, are they?'

Cato shrugged. 'No better or worse than the batch I joined the Second Legion with.'

'And you can tell, of course.' Macro shook his head. 'Trust me, Cato. I've seen 'em come and go for years and this lot are from the bottom of the barrel.'

Cato turned towards him. 'Is that experience talking, or prejudice?'

'Both,' Macro smiled. 'But we'll see who's right soon enough. I'll bet you that we lose a quarter of these men before we reach Ravenna.'

Cato looked over the men gathering by the wagons. The majority of the recent recruits certainly looked like poor specimens. A few had no boots at all and most were thin and drawn, and clothed in little more than rags. They were, as Macro had said, the dregs of the city: men with little hope of employment and no prospects for a better life. And now, in an act of desperation, they had volunteered for the marines. No legion would have had them, that's for sure, Cato reflected. And a good few of them would still be thrown out of the marines before training was completed. So this was their last chance. Men in such circumstances either caved in quickly, or found some last reserve of strength and determination from deep inside themselves. As Cato once had. He turned back to Macro.

'How much?'

'You'll take the bet?'

Cato nodded.

'More fool you,' Macro smiled. They had made wagers before, and Macro had won more often than not, his experience triumphing over Cato's attempts to rationalise the odds. It was typical of the lad to persist, and Macro was touched by Cato's confidence in his own judgement. But not touched enough to refuse the chance of easy money.

'All right then. The first month's pay.'

Cato stared back at him.

Macro arched an eyebrow. 'Too rich for you?'

'No. No. Not at all. A month's pay it is.'

'Done!' Macro grasped his friend's hand and shook it firmly before Cato could think of changing his mind.

A shout from the centurion in charge of the convoy drew the marines up in their ranks and they stood silent and shivering as the optios strode down the column and dressed the ranks with their long wooden staffs, clipping the odd unfortunate who failed to move with sufficient alacrity. Macro and Cato made their way over to the front of the column. They had already introduced themselves to the centurion, a skinny veteran by the name of Minucius. He was a friendly enough man and told them that he had transferred back to the marines, with a promotion, after a stint in the auxiliaries many years before. Clearly, Minucius had remained true to the hard training of his former service arm and showed no pity for his new charges. Once the introductions had been made and Macro and Cato had shown him their orders, Minucius offered them space in the lead wagon. There was one vehicle in front of the recruits and another three behind, carrying rations and tents for the journey, a small chest of money for expenses and a parcel of letters.

Cato looked round. 'Where's Vitellius?'

Centurion Minucius glanced at Cato. 'Gone. He left an hour ago, with his escort. Seems that the prefect is in a tearing hurry to take up his new command. So, I'm afraid we'll be denied the pleasure of his aristocratic company for the rest of the journey. Shame that.' He grinned.

'You don't know the half of it,' Macro said quietly.

Minucius looked at him searchingly. 'Something I should know?'

'No,' Cato interrupted. 'It's nothing.'

'Nothing?'

'We've served with Vitellius before. Back in Britain.'

'And?'

Cato frowned. 'And what?'

'What's he like?' Minucius observed the two centurions as they exchanged a wary look. 'Come now, lads. We're grown-ups. We'll be serving together for months, maybe years. If you've got some information on the prefect you should share it. After all, who's going to show you the ropes when we get to Ravenna, eh?'

Cato coughed. 'Let's just say that we didn't see eye to eye with Vitellius on a few issues.'

'Didn't see eye to eye, eh?' Minucius looked at the other centurions shrewdly. 'He's a thorough-going bastard then?'

Cato pursed his lips and shrugged.

'You could say that,' Macro said softly. 'But you didn't hear it from us. Right?'

'Got you.' Minucius winked good-humouredly. 'Forewarned is forearmed. I'll watch my back around our new prefect.'

'Yes,' Macro added, as Minucius strode off to make sure that the convoy was ready to set off, 'so will we all.'

From Ocriculum the Flaminian Way led north, the landscape became more hilly, and the column marched through great vineyards that rolled down the hillsides either side of the road. Everywhere, the stark brown of leafless trees and shrubs of winter looked bleak and depressing, and frequent showers of icy rain lashed down on the hapless recruits. But no one dropped out of the line of march for the first few days, much to Macro's frustration.

On the fourth day after leaving Rome, the column reached the foothills of the Appennines, and crossed torrential streams that fed into the upper reaches of the Tiber. The road then wound its way up to the town of Hispellum. The villas of the rich were closed for the season and would not open again until the summer heat drove the owners up into the cooler air of the mountains, so the streets were quiet as the column tramped through the town to the barracks beyond the far gate.

From the situation of the barracks and the unfriendly glances from passing townsfolk, it was clear that the good people of Hispellum wanted little to do with passing military traffic. Not that Cato could blame them. The soldiers of the Emperor were inclined to regard themselves as being above the law in some respects, a view that was encouraged by the emperors themselves, who had been wise enough to realise that the military were the ultimate guarantor of their power and authority. The odd theft, drunken brawl and non-payment for goods or services were overlooked – mostly because any victims of such crimes were loath to make things worse for themselves by seeking recourse to the law. The people in the towns that lined the main military routes just kept their heads down each time a column appeared, and prayed that it would pass through without causing too much trouble.

The barracks outside Hispellum were well maintained by the town council and, having spent the previous two nights in goat-leather tents, the recruits and their officers were glad at the prospect of a warm and dry night's rest.

As night fell the officers met in the small mess where a slave had laid a fire and the town council had sent several jars of wine and some cured sides of venison to the new arrivals. No doubt they hoped that the soldiers would get drunk in the barracks and not need to venture inside the town walls. The officers were joined by a merchant, who said that he had been unable to find a room in the town. He sat apart from them and watched in silence as the soldiers talked.

'Any more drop out today?' Macro asked hopefully.

Minucius nodded. 'One. An old boy. Claudius Afer. He collapsed on the road this morning. I told him if he didn't catch up he was on his own. Looks like that's one we can scratch off the intake.'

'How many so far?' Macro asked.

'Aside from Afer, let me think. Eight. And we'll lose more as we cross the mountains. We always do. There's no more shelter for three days after Hispellum and we'll spend two nights high up. At this time of year there'll be snow and ice, and the new boys will hate every moment of it. By the time we reach Ravenna we'll have winnowed out most of the weaklings. Those that are left should make good enough marines. Cheers!'

As he raised his cup and drank deeply Macro was busy doing some mental maths. Eight men down, from a total strength of a hundred and fifty, was, on the face of it, disappointing. They'd need to lose another thirty-odd for him to win the bet safely. He looked up as Minucius emptied his cup and reached for the wine jar.

'How many do you expect to lose before we get clear of the mountains?'

'How many?' He puffed out his cheeks. 'Usually something like a fifth to a quarter of the new recruits. I'd expect a lesser proportion if these were men destined for the legions. The fitness test sees to that. For marines, alas, the standard is somewhat lower.'

'A fifth to a quarter,' Macro mused with a smile, and caught Cato's eye. 'Better get used to the idea of a quiet first month in Ravenna.'

'We're not there yet,' Cato replied. 'So don't go spending my money before it's yours.'

Minucius looked at them with a confused expression. 'Now, what's that all about?'

'It's nothing,' Macro smiled quickly. 'Drink up. There's plenty more to get through before the night's done.' Macro turned back to Minucius. 'You've served with the auxiliaries, you say?'

'That's right. Four years with an infantry unit. In Syria.'

'Syria!' Macro's expression gleamed with sudden excitement and he scraped his stool closer to Minucius.

Cato raised his eyes despairingly. 'Here we go again. Bloody Syria . . .'

'Quiet, boy!' Macro snapped. 'The grown-ups are talking. Now then – Syria. Tell me all about it. Especially the women. Are they as loose as I've heard?'

Minucius shrugged. 'Wouldn't know about that. I was posted at some shitty little frontier fort beyond Heirapolis for the best part of five years. Hardly saw a woman from one month to the next. Plenty of sheep, though.'

Macro's expression soured. 'You mean . . .?'

Minucius scratched his chin. 'That's why the cohort was known as "The Rams".'

'Oh. I'm sorry.'

'Sorry?' Minucius looked confused. 'Nothing to be sorry about. Most of them were good lays. And they didn't charge and give you any stupid back chat. Mind you, it was a bloody hard job catching any of the buggers in the first place. You'd have better odds on getting a dose of the clap from a vestal virgin. On second thoughts . . . Anyway, it took me a while, but I discovered the trick of it in the end. Want to know?'

Macro's distaste had given way to a prurient compulsion to know the sordid details, so he took another sip of wine and nodded. Minucius leaned forward conspiratorially and lowered his voice. Though not so low that some of the optios sitting nearby could not overhear and Cato noticed them giving each other knowing looks.

'The trick of it,' Minucius explained, 'is to creep up on them nice and quiet, like. Take your boots off first, and balance on the balls of your feet. Approach from downwind and move very slowly. Too fast and you'll startle the buggers and have to start all over again. With a bit of practice you should be able to get within ten feet of 'em. Now's the clever part.' He paused and looked at Macro.

Macro nodded. 'Go on.'

'You crouch down low. Take a deep breath, and make a sound like grass . . .' He stared at Macro a moment, then nodded seriously and leaned back on his stool.

After a moment Macro frowned. 'Like grass?'

'Yes, grass.'

Macro glanced at Cato to make sure that he wasn't going mad. 'But . . . you're taking the piss. Aren't you?'

'Taking the piss?' Minucius glared at him in outrage for a moment, then the expression crumbled and he roared with laughter. The optios joined in and soon tears were rolling down the old centurion's weathered face. 'Of course I fucking am! You dozy twat.'

Macro's expression darkened dangerously and Cato leaned towards him. 'Take it easy. You asked for that.'

For a moment it looked as if Macro would not control his anger, then he glanced round the room and saw that expressions on the other men's faces were good-humoured enough, and he relented.

'Yes. Very fucking funny. You're a bloody riot, Minucius.'

'No harm intended, son.' Minucius slapped him on the shoulder and recharged Macro's cup. 'Come on. A toast. To the harems of Syria. To the best watering holes, so to speak, and the best posting any clapped-out centurion can hope for!'

He downed the wine in one go, and after the briefest of hesitation Macro followed suit as Cato let out a sigh of relief.

'Seriously, though,' Minucius continued, 'I doubt I'll ever get the chance to return there. Too old now.'

'How old?'

'Fifty-six. Joined up when I was twenty, to get away from the family of a girl I got pregnant. That was a long time ago,' he mused. 'Anyway, I'm happy enough in the marines. I've settled down and found myself a good woman. It's a nice, quiet life,' he added fondly, and then frowned. 'At least it was, until several months ago. When those pirates started causing trouble.'

Cato leaned forward. 'Tell us about the pirates.'

Minucius ran a hand through his grey thinning hair as he collected his thoughts. 'It began with a few ships failing to make port. As I said, this was nearly a year ago, and there's far less shipping over the winter season. So at first we thought they must have foundered. Trouble was, when spring came, more ships went missing, enough to look suspicious. Then, one evening, a small cruiser made port. You know, one of those fancy yachts that rich men use. They'd been cruising down the coast of Illyricum when two pirate ships jumped them. It was touch and go for a few hours. The pirates damaged some of their running gear, and killed most of the crew with missile fire. But the survivors managed to get a small lead over the pirates, just enough to pull out of range, and they cut across the sea towards the Umbrian coast and made Ravenna. It was them that told us about the pirates.

'I guess that they must have known that their secret was out, and since then they've been operating freely up and down the coast – mostly their side of the sea, but there have been isolated raids into small ports on our coast. They're getting quite bold.'

'And what about our navy?' Cato asked. 'Surely they've done something about it.'

'Not that easy, lad. We can patrol our coast easily enough but the far shore is riddled with small islands and inlets, some of which have never been charted. You could hide a fleet there and not be discovered for months. And that's what they've got. The pirates must have been converting some of the vessels they'd taken. Last I heard they'd got hold of a couple of triremes. We've even lost some of our own ships.'

'They've been captured?'

'They've not returned from patrol. No one knows what's happened to them. So you can see,' Minucius concluded wearily, 'we've got our hands full. But we'll track 'em down in time. We always do, without much help from Rome. Until now.'

'Oh?'

'Someone high up has finally noticed the good work we're doing. That's why Rome has authorised the raising of several new centuries of marines, and transferred two squadrons from the fleet at Misenum. This latest gang of pirates has really rattled them. And if we don't stamp them out soon, they might start interfering with the grain convoys from Egypt. Once that happens they can pretty much hold Rome to ransom.'

Cato leaned back. 'I had no idea the situation was so serious.'

'It is serious,' Minucius smiled. 'It's got the wind up the powers that be and they're not keen for word to get out. Last thing the Emperor needs is grain riots in the capital. We've been told to have everything in place for a major operation as soon as spring comes. So, a busy time for all concerned.' Minucius reached for the wine jug and frowned when he discovered it was empty. 'Hang on, lads. I'll get us another.'

As the old centurion weaved his way unsteadily towards the stack of jars leaning against the far wall, Cato moved closer to Macro.

'We're in trouble.'

'I heard.'

'No, I mean it. Forget the offensive against these pirates. That's bad enough. But how the hell are we supposed to get our hands on those bloody scrolls? That's why we're here.'

Macro shrugged. 'I suppose Vitellius must have a plan.'

'You can count on it,' Cato replied.

CHAPTER TEN

The next day the column began to climb up into more mountainous terrain where the road was hemmed in by pine forests as it traced a winding route through gorges and up the sides of precipitous slopes. The marines had to lend a hand with the wagons when the slope became too steep for the mules alone. There followed hours of back-breaking labour as the wheels ground up the road and wooden wedges had to be driven under the wheels whenever a stop was called. By noon they had passed beyond the snow line, and slush and then ice made the going far more exhausting and hazardous. The branches of the trees were laced with fine crystals, and as they climbed higher the snow had drifted in places and a passage had to be cleared by the recruits.

The weariness and discontent in the men's faces raised Macro's spirits by the hour. He was now certain that he would win the bet. A few more days of this hard-going and he'd be home and dry. Well, not quite dry, he smiled to himself. As soon as Cato had paid up he was going to get as drunk as possible. He almost felt pity for his friend's rashness in taking the bet in the first place. One day the lad would learn . . .

As night drew in Minucius called a halt when they reached a patch of level road with some open ground off to one side. Ahead the road disappeared round a rocky outcrop; part of the large hill rising up beyond the ground Minucius had chosen for their camp site. The wagons rumbled off the road and the marines slumped on to the snow beside them.

'What the fuck are you ladies doing?' Minucius roared at them. 'Back on your feet! Get the tents up. You try and sleep without any cover and half of you will freeze to death by the morning. Now move yourselves!'

The men dragged themselves to their feet and trudged over to the equipment wagons where the optios handed them their tents, guy ropes, wooden pegs and mallets. It began to snow, heavy white flakes that swirled out of the darkness and muffled the sounds of the men toiling away with the leather folds of the tents, and then struggling to drive the pegs far enough into the hard ground to keep the tents up. So it was long after dark by the time the tents had been erected in standard rows and the men had piled inside with their blankets and pine branches cut from the nearby trees to provide some comfort and insulation from the frozen ground. All about them was the easy sweep of snow and the boom and flap of tent leather.

There had not been time to light a fire, and rations were issued cold. The recruits sat hunched in their blankets, chewing on hard biscuit and strips of dried mutton.

In the centurions' tent Minucius finished his meal and gathered his cloak about his shoulders.

Cato looked up in surprise. 'You're going out in this weather?'

'Of course I am, lad. Have to set the watch for the night.'

'The watch?' Cato shook his head. 'We're hardly likely to be attacked by a pack of mountain goats.'

'Not goats. Brigands. The people who live in these mountains are pretty lawless. There's even supposed to be a few hidden settlements inhabited by descendants from the slaves of Spartacus' army.'

'You don't believe that, surely.'

'That's what people say. Personally, I think it's bollocks. Anyway, I have to set a watch. Better get the men used to the idea.'

Minucius undid the fastenings on the flap and the other centurions narrowed their eyes as an icy blast of wind gusted into the tent and swelled its sides, straining the seams. Macro shuffled over and struggled to get the pegs back into their slots.

'What's the point?' Cato muttered. 'He'll be back soon.'

'Well, there's no point in us freezing our balls off while we wait, is there?'

Cato shrugged and clutched his blanket more tightly about his thin frame. He doubted there would be any sleep for him that night. It was just too uncomfortable, no matter how tired he felt. Soon his teeth were chattering and Macro shot an irritable glance at him before turning round and curling up, inside his waterproof cloak on a thick bed of branches.

Minucius returned shortly afterwards and nodded a good night at Cato before he took to his makeshift bed, and soon both of the veterans were asleep and snoring loudly.

'Shit,' Cato muttered, bitter with envy. He shuffled around, trying to find a comfortable position, but lying on either side left the other exposed to the icy chill that somehow reached through the entrance of the tent and clutched at him with frozen fingers. He endured over an hour of this torment, becoming steadily more miserable, before he gave up and rose into a sitting position, hugging his knees tightly to his chest and rubbing his shoulders vigorously to try to get some warmth back into his muscles. Outside, the wind was dying down, only rising to a keen moaning on the occasional gust. But that was small comfort to Cato, shivering in his tent.

He tried to think about something else, anything else, and his mind turned again to the mysterious scrolls that meant so much to Narcissus. More important, it seemed, than the pirate menace itself. The operation being mounted to deal with the pirates was largely a front, a disguise to hide the real object of Rome's attention. If that was Narcissus' game then the scrolls must be worth the lives of a good many men. But what could be so important? Lists of traitors? State secrets from Parthia? It could be anything, Cato decided in frustration.

The wind died away completely for a moment and the sides of the tent hung limply about him. Then Cato heard a scream – short, shrill and some distance off. It seemed to echo off the mountainside for an instant, and then the wind rose again and the sound was gone. He threw back the blanket from his head and strained his ears to try to catch the sound again. And there it was: a thin tortured cry, just audible above the moaning wind and irregular slap and thud of tent leather. He reached over and shook Macro's shoulder. There was no response and he shook again, harder this time, and pinched his fingers into the bulk of Macro's muscles. The older centurion stirred into startled consciousness.

'What? What is it? Where's my sword?' His hand immediately went for the blade, then he focused on the dark outline of Cato, squatting beside him.

'Quiet!' Cato said softly. 'Just listen!'

'Listen? What for?'

'Shhh! Just listen . . .'

Both men stayed still, ears straining, but all that they

could hear was the sound of the wind outside. Macro gave up.

'You mind telling me what I'm listening for?'

'I heard a scream.'

'A scream? Up here in the mountains? Sure it wasn't the wind?'

'I'm positive.'

'Maybe some bacchanalian revelry of the mountain folks then.'

'Quiet! There it is!'

This time Macro did hear the sound: unmistakably human and carrying with it a clear sense of torment and agony. The scream was abruptly cut off, and Macro felt the hairs rise on the back of his neck.

'Shit. You're right.'

'What should we do?'

Macro threw back his blanket and groped for his boots. 'Check it out, of course. Come on. Bring your sword.'

'What about Minucius?'

'Leave him. I'm not going to look like some jumpy recruit. We'll just check it out and come back for help if we need it. Let's go.'

As they emerged from the tent they saw that the snow had stopped falling, and a thick blanket of white covered all the tents and the wagons. A pair of sentries stood watch at each end of the camp site and stamped their feet to keep them from going numb. The wind had died down to a flukey breeze, and overhead thin shreds of silvery cloud flitted across the bright points of star constellations.

'This way,' Macro said quietly, and softly crunched through the snow towards the nearest sentry. The man stiffened as he noticed the officers approaching.

'Halt! Advance and be recog—'

'Shut up. If you don't know who we are yet you never will. You're supposed to be keeping watch for people approaching the camp, you dozy bastard, not those moving around inside it.'

'Sorry, sir.'

'It doesn't matter,' Cato cut in.

'Yes, it bloody does,' Macro grumbled. 'If he can't keep a decent watch he's no use to anyone, even the marines.'

Cato ignored him and concentrated his attention on the sentry. 'Did you hear anything a moment ago?'

'Hear what, sir?'

'A man's voice, a scream.'

The sentry looked wary. 'I might have.'

'Don't fuck about, son.' Macro poked him in the chest. 'Did you hear something, or didn't you?'

'Yes, sir. But only for a moment. I might have imagined it. Thought it came from over there.' He gestured towards the rising mass of the hill behind the camp site. 'Up the hill, or more likely round the other side, I should think, sir.'

'Why didn't you raise the alarm?'

'For something I might have heard, or imagined, sir?'

'You don't take risks with other people's lives, lad. Understand?'

'Yes, sir. Want me to call out the rest of the men?'

'No,' said Macro. 'We'll investigate. If we're not back by the next change of watch, then you can raise the alarm. It's probably nothing to wet yourself over – just a wolf or something. Now get back on watch.'

The recruit saluted and turned to face away from the camp site.

Macro pointed up the side of the hill. 'That way, I think. Let's go.'

When they were out of earshot of the sentry Cato nudged him. 'A wolf?'

'Might be. I've heard them sound like that before.'

They reached the foot of the slope and waded through a drift until they came to the treeline, where a dense forest stretched up the slope. Very little snow had penetrated the heavy lower branches and the air was thick with the scent of pine. The incline was steep and they had to scrabble up on hands and feet, weaving between the tree trunks, making little sound as their boots trod on generations of dead pine needles. Sheltered from the breeze and warmed by their exertions, they emerged panting and sweating from the far side of the trees. By the loom of the snow they could see that there was a low craggy outcrop above them, and then the crest of the hill. Cato glanced back and saw the camp site some distance below them, hardly recognisable as tents and wagons under a thick blanket of snow. The scream came again, much more distinct this time, and the two centurions looked at each other.

'What do you reckon?' asked Cato.

'Sounds like some poor bastard's being given a hard time of it.' Macro took a deep breath and climbed towards the rocks. Cato followed, stepping into the deep footprints Macro had left in the snow. The rocks were loosely jumbled and there were sufficient handholds and ledges to make it easy going, and moments later Macro lent a hand to Cato and heaved him up on to a flat slab that overlooked the gorge the convoy had wound its way up that afternoon. Below them the road turned round the mass of the hill and rose up the other side.

They both saw the fire at once, a small glittering yellow glow at the edge of the road no more than a hundred paces below them. Four horses were tethered nearby, and the shapes of three men sitting on a fallen tree trunk close to the fire. A fourth was leaning over the end of the tree trunk and an agonised wail carried up the slope. The man stepped back towards the fire and revealed a fifth man, stripped to his waist and bound to the tree trunk. By the wan glow of the fire Macro and Cato could see black marks across his chest. The source of the marks was quickly apparent when the man who had been standing over him moved to the fire and lowered the tip of his sword into the heart of the small blaze.

Cato turned to his friend. 'I've seen that man before. The one tied to the tree. He's that merchant.'

'Merchant?'

'The one from Hispellum . . . What do you think's going on? Who are those men?'

'Not sure. Brigands, most likely. But I'm not going to sit here and let them carry on with that.' Macro looked over the ground and thought for a moment. 'It'd take too long to go back and rouse the others. By the time we got 'em back up here that poor bastard will be finished. Besides, with that bunch of marines on our hands there'd be no question of surprising them. They'd kill him, get on their horses and slip away long before we could get down the slope.'

'I see.' Cato nodded slowly. 'So, what you're saying is that it's down to us.'

'Got it in one, lad.' Macro clapped him on the shoulder. 'Come on.'

They eased themselves down from the rock slab, and then followed the crags along until they came to a thick growth of trees that stretched down to the road, just as the prisoner cried out again.

'Please! Please, no more!' The wail carried clearly up the

slope to the two centurions. 'I swear I don't know anything! . . . Please! No!'

A tormented shriek cut through the night, and spurred Macro and Cato on. They moved into the shadows of the trees and half-scrambled, half-slid down beneath the snow-laden boughs of the trees. They kept the fire in sight, and it twinkled through tangled skeins of slender pine branches as they descended. At length Macro stopped and put out an arm to warn Cato that they were close enough. Through the trees, no more than fifty paces away, the four men and their prisoner were clearly visible in the flickering firelight.

Macro drew his sword and took a step forward.

'Wait!' Cato hissed. 'You're not just going to charge in there.'

'What else?' Macro whispered. 'The two of us are hardly going to surround them.'

'No,' Cato muttered. 'We should have gone back for help.'

'Too late for that now.'

'All right then. We'll go in. But let's try and even the odds first. See there.' Cato pointed out a shallow fold in the ground beside the road, and Macro realised that it was the snow-covered drainage ditch. It passed close by the fallen tree trunk, and the men sitting there had their backs to the road.

Macro sheathed his sword and nodded. 'Looks good enough for me.'

They crept down through the trees and when they reached the open ground beside the road, both men crouched low and crunched softly across the snow until they reached the ditch, and then lowered themselves on to their stomachs. With Macro in the lead they cautiously crept forward, fighting back the urge to move more quickly when a fresh chorus of screams cut the air. They passed the edge of the trees, and drew level with the orange hue of the fire.

'Keep down,' Macro whispered over his shoulder. He eased his sword from its scabbard, took a deep breath, and slowly raised his head. Over the lip of the ditch he could see the silhouettes of the three men sitting on the tree trunk. They were silent, just watching the fourth man as he bent over the prisoner, who was invisible from the ditch. Macro mouthed a curse. The fourth man was facing them. He would see them the moment they rose up from the ditch.

Macro lowered his head and watched in frustration, until he felt a gentle tug on his foot. Glancing back, he saw Cato open his hand questioningly. Macro shook his head, then eased himself down until he could whisper to Cato without any risk of being overheard.

'We have to wait. Watch me. When I give the signal we get up, quiet as we can, and move on them. You strike when I strike. Not before.'

'Right,' Cato breathed.

They lay in the snow, swords in hand, waiting for their chance. As the snow melted beneath him Cato felt it soaking into his tunic, and chilling the bare skin beneath. He started to shiver again, even though his heart was pounding with terror and excitement. Ahead of him, Macro was still as a rock; only his eyes followed the movement by the tree trunk. The torturer continued his grisly work, and they could catch everything he was saying to his victim.

'Come on, man! You'll tell us in the end. Make no mistake, though. You will die, but you can make it easier on yourself. Much easier.'

'I swear I know nothing,' the victim choked. 'I don't know what you're looking for. I swear it!'

There was a pause before the questioner spoke again, in a

low voice that dripped with menace. 'Time, I think, to fry your balls off. Let's see if that loosens your bloody tongue.'

He backed away, turned towards the fire and leaned forward to place his sword blade in among the coals. Macro tensed his muscles and waved a hand at Cato. Then both men rose into a low crouch, swords held ready, and stepped softly towards the tree trunk. The snow creaked under each footfall, and Cato placed each step as carefully and as slowly as he could, all the time keeping his eyes fixed on the back of the man in front of him. He was aware of the dark mass of Macro to his left, easing towards the man at the other end of the trunk. Then he caught a scent of woodsmoke, horse-flesh and the sharper tang of burned meat, and fought down the bile in his stomach.

The torturer straightened up and raised his blade, glowing a dull red against the dark background of the hill. He turned round and froze as he caught sight of the two shapes beyond the tree trunk.

'What the fu—'

'Get 'em!' Macro bellowed, and threw himself forward, kicking up snow as he thrust the point of the sword into the back of the man in front of him. Cato didn't have time to brace himself and just stretched out an arm and launched an attack on his man as the latter began to turn round. Cato's point went high, and straight into the man's ear with a wet crunch. The head snapped to one side under the impact of the blow and he crumpled over. The man in the middle leaped up and back from the tree trunk. He had his sword out in an instant, raising the blade to counter any attack. The torturer stood by his side, eyes flickering left and right. He smiled.

'There's only two of them. We can take 'em.'

Having cut down half the opposition, Macro and Cato

paused on their side of the tree trunk. The surprise of the attack was gone. Now it was a straight paired duel. Without taking his gaze from the other men, Macro called out to Cato, 'The one with the hot blade's yours. I'll take the other bastard.'

Cato nodded and moved round the edge of the tree trunk, crouched low and ready to spring into an attack. He didn't get the chance. With a roar, the man with the glowing sword charged at him. The tip of the sword slashed through the air in a bright sparkling arc and Cato just had time to thrust his blade up to parry the blow, and the glowing tip glanced off his handle and landed in the snow with a sputtering hiss. Cato recovered quickly and thrust at the man's chest, but the torturer was too quick for him and recovered from his attack, lurching backwards so that Cato's point met only thin air. The two men paused to size each other up, and Cato was dimly aware of Macro slashing away at the other man, but dare not shift his gaze from his immediate foe.

The torturer waved his free hand at Cato. 'Come on, boy, if you think you're good enough.'

Cato sneered. He wasn't going to fall for the bait that easily. 'Fuck you.'

The man laughed, then his face froze into an intense and deadly concentration. He quickly stepped forward and feinted. Cato knew he was being tested and flinched slightly, but kept his blade still. The man grunted, and then launched a real attack; a whirling series of slashes and cuts, forcing Cato backwards, towards the tree trunk as he desperately countered each blow with a sharp ring as the blades connected, sending jarring waves of pain down his arm. Then he felt the bark against the back of his thigh and knew there was no further retreat. The attacker came on with renewed frenzy. Then, with a guttural shout of rage and triumph, the man smashed Cato's sword down on to to the top of the tree trunk and made to cut his blade up and sideways into Cato's face. But it had lodged in the wood and his arm shuddered as the blade refused to budge. He frowned. Without thinking, Cato lashed out with his left fist and caught the man on the bridge of his nose, crunching bone and dazing him. Cato felt his blade trapped beneath that of his foe, and released his grip before slamming his right fist into the man's face, following that with a flurry of blows that sent the man reeling back, step by step until he collapsed into the snow.

Only then did he glance up and see how his friend was doing. But Macro needed no help. His man was already down, and the centurion was standing over him, one foot braced on his enemy's chest as he wrenched the blade out from between the man's ribs.

Macro glanced round. 'You all right, lad?'

'Not a scratch.' Cato turned round and went to retrieve his blade. A hand shot out and grabbed his ankle and he sprawled on the ground. He turned on his side at once and lashed out with his foot. The man he had stabbed in the ear snarled at him through clenched teeth, even as he glared at Cato with a strange unfocused expression. But his grip was as firm as a vice and his fingers locked painfully around the flesh of Cato's ankle. Cato kicked out with his free boot, bringing the iron studs down on the man's knuckles. Still he held on, blood streaming from the gouged flesh. Beyond him Cato could see that the torturer had scrambled back on to his feet. He looked at Cato, then Macro, and turned and ran towards the horses.

'Stop, him!' Cato shouted.

Macro reacted at once and dashed forward, sending sprays of powdery snow flying in his wake. Cato turned back towards the tree trunk, grabbed the handle of his sword and with a convulsive heave he wrenched the blade free. He sat up and, gritting his teeth, he slashed it down into the injured man's forearm, cutting deep into flesh and shattering the bones. The grip on his ankle loosened and Cato wrenched his boot free of the nerveless fingers. The man grimaced, then his eyes slowly rolled up and he slumped face first into the snow, blood and grey matter oozing out of the side of his shattered skull.

A sharp neigh drew Cato's attention towards the trees and he saw the torturer leaning low across the back of a horse as he wheeled it round and spurred it across the drainage ditch and on to the road. Macro scrambled after him, but it was too late, and he stopped when he reached the ditch and could only slap his sword against his thigh in frustration as the horse galloped off up the road and into the night.

Cato turned his attention to the prisoner and kneeled down beside him. He was a tall man, well-built, of middle age with short dark hair. He wore riding breeches and soft leather boots. His bare chest had several patches of scorched flesh and there was a burn on his cheek. He forced a smile as Cato loomed over him.

'My rescuers, I hope.'

Cato reached round and fumbled with the thongs that bound him to the tree trunk, found the knot and then worked it apart. When the bindings came free the man slumped forward and rubbed his wrists.

'Oh, shit . . . I'm in agony.'

He trembled, and Cato fetched the cloak from the nearest of the bodies, wrapping it about the man. 'Can you walk?'

Macro crunched across the snow to join them. 'You all right, mate?'

The man glanced up with a forced grin. 'Oh, I'm just fine, thanks. May I ask who you two are? I seem to recognise you.'

'Centurions Macro and Cato, part of a marine column heading for Ravenna. You?'

The man winced and was silent for a moment before he replied, 'Marcus Anobarbus, merchant.'

Macro nodded, and then gestured towards the bodies of the three men they had killed. 'And who the hell are these jokers?'

Anobarbus looked up. 'Mind if we get some shelter before I tell you my story? I'm feeling a bit faint.'

'Sorry.' Macro leaned over and offered his hand. The merchant grasped it and heaved himself to his feet with a grimace, then passed out.

'Give me some help here, Cato,' said Macro, as he slipped an arm round the merchant's back.

With Cato supporting him on the other side the three men crossed to the road and began to walk slowly down towards the marines' camp site.

CHAPTER ELEVEN

Centurion Minucius was waiting for them on the road beside the camp. As the centurions slowly approached either side of Anobarbus, he crossed his arms.

'And this is . . .?'

'Marcus Anobarbus,' Macro grumbled. 'We've met him before. He was at Hispellum the night we stayed there.'

'And you just went out for a walk in the middle of the night and found him, I suppose?' Minucius said with scarcely veiled suspicion. 'For that matter, just who exactly are you two?'

'Centurions, on our way to a new posting, like we said.'

'Like you said.'

'You've seen our documents,' Cato added. 'They carry the stamp of the Imperial army bureau, right?'

'Any half-competent child could have faked those.'

'Maybe, but who would want to?' Cato persisted. 'Now, please, can we get this man into our tent and tend to his injuries?'

Minucius raised his eyebrows. 'Injuries? What kind of injuries?'

'When we found him, some men were amusing themselves by seeing how painful they could make Anobarbus' last moments.'

'Why?'

Macro shrugged. 'Let's get him inside and find out.'

The centurions laid Anobarbus down on Macro's bedding. A moment later Minucius appeared from the wagons with a box of salves and dressings. He set the box down beside the merchant as Cato gently peeled back the cloak and exposed the injuries.

'Shit,' Minucius grimaced. 'What the hell were they doing to him?'

'Trying to loosen his tongue,' Cato replied. 'We heard them asking him some questions.'

'What questions?'

'Not sure. They were after something and he said he didn't have it.'

'Oh, that's very helpful.'

Macro nodded at the merchant. 'He's stirring. Let's ask him.'

Anobarbus' eyes flickered open, and he glanced anxiously at the faces looming over him before he recognised Cato and Macro, and the terror eased off. He licked his lips and forced a smile. 'My rescuers. For a moment I thought you were . . . What happened to them?'

'One got away,' Macro replied. 'The others are dead. Care to tell us who they were?'

'In a moment,' Minucius interrupted. 'Let me see to the burns first.'

He lifted the lid off his medical box. In the bottom lay a selection of jars of ointments and dressings. Minucius rummaged about and took out a small pot with a cork lid. Inside was an oily cream which he applied carefully to the merchant's chest and the burn on his face.

'Goose fat,' he explained. 'It'll protect the burns. Now lift him up while I get the dressing on.'

The merchant gritted his teeth as Minucius wrapped a

clear linen bandage round his torso and tied it off under one arm. Anobarbus gratefully slumped back on to the bedding while Minucius closed the medical box and placed it to one side.

'All right then,' Macro said. 'Tell us what happened.'

Anobarbus closed his eyes for a moment before he started. 'I've already told you I'm a merchant. I deal in artworks. I buy stuff that's shipped into Ravenna from Greece and have it transported to my clients in Rome. I came down from the capital a week ago. I had quite a large sum of money with me when I set off from Rome. I was making good time. Then a blizzard set in and closed the Flaminian Way. When it cleared I saw those men, some distance ahead on the road. They must have been waiting for travellers. I turned my horse and raced back the way I'd come. Soon as they had mounted they came after me. My money box was still filled with gold and weighing me down. I could see that they must catch me if I didn't move faster. So I stopped and hid the gold before continuing.'

'Hid it?' Macro interrupted. 'Where?'

Anobarbus looked at him. 'Why should I tell you?'

'For fuck's sake, man! We rescued you. We're centurions in the service of the Emperor, not more bloody mountain brigands.'

Anobarbus thought for a moment. 'All right. There's a small shrine by the side of the road. I slipped the box into a fox-hole close by. It'd better still be there when I get back to it, or I'll know who to blame. I've got contacts, I have. Powerful contacts.'

Macro shook his head sadly. 'So have we all, mate. The trick is to avoid getting shafted by them all the time. Anyway, on with your story.'

'You can guess the rest,' Anobarbus continued. 'I rode on, but they were better mounted, and they caught up with me just as it was getting dark. They were going to kill me straight away but when they saw I no longer had the money box they knew I had hidden it somewhere. At first they just slapped me about a bit, and when I refused to speak, the leader threatened to kill me on the spot. But I knew that I would be dead the moment I told them where to find the money, so I clammed up. They settled down, stripped me, tied me to that tree trunk and lit themselves a nice little fire. I had no idea what was in store for me until I saw him start to heat his sword. Well, you know the rest. You came on the scene just in time. Frankly, I'd have spilled my guts the moment he put that blade anywhere near my balls.'

Cato winced. 'Who wouldn't?'

'So, then you two charged on to the scene. Against four of them.' Anobarbus smiled. 'Now that does take balls.'

'Use them while you still have 'em,' said Macro. He turned to Minucius. 'We surprised them. Took the first two out before they could react. I sorted one, and the other man gave Cato the slip.'

'Just a bloody moment!' Cato flared up. 'Some bastard had me by the ankle. You went after him. He gave you the bloody slip.'

Macro raised his hands placatingly. 'Figure of speech, lad, that's all. Anyway, he got away, and headed off down the road.'

Cato pointed a finger at the merchant. 'You said you deal in antiques.'

'Yes. So?'

'What kind of antiques?'

'Usual stuff. Statues, ceramics, furniture, books. Anything that commands a premium price amongst collectors in

Rome. You'd be horrified to know what they're prepared to pay for some things. Of course, I'm delighted.'

'What about scrolls?' asked Cato.

Anobarbus frowned. 'Scrolls? What kind of scrolls?'

'I don't know. But tell me, in your experience, what makes a scroll valuable?'

'Depends. Some people will pay a fortune for an original book of recipes. Others collect histories. Or stories, sayings, predictions. That type of stuff. Of course, some of the best material, from an investment point of view, is erotica, especially material from the Far East. They could teach a Subura streetwalker a trick or two.'

'No doubt,' Cato smiled. 'But is that it? Nothing else that might make a scroll so valuable?'

Anobarbus thought a moment and then shrugged. 'Sorry. That's all I can think of right now . . . Ouch!' His face contorted and he reached up to his chest.

'Don't!' Minucius snapped and slapped his hand aside. 'Best to leave it alone. You should try and get some rest.'

'Yes. Rest.' The merchant nodded. 'Now, I think I've had enough questioning for the night, if you gentlemen don't mind?'

Macro shook his head, and Cato sat back and puffed his cheeks. Anobarbus closed his eyes and, with a strained expression etched on his face, he tried to breathe easily. Gradually, the rise and fall of his chest became less laboured and his face relaxed into a deep sleep.

'What do you think?' said Cato.

'About what?'

'About his story? Does it hold up?'

Macro shook his head. 'Why not? Cato, you see conspiracies everywhere. Why shouldn't the man be what he said he is? It's simple enough to believe.'

'Too simple,' mused Minucius.

Macro looked round in exasperation. 'Not you too?'

'Why not?' said the old centurion. 'And, by the way, I'm still not even sure about you and the lad here. What was all that nonsense about scrolls?'

'I've had enough of this,' Macro grumbled. 'I need some sleep.'

'Tough.' Minucius nodded at the merchant on Macro's bedding.

'Oh, great,' Macro gritted his teeth. 'That's all I need.' He rose up and made for the tent flaps.

'Where are you going now?'

'For a piss. If you don't mind. Then I might just go and cut myself some more bloody bedding.'

CHAPTER TWELVE

The column reached Urbinum two days later, having paused a short while along the way to retrieve a small wooden chest from behind a shrine. Anobarbus decided to remain with them, explaining that he had friends in Ravenna who would put him up until he recovered from his wounds.

Two more men had been lost in the mountains, simply vanishing in the night in a foolhardy attempt to return to their families in Rome. Minucius doubted they would get out of the mountains alive, and Macro was in spitting distance of winning his bet.

By the time the marines reached the port of Ariminum the roadside inns were full of stories relating the latest exploits of the pirate fleet terrorising the seas off the coast. Although the barbarians were hardly at the gate, there was no denying the palpable hysteria that was gripping the people of Umbria. In Ariminum itself the local garrison had moved into the citadel, along with most of the wealthiest townspeople. There were few ships in port and the azure horizon of the sea was bare of sails.

Ten days after they had picked up Anobarbus, the column marched through the town gate of Ravenna, one man over the total number Macro needed to win his bet. It had taken a great effort of will for Macro not to quietly dispose of one of the recruits the night before they reached their destination, and he reluctantly conceded the bet to Cato as the last of them marched inside the town.

'Want me to start a tab?' Cato grinned.

'Only if you want me to knock your teeth out. You'll get your money, just as soon as we're paid.'

'I can hardly wait to spend your first month's wages. Three hundred denarians goes a long way.'

'Three hundred?' Minucius laughed at the exchange. 'You'll be lucky. I assume you two are on the marine payroll?'

'Yes,' Macro replied. 'What of it?'

'I don't suppose for a moment that the officials who posted you here were kind enough to mention the rate of pay?'

'No.' Macro's heart was sinking like a rock. 'What of it?'

'We get the same as the auxiliaries.'

Macro stared at him in horror for a moment, and then smiled nervously. 'You're having me on again, aren't you? Just give it a rest, Minucius.'

'I'm serious.'

'Bollocks.'

'No, really. I'm serious.'

Macro shook his head, and then slapped his thigh in fury. 'Shit! . . . That tight bastard Narcissus has shafted us again! I swear I'll kick his head in one day, if it's the last thing I ever do.'

'More than likely,' muttered Cato. 'And pipe down about Narcissus, unless you want the whole town to know our business.'

'I don't bloody believe this,' Macro continued. 'Not only does he stick our heads in the bloody noose, he does it on the cheap into the bargain.'

Macro persisted in his grumbling as the column worked its way down the main thoroughfare of Ravenna towards the docks. As in most provincial towns, the streets were narrow and few of the buildings were more than two storeys tall. Even before they reached the waterfront, Cato could see a dense forest of masts and rigging packed into the harbour. On the main quay itself scores of sailors sat around disconsolately and gazed out at the ships moored tightly together in the gentle swell. They stood up as the recruits marched by, and stared at them with open hostility.

'I don't understand,' said Cato. 'I thought all the shipping had tried to get as far from the pirates as possible. There was a handful of ships in Ariminum.' He waved a hand across the harbour. 'I've never seen so many before. Aren't they afraid of the pirates?'

'Of course they are, lad,' Minucius grinned. 'And that's precisely why they're here. What better place to be than right beside a naval base. Over there's the guarantee of their safety.'

Cato followed the arm that Minucius had raised and saw what he was pointing at. At the end of the quay was a large fortified gateway, leading into the naval dockyard. Riding at anchor in the open waters of the navy harbour was a fleet of sleek warships. He counted over thirty of them. Most were small patrol craft, but further out lay a squadron of larger triremes, the formidable backbone of the Roman fleet. Each trireme boasted three banks of oars on each side, with fortified towers at the bow and stern, upon which catapults were mounted. A large bronze-sheathed ram extended from the prow of each ship.

Beyond the triremes there was one even bigger vessel. Cato stood up on the bed of the wagon and pointed. 'What's that?'

'That's the *Horus*, our flagship. She's a quinquireme, a five, as we call 'em. Quite a history behind that one.

She was Mark Antony's flagship. Captured at Actium and taken into the imperial navy by Augustus. Built to last and tough as old boots. There's nothing afloat that can match her.'

Cato stared at the *Horus* a moment longer, then resumed his seat as the convoy moved along the quay towards the gates of the naval base. The sailors and dockers lining the route closed in on each side, watching them in bitter silence.

A voice cried out, 'When are you going to do something about them pirates?'

The complaint was instantly taken up by other voices, and soon the marines and their officers were surrounded by angry shouts and shaking fists. The recruits glanced around nervously.

'Eyes front!' Minucius roared out. 'Eyes front, I said. Ignore the bastards.'

A clod of filth sailed through the air and struck the centurion on the shoulder. He clenched his jaw and stared straight ahead. Unfortunately, the example had been set and suddenly the air was filled with mud, excrement and other stinking refuse, and it pelted down on the hapless marines and their officers. The men at the front of the column faltered as they tried to shield themselves from the bombardment, and Minucius rose to his feet and cupped his hands to his mouth.

'Keep marching at the front there! Don't bloody stop!'

The optios lashed out at their men with their staffs and the pace picked up. Minucius opened his mouth to shout further encouragement and, as Macro watched, a turd flew through the air and caught the veteran right in the mouth. There was a spontaneous roar of laughter from the nearest townspeople at the sight.

Minucius ducked down, spitting and wiping his lips on

his sleeve. 'If I ever find the bastard responsible for that, I'll make him eat shit for the rest of his bloody days.'

Macro, struggling hopelessly to keep a straight face, nudged Cato. 'I thought that sort of thing only happened to me.'

'It has. Look.' Cato pointed to his tunic and, glancing down, Macro saw a nasty brown smear on the wool.

The watch officer on the gate had seen the trouble brewing along the wharf and as the recruit column approached a squad of marines piled out of the entrance to the naval base and charged into the crowd to clear a route for Minucius and his men. The barrage intensified as the townspeople made the most of their last chance to have a go at the men they held responsible for the loss of their livelihood. Macro and Cato covered their heads and ducked down behind the sides of the wagon.

'Some fucking welcome,' Macro grumbled. 'This job is just getting better by the instant. Wonder what's in store for us next?'

Cato did not reply. He was looking intently at the sea and for the first time he realised just how afraid he was of this element. Not only was he a poor swimmer, he had suffered acutely from seasickness on the few occasions he had actually been at sea. And now he was destined to spend the foreseeable future on, or worse, in the sea. He felt sick just thinking about it.

When the wagons at the tail of the convoy had entered the naval base the marines retreated inside and quickly closed and bolted the gates. The watch officer, another centurion, strode up to Minucius' wagon, grinning widely.

'A fine welcome home that, eh?'

'Great,' Minucius growled as he reached for his canteen and rinsed his mouth out. He spat the contents to one side.

'Varro, what the hell's been going on since I've been in Rome? The whole of Umbria's gone mad with this pirate nonsense.'

The watch officer's smile faded. 'You can't have heard then?'

'Heard what?'

'They landed near a veterans' colony at Lissus a few days ago. Sacked the place and slaughtered everyone there. Women and kids put to the sword and all the men impaled. They burned the colony to the ground.'

Minucius stared at him. 'Lissus? I know some people there . . .'

'You did. Not any more.'

'Shit . . .' Minucius slumped down on to the driver's bench. The watch officer reached up and gave his arm a gentle squeeze, before he turned to the other centurions.

'Are you Macro and Cato?'

They nodded.

'You're to come with me. The prefect gave orders to send for you the moment you arrived.'

'Just a moment,' said Cato. He climbed down from the wagon and trotted back to the vehicle carrying Anobarbus.

The merchant was sitting up and brushing some mud off his cloak. He glanced up at Cato. 'Nice town, Ravenna.'

Cato held out his hand. 'The prefect's sent for us. I'll say goodbye for now. Send us word when you've found a place to stay.'

'I will.' Anobarbus clasped his hand. 'And the drinks will be on me.'

Cato nodded at his money box. 'You can afford it.'

The merchant gave Cato a queer smile and then nodded. 'I owe you and Macro my life. I shan't ever forget.'

'I'll hold you to that!' He winked and hurried back to

Macro and Varro, who was twitching his vine cane impatiently.

The watch officer turned away and strode off towards a massive porticoed building that looked out over the naval base.

'Nice going,' Macro hissed. 'You've managed to piss them off this side of the gate as well.'

'Maybe, but there's a drink in it for us.' Cato jerked his thumb back at the merchant's wagon. 'And it's on our friend.'

'That's more like it.' Macro's contented smile lasted all the way across the parade ground.

The prefect's office was imposing – a long room that gave out on to the upper level of the portico, which provided access to all the offices along the second floor of the fleet headquarters building. The view from the prefect's office took in the broad sweep of the naval harbour, the marine barracks and the sprawl of store sheds and workshops beyond. To one side of the harbour was a timbered hard where men toiled over a beached trireme, covering the bottom with black tar from steaming vats – further evidence of the preparations for the campaign against the pirates.

Inside the prefect's office, the floor was laid with an attractive mosaic featuring Neptune skewering some demon of the deep with his trident while the other hand directed a storm to wreck a Punic fleet. Vitellius had a small, but expensive desk by a window at one end of the room, and the other end was covered with a huge map of the fleet's theatre of operations, painted on to the wall in minute detail.

Macro and Cato approached the prefect's desk and stood to attention. He was signing a stack of documents and glanced up at them before turning back to his work and completing it unhurriedly. At length, he replaced his stylus in its holder and looked up at the two centurions.

'Well,' Prefect Vitellius smiled as he leaned back in his chair, 'I take it you had a pleasant tour through our idyllic countryside?'

'Yes, sir,' Cato replied flatly.

'Good, because the holiday's over. We've got plenty of work to do over the following months. Things have moved on since Narcissus briefed us back in Rome. The situation is far more serious.'

'We noticed, sir.'

'Really?' Vitellius looked amused. 'I doubt you have been given the full picture, Centurion Cato. The Imperial Secretary has only provided that to his most trustworthy agents.'

'Meaning you?' Macro chuckled bitterly.

The prefect was still for a moment, fighting to control his temper, and Cato feared for a moment that his friend had overstepped the mark, by about a mile. Then Vitellius' expression eased.

'Please dispense with the uncooperative attitude.'

There was a pause as the two men stared silently at each other in mutual loathing.

Finally, Macro nodded. 'Very well.'

'That's better. And from now on, you'll supply the required respect due to my rank. You will call me "Prefect", or "sir". Understand?'

'Yes, sir.'

'Good. Come over here.' Vitellius stood up and walked over to the map. He picked up a long cane from a rack beside it and rapped on the coastline of Illyricum. 'The pirates must be operating out of a base somewhere along this coastline. So far we have gathered only very limited intelligence on them, but we do have a name. The leader is called Telemachus. A Greek. I expect he's trying to drum up some support from locals. He's a shrewd man, and won't be easy to beat.'

Cato coughed. 'Getting the scrolls back isn't going to be easy either, sir.'

Vitellius turned round and tried to read Cato's face. 'What do you know about the scrolls?'

'Enough, to know how valuable they are to the Emperor, sir.'

'Really?' Vitellius gave him a searching look. 'I think you're bluffing, young Cato. Or fishing for information. Nice try. Anyway, it seems that our pirate chief is quite a player. He sent a message to inform us that there are now other parties interested in the scrolls, and they're willing to match any price that Narcissus will pay.'

'Who are these other people, sir?'

'Telemachus didn't say.'

'He's trying to drive the price up.'

'Maybe, but we can't take the risk that he's lying. Narcissus wants those scrolls, whatever the price. In men as well as money.'

'But who else would want these bloody scrolls, sir?' Macro asked.

'It doesn't really matter. Whoever it is, they can't be allowed to have them.'

'Look here, sir. It would help us if we had some idea of who we are up against.'

'No doubt,' Vitellius smiled. 'But ask yourself, if these scrolls are so vital to the Emperor, then who else would be as interested in them?'

'Aside from you, sir?'

'We've been over that, Macro. Don't try my patience any further.'

'The Liberators,' Cato said quietly. The secret organisation of republicans dedicated to the overthrow of Emperor Clandius seemed to be the obvious suspects.

Vitellius turned to look at him and shrugged. 'Who else?'

'Great.' Macro shook his head wearily. 'That's all we bloody need. If they're in on the act we'll be jumping at our own shadows.'

'Quite.' Vitellius ran a hand through his oiled hair, and wiped it on the side of his tunic. 'So you can see we must proceed carefully, on a number of fronts. Firstly, we have to keep the negotiations going for as long as we can. That'll give us time to try to identify these other parties who are after the scrolls. Then we can seize them. In the meantime, we'll continue preparations for an amphibious campaign along the coast of Illyricum. We must find and destroy the pirate base, and sink or capture their ships. More importantly, we must find those scrolls. It's possible, likely even, that the Liberators have sympathisers or agents here in the fleet already. When we engage the pirates, it'll be a dirty and confusing business. That's when the Liberators are most likely to try and grab the scrolls. That's what we have to look out for and make sure we get to them first.'

Macro sighed. 'Not much to ask for, then.'

'That's in addition to the tasks you'll have to carry out for your cover. You and Cato have been assigned to regular duties. I want you to carry them as conscientiously as if you were back in the legions you so admire. The marines must be as good as you can make them if we're going to have the edge over the pirates when it comes down to the fighting. Furthermore, when the men and ships are ready to take the offensive, I'll be appointing each of you to command a ship.'

'Take command of ships?' Macro shook his head. 'Sir, I don't know the first thing about bloody ships.'

'Then you'd better learn. I wouldn't worry too much. The trierarchs will be handling the day-to-day running of the ships. You just have to tell them the direction you want to go and act as a kind of figurehead in battle.' Vitellius smiled. 'That means being thick and hard, standing at the front of the ship and shouting. Shouldn't present much of a challenge to you, Macro. At any rate, you'll meet your marine officers and the trierarchs at tonight's meeting. You may go now, Centurion Macro. There's a clerk outside who will take you to your quarters.'

'Yes, sir.' Macro exchanged a glance with Cato, then turned and marched out of the office, closing the door behind him.

For a moment Vitellius gazed at the map, and then turned to Cato. 'Let's take a seat.'

'Yes, sir.'

They crossed the room back to the prefect's desk and Cato pulled up a chair, wincing slightly as the iron feet grated across the mosaic tiles. He had no idea why he had been kept back by Vitellius and was afraid, because he knew what the scheming aristocrat was capable of.

Vitellius was a good reader of men's expressions and appraised the young centurion with cold eyes. 'I don't mind that you hate me so much, Centurion. I can understand your reasons. But you must accept that I am out of your league. You raise one hand towards me and I'll have you crushed under foot like a cockroach. It would be a shame to have you killed, since you have much to offer in the service of Rome. But I must look to my own interests first, and I have to be sure that I can rely on you and that you pose me no threat.'

Cato shrugged.

'Very well, then I propose a truce between us, for the duration of this matter. For both our sakes. There's already enough danger to be faced out there without needlessly adding to our perils. You understand?'

'Yes, sir.'

'Good. Feel free to hate me again the moment we have found those scrolls.'

Cato shook his head. 'I'll always hate you, and despise you, sir. But I can endure that without it affecting my duties, for a while at least.'

Vitellius stared at him, and gave the slightest of nods. 'That will have to do, then . . . Now, there's one other matter to deal with. I need you for something that might be quite dangerous.'

'How convenient, sir.'

'Useful rather than convenient. Telemachus' message ended with a demand that we make a payment up front to keep us in the negotiations for these scrolls. "A token of our commitment", as he puts it. So, you will meet him, assure him that we're still keen and give him the gold he's demanded.'

'Why me?'

'Because it's important that one of us can identify Telemachus by sight. When the time comes to put that bastard in his place, I want to be sure we have the right man. He may be the only one who knows where the scrolls are being kept.'

'Why send me alone? Surely it would be useful if Centurion Macro was there as well?'

Vitellius smiled. 'Your friend Macro has many admirable

qualities, but diplomacy is not one of them. I dare not send him with you. This job requires more subtle skills. And you're young enough to make our man feel he's dealing with someone lacking in experience and guile. That should put him at his ease.'

'Where will this meeting take place, sir?'

'At sea, like last time. He needs to be sure that it isn't a trap. You'll take one of the scout craft. Anything bigger might scare him off.'

'Anything smaller might put us at risk.'

'Well, that's a chance I'm prepared to let you take.'

'Thank you, sir.'

'You're to meet him ten miles off the cape at Mortepontum shortly after sunrise so he can be sure that you're alone and that he can escape if you're not.'

'He's a cautious man, sir.'

'He has to be. You know the saying: there are old pirates and bold pirates but no old bold pirates.'

Cato nodded thoughtfully and looked Vitellius in the eye. 'You know, sir, this Telemachus sounds like the kind of man *you* could learn from.'

'Thanks for the advice, Centurion. But I think I'll cope well enough on my own. Now, I'm sure there's at least one more question you'd like to ask.'

'When is this meeting?'

'In two days' time. You're leaving tonight.'

CHAPTER THIRTEEN

The bireme heaved to before the first hint of dawn. It wallowed in a heavy swell that rose under the stern, lifted it up and then let it fall back with a sickening swoop. Cato leaned on the stern rail, head pitched forward, and vomited into the dark oily abyss below. It had been bad enough while he had been able to see the horizon as a reference point to steady his sense of balance, but as darkness had closed round the small ship the chaotic and nauseous movement under his feet had increased his misery tenfold. All night he had been at the rail, head swimming, with regular bouts of retching that felt as if the pit of his stomach was being ripped up and wrenched out of his throat.

Cato was glad that Macro had been ordered to stay at Ravenna. Macro's cast-iron constitution took sea travel in its stride with the same blithe confidence and comfort as every other mode of transport. No doubt Macro would have found the chilly sea breeze 'bracing' or some equally annoying sentiment.

When his friend had heard about the meeting Cato had been roundly accused of keeping secrets. At the time Cato had been secretly flattered to be chosen for this duty; now he would have paid any price to swap places with Macro.

'Any better?'

Cato turned from the rail and saw Decimus, the bireme's

trierarch, emerge from the darkness. Cato shook his head.

'I thought you were one of the new centurions appointed to the marines?'

'That's me.'

'Well, I hate to be rude, or anything, but you're not exactly taking to the vocation.'

'I hate the sea.'

'I assume you're a landsman.'

'Yes . . .' A fresh wave of nausea gripped his body and Cato lurched back to the rail and retched until the attack passed, then wiped the stringy spittle from his lips before turning back to Decimus. 'I was transferred from the legions.'

'Transferred? I see . . .' Decimus nodded, tactfully avoiding asking the reason for what was in effect a demotion. 'Can't be doing with all that marching and civil engineering nonsense. Give me a simple life on the sea any day.'

Cato stared at him, thinking that he'd rather build an aqueduct all by himself than spend another moment on the ship.

Decimus leaned on the rail next to Cato, upwind, and sniffed the air. 'Fresh and salty. We're in for a good day. Bit choppy, but no chance of a storm.'

'Choppy . . .' Cato swallowed and tensed his jaw. 'Where are we?'

'Some miles from the Cape. I gave the order to heave to so that we don't get too close in the dark.'

'Why not?'

'Why not?' Decimus laughed. 'You've never seen the Cape before?'

'I've never seen many things before. Your bloody Cape Mortepontum amongst them.'

'How do you think it got the name? "The Bridge of Death" – bit of a giveaway, don't you think?'

Cato glanced round. 'Dangerous then?'

'More ships are wrecked on the Cape than anywhere else along this entire coastline.'

'How so?'

'When the sun rises and we get closer, then I think you'll understand why I give it a wide berth. Now, if you'll excuse me I'll see to my men. They need to be fed and at their stations before first light.'

'Expecting trouble?'

'Are you serious?' Decimus shook his head in wonder. 'You've not had dealings with pirates before?'

'No.'

'They're as trustworthy as a shark in a sausage factory. And twice as dangerous.'

Cato raised his eyebrows. 'Colourful. But not entirely coherent.'

'What?' Decimus frowned.

'The analogy doesn't work. The shark is not a land creature.'

Decimus shrugged. 'You obviously haven't met my banker.'

As the first hint of dawn spread along the eastern horizon Cato could just make out the pale shadow of the mountainous coastline.

Decimus pointed out a darker patch. 'That's the Cape. We'll move close in.'

He turned to face the bows and cupped his hands to his mouth. 'Raise the sail! Put a reef in her!'

Several sailors clambered up the rigging and swung out along the yardarm, bare feet pressing down on the toe-line as they shuffled along. When every man was in place the mate called out an order and the sailors undid the ties and began to unfurl the sail. Its billowing expanse slowly filled up and became taut as more sailors on deck hauled the mainsheets in and fastened them to the stout wooden cleats on the ship's side rails. When the rectangular sail had been let out as far as the first reefing lines, the sailors on the yard tied it down and returned to the deck. The motion of the bireme began to settle as it got under way and Cato could hear the rush and hiss of the sea sliding along the waterline.

'Steersman!' Decimus called out. 'Heading, three fingers off the port bow.'

'Three fingers off the port bow. Aye, sir.'

Just behind Cato the powerfully built sailor braced his legs on a foot rail and heaved at the great steering paddle that was suspended over the side of the bireme, a short distance from the stern. Slowly, the vessel began to respond, and the bows turned downwind, towards the distant shore. Then the bireme was running before the wind and left a swirling white wake across the sea behind her.

Decimus was clearly in his element and turned to Cato with a twinkle of delight in his eyes.

'Feeling better now?'

'Much.'

'We'll be at the meeting point soon with this following wind. Of course, it'll be difficult going if we have to beat back towards Ravenna. Might have to take down the sail and get the rowers to work.'

He nodded at the deck and Cato glanced towards the main grating. The dim forms of men sitting at their benches were just visible in the pale light.

'Will they be fast enough to get the ship out of danger if it's a trap?'

'They should be. This class of vessel is designed for speed. The real question is how long they can keep it up. I generally keep my men well fed and rested so we have that extra reserve of strength at the oars, should we need it. Let's just hope we don't need it, eh?'

'Sail! Away to port!' the lookout cried down from the masthead, and thrust his arm out, pointing a short distance off the coastline.

Cato automatically turned and squinted towards the horizon but saw nothing along the unbroken line.

Decimus called up to the lookout, 'Can you make anything out?'

There was a short delay before the report came back. 'Black sail. I can see the hull now. Big ship.'

'Is that him?' asked Cato.

'Most likely. There'll be few ships at sea in winter. Even fewer with pirates out on the prowl.'

'Deck there!'

Cato and Decimus tilted their heads up towards the masthead. The lookout was pointing to the south. 'Another sail.'

Cato felt an icy tingle at the back of his neck. 'It's a trap.'

'Calm yourself,' Decimus smiled. 'There's still plenty of time to head back out to sea.'

'Another sail! And another!' cried the lookout, pointing his arm out over the stern of the bireme.

Cato nodded in resignation and then forced a smile as he turned back to Decimus. 'You were saying?'

The trierarch ignored him, and stretched up on to his toes as he stared out over the swell behind his ship. There, faintly visible on the horizon, were two triangular sails.

'Bloody fine piece of seamanship,' Decimus growled. 'They must have been watching us from the east, long before we heaved to last night.'

'How do you know?'

'They'd have been hidden in the dusk while we were silhouetted against the sunset.'

'So what now?'

'Now?' The trierarch shrugged. 'They've got us by the balls. Let's just hope they aren't planning any treachery. No point in trying to escape. We'll have to heave to and wait for them to run down to us.'

The bireme rode out the swell. A small foresail had been set to steady the bows and give just enough forward motion for the steering paddle to bite. Around Cato the deck had been cleared for action and the bireme's complement of marines were at their stations. The catapult mounted to the foredeck was loaded and the crew were winding back the torsion arms with a steady clank from the locking ratchet. Boarding nets had been rigged and a handful of men armed with bows lined the stern rail. Cato had put on his armour and stood beside Decimus, one hand resting on the pommel of his sword. He gazed at the four ships steadily closing in on the bireme. Three were not much larger than the bireme, and used a lateen sail of eastern design. They looked sleek and cut easily through the blue-grey rollers sweeping across the sea. Decimus shook his head in despair as the fourth vessel drew close enough for them to make out the details. Even Cato's unpractised eye was familiar with the silhouette.

'That's a Roman ship, isn't it?'

'She was. That's one of the triremes that went missing.'

The smaller ships heaved to some distance from the bireme and waited for the fourth ship to close up. The trireme, like the other pirate ships, carried a dark sail, and as they turned on the final tack, tiny figures appeared on the yardarm and hurriedly furled the sail. A moment later the oars were run out and after a brief pause to get the timing right, they dipped down and churned up the sea as the trireme manoeuvred directly towards the Roman ship.

Decimus glanced at Cato. 'The moment of truth, I think.'

'Yes.' Cato's eyes were fixed on the approaching warship and he wondered if the real reason Vitellius had picked him for this task was the hope that he wouldn't come back.

When the trireme was no more than a hundred paces away, it began to turn up into the wind, and the oars stopped moving and were neatly drawn back into the hull. Almost at once, a small skiff was lowered over the side and it bobbed across the gap between the two ships, steering clear of the catapult in the bow of the bireme. It stopped and stood off a short distance from the beam of the Roman ship.

A tall, thin youth with curly black hair poking out from under a Phrygian cap sat on the aft thwart of the skiff. He cupped a hand to his mouth and called across to the bireme in fluent Greek.

'Is the negotiator on board?'

Cato moved over to the rail and raised a hand. 'I'm here.'

'Do you have the money with you?'

'I do.'

'You will come with us.' The man called an instruction to his oarsmen and the skiff darted over the water towards the bireme and one of the pirates took a firm hold of the boarding ladder.

Cato turned to the nearest marine. 'Go down to the cabin. There's a chest under my bunk. Bring it here.'

The marine saluted and hurried over to the hatch coaming that led down to the small cabin in the stern. Cato gripped the side rail and swung himself over, his boots scrabbling for the steps on the boarding ladder.

'Roman!'

Cato glanced round and saw the man in the skiff wagging a finger at him. 'No sword!'

Gripping tightly to the rail with one hand Cato drew his

sword and tossed it up on to the deck of the bireme. Decimus eyed him anxiously. 'Is that wise?'

'Who knows?' Cato responded bleakly. Then he realised that the trierarch was probably even more nervous than he was. He made himself smile up at Decimus. 'I'll have that back when this is over.'

He looked round, timing the rise and fall of the skiff beneath him, and then dropped down heavily. The little craft rocked from side to side, and for a moment Cato was sure it was going to turn over and pitch them all into the sea. In his armour, he was sure to sink like a stone. But then the young man in the stern grabbed at his shoulder and steadied the centurion.

'Sit down, you fool! Where's the gold?'

'Coming.'

A moment later the marine appeared at the side of the bireme and lowered the box in some netting. The pirate stood up, with the instinctive balance of a man who has spent many years at sea. He stretched up his arms to the chest and steered it down into the bottom of the skiff. He dragged it free of the netting, before placing the chest under the thwart in the centre of the boat, then nodded to his oarsmen. The skiff turned and made for the trireme as Cato squatted down, icy sea water sloshing over his boots and breeches. He had thought the motion of the bireme unsettling enough, but now the sea seemed to be almost level with his face and the boat bobbed up and down in a terrifying manner. When they reached the trireme he grasped the rope that was lowered to him as if it was a lifeline and scrambled up the side and on to the broad deck in a most undignified manner. The relative firmness of the deck beneath him went someway towards calming his nerves as Cato rose to his feet and stiffened his back. An instant later the chest was heaved up and placed by his feet. The young man from the skiff scrambled up and stood beside Cato.

'Welcome!' a voice called out from the stern, and Cato turned and saw a man striding towards him. He was tall and broad-chested, with the unmistakable features of a Greek. A gold earring gleamed from each side of his face, which was so terribly scarred that Cato could not help but stare at it. The pirate smiled as he stood before the centurion, and stretched out his hand. Cato had not expected anything resembling a warm welcome and was momentarily thrown off guard. Then he swallowed, and was determined to play the part of a true Roman. He glanced coldly at the outstretched hand and shook his head.

'I regret to say I am under orders not to fraternise with pirates.'

The Greek stared at him in surprise for an instant and then roared with laughter. 'I've never known such a stiff-necked people! Aren't you Romans taught any social graces?'

'Of course. We just don't consort with criminals. I assume you are Telemachus.'

'I am.' The Greek bowed his head. 'And this is my lieutenant, Ajax.'

The young man beside Cato nodded, as Telemachus continued. 'We'll have to make this quick, Roman. I have business to attend to.'

'Business? Is that what you call piracy and pillaging?'

'You can call it what you like, Centurion . . . I didn't catch the name?'

'I didn't mention it.'

Telemachus shrugged. 'Please yourself. Is this our retainer?' He tapped the box with the toe of his boot.

'It is.'

'Good. Then I have a message for your masters. Tell them

that the merchandise is still with me, but that other parties have also demonstrated their interest – in gold. They will be paying their retainer in the next few days.'

'Who are they?' Cato asked.

'You know I can't tell you that. They wish to remain anonymous, and alive.'

'The Liberators,' Cato sneered. 'Who else could it be?'

'You tell me. It's not as if the world is short of people who have every cause to hate Rome and all it stands for.'

'How do I know that you're not bluffing just to drive the price up?'

'You don't,' Telemachus grinned. 'But can your masters afford to call my bluff? Given the nature of the merchandise, I doubt it. Now then, you will tell them that the competition has offered me twenty million sestertians. Your masters have two months to improve on that.'

Cato struggled to contain his astonishment at such a vast demand. It was a fortune, enough to ransom a kingdom, let alone a king. He stared at Telemachus. 'When you say the merchandise, you are referring to the scrolls, aren't you?'

The pirate chief exchanged a glance with his lieutenant and chuckled. 'That's right.'

'But no scroll is worth such a sum.'

Telemachus poked the centurion in the chest. 'These scrolls are. Believe me.'

'Why?'

Telemachus stared at Cato with amusement. 'You have no idea what they are, do you?'

Cato thought about trying to deceive the pirate chief, and then realised he would be seen through in an instant. 'No.'

'But you would like to know?'

Cato stared back at him for a moment, but could no longer deny his curiosity.

Telemachus nodded before the Roman could reply. 'I thought so. If I told you what they were . . . if I told you any detail of what they contain, you would be in mortal danger, Roman. Be content in your ignorance. If you want to survive.'

He watched Cato closely to make sure the young officer understood the peril, then continued, 'Now, before you run along, there's one other message I'd like you to carry back.' He clicked his fingers and a Nubian came trotting up with a small wicker casket, which he handed to the pirate leader. Telemachus flipped the lid open and tilted it towards Cato. Inside there was a shock of black hair plastered down on to a scalp. 'May I introduce you to the former governor of the former colony at Lissus? Gaius Manlius, I think his name was. Take this back to Ravenna as a little memento of our meeting. Tell your masters that I will begin to raid more colonies from now on, unless I am paid a tribute of ten million sestertians a year, or the equivalent in gold.' Telemachus looked at him closely. 'Can you remember all that?'

'Yes.'

The pirate chief looked a little uncertain. 'How old are you, boy?'

'Nineteen.'

'Why did they send you?'

'I'm expendable.'

'Indeed you are,' Telemachus replied as he scratched his chin. The rasping noise drew Cato's eyes and there was a blur of motion and then a curved dagger was at the centurion's throat. Cato froze, and Telemachus leaned closer, dark eyes narrowing to slits. He spoke softly. 'I'll remember you, you arrogant young pup. I could cut your throat right now and send your head back as a companion piece.' He leered into Cato's face, and the warm odour of fish sauce filled Cato's nose. Then the dagger dropped away. 'As it happens I want to close negotiations reasonably soon and I'm not prepared to wait until you Romans send out an envoy with some manners. If we meet again, I swear I'll gut you with my own blade. Now, take that.' He thrust the casket towards Cato. 'And get off my ship. If you make any attempt to follow us once this meeting is over, we'll turn on you, sink your ship and kill any survivors. Go.'

Cato hurried down the side of the trireme and back into the skiff, and the casket, with the lid fastened, was tossed down to him. Cato quickly tucked it under the thwart and tried not to think about what it contained.

Ajax watched him with an amused expression. 'You've got guts, Roman. There's not many people who speak to Telemachus in such a manner, and live to tell the tale.'

'Oh, really?' Cato looked at him for a moment before he continued. 'You can't have served him for long enough to know the man.'

A strange smile flickered across Ajax's face. 'You're wrong. I've known him all my life. He's not the dandy you think he is. If you meet again, he will kill you.'

'Not unless I kill him first.'

The pirate laughed. 'Roman arrogance. I've never known anything like it.'

As Decimus helped Cato on to the deck the centurion passed the casket to the marine he had sent to fetch the chest. 'Put this in the cabin, but don't open it, unless you want to be flogged. Understand?'

'Yes, sir.'

Cato crossed the deck to the far rail and threw up.

'What happened over there?' Decimus asked.

'Don't ask. Just take the ship back to Ravenna. Get me out of this place.'

CHAPTER FOURTEEN

Prefect Vitellius looked up from Cato's report. 'He gave us two months?'

'Yes, sir.'

Vitellius closed his eyes and thought aloud. 'That gives us enough time to send a message back to Rome, and for Narcissus to make a decision about his offer, and send us a reply to pass on to Telemachus.'

'Excuse me, sir, but do you think it's likely that the Imperial Secretary will top the opposition's offer?'

'Oh, yes. He has to. If the scrolls fall into the wrong hands, they could make life very difficult for Rome . . .' Vitellius looked up and saw Cato shake his head. 'You don't believe me.'

'How can I, sir? I have no idea what's in these scrolls. It all seems too far-fetched.'

'You don't have to worry about it. You're a soldier, and you must obey orders. That's all you do. Your superiors can deal with the finer details.'

Vitellius glanced back at the wax tablets. 'Now, to this other matter. The tribute he's demanding for not attacking our colonies. That's his first big mistake.'

'Sir?'

'Telemachus is getting too greedy. The scrolls are one thing, but this demand for tribute is quite another. There's no question of us paying it. The Emperor would never stand for it.'

'Why not, sir? We already pay off any number of tribes in Germany to keep the peace.' Cato was struggling to work through the logic of the situation. Rome would pay upwards of twenty million sestertians for some scrolls, yet balk at half that for saving the lives of thousands of her people and dozens of her colonies.

'That's different. The Germans act as a buffer between the Empire and other barbarians of an even more violent and distasteful disposition. Pirates are different – no more than a gang of thieves and murderers.'

'It would seem they have grown to become more than just a gang, sir.'

'True. But I can tell you now that Claudius will not demean himself by permitting these pirates to run a protection racket. He'll give orders for them to be found and destroyed, and we'll not be allowed to rest until that has been carried out.'

'Even at the risk of losing the scrolls, sir?'

'Maybe we can combine the two tasks.' The prefect rose from his chair and crossed the office to the map. Cato followed him. Vitellius stared at the Illyricum coastline for a moment before he spoke.

'Centurion, where would you position your base if you were Telemachus?'

Cato concentrated on the detailed map as he collected his thoughts, and then offered an answer. 'Going on what you've let me read of the intelligence reports, it would have to be somewhere off the trade routes, by land and sea. He couldn't afford to be near any spot where a passing merchant vessel might beach for the night. So that rules out the Liburnian coastline, and there, further to the south, in

Macedonia – far too many colonies and ports. At the same time he needs to be sufficiently close to the trade routes to prey on them. Some of his ships carry oarsmen. If he provisions his ships like we do then that gives him an operating radius of five or six days' sailing at most. That places him somewhere between Flanona and, say, Dyrrachium. Most probably in one of those inlets, or on one of the small islands just off the coast. Could be hundreds of them.' Cato turned from the map. 'That's my best guess, based on the information I've seen, sir.'

Prefect Vitellius nodded. 'I agree. So that's where we'll start looking for them. We'll leave a garrison here, and I'll take the fleet over to Illyricum and establish a base near . . .' his eyes scanned the map, 'Birnisium. Looks sheltered enough and we can draw supplies from that cluster of colonies nearby. Birnisium, then.' He glanced round at Cato. 'I'll brief all the officers at noon tomorrow. You may go, Centurion. Send my chief clerk to me on the way out.'

Cato saluted and marched out of the office, leaving the prefect to ponder on his plans.

Cato returned to the officers' quarters, changed into a fresh tunic and made for the bath house. As he entered the caldarium he saw Macro sitting on one of the marble benches. His friend looked up and smiled with genuine relief. 'Cato! Good to see you. How did it go?'

Macro listened attentively as Cato recounted the meeting with the pirates, and when he had finished Macro dabbed at his face with a sponge, then turned back to Cato.

'This Telemachus, what was he like?'

Cato described his appearance, shutting his eyes for a moment as he recollected as much as possible of the details of the encounter. 'He seemed capable enough. Tough and fast with a blade. And his ships seemed to perform well. Of course, I'm no judge of seamanship, but that's what Decimus reckoned. And he's ruthless.' Cato shuddered as he recalled the memory of Vitellius ordering a marine to empty the casket on to the wharf when the bireme had returned to Ravenna shortly after noon. Cato shook off the image as he carried on talking to Macro. 'Certainly his men seemed afraid of him.'

'Sounds like a tough nut to crack,' Macro mused. 'They'll put up quite a fight.'

'Maybe,' Cato shrugged. 'But, as I've always said, men fight hardest for the things they believe in, not for what they fear.'

Macro smiled, dipped the sponge in a tub of water and lobbed it at Cato's face, dowsing his friend. 'Honestly, Cato, now you think you're an expert on what motivates men.'

Cato wiped the water and sweat from his brow. 'I believe I have some idea of what works.'

'All right then,' Macro conceded, 'some idea. But I'm telling you, these pirates are like us. Harsh discipline is the best motivation for fighting men. Inspiration, ideas, they're for artists and those pansy philosophers like . . .'

'Like me?'

Macro shrugged. 'You said it. Now don't go and sulk on me.'

'Sulk?'

Macro laughed. 'Come on, let's go.'

'Go where?'

'For a drink. We're meeting Anobarbus and Minucius in the port.'

'Are we?' Cato was a little put out by his friend's presumption. 'I'm tired. I just came in here to relax, not to be roped into one of your all-night benders.'

'It won't be like that. We're going to be respectable tonight. Minucius is taking us to meet his woman. She owns a tavern.' Macro smiled. 'Every soldier's dream girl.' He looked round at Cato. 'Any normal soldier's dream girl, I should say.'

'Macro?'

'Yes?'

'Just fuck off, eh?'

Macro slapped him on the shoulder and laughed. 'That's my boy. Come on then, we're wasting good drinking time.'

They borrowed some plain tunics and capes from stores rather than wear their distinctive red military tunics. With popular feeling in Ravenna being the way it was, neither man was keen to draw attention to himself. They slipped out of a side gate and followed Minucius' directions through the narrow streets to a run-down area of the port that was filled with taverns, brothels and cheap tenements. The streets were packed with drunken noisy sailors and marines from the naval base, but the local men looked hard and hostile as they clustered together around the public drinking fountains. A handful of provosts patrolled the area, keeping a wary eye on proceedings.

'Feels like a fight's going to break out at any moment,' Cato muttered. 'We should have stayed back at the barracks.'

'Oh, come on!' Macro elbowed him. 'Not frightened of a few surly teenagers, are you?'

'Yes, I am,' Cato readily confessed. 'These ones at least. They look as if they'd kill to start a fight.'

'Ooooh,' Macro pretended to shiver. 'Better find shelter quickly then . . . Here we are. Crab Lane.'

He turned into a wide thoroughfare, every foot of it

given over to taverns. The drunken din of their customers assaulted Cato's ears. Macro shouted something to him and pointed across the street to a brightly painted sign, high up a grimy wall.

' "The Dancing Dolphin – we don't water our wine . . ." ' Cato muttered to himself. 'Cute name.'

The two centurions pushed their way across the street and through the arch that led into the tavern. Inside, the air was thick with cheap incense and dimly lit by just enough lamps for the clientele to see their way up to the bar, or out the back to the latrine. Two well-built and tough-looking men were working behind the bar, together with a tall, grey-haired woman who had her back to the entrance as she dealt with a drunken customer who was trying to grope her. Cato watched as one of the barmen leaned over and floored the drunk with a quick upper cut.

The centre of the tavern was packed with benches and trestle tables, at which large groups of rowdy men were drinking, or chatting up the local tarts and negotiating a rate for their transaction. To the side of the tavern were a number of alcoves with curtains that could be drawn across for a degree of privacy.

'Cato!'

The two centurions turned towards the sound and saw Minucius beckoning them to the alcove in the far corner, closest to the bar. Opposite him sat Anobarbus, who smiled a greeting as Macro and Cato squeezed through the drinkers towards them. They slipped on to the benches either side of the battered table, and Minucius immediately filled two leather cups and pushed them towards Macro and Cato, sloshing some of the wine over the brims.

'Thought you weren't coming.'

'Wouldn't miss it for the world,' Macro replied. 'Looks

like we've got a bit of catching-up to do. Cheers!' He raised his cup and took a gulp.

Cato was sitting next to Anobarbus and turned towards him. 'How are the injuries healing?'

'Not bad. Still a bit painful. Skin on my chest feels like it's shrunk to fit a man half my size.'

Cato nodded. 'I know. I've had some burns. You'll be all right. Give it time.'

'That's what the quack says. Cheers.'

They tapped cups together and took a sip. Cato noted, with approval, that Anobarbus was a kindred spirit and merely sipped at his wine rather than gulping it down like there was no tomorrow, as was the case on the other side of the table. Anobarbus lowered his cup.

'Minucius tells me you've already been out with the navy.'

Cato glanced up at him. 'That's right. A patrol.'

Anobarbus smiled. 'So, how have you taken to a life on the ocean waves?'

'Not at all. I was sick as a dog for most of the trip.'

'Where did they take you?'

'Just a patrol,' Cato said carefully. 'Over to the coast of Illyricum and back.'

'Really?' Anobarbus looked surprised. 'I wouldn't have thought it was safe to venture that side of the sea with all these pirates about. Don't suppose you actually got to see any?'

Cato shook his head. 'No. One or two sails. That was it. Quite boring really. How about you? Picked up any more artworks for your clients?'

'No. The market's dead right now. I'll stay a while longer, until I've fully recovered. Might try one of the ports further up the coast in the next few days, see if they have anything worth buying, then head back to Rome.'

'Well, I hope you have better luck with your next journey.'

'Yes,' Anobarbus replied quietly. 'I'll need it.'

'Come on, lads!' Macro leaned over the table. 'Drink up. It's on the house! Let's have a toast to Minucius' woman, bless her!'

The cups thudded together, spilling yet more wine, and the toast was drunk, to the bottom of the cup. Cato was surprised that the wine was of a decent quality and wished that Macro would take the time to actually savour it. Unfortunately, the other two centurions had already finished the first jar of wine and Macro rose up from the bench.

'Next one's on me.'

'No need!' Minucius smiled. Pulling Macro back down with one hand, he reached under the table and brought out another jar.

Macro's eyes widened. 'How many more of those have you got under there?'

'Enough to keep us going for a while yet. Drink up!'

'Where's this woman of yours?' Macro looked round, but his view of the bar was obscured by a crowd of customers standing in the way. 'I want to give her a hug.'

'She'll join us a bit later. When it quietens down.'

'Oh, all right then.' Macro turned back to the others. 'Hey! Have you heard the news?'

'What news?' Anobarbus asked.

'The prefect's going to stick it to the pirates. Taking the whole fleet and the marines over to Illyricum to hunt the bastards down.'

Cato leaned across the table and laid a hand on his friend's arm. 'Macro!'

'What?'

'That's not for general consumption.'

Macro looked at him blearily. 'General who?'

'It's supposed to be a secret.'

'Secret? Secret from who? Soon as we start loading up the ships everyone'll know anyway.'

'That's not the point. The prefect doesn't want word of it getting out to the pirates any sooner than can be helped.'

'You told me.'

'I trusted you.'

Macro shifted guiltily. 'Well, yes. Look, I'm sorry, lad. Anyway, it's not going any further than the four of us, then. All right, boys?'

'Sure,' Minucius smiled. 'Let's make an oath, and seal it with a toast.'

'No,' Cato said firmly. 'Just don't mention it again. Goes for you too. And you, Anobarbus.'

Anobarbus nodded. 'My lips are sealed. Don't you worry.'

'Don't worry? Easier said than done, with those two soaks around.'

Minucius suddenly beamed and stood up, knocking the table with his hip and nearly sending the fresh jar of wine flying. Anobarbus' arm shot out and steadied the jar before it could spill a drop.

'Nice hands!' Macro winked at him.

'Here she is now, boys!' said Minucius. 'My woman. My girl. The love of my life.'

Cato turned round and scanned the crowd. Suddenly it parted before him as a tall, thin and elegant old lady cast a withering glare at the men around her. From the pattern of her stola he realised she was the woman he had seen earlier at the bar. She walked up to the table and smiled back at Minucius.

Flushing with pride the veteran centurion turned to his companions. 'Lads, may I introduce you to Portia, proprietress of this fine establishment and soon to be my blushing bride.'

'Ignore him,' Portia smiled. 'He's been saying he'll make an honest woman of me for the last twenty years.'

Minucius laughed, then turned to the other men. 'Portia, these are the men I was telling you about. We shared that little adventure back in the mountains. That's Anobarbus, the young lad there is Cato and this incorrigible is Centurion Macro.'

Anobarbus and Cato nodded their greetings but Macro just sat still, an ashen expression on his face.

Portia looked worried. 'Are you all right?'

Macro swallowed nervously before he could manage a reply. 'Hello, Mum.'

CHAPTER FIFTEEN

The silence was finally broken when Portia gave a little cry of shock and clasped a hand over her mouth. Her eyes fluttered and she collapsed like a broken laundry rack.

'Portia!' Minucius clambered over Macro and cradled her head in his hands. 'Portia, my love! Speak to me!'

While he tried to revive the woman, Cato's gaze switched from her to Macro and back again in total bewilderment. Macro just stared fixedly at Portia as if the old woman was the most astonishing vision in the entire world. When the enormity of what had just happened fixed itself in Cato's brain he began to understand Macro's paralysed reaction.

'What's going on?' Anobarbus asked, tugging at Cato's sleeve. 'What did he call her?'

'Mum. He called her Mum.'

'She's his mother?' Anobarbus smiled. 'What is she doing here? I thought you two had come down from Rome.'

'I don't know.' Cato shook his head. 'Macro told me that she'd abandoned him as a child. Ran off with some marine . . . oh . . .' Cato looked at Minucius, who was now squatting on the floor and stroking the old woman's grey hair. 'Oh, no! Macro.'

Macro was still staring down at Portia with a stupefied expression. Cato grabbed his arm and shook him hard.

'Macro! Come on! We have to go.'

Macro tore his gaze away and looked vaguely at Cato. 'Go? Go where?'

'Trust me, we just have to go. Right now.'

'But that's my mum.'

'I know. We'll pop back and see her when you're sober.'

'I haven't seen her for twenty years.' Tears brimmed in the corner of his bleary eyes. 'Since I was her little boy.'

'Yes, yes.' Cato patted his arm gently. 'Wonderful, isn't it? Now we don't want her to see you in this drunken state, do we? Let's go and get you sobered up first. Come on.'

Cato rose from his seat, moved in between Macro and his mother, and her lover, and tried to lift Macro off his bench.

'Here, Anobarbus, lend us a hand.'

The merchant looked at Macro warily. 'Why? What's going on here?'

'Just give me a hand. We have to get him out of here.'

'She's my mother,' Macro mumbled, tears rolling down his cheeks. 'She's my mum, and she ran away from me. Left us for a marine.' Macro suddenly froze, staring at Minucius with wide eyes. 'Him!'

'Oh, no!' Cato's heart sank. 'Quick! Let's go!'

He snatched at Macro's arm and heaved with all his strength, raising the centurion off the bench, but by now full realisation of the situation had flooded drunkenly into Macro's mind. His head snapped towards Minucius.

'You! . . . You bastard!' he snarled, and then a raw shout of hatred ripped out of his throat. 'It was you! You stole her away from us!'

Minucius looked up, startled by the bellow of rage. He snatched up his hands to protect himself and Portia's head bumped on to the floor. Her eyes flickered open, fixed on Macro and she screamed.

Before Cato could react, Macro roared something

incomprehensible and charged into Minucius, picking him up by the shoulders and thrusting him back, through the crowd of marines. Men went flying to either side, tables went over, jars of wine crashed to the floor and shattered, spilling their red contents like blood. There were outraged shouts and screams of panic from the whores as Macro continued to plough through them like an enraged bull with a lithe acrobat pinned on its horns.

Cato turned to Anobarbus and shrugged. 'Here we go again . . .'

The merchant frowned. 'Does he do this sort of thing often?'

'Not really. But this is something of a special occasion. A family reunion.'

On the far side of the tavern Macro had Minucius pinned up against a wooden post and was busy head-butting him. Customers were piling out of the archway and into the street, most of them keen to avoid any fight that might attract the provosts, and some hoping to get out in the confusion without having to settle their bills.

Portia had recovered from her shock and now flew across the room, snatching up an iron skillet on the way.

'Let go of him!' she shrieked. 'Let go of him, you little horror!'

Macro ignored her intervention and continued battering her paramour with commendable single-mindedness.

'All right then, you little bastard!'

Portia swung the skillet back, took aim and then smashed it into the back of Macro's head. There was a dull gong-like noise, and Macro's knees buckled under him, revealing Minucius, bloody-faced and dazed. A moment later he too slumped to the floor. Portia dropped the skillet and started to cry, an awful screeching sound like a parrot inadvertently caught in a meat-grinder, as her shoulders flapped up and down.

'Look out! The provosts are coming!' a terrified voice shrieked from outside in the street.

'Come on,' Cato said to Anobarbus. 'We have to get them out of here. Before the provosts kick seven shades out of them, and us.'

'But surely they won't strike a centurion.'

'How will they know? We're out of uniform.'

They scrambled over the wrecked furniture of the tavern as people stampeded past the archway. Cato gently turned Portia towards him.

'We have to move them. Is there anywhere at the back of the tavern?'

Macro's mother stared at him for a moment before her mind cleared. 'Yes. That way!' She pointed to a small door behind the counter. Anobarbus and Cato picked up the limp form of Macro, dragged him over to the door and thrust him through before they came back for Minucius. Portia held his hand and stroked his hair as they carried him to safety. Outside the Dancing Dolphin an open brawl was breaking out and spilling in through the arch as drunken marines tried to take on club-wielding provosts.

Portia looked up in alarm and screamed, 'Watch them fixings! I paid good money for them!'

One of the provosts nodded. 'Sorry, ma'am.' Then continued pounding the marine lying at his feet.

With the two centurions dragged to safety Cato shut the door and slipped the catch to prevent anyone following them. He looked round and saw that they were in a large stockroom lined with wine jars standing almost as high as a man. A small desk was built into the wall and a ledger lay open on its worn surface. There was a locked gate to the street, and the shadows of people running past in blind panic flitted past the splits and gaps in the timbers. Almost hidden between large jars was a small doorway, which Portia waved them towards.

'Through here.'

Cato gritted his teeth as he lifted Macro up, flung an arm round his friend's back and half carried and half dragged him to the doorway. Anobarbus followed with the lighter Minucius, who was slowly recovering his wits. The doorway led into a long narrow passage that was lit by a single oil lamp at the far end. Portia fumbled with a key before opening another door and led them through into a large, poorly illuminated space beyond. Cato eased Macro down on to the tiled floor and stood up. They were standing in a neat, modestly sized atrium. A small pool glimmered in the centre, beneath an opening that revealed distant starlight. Oil lamps flickered beside a small shrine to gods of the household standing in one corner. A gentle tinkling of running water came from a door at the back of the atrium.

'Nice place you have here,' Cato muttered as he caught his breath.

'That's how I'd like to keep it,' Portia said bitterly. 'You might tell your friend that when he comes round. Then you can get him out of here as quickly as possible.'

'My friend?' Cato raised his eyebrows. 'He's your son, if I'm not mistaken.'

Portia stared back at him. 'So it seems . . . Very well, bring him into my dining room, through here. We'll sort him out and try to talk some sense into his thick skull.'

The dining room was just as tastefully decorated at the atrium and had the usual three couches arranged around a communal table. They heaved Macro on to one while Portia helped Minucius to their bedroom.

Anobarbus looked round admiringly. 'I had no idea one could make such a good living out of running a tavern, particularly one that doesn't water its wine.'

Cato ignored him, and was holding an oil lamp up to the back of Macro's head. The hair was matted with blood, but the skull seemed to have held up well to the impact of the skillet. Macro groaned, and his shoulders twitched violently as he muttered something that made no sense.

Portia returned a short time later with a bowl of water and some old rags. 'Out of my way, young man.' She sat down on the couch next to Macro. 'If you must loiter, then please hold that lamp where it'll do some good. There, by his head.'

'Sorry.'

Cato watched as she gently sponged the blood away to reveal a cut in his scalp. As quickly as the blood was wiped away, more welled up. Portia rinsed the cloth and then held it against the wound.

She laid her spare hand on Macro's cheek and stroked it gently. 'I never thought I'd be doing this again. The number of times I've had to sort out this boy's cuts and scrapes is anybody's guess.'

Cato was intrigued. 'Clumsy lad, then?'

'Clumsy? No. He was a complete thug as a child. Always getting into fights, and never having the sense to pick on people his own size. Just like his father. The pair of them drove me to my wits' end.'

Cato coughed nervously. 'Er, is that why you left them?'

Portia turned towards him with a cold expression. 'And who are you exactly, young man?'

'Quintus Licinius Cato, ma'am. I'm a friend of your son. I've served two years in the Second Legion with him.'

'A legionary?'

'No, I'm a centurion, like your son.'

'Macro a centurion? The good-for-nothing's a centurion?'

'And a good one, ma'am.'

She pointed an elegant finger at him. 'My name is Portia. I'd rather you didn't call me ma'am. I'm not your grandmother and I won't be treated like one, young man.'

'Fair enough.' Cato nodded. 'By the same token I'd prefer you to call me Cato, and not young man.'

She glared at him for a moment, before her stern features abruptly melted into an amused smile. 'Well said.'

Portia turned back to her son and ran her fingers through his hair, then paused. She leaned closer. 'What on earth . . .? Is that a scar? Why, it's enormous. It's a wonder the boy's still alive.'

'Yes it is,' Cato replied quietly. 'I was there when it happened. A celt nearly took off the top of his head. He was in the legion's infirmary for months. We shared the same room.'

'You've been in battle? You don't look old enough.'

'I've been in battle. And I've survived, largely thanks to Macro.'

Portia smiled. 'You're very fond of him.'

Cato thought about it for a moment. 'Yes. Yes, I am. He's the nearest thing I've had to family since my father died.'

Anobarbus coughed. 'Er . . .'

'What is it?' Portia resumed her brisk, businesslike mask. 'What do you want?'

'Latrine.'

'Down the corridor, last door on the left. Make sure you clean it after you. I know what you men are like.'

After the merchant had left them Cato wanted to pick up the conversation about Macro but the brief display of maternal feeling had dried up. Portia rose and picked up the bowl with its bloodstained water. She went over to a potted plant in the corner and threw the water on to its soil, and placed the empty vessel beside Macro's couch.

'Keep pressing that cloth to his wound. When he comes round, he'll probably want to throw up. Make sure he gets it in the bowl.'

'Where are you going?'

'To see if my intended has survived your friend's assault. Then I'm going to look over what he's left of my tavern. Is that all right with you?' Portia concluded tartly.

Cato nodded, and she disappeared in the direction of the atrium.

He glanced down and saw that the blood was flowing more slowly and pressed gently against the wound. Macro moaned and rolled on to his side.

'Ohhhh, shit . . . What the hell hit me? Feels like a bloody house collapsed on my head.'

'Shhh. Lie still.'

Macro's eyes flickered open and his forehead creased into a frown as he tried to identify his surroundings. 'Where am I?'

'Well, you may not like this, but it seems that you're at home.'

'What?' Macro turned round quickly. Too quickly. His eyes rolled up and with a convulsive heave he vomited, completely missing the bowl Cato had snatched up from the floor.

CHAPTER SIXTEEN

'I made a bit of an arse of myself, didn't I?' Macro groaned. He sat up on the bed and winced at the light coming in through the window of the officers' barracks. 'Cato! Push that shutter to. The light's killing me.'

Cato half closed the shutter and lowered the catch so that it would not swing open in the morning breeze coming off the sea. He returned to the side of Macro's bed and leaned over to inspect the cut on the back of his friend's head. The blood had congealed into an ugly black and purple gum.

'You'll need some kind of dressing on that.'

'Why? I'm not going round looking like some bloody Parthian.' Macro groped a hand over his head and cried out as his rough fingers pressed on the injury.

Cato clicked his tongue. 'That's why. Now leave it alone while I get a bandage.'

Cato left his friend in his room and stepped out into the corridor that ran down the middle of the officers' quarters. The hospital block was on the other side of the parade ground, a fair distance away. Then he remembered Minucius' medicine box and stopped outside the centurion's room, listening at the door. But there was no sound from inside and Cato guessed that he must still be at Portia's house.

Cato sighed. There was going to be bad blood between Minucius and Macro over this business. Just one more complication to add to all the other details and dangers facing them in coming months. Cautiously opening the door, Cato looked in, but there was no one inside, and he entered and scanned the room for sign of the medicine box. The room was neatly kept and he saw the box quickly enough, tucked under the end of the bed. Cato grasped the handle, braced himself, and pulled it out. It was much heavier than he had anticipated and he tightened his grip and gritted his teeth as the box scraped across the floorboards.

Cato bent over the box, unfastened the catch and raised the lid. He ignored the jars of ointments and salves at the top, and sorted through the bandages, selecting a long roll of linen. He closed the lid and shoved the box back under the bed and returned to Macro.

'Hold still; this might hurt.'

'What's new?'

Taking as much care as he could, Cato slowly began to wind the bandage around Macro's skull, and once he had made several passes over the wound and was satisfied that it would be well protected, he tied the bandage to one side of Macro's head and tucked the ends out of sight. 'There. Now don't fiddle with it.'

'Yes, Mum,' Macro mocked him, then immediately wished he hadn't as memories of the previous evening flooded back. He tried to put them to one side and glanced up at Cato. 'How did I get back here?'

'We carried you.'

'We?' Macro asked suspiciously.

'Portia lent me a couple of her slaves.'

'Oh no . . .' Macro groaned. 'Did anyone see us return?'

'A few people,' Cato replied quickly. 'Probably won't talk.'

'You think so?' Macro asked coldly. 'Where's that bastard Minucius?'

'I imagine he's still with your mother.'

Macro winced at the word and he slumped back down on to his bed. 'What a bloody mess . . .'

Cato nodded as he crossed to the window and gazed out through the half-open shutter. The officers' barracks looked across the navy harbour to the fortified mole and beyond that the sea, twinkling brilliantly in the late morning sunshine. The sky was clear of clouds and seagulls wheeled overhead, filling the air with their shrill cries. Preparations for the campaign against the pirates were already under way. Several of the triremes had been moored alongside the wharf, and sailors were busy erecting some kind of gangway to the foredeck of each vessel. Cato turned his back on the view and leaned against the wall.

'What are you going to do about it?'

'Besides throttling that randy old bastard and my bitch of a mother? I don't know. I'm not sure what to do right now. I'm too . . . confused.'

'You know, I'd have thought you'd be a little pleased to see her again after all these years.'

'What do you know about it?' Macro growled. 'You never knew your mother.'

'No,' Cato said quietly, and an awkward silence filled the air.

'I'm sorry,' Macro said at last. 'I didn't mean to say that.'

'Forget it.'

'It's just that she left me without saying a word. Last I saw of her was in the harbour at Ostia. I had gone to fish off the harbour entrance, and was watching a warship pass by, and there she was on the deck, cuddling up to some bloody marine. I called out, but I guess she didn't hear me, or maybe just ignored me. At first I thought it had to be someone else, but she wasn't there when I got home. Sometimes, when my parents had been fighting, she went to her sister's for a day or two. But she hadn't turned up there either, and after a few more days I told my dad what I'd seen. He went mad, and beat me up and then went and got drunk. He came back crying, and beat me up again. That's how it was for years, until I'd had enough and left home to join the Eagles . . . So I've never forgiven her.'

'I'm sorry.' Cato felt helpless. There were no adequate words of comfort he could offer his friend. At the same time he was aware that there was another side to the story, which Portia had hinted at last night. But now wasn't the time to mention that to Macro.

'Sorry?' Macro glanced up. 'What've you got to be sorry for, mate? It's not your fault. Nothing to do with you.'

'I know. But you're my friend. I don't like to see you like this.'

'Like this?' Macro was quiet for a moment, and then sat up. He rose to his feet. 'No point in brooding over it. I'm getting dressed. We've got that briefing with the prefect at noon.'

'You know, you might try talking to your mother about all this. Not right now, maybe . . .'

'Over my dead body, or preferably hers, and that old goat Minucius.'

Cato recognised his friend's mood well enough and knew that there was no point in discussing the issue further, for the present.

'Very well then, but promise me you'll keep well clear of Minucius.'

'Cato, I'm not a little boy, so don't bloody speak to me like I'm one. As long as we're in uniform I'll work alongside that bastard without a word. But when we're off duty, that's different. He'd better stay out of my way if he wants to live to see retirement.'

As the last note of the midday signal died away the officers of the Ravenna fleet assembled in the prefect's office. His clerks had pushed all the furniture aside and filled the space with benches from the officers' mess, arranging them to face the map on the far wall. All the centurions and optios from the marines were present, as well as the trierarchs of every vessel in the fleet. Cato, sitting next to Macro near the front of the audience, surreptitiously glanced round, looking for Minucius, but there was no sign of him. As soon as all the officers had entered the room and taken their seats, the air filled with an excited hubbub of conversation. Rumours had already flown round the base, fuelled by the activity down on the wharf, and every officer was keen to know what the prefect had planned.

Vitellius' chief clerk, Postumus, stepped smartly into the doorway and called out, 'Commanding officer present!'

The benches grated as the officers rose quickly and stood to attention. The prefect entered the office and strode down the gap left in the middle of the rows of benches and took up position to one side of the map. He glanced over his officers for a moment before he spoke.

'You may be seated, gentlemen.'

When everyone had settled down Vitellius stared at Macro. 'You look as if you have already seen some action, Centurion.'

A ripple of laughter went through the assembled officers. 'So what happened to you, Macro?'

'I, er, slipped and fell down some stairs, sir.'

'Really?' Vitellius' eyes glinted mischievously. 'Was that before or after your mother gave you a hiding?'

More laughter, louder this time, and the blood drained from Macro's face.

'Steady,' Cato whispered. 'Don't give him the satisfaction.'

The door to the office squeaked on its hinges as Minucius slipped through the gap, closed the door behind him and quickly sat down on the nearest bench. His face was black, purple and yellow with bruising and his nose was broken.

'Ah, the prospective stepfather, I presume. Now that the family's all here, let's get down to business.'

The laughter subsided and the officers looked intently towards the prefect. Vitellius clasped his hands behind his back and began.

'As you know, in recent months the coastlines of Apulia, Umbria, Liburnia and Illyricum have been ravaged by a new pirate threat. A few days ago they destroyed the colony at Lissus. This morning I have had news of the sacking of a second colony. This is a most disturbing development, gentlemen. It's bad enough that they have been preying on our trade routes without being punished, but wiping out our colonies demands action, and punishment of the utmost severity. Their leader, Telemachus, has recently communicated to us a demand for tribute to refrain from destroying any more colonies. My answer to him is unequivocal: Rome does not negotiate with pirates. My orders were to remove the pirate threat, and today we take the first steps towards achieving that end. I am leaving six biremes for the defence of Ravenna. The rest of the fleet and the marine reinforcements will be leaving the port in five days' time to sail across to the coast of Illyricum.'

Vitellius picked up a cane and pointed to the map. 'We will land near Birnisium, and establish a fortified camp.

From there we will search the coastline, mile by mile, until we locate the pirates' lair. We will take it, and destroy their ships and kill or capture their crews. Any prisoners will be sold into slavery. Except the leaders, who will be executed.'

Macro leaned slightly towards Cato. 'And no doubt our friend will soak up the popular acclaim.'

Fortunately Vitellius did not hear the remark as he turned from the map. 'Any questions?'

'Sir.' A hand went up towards the back of the room.

'Yes, Decimus?'

'Those alterations being made to those triremes on the wharf . . .?'

'Yes, what of them?'

'One of the men told me they were installing a crow.' Cato recalled the apparatus he had seen being fitted to the triremes earlier. The crow was the navy's term for the rotating boarding ramp used on some ships.

'That's right. We'll be engaging the pirates ship to ship. I've heard how manoeuvrable their vessels are. We need a method of fixing them so that our marines can decide the issue. So, I have decided to fit each of our ships with the device. I can't wait to see the pirates' faces when those boarding ramps drop down and pin them in place. It'll be just like sticking a pig.'

'But surely you won't be fitting them to the biremes as well, sir.'

'Like I said, every ship.'

The trierarchs exchanged concerned looks and there was some muttering. Vitellius rapped the bottom of his cane down on the mosaic floor to signal for silence.

'Is there a problem with my decision, Decimus?'

'Well, yes, sir.'

Vitellius bristled at the condescending tone. 'Please explain yourself.'

'With the load they're carrying, the biremes aren't really big enough for a crow, sir. Aside from the deck collar, there's the ramp itself, the sideguards and all spars and tackle needed to raise it and swing it out towards the enemy ships. It'll make the biremes top-heavy. If there's a storm, or even heavy seas, they'll be dangerously unstable.'

'I've thought of that,' Vitellius replied sharply. 'The ships will be taking on extra supplies and equipment. That ballast – as I believe you navy types call it – should counteract the weight of a crow.'

Decimus considered the idea for a moment and then shook his head.

'What is the problem?' Vitellius' irritation was apparent to all.

'Sir, the amount of ballast required would overload the vessels. They have a low enough freeboard as it is.'

'Freeboard?'

'The measurement from waterline to deck, sir.'

'Ah. I'm sure the, er, freeboard, will be adequate for our crossing. And once we have crossed the sea and unloaded our supplies and equipment, that need not concern you any more. As for being top-heavy, well, we can experiment with the required ballast when the time comes. Any other questions? . . . Good. Then, gentlemen, you may collect your orders from my chief clerk as you leave headquarters. You'll need to see to your men and make sure they're fully prepared and equipped for a lengthy campaign. We're in for a busy few days, and a hard fight. But, if these pirates have been half as successful as we're led to believe, there'll be plenty of booty for all. On that happy thought I bid you good day.'

The officers rose as Vitellius strode towards the door, and

only stood easy once he had left the room. As the centurions, optios and trierarchs shuffled towards the door, Cato was relieved to see Minucius push his way through the throng and leave the prefect's office as swiftly as possible. Macro stared after him, glowering with hatred.

Cato slapped him on the shoulder and gave Macro an exaggerated smile. 'You heard him. Booty for all. If it goes to plan, we'll be rolling in it. No more squalid digs in the arse-end of Rome for us.'

'If it goes to plan?' Macro shook his head sadly. 'When does it ever go to plan? And aren't you forgetting something?'

'The scrolls?'

Macro nodded. 'It's all down to the scrolls as far as we're concerned, lad. That's why we're here. Giving the pirates a good kicking and grabbing a share of their loot is just a side issue.'

'I know.' Cato dropped the light-hearted expression. 'Just trying to raise your spirits.'

'Well, thanks for the thought. Now we've got work to do. Let's go.'

CHAPTER SEVENTEEN

Over the following days the naval base was a chaos of activity. Most of the ships in the fleet had been laid up for winter, and some of the larger vessels had not left port for several years. These ships had to be beached and cleared of the foul-smelling weeds and barnacles that had fixed themselves to the hull below the waterline. A fresh coating of pitch was painted on to the scoured timbers and the acrid stench caught in the throats of men across the base. Standing rigging had to be checked and any worn or frayed ropes replaced. The heavy sails were carried over to the workshops and closely examined for any signs of weakness, before being patched up and returned to their ships.

Only when the vessels were deemed ready for action were the supplies loaded aboard: spare armour, stacks of javelin shafts and heavy chests filled with replacement iron tips, arrows, lead slingshot, boots, more boots and finally the provisions that were to feed the men for the voyage across the narrow stretch of sea, and sustain them for the first few days on the far shore.

While the ships were readied for action by their crews, the marines practised ship-to-ship fighting, and familiarised themselves with the tackle for operating a crow. A series of pulleys fixed to spars raised and lowered the ramp, and allowed the marines to rotate it towards an enemy vessel approaching on either side of the bows.

Cato and Macro were introduced to the rudiments of fighting at sea. To prevent further friction between Macro and Minucius, the older centurion was sent north to Hispontum to purchase spare cordage for the fleet, leaving Macro and Cato in the charge of another officer.

'As far as I can make out,' Macro said at the end of the first day's instruction, 'it's just like fighting on land, except that the navy ferries you to and from the fighting. Beats all that marching about we had to do in the legions.'

Cato shrugged. 'As long as I get ferried back from the fight I'll be a happy man.'

At the end of each day's training the marines returned to their barracks to clean and check their kit, record their wills, and those with families in the port were allowed to spend their nights in Ravenna.

In order to preserve the secrecy of their operations as far as possible, Vitellius had closed the port and no shipping was allowed in or out, not even fishing vessels. Every day the prefect had to deal with angry representatives of the town's council and merchant guilds. But Vitellius was unmovable and the town's worthies could only fume at the loss of trade and business, already reduced by the depredations of Telemachus and his pirate fleet.

On the fifth day the ships were fully provisioned and ready for sea. Loaded with extra stores and equipment, they floated low and sluggish in the calm waters of the navy harbour. Beyond the mole the sea was rough, and huge grey waves shattered on the breakwater in thunderous clouds of spray. A keen wind snatched the falling spray and swept it across the decks of the nearest vessels, drenching the men still on deck. The air was filled with the clatter of halyards rapping on the masts, and there was a low moaning undernote from the wind sweeping through the rigging. It had taken all the persuasive skills of the trierarchs to talk the prefect out of giving the order to set sail. Loaded down as they were, most of the ships would have foundered before they were even out of sight of land. At length Vitellius gave the order for the crews to be stood down and the marines tramped back to barracks. The less experienced men played dice or drank and swapped jokes and stories to try to take their minds off the delayed operation. The older marines took the chance to get some sleep, knowing well how miserable a rough sea-crossing could be.

All day the wind strengthened and the sea became more wild as dark clouds gathered on the horizon. The storm swept in towards the shore and battered Ravenna with a deafening shower of hailstones that rattled off the rooftiles and bounced off the paved streets before gathering in little drifts where the wind settled them. Even in the comparative shelter of the harbour the wind and waves engulfed the ships moored at the docks or laying at anchor. As darkness fell, anxious trierarchs set their crews to bailing the water that their vessels were shipping from sea and sky. Watches were set on the anchor cables to make sure that they weren't dragging, and the more nervous of the crews laid down spare anchors, and prayed that their gods would see them through this terrible night.

When, at last, the pale glimmer of dawn feebly struggled for purchase on the horizon, the fury of the storm finally began to abate. The sky remained overcast, clear of rain and hail. The wind died away to a hushed breeze while the waves subsided into an oily smooth swell. The officers of the naval base emerged from the shelter of their barracks to survey the damage. The shattered remains of loosened tiles lay scattered about the buildings but the worst of the damage, as ever, had been wreaked on the shipping. Inside the mole, the breakwater was strewn with the timbers of vessels washed ashore and wrecked on the rocks. Here and there lay the twisted shapes of men, like discarded toys. A handful of ships had foundered at their anchors and only the tops of their mast, with sails furled on the yards, were visible above the surface of the sea.

Glancing over the naval harbour Cato and Macro counted the vessels that had survived the night.

'What did we lose?' asked Cato.

'I make it two triremes and four of the biremes,' Macro said. 'Seems that those sailors were right about the boarding devices. Not that Vitellius will admit it. Maybe he'll listen next time.'

Cato turned to him with raised eyebrows.

'All right,' Macro conceded. 'Maybe he won't. This isn't the best start to this campaign of his. Think he'll go ahead with it?'

'He has to. He's on the same mission as us. Narcissus won't stand for any excuses.'

Sure enough, the moment the clouds began to disperse, the assembly signal rang out across the base. The marines tumbled out of their barracks and formed up in their ship's companies, ready for the order to board. Vitellius consulted with his senior sea-going officers, and the men of the ships that had been lost were distributed among the surviving craft. Then, when the final signal sounded out, the men tramped aboard the warships moored along the quay. Once each vessel had taken on its marines, it moved off and waited in the harbour as its space was taken by the next. Macro's ship, a bireme with the name *Trident* painted on its bow, tied up and lowered its gangway.

'I'll see you on the other side.' He held out his hand to Cato as if in final farewell, and Cato smiled.

'It's a narrow stretch of sea, Macro, not the River Styx.'

'Really?' Macro glanced out, beyond the harbour towards the horizon. 'I can't see the difference from where I'm standing.'

'Oh, come on. We'll be back on dry land by the end of tomorrow.'

'I thought you were the one who was afraid of water?'

Cato made himself smile. 'I am.'

'Me too . . .' Macro shook his hand. 'I swear, if we get through this alive, I'll never work with ships again.'

'Let's hope we have that choice.'

Macro nodded, and then turned briskly away and marched over to the *Trident* and stepped gingerly along the boarding plank behind the last of his men. As soon as his boots thudded down on the deck the plank was hauled aboard, the mooring cables slipped from the stout wooden posts on the quay, and the sailors strained at long shafts of wood to ease the ship out into open water. At the side of the ship Macro glanced back at Cato, waved once and then took up his position behind the captain on the raised aft deck.

Cato's bireme was one of the ships that had sunk, and his century was transferred on to the *Spartan*, a trireme. The unit that boarded ahead of him was commanded by Minucius. The veteran still bore the livid bruises from his encounter with Macro and was not pleased to see Cato.

'We're overloaded. Get your men forward. I'll keep mine aft. That should help the ship's trim.'

Cato stared at him a moment before passing the order on to his optio. Then, as the men shuffled forward of the mast and sat down beside their packs, he turned back to Minucius.

'A word, if I may?'

Minucius shrugged as Cato stepped closer to him so that they would not be overheard.

'I don't care about the issue between you and Macro. It's none of my business.'

'Just keep him away from me. Next time he won't be so lucky.'

'Lucky?' Cato smiled. 'You should consider yourself lucky still to be walking. Macro's not known for handling people with kid gloves.'

'So his mother says. Sounds like he's always been a right little thug.'

'Then I'd say he's found the right vocation. Wouldn't you? Take my word for it, he's good at what he does. So steer well clear of him. I'll do what I can to talk him round. We've got enough trouble on our hands with these pirates, without any family feuding.'

'We're not family,' Minucius replied through clenched teeth.

'As good as.' Cato winked. 'So I'll see what I can do.'

Minucius glared at him a moment, then his expression softened. 'Fair enough. For his mother's sake.'

'That's settled then. There's one other matter.'

'Oh?'

Cato stiffened his back so that he could look down at the marine officer. 'I'm a legionary centurion. I have seniority here.'

Minucius chuckled. 'Don't tell me you're pulling rank?'

Cato nodded.

'For fuck's sake, you're barely a man. I was in this job before you were even born.' Minucius' eyes glinted angrily. 'Who the hell do you think you're talking to?'

Cato's face was expressionless. 'You respect the rank, not the man, Minucius. And you will call me "sir" from now on. In front of the men.'

'Sir?' Minucius laughed. 'I'll do no such thing!'

'Then you leave me no choice. I'll have you charged with insubordination. Unless you'd prefer that to be mutiny?'

'You wouldn't dare . . .'

Cato drew a breath and called out over his shoulder. 'Optio Felix!'

Cato's subordinate hurriedly rose from the deck and marched towards the two centurions. A look of uncertainty flashed across Minucius' face and he poked a finger at Cato.

'All right. You win, sir.'

The optio stood to attention beside Cato, waiting for orders. Cato said nothing for a while, to make Minucius sweat it out. Then he turned to the optio.

'Tell the men not to move about. The centurion here tells me that we're overloaded. No sense in making the ship any more unstable than she already is. See to it.'

'Yes, sir.' Optio Felix saluted and made his way forward. Cato fixed his eyes on those of Minucius.

'I know you have far more experience than me. I'll look to you for any advice that I need. But while I'm on this ship, I'm the senior officer. Understand?'

'Yes . . . sir.'

'Good.'

'May I go now, sir?'

'Yes.'

Minucius saluted and turned away, marching stiffly towards some of his men who were leaning on the side rail. 'What's the matter? Never seen the bloody sea before? Get inboard, you dozy bastards!'

Cato watched him for a moment, awash with relief. He had been afraid that the veteran would see through him and call his bluff; dare him to exert his authority. In the end, despite his outrage, Minucius had known that Cato was right. Legionary rank took precedence over auxiliary rank and there was nothing Minucius could do about it. Now, thanks to Cato's assertion of his seniority, there would be a gulf between them. That suited Cato perfectly. He would sooner have the man's resentment focus on the difference in authority, rather than any simple personal animosity due to Cato's friendship with Macro. Of course, it was likely that Minucius would be hostile to him on both counts. Cato could live with that. Just as long as their relationship maintained a thoroughly professional edge. He nodded his satisfaction with the situation, turned and made his way forward to join his men.

The prefect was the last man to join the fleet, striding up the gilded ramp that led up to the wide deck of his flagship, the quinquireme *Horus*. Vitellius climbed the narrow gangway to the aft deck and acknowledged the salute of the trierarch of the flagship.

'Signal the fleet to leave the harbour.'

'Yes, sir.'

'They're to form up on the flagship as soon as we make open sea.'

'Yes, sir.'

'I'm going below. Make sure I'm not disturbed. Carry on.'

Without waiting for the man to reply Vitellius ducked through the low hatch into the cabin that ran the width of the quinquireme's stern. He ignored the boxes of scrolls awaiting his attention at the desk built round the sternpost, and flopped down on the narrow cot at the side of the cabin. Like most of his men he had not slept much the night before, but unlike them, he had the luxury of command and could permit himself this indulgence. Feet pattered across the deck as the crew of the flagship eased the vessel away from the quay, ran the oars out and began to get the quinquireme under way.

Sporting a long purple pennant that lifted lazily in the light airs, the flagship slowly made its way through the naval base, and out to sea through the gap in the overlapping moles that sheltered the harbour. As the great bronze ram cut into the gentle swell the men at the oars gritted their teeth and bent to the task, thrusting the large warship towards the ocean beyond. Behind the *Horus* the rest of the fleet put to sea under the gaze of the small garrison left behind, and a crowd of townspeople, who had gathered along the harbour front of Ravenna. Most of them were the families and sweethearts of the men in the fleet, and they waved their sad farewells as the warships pulled out to sea, took up position behind the tall stern of the flagship and headed slowly towards the distant horizon.

CHAPTER EIGHTEEN

For a few hours it seemed as if the storm was merely drawing its breath before sweeping back across the sea. There was an unnatural calmness to the gentle swell, and a stillness and tension in the air. The sky remained a gloomy grey and veiled the sun so that only a vague patch of lighter haze indicated that it was there at all. The sailors on Cato's ship had had enough experience of the sea in winter to know just how swiftly it could change and they watched the weather with considered apprehension. The marines caught their mood and so there was little of the usual conversation aboard the *Spartan* as she followed in the wake of the flagship, oars rising and cutting back into the sea in an endless rhythm.

Cato tried to ease his growing sense of dread by walking slowly around the deck, his hands clasped behind his back. He tried to divert his mind but each time he paced by the mast and headed aft, the presence of Minucius loomed at the periphery of his vision, and in the end Cato gave up and joined the trierarch on the aft deck.

'How long do you think the crossing will take?'

Titus Albinus pursed his lips for a moment before replying, 'That depends, sir. With no wind, we have to rely on the oars. We can keep the men shift on shift for a while yet. If we can keep this pace up then we should make the coast of Illyricum by late afternoon tomorrow. Assuming that the weather doesn't break.'

As he glanced round at the other warships, a sudden thought struck Cato. 'What happens when it gets dark? Isn't there a risk of the ships colliding or getting lost?'

Albinus smiled and nodded towards the stern of the trireme. 'Soon as it's dusk, each ship hoists a lantern. It'll keep us in formation until dawn. At least, that's the theory.'

'Theory?' Cato turned towards him sharply. 'What do you mean? This can't be the first time you've sailed at night?'

'Of course not, sir.' Albinus sounded aggrieved. 'It's part of the basic drill. It's just that most ships tend to hug the shore as much as possible and find a safe anchorage at the end of each day. I've had the *Spartan* out overnight, but never as part of a fleet.'

'Never?' Cato was incredulous.

'Never.' Albinus smiled. 'Should be an interesting experience.'

Cato looked at the trierarch as if he were quite mad. As the day wore on a light northerly breeze stirred the surface of the sea and the flagship signalled the rest of the warships to ship oars and make sail. The soft rush and hiss of the sea passing alongside seemed hushed and soothing after the monotonous creak and splash of the oars, and Cato stood to one side as Albinus ordered his crew to trim the sail to his satisfaction. Then he glanced at the flagship, a few hundred feet ahead.

'First mate!'

'Sir?'

'Make sure you maintain our station.'

The *Spartan*, being a lighter vessel, was inclined to sail faster than the lumbering quinquireme and the mate had to frequently order the men at the sheets to spill the wind from the rectangular sail to prevent the ship closing on the *Horus* and the other ships ahead.

As dusk gathered around the fleet, and sky and sea merged into one gloomy mass, one of the crewmen brought a lantern up from below deck, a heavy bronze affair with a glass pane. The oil lamp inside had already been lit and the dull flame reflected brightly off the highly polished tin mirror at the back of the lantern. An iron hook protruded from the sternpost and the crewman offered the lamp up and slipped the handle over the hook. The lantern swayed gently with the easy motion of the vessel, and as Cato watched, more lights winked into being in the ships ahead of the *Spartan*. It reminded him of the torchlight processions held by the followers of Mithras he had seen occasionally in the camp of the Second Legion.

'Deck there! Sail sighted!'

Cato looked up at the masthead where a figure sat astride the yard with one arm anchored on the mast. The other arm was pointing out to the side of the fleet. At once all eyes on the deck followed the direction indicated and Cato squinted into the shadows, and saw nothing.

'What d'you see?' Albinus called to the lookout.

'A lateen sail, sir. Just been raised. No more than two miles off.'

'Two miles . . .' Albinus started in alarm. 'Can you make it out?'

The last of the light was failing fast and there was a pause before the lookout called down his reply. 'She's hauled her wind and gone about. Must have seen us, sir . . . I can't see her any more.'

'Shit,' Albinus muttered.

'Do you think that was a pirate vessel?' Cato asked.

'Most likely, sir. If she saw us, the chances are she would

have seen some of the other warships and realised it's the fleet. If that was a merchant ship then there's no reason to turn and run. I'd lay good money on her being a pirate.'

Cato glanced in the direction the lookout had pointed. 'I don't suppose they fancied their chances against a force our size.'

Albinus laughed. 'Not even your cockiest pirate would be foolish enough to do that.'

Cato blushed, angry with himself for sounding like such a raw recruit. He looked round and saw Minucius shaking his head. The veteran had obviously overheard the remark and lowered his opinion of Cato even further.

'Don't worry, Centurion,' Albinus continued. 'You're safe for the moment. As long as the enemy doesn't know we've got a landsman like Vitellius running the show.'

Cato knew well enough that the lack of faith in inexperienced officers extended to him as much as the prefect, and he tightened his lips to prevent any bad-tempered response.

'What will he do then?'

'He'll report back to Telemachus. By the time that bastard gets the message we'll be ashore and getting ready to hunt him down.'

'What if that ship was looking for us?'

'No.' Albinus shook his head. 'Had to be a chance encounter. They don't know we're coming.'

'What if they did know?' Cato's mind raced ahead as he thought through the implications. 'What if he's put to sea to intercept us?'

'Now you're just jumping at shadows, sir,' Albinus said with a trace of irritation. 'I'm telling you, they don't know. How can they, with all the security the prefect slapped on this operation? Even if they did know, you've seen our ships. You've even seen some of his, come to that. You know he can't take us on.' Albinus glanced round to make sure that none of his men could hear his next words. 'Now do keep a lid on that kind of scaremongering, sir. Doesn't do my lads any good to see officers losing their heads at the first sight of a strange sail. Won't do your men much good either.'

'All right.' Cato nodded. 'It won't happen again.'

'That would be for the best, sir. Now, if you don't mind, it's going to be a long night. I need to look after my ship.'

'Yes. Yes, of course.'

Albinus saluted and turned away, padding barefoot along the deck towards the bows. Cato watched him disappear into the dark mass of figures crowded in front of the mast, and then clenched his hand into a fist and smacked it against his thigh. This was not the first time he had been made to feel like an ignorant dilettante. Yet, no matter how often he determined not to let his lack of experience and expertise show, he always seemed to get caught out, and be left feeling deficient. A deficiency that he felt compelled to wipe out, whatever the cost.

The night passed slowly. For Cato the experience was completely unnerving. All around, the noises of the sea sounded alarmingly close, as if it would rise up and engulf the ship at any moment. Cato was tormented by nightmarish images of himself struggling to stay afloat, alone and forsaken in the heaving immensity of the dark ocean, until at last his strength gave out and he slipped beneath the surface into a suffocating inky black oblivion.

There was no possibility of sleep while his mind was consumed by such fears and he looked on the still forms of the marines in his century in frank admiration and envy. For a while he paced round the deck, gazing at the winking stern lights of the surrounding fleet. Occasionally voices carried across the surface of the water, sounding flat and indistinct and at times inhuman so that he stared hard into the darkness and wondered if the myths of sea monsters might not have some kernel of truth in them after all.

'Quiet night, sir.'

Cato started and turned to see a dark figure a short distance along the ship's side. He recognised the voice readily enough and nodded a greeting.

'Yes, Optio. Quiet enough, I suppose.'

He sensed the amusement in Optio Felix, even before the other man continued, 'You'll get used to it, sir. Give yourself a few months and the sea will seem like a second home.'

'I sincerely doubt it,' Cato replied before he could stop himself. He had known his optio for a matter of days and should not take him into any kind of confidence, let alone any admission of fear or weakness. He cleared his throat and eased himself up from his elbows so that his back was straight and his hands gripped the wooden rail tightly. He spoke in a nonchalant tone. 'It's an interesting enough experience, but I imagine it becomes boring soon enough.'

'Boring?' The optio was surprised. 'There's nothing boring about the sea. She's a strange creature, sir. Never quite still. And she's as fickle as a drunken bitch. Just when you think you know her, and begin to take her for granted, she'll hit you with the full force of her fury . . . She's not boring, sir. She's terrifying, and you'd do well to respect her.'

Cato stared at the shrouded features of his optio, and silently cursed the man for adding to the sum of his fears.

'That's, er, an interesting perspective, Felix. I'll bear it in mind. Thank you.'

'Best get some sleep, sir. You never know what the morning will bring.'

'Sleep. Yes, in a moment. You too, Optio.'

Felix saluted and retreated towards the dense mass of dark shapes sprawled across the deck of the *Spartan*. Cato watched him go, and then turned back to gaze out into the night, more unnerved than ever.

At length the strain on Cato's senses became too much and he found a vacant stretch of deck close to the bows. Leaning his back against the base of the canted foremast, he closed his eyes and feigned sleep. If his men could sleep under such conditions then he must be seen to as well. Little by little, the gentle heave and fall of the deck, the creaking of the rigging and the soft churn and hiss of the sea alongside lulled him into slumber.

'Sir!' A hand shook his shoulder. 'Sir! Wake up!'

Cato blinked his eyes open and found himself staring along an unfamiliar plane of wood. For a moment he was confused, then memory flooded back and he raised himself up, wincing at the numbness of the arm he had been resting his head on. He twisted and looked up at Felix.

'What is it?'

'Lookout reports sails to the north of us, sir.'

Cato thrust himself up from the deck and rose stiffly to his feet. Most of his men were already on their feet and silently staring out to sea. Cato pushed past them and made his way up on to the aft deck where Albinus acknowledged him briefly. Cato nodded back.

'My optio says you've sighted something.'

'Several sails. More appearing all the time. Over there.' He raised an arm towards the horizon. 'From the coast of Illyricum.'

'Pirates?'

'Almost certainly. There's no other fleets operating in

these waters.' He turned away from Cato and bellowed up to the masthead, 'How many can you see now?'

After a short pause the lookout called back, 'Fifteen. Still hull down, but some of them look big, sir. Biremes or better.'

Cato coughed. 'Seems they knew we were coming. As I feared.'

'They must have known all along.' Albinus frowned, and added, grudgingly, 'Seems you were right, sir.'

'Thank you.'

Albinus suddenly craned his neck forwards. 'Look there!'

Cato stared towards the horizon, and as the *Spartan* lifted on a swell, he glimpsed several tiny dark shapes on the very rim of the ocean.

'How long before they can reach us?'

Albinus pursed his lips. 'Three, maybe four hours. But it won't come to that. The prefect will have to turn south until we make the coast.'

'Why retreat? Surely we can take them on?'

'Not loaded down like this, and not while they have the advantage of the wind at their backs. Once we've landed the supplies and equipment we can turn on them quickly enough. Then you'll see the buggers turn about and run for it,' Albinus smiled.

'Captain!' the mate called out. 'Flagship's signalling!'

Albinus faced forward and squinted at the *Horus*. A long red pennant was rising up the mast, and the breeze lifted it up and out in a flickering ripple. Albinus shook his head slowly.

'What's the matter?' Cato asked. 'What does that mean?'

'It means that the prefect is a bloody fool,' Albinus replied softly.

'What?'

Albinus waved a hand towards the red pennant. 'That's the signal for the fleet to attack.'

'Attack? I thought you said we couldn't.'

'No . . .'

Cato was confused. 'So what's he doing? There must be some mistake.'

But even as he spoke the crew of the *Horus* let fly the sheets of their mainsail. The tiny figures of sailors spread out along the yardarm quickly furled the sail, and a moment later the sides of the flagship bristled with oars.

As Captain Albinus bellowed out a series of orders to his own crew, Cato could only watch in horror as the sternpost of the flagship turned away from him. Slowly the *Horus* gathered speed as the oars churned up the grey surface of the sea, and the quinquireme surged forward, directly towards the pirate fleet.

CHAPTER NINETEEN

'Beat to stations!' Albinus roared across the deck. 'Sail in! Oars out!'

This was the moment for which sailors and marines had trained over many years, and, at the sound of the ship's drum, the men on the deck burst into activity. Sailors swarmed up the rigging, and spread out along the yard to take in the sail. Cato ran forward to join his century, the heavy thud of his boots accompanied by the clattering and scraping of oars being run out below the main deck. All around him marines scrambled into their armour, then snatched up sword and dagger belts and strapped them on, before reaching for their helmets and shields. When he reached his kit Cato found Felix already there, holding out his chain-mail corselet.

Cato nodded his thanks. 'Soon as the men are kitted up, get the javelins issued. And bring some more cases up from stores.'

'Yes, sir.'

As Cato fumbled with the leather ties of his helmet he glanced back towards the aft deck. Albinus was leaning on the rail, staring over the side towards the *Horus*. As the *Spartan*'s sail was furled the trireme began to slow down. Then, from below deck, the sharp rap of the pausarius' hammer began to sound the pace for the men at the oars.

The blades dropped down into the sea with a rolling chorus of splashes, then with an audible collective grunt of effort, the *Spartan* lurched forward. It took a moment for the crew to find their rhythm, and then the deck steadied as the warship ploughed forward. The moment they were immediately behind the flagship, Albinus shouted an order to the steersman, who threw his weight against the shaft of the huge oars hanging over the stern of the *Spartan*. As the broad blades of the steering oars bit into the sea, Cato felt the deck shift beneath his boots and instinctively grabbed at the side rail. Beside him Felix saw the gesture and smiled.

'Better get used to the feeling, sir. There'll be plenty of turning when we close with them pirates.'

'Let's hope they decide not to make a stand.'

Felix looked at his centurion guardedly. 'Why's that, sir?'

'We're overloaded. They'll have the advantage in speed, if not strength. I just hope they count the numbers and beat a retreat.'

Optio Felix glanced forward over the bows at the cluster of distant sails on the horizon. As the trireme rose on a swell the dark hulls of the pirate ships were clearly visible against the gleaming blue of the sea.

'Doesn't look like they're going to run for it.'

'No.' Cato pressed his lips together. The enemy fleet was steadily closing on them, with no sign of changing course. 'Tell Minucius to get the crow ready.'

Felix saluted and turned forward. A moment later Minucius was bellowing orders at his men to drop their shields and javelins, and follow him back to where the boarding device was lashed to the deck in front of the mast. As they set to work, Cato glanced back down the length of the ship, and noted the time it took for the *Spartan* to make the quarter-turn into the wake of the flagship. To his mind the trireme was an unwieldy vessel, a perception confirmed by the far quicker turns of the biremes as they fanned out on either side of the *Horus* and took up position on the flanks. It was just like on land, Cato reflected. The heavy bulk of the quinquireme and the triremes in the centre, like the legions, and the lighter vessels on the flanks, like cavalry, waiting to exploit their speed over the open space before them. Slowly, as the two fleets crawled across the sea towards each other, the Roman vessels took station on the flagship and the formation flattened from a chevron into a broad line, with a small reserve of two triremes and four biremes held back to plug any gaps that opened in the Roman fleet.

Cato raised a hand to shade his eyes as he gazed round, looking for Macro's ship. Then he saw the small three-pronged design on the bows of a bireme, out on the left flank. Cato squinted and just made out a red crest on one of the helmets packed in at the bow. He smiled, wondering what Macro was making of his new cavalry role. No doubt his friend was itching to get stuck into the pirates and would order his trierarch to ram the first available enemy. As Cato watched, the distant outline of a crow rose above Macro and his men and hung at an angle, ready to plunge down and impale an enemy vessel.

On board the *Spartan*, Minucius and his men heaved the boarding device forward towards the bows. As the warship rose and fell on the swell they struggled to line up the thick wooden pivot with the iron socket that had been fixed on to the foredeck. At length, and after much cursing, the crow was lowered into position and ropes fed through the tackles that would raise and swing the boarding ramp. When the men were ready, the ramp was lifted far enough for the iron spike to be attached underneath the front and the ropes were fastened tightly to the cleats to hold the device still, until it was needed. Cato noticed that the weight of the crow and the marines had canted the bows down, and the trireme seemed markedly more sluggish as the oars drove it through the swell.

The Roman fleet was heading directly into the wind, and the bows thudded into the oncoming waves, sending up clouds of spray that fell back into the faces of the men on the foredeck. Cato blinked away each salty deluge as he stared intently at the approaching enemy. The pirates, still under sail, closed swiftly with the Roman ships, and within the hour were in clear view, barely a mile off. Most of the pirate ships were in the same class as the biremes, and at the centre of their line was the trireme Cato had seen several days earlier, its dark pennant flickering in the stiff breeze like a serpent's tongue. Despite what Albinus had told him about the dangers of fighting with overloaded ships, Cato still felt that the coming fight looked one-sided.

'Hello . . .' Optio Felix muttered. 'What's that big bastard up to?'

Cato glanced back towards the trireme. The main sail was flapping wildly, then a moment later tiny figures on the yardarm hurriedly gathered in the sail as oars were thrust out from the sides of the ship. On either side the biremes and lighter liburnians continued forward, into the teeth of the Roman fleet. But as the trireme's oars splashed down into the sea there was something odd about their motion and Cato frowned for a moment, before the truth dawned on him.

'She's rowing backwards.'

Felix stared hard for an instant, then nodded his head. 'So she is! What's he playing at? Think the bastard's running for it, sir?'

'I don't know.' Cato felt a sudden icy pang of anxiety

deep in his guts. Something was wrong, he was sure of it. Even though he knew little of naval tactics – only what he had been hurriedly taught since his arrival at Ravenna – he was sure that this was some kind of ruse. But all around him his men, and the sailors, were cheering in triumph at the sight of the retreating pirate ship, as if the battle was already won.

'Quiet!' Cato bellowed. 'Silence there! Next man to open his bloody mouth is on a charge!'

The cries died away and Cato turned his attention back to the enemy fleet, now close enough for him to make out the details of the men scurrying across the decks of the closest vessels. Telemachus' trireme was steadily withdrawing ahead of the *Horus* and the excited cries of the men aboard the Roman flagship carried clearly across the waves to the ships following behind. Some of the men close to Cato glanced at him resentfully, but were wise enough to keep their mouths firmly shut. High up, at the stern of the quinquireme, a red-cloaked figure brandished a sword that flickered like a sliver of fire in the morning sunlight as Vitellius urged his men on. Beyond the *Horus* a flash of colour drew Cato's eye and he saw a bright yellow pennant flutter up the mast of the pirate vessel. At once the other ships in the enemy fleet began to turn to either side, sails shifting round as they filled with the wind blowing over the aft quarter. They had divided in two and now each half of the pirate fleet was sailing directly at the lighter craft on the wings of the Roman fleet.

As if oblivious to the danger to his biremes, Vitellius ploughed on through the waves, in pursuit of the pirate leader. From the foredeck of the *Spartan* Cato could only watch in growing desperation as the enemy fleet swept across the bows of the largest Roman warships. He could understand the prefect's thinking well enough. If they could only capture, or kill, Telemachus, then the pirate fleet might be broken in this first battle. Sure enough the *Horus* was slowly closing on the enemy commander's ship. Too slowly. And all the time she was drawing them away from action that would be fought on the flanks of the Roman fleet. It was cleverly worked, Cato realised with despair. Telemachus would hold himself out as bait, knowing that the Roman prefect would be hellbent on winning himself a triumphant victory to further his career. The trick was to make it look as if the Romans stood a good enough chance of catching up with his ship, yet still have sufficient time to turn and make an escape.

'There they go,' Felix muttered, and Cato turned to look towards Macro's ship. Half a mile away across the rolling sea the sails of the pirate ships were mixing in with the bare masts of the biremes. Even as Cato watched, one of the enemy vessels raced down the side of a Roman ship and sheered off its oars in an explosion of splinters and wooden shafts. The pirate ship was moving so swiftly that the marines had no chance to deploy their crow, and had only begun to swing it round as the pirate ship snapped off the last of the oars and passed beyond reach. The oars on the far side were still being worked and the bireme started to spin round, heeling the ship over in the direction of the boarding ramp. As the marines on the *Spartan* watched in horror, the bireme turned on to its side, the sea closing over the rail as men and equipment spilled into the churning water. A moment later there was a dull crack as the mast broke and the ship capsized completely, leaving a glistening hump above the surface, surrounded by men frantically splashing as they tried to find some debris to keep them afloat.

'Oh, shit.' A marine close by Cato shook his head. 'Did you see that? Poor bastards . . .'

Cato was already casting his gaze over the other ships, searching out Macro's. The *Trident* had passed through the pirate fleet unscathed and was already struggling to turn round and seek out an enemy to close with. Elsewhere, another bireme had been rammed, the shock of the impact breaking the yardarm of its attacker. But the pirates had their oars out in an instant and as they furiously backed away from their victim the sea rushed into the shattered hull and a moment later the overloaded vessel also capsized. Cato turned back to the *Horus*, still plodding towards the retreating trireme of Telemachus.

'What the hell is wrong with the prefect?' Felix slammed his fist down on the side rail. 'Can't he bloody well see what's happening?'

'He knows all right,' Cato replied quietly. 'He just thinks it's a justifiable sacrifice.'

'Sacrifice? It's going to be a fucking slaughter. Look! There goes another one.'

Cato stared in silence as the pirate ships continued to cut through the ships on each Roman flank. Only a handful of the biremes had managed to strike back. One had pinned a pirate vessel with its crow and the marines were already pouring across the ramp and dropping on to the pirates, striking them down with desperate savagery. A short distance away another bireme had managed to ram an unwary pirate ship and the latter's decks were already awash as it settled into the sea. Every other Roman ship was either engaged or struggling to close with the pirates.

Optio Felix was right, Cato decided. It was going to be a slaughter, unless someone acted. He took one last look at the flagship, still pursuing Telemachus, then turned and pushed his way through his men, and ran aft towards Albinus. Minucius glanced at him as Cato passed, and there was what looked like contempt in the older man's eyes.

'Turn us round!' Cato called out.

The trierarch stared at him blankly, as if he had not heard the order. Cato clambered up the steps to the aft deck and thrust his arm out towards the flank where Macro and the others were battling for their lives. 'I said, turn us round.'

'No.' Albinus nodded forward. 'There's been no signal from the flagship.'

'Forget the flagship. Look over there. Our comrades need us. Right now.'

'We haven't had orders.'

'Fuck the orders! Our ships are being cut to pieces. If we don't act now – right now – we'll lose them all.'

'But—'

'Turn the ship around. That's an order!'

For a moment the two officers stared at each other, and more and more of the marines and sailors turned to watch them, as they became aware of the crisis. At length, Albinus nodded his head.

'All right, Centurion. But I'll want it in writing that you gave the order.'

Cato sneered at the man. 'You can have it in writing, if we survive. Now, do it.'

Albinus turned to the steersman. 'Turn to port, hard over!'

'Aye, sir!' The steersman hauled on the oar shaft, straining every sinew of his brawny arms, and the water churned under the stern of the trireme. Cato found it hard to restrain his impatience as the bows slowly swung away from the *Horus* and eventually lined up with the sea battle over a mile away. Glancing round at the other triremes, he saw faces turned towards them, and could even read the surprise in those on the nearest ship. Cato drew his sword and thrust it forwards, pointing out over the bows of the *Spartan*. He cupped his spare hand to his mouth and bellowed across the water.

'Follow us! For pity's sake, follow us!'

At first there was no response, then the trierarch called out orders to his men and Cato's heart lifted as he saw the bows of the trireme start to turn after the *Spartan*. Two more of the large warships altered course, steering towards the other flank, but the remainder held their course in the wake of the flagship.

'Better than nothing,' Cato muttered wryly. Then he turned to Albinus. 'Steer right at the middle of that lot. Pick out any target that looks promising.'

'Where are you going?'

'We have to lighten the ship.'

Albinus nodded. 'All right. But do it quickly!'

Cato ran back down the deck and sought out Centurion Minucius. 'Get your men down into the hold. I want anything that's portable brought up on deck and dumped over the side.'

'Dump it?' Minucius raised his eyebrows. 'But we'll need that later.'

'There's not going to be any later if we don't dump it.'

Minucius shook his head. 'You don't have the authority.'

Cato stared at him, eyes wide and glaring. 'Yes I do. Now carry out your orders or I'll have you taken below and hand your command over to your optio. I mean it.'

Minucius saluted and immediately started to give the necessary orders as Cato headed towards his men, seeking out Felix.

'Optio!'

'Yes, sir!'

'Take a section. Go below and bring up the slingshot stores.'

'Yes, sir. How much do you want?'

'All of it. Get moving.'

The optio had served long enough to know not to question orders, however unexpected they might be. He turned to the nearest men. 'Drop your shields and javelins and follow me.'

Felix drew back the cover of the forehatch and dropped down below the deck, quickly followed by the others. A short time later they were handing up small sacks filled with lead shot to the men on the deck. Felix's head popped up through the hatch. 'Slings as well, sir?'

'What? . . . Yes, why not? Might as well put them to some use while we lighten the load.'

As the marines began to stack the sacks in the centre of the deck Cato looked aft and saw that Minucius and his men were already heaving sacks of grain and spare sheets of plate armour over the side. A quick glance at the trireme following a short distance behind revealed that they too had realised the need to lighten their ship. Cato nodded his satisfaction and then pushed his way to the thick timber post at the *Spartan*'s bow. Below him, the bronze mass of the trireme's ram lifted and plunged into the sea, aiming at the heart of the sea battle being fought out barely a third of a mile ahead.

Cato scanned the vessels still fighting it out amidst the flotsam, wreckage and bodies littering the surface of the sea. The *Trident*, which had passed through the enemy, had turned about and charged back into the fight, ramming into the stern of a pirate ship that had already wedged its ram into the side of a bireme. The crews of all three vessels were locked in combat on the deck of the pirate ship and, as far as Cato could make out, the Romans had the upper hand.

The sound of forlorn cries reached his ears and Cato noticed that there were men in the water directly ahead of the *Spartan*, Romans as well as pirates. He was on the verge of crying out a warning to Albinus, before he realised that there was nothing that could be done for these men. The trireme was too unwieldy to set a course to avoid the men in the water. As the warship surged into the fringe of the battle, Cato glimpsed the desperate expressions of the men in their path, and saw them frantically swim out of the trireme's path. Those who were too badly injured to swim fast enough, or who simply clung to debris, could only watch in despair as the bronze ram bore down on them. A handful of men grasping a shattered length of mast were swept from sight as the bow crashed into them with a dull thud, then there were screams as the survivors of the impact swept along the sides of the warship and were crushed by the blades of the oars churning through the sea.

Cato tried to ignore their cries and glanced round. He looked back at the *Trident* and froze. A short distance beyond Macro's ship Cato saw the front of a pirate ship powering forward under its oars. As the crew of the Roman vessel became aware of the danger their shouts of alarm carried clearly across the water. The marines were still fighting aboard the enemy they had managed to pin with their crow. But now they hesitated and looked back over the deck of their own ship. With a triumphant roar, the pirates they were fighting surged back at them.

'Over there!' Cato shouted over his shoulder as he pointed towards Macro's ship and thrust out his arm. 'Steer over there!'

Albinus relayed the order to the steersman and the *Spartan*, a little more nimble now that she had shed some weight, slewed round towards the three ships still locked together, and the fourth rushing in to finish off the *Trident* and her crew.

'Ready your slings!' Cato shouted to his men and pointed out the target. 'Aim for that bastard on the far side! You men, give the slingers some space!'

Only two hundred paces separated the *Spartan* from the ships locked together when the pirate vessel slammed into the side of Macro's ship. The grinding, splintering crash filled the air as the *Trident* recoiled under the impact, the shock tearing the rigging apart. The mast splintered and crashed down on to the deck moments later. The collision knocked every man off his feet in the three ships that had been locked together, and there was an instant of silence before they recovered, scrambled back to their feet and continued fighting. The pirates aboard the ship that had rammed the *Trident* launched their grappling hooks over on to the Roman deck and began to haul the vessels closer together as a boarding party crowded the foredeck, brandishing their weapons as they waited impatiently for the moment to spring on board the bireme and wipe out her crew and marines.

Cato turned away and filled his lungs. He stared down through the grating on the trireme's deck to the dim faces of the oarsmen below. 'Come on! Faster, you worthless bastards! Faster!'

The pausarius increased the rhythm and with the oarsmen straining every sinew of their muscles the *Spartan* leaped forward, closing down on the tangle of ships ahead. Suddenly Cato was aware that the bows were swinging away from the ships and he felt a surge of cold fury as he turned towards Albinus and began to raise his fist. Then he realised the trierarch's intention was to pass round the stern of the *Trident* and take the pirate ship in the side.

They were well within slingshot range now and Cato bellowed an order to his men. 'Slingers! Loose! Let 'em have it, lads!'

The air was filled with a whirring of slings and then lead shot zipped out across the sea in a low arc, before striking down into the pirates massing on their foredeck. The chorus of sharp cracks and thuds, and cries of pain were clearly audible to the men on the *Spartan*, and they responded with a ragged cheer of cruel satisfaction before more shot flew across and struck down yet more men, some falling helplessly into the narrowing gap between the hulls of the two warships where they were crushed moments later. But Cato had no time to observe any more. The trireme was already slewing round the stern of the *Trident* and there ahead of them lay the defenceless beam of the pirate ship. Some of her crew gazed helplessly at the large warship speeding towards them. Others, with more presence of mind, ran from the side and sought cover as more slingshot rattled across her deck. As the gap between the two ships rapidly closed, Cato found that he could now look down on the enemy and he gritted his teeth as he waited for the collision.

At the last moment, Optio Felix turned and saw his centurion leaning across the bows of the trireme. He leaped forward, grabbed Cato by the arm and hauled him back as hard as he could. As both men tumbled back on to the foredeck the worn planking leaped up with a great grinding crash and sent men tumbling all across the deck. The impact hurled Cato forward and he cracked his helmet on the bow strake. He gasped at the searing pain, before he looked round at his men. Most were picking themselves up, snatching up their weapons and moving towards the boarding ramp. But there were several casualties: men hurled forward and knocked senseless, others with broken limbs, and a steady chorus of groans and cries of pain from below deck where the oarsmen had been thrown from their benches.

Felix was already on his feet and he shoved a shield towards Cato. 'Here, sir. On your feet now.'

While Cato shook his head to try to clear it of the blurring pain the optio was thrusting men towards the crow. The trireme had struck the pirate ship at an angle, and aft of the mast Minucius already had his men hurling grappling hooks across the gap to try to draw the ships closer together. Cato stood erect and, raising his shield, he approached the prow cautiously and looked down. The ram had crushed the enemy's timber hull and penetrated six or seven feet inside. Water gurgled and bubbled as it poured in through the breach. He sensed a blur from his left and ducked down just as a light javelin glanced off the angle of his shield with a sharp crack. The men on the foredeck of the pirate ship had also recovered from the impact and now a handful turned to face their attacker as the rest hurried aboard the *Trident.* The pirates' trierarch must be fairly cool-headed, Cato realised. He saw that the first fight had to be won before he could afford to take on the crew of the trireme. As Cato glanced at the men dropping down on to the deck of the *Trident* he saw Macro and a score of his men fighting for their lives in a tight circle about the mast.

'Get that boarding ramp moving!' Cato shouted over his shoulder.

As Minucius' men hauled on the grappling lines the trireme gradually swung in towards the pirate ship. The marines on the crow's tackle heaved and the pivot groaned and squeaked as the ramp swung out over the side of the *Spartan*, across the surface of the water and then its shadow fell across the deck of the pirate ship.

'Let go!' Felix yelled.

As soon as the men released their grip on the tackle the heavy iron spike under the ramp swung down and pierced the planking with a splintering crash. Cheering, the marines swarmed on to the ramp and ran across to meet the enemy. A few javelins and arrows flitted towards them, but hammered into the protective wooden hoardings on either side and injured no one. Felix was standing by the near end of the ramp, thrusting men along it.

'Go! Go! You lazy bastards! Or there'll be none left for you! Go!'

Cato drew his sword and pressed himself in amongst the stream of men crossing to the enemy ship. At the far end of the ramp there was a short jump down on to the deck, then he raised his shield and held his sword ready as he looked around. Several of his men had rushed towards the bows, hacking and thrusting at any pirate that stood in their way. Cato turned towards the stern. A small party of men stood there, heavily built and well armed.

'You there!' Cato called out to the marines who had been immediately behind him on the boarding ramp. 'Follow me!'

They trotted steadily towards the stern, slowing to pick their way over the tangle of fallen rigging. The gratings had been thrown open and as Cato glanced down he could see that the oars had been abandoned as the crew had armed and thrown themselves at the Romans aboard the *Trident*. Now there was the glint and glimmer of water sloshing through the bilges as the sea poured through the breached hull. Ahead of them the group of men closed ranks and hefted their round shields towards the Romans. There was no time for formations and tactics, and Cato filled his lungs and roared, 'Get them!' before lowering his head, leaning into his shield and throwing himself at the pirates.

On either side his men charged home and the air was filled with grunts and shouting and the scrape and clatter of sword blades. Cato's shield slammed back towards him as one of the pirates charged with a savage cry of rage. Light glittered off the side of a blade rising above Cato and he saw the man draw back a heavy falcata to slash it down and through Cato's helmet. He threw his sword up and parried the blow with a jarring clang and, before the man could recover, Cato slammed the pommel of his sword into the snarling features of the pirate's face. The man's head jerked back with a grunt and flecks of blood flickered into the air from a deep gash across his forehead. At once Cato snatched back his arm and slashed his sword into his enemy's face, the edge cutting through the bridge of the nose and into his eyes. With a scream the pirate stumbled back against the side rail. Raising his shield, Cato shoved him over the side and turned on the next pirate.

A short, stocky man with blond hair spiking out under a leather skullcap stood in a crouch, weighing the Roman centurion up with narrowed eyes. Then he raised the point of his sword and crept a step closer. Cato tensed up, ready for the man to explode into an attack. Instead, the pirate suddenly stopped, frowned and glanced down at his chest where the bloodied point of a sword tip had pierced his leather jerkin. His legs folded under him and he pitched forward. Behind him stood a marine, grinning with satisfaction as he yanked his blade out of the pirate's back. Cato opened his mouth to thank the man, but a glittering whirl scythed through the air, and right through the marine's neck, sending the head flying several feet to where it thudded on to the deck. Still swinging the sword in a wide arc the pirate jumped in front of Cato with a triumphant snarl.

Cato threw up the edge of his shield and the blade slammed into the metal trim, sending sparks flying, and throwing Cato back against the sternpost. As the man recovered his sword and stepped back a pace, Cato's eyes swept round and to his horror he discovered that he was the last Roman standing at this end of the pirate ship. All the men who had followed him were sprawled in bloody heaps on the deck, amongst the bodies of their enemies. The two pirates had the centurion to themselves.

The man with the long sword whirling overhead was dark-skinned and fat. A few feet from him stood another pirate; thin and swarthy. He wore scale armour and carried a buckler and light, curved blade that dripped blood on to the sun-bleached planks of the deck. Cato's eyes flickered from man to man as he crouched low to receive the first attack. The thin man shouted an order, and the long sword sliced through the air towards Cato's head. Dropping his knees, he hunched down and the edge of the sword cut deeply into the sternpost. So deeply that it was wedged in place and the pirate grunted savagely as he tried to wrench his weapon free. Before Cato could take advantage of the situation the younger pirate sprang forward, his light blade whirling in a flurry of attacking strokes that Cato parried desperately. When his fat comrade was clear of the Roman and had snatched up another sword, the young pirate stepped back, breathing hard.

Cato knew he was in a desperate situation, and the thought that his only line of escape lay in jumping over the side flashed through his mind. But armoured as he was, he realised he would sink straight to the bottom of the sea. So, he clenched his sword tightly, eased his shield forward and waited for the next attack.

'Sir!' Felix's voice carried across the background din of fighting from the other ships. 'Sir, get down!'

Cato and the two men facing him heard the whirring sound at the same instant, but only the Roman realised the danger in time to act, and threw himself down on the deck and covered his body with his shield. Slingshot whipped overhead, cracked into timber and several thudded into the bodies of the two pirates. Both men crumpled to the deck and lay groaning.

'Hold fast!' Felix shouted to his men.

Cato waited a moment to make sure that no more shots were coming his way, then he rose up. He glanced at the last two pirates. The big man was already dead, his skull crushed by a direct hit. His young companion had been struck in the back, smashing his shoulder blade and some ribs, and as he gasped for breath, blood trickled from the corner of his mouth. He glared up at Cato, as his hands groped across the deck towards the handle of a sword. Cato kicked the weapon away and leaned over him.

'Are you their leader?' he said in Greek.

The injured man said nothing, but continued glaring with hate-filled eyes, and then spat a globule of bloody saliva at Cato's face. The centurion wiped it away.

'Have it your own way.'

Cato raised his sword to strike and the pirate commander clenched his eyes shut and flinched. Cato smiled, and walked away, back towards the boarding ramp, where the last of Minucius' marines were crossing over. With nearly two centuries of marines crowded on to the deck there was little room, and Cato had to squeeze through to find Minucius and Optio Felix.

'We have to move fast. This ship's sinking, and I doubt the others will stay afloat for much longer. Come on!'

Cato pushed forward to the bows where a handful of the marines were skirmishing with the pirates on the deck of the *Trident*, neither side willing to be the first to leap across the narrow gap between them.

'Give the front rank space!' Cato shouted, thrusting men aside. 'Get back there!'

As soon as there was enough room for the men at the side rail to swing their arms effectively Cato grabbed a javelin from one of the men and thrust it towards the pirates. 'Use javelins! Clear that deck!'

The marines who still had javelins took aim and hurled their weapons at point-blank range, skewering those pirates who did not have the sense to fall back. As soon as the deck was free of the enemy, Cato clambered up on to the side rail, checked his balance and leaped across the gap, landing clumsily on the *Trident*'s deck. He straightened up, raising his shield and sword as he called back to the others, 'Come on!'

He didn't wait for them, but charged towards the men fighting about the mast. Some of the pirates were aware of the new danger and had already turned to face the fresh wave of Roman marines. Beyond them, Macro's voice rose above the din as he shouted encouragement to his men and foul abuse at the enemy. Cato smiled. Then he clenched his teeth as his shield slammed into that of the nearest pirate, the impact jarring his arm right up to the shoulder. Cato swung the weight of the shield back as his sword arm thrust forward, knocking aside a desperate parry and sinking the point deep into the man's stomach. Wrenching the blade free, he swung the shield forward, knocking the pirate down to one side, and made for the next enemy, an axe-wielding giant who screamed a high-pitched war cry as he staggered towards the centurion. The axe thudded into the shield, unbalancing Cato long enough for the giant to recover, swing the shaft round again, this time aiming low at Cato's legs. Cato was forced to leap back against his own men, and with a cry of glee the huge man raised the axe up for an overhead blow. There was nowhere for Cato to retreat. Instinctively, he crouched low, tipped his head down and charged forwards, under the blow, and the iron cross-piece of his helmet smashed into the pirate's face, knocking him senseless.

The marines swept forwards, hacking and thrusting at the enemy, and the ferocity of their assault instantly broke the pirates' will. They retreated, then turned and ran, foolishly hoping to find a safe haven from the marines. Only a few small knots of the enemy fought on, back to back, or forced up against the side rail. And there they died, cut down without mercy. A few dropped their weapons and pleaded for mercy, but the marines were in no mood to take prisoners and they fell across the bodies of their comrades who had gone down fighting.

Cato drew back from the mêlée to draw breath and take stock. There was only a handful of the enemy fighting about the mast, trapped between Cato's men and the survivors of Macro's century. When the last man had been killed, Cato pushed through his marines, anxious to seek out Macro and make sure that his friend was still alive.

The scene around the mast appalled his eyes. Twisted bodies, Roman and pirate, were heaped on the deck, which was drenched in gore that ran in livid red streaks towards the scuppers. No more than a dozen wounded and breathless marines still stood in a tight circle around the base of the mast. Macro stood amongst them, spattered with blood as he looked around wildly. Then his eyes fell on Cato and he slowly smiled.

'What the bloody hell kept you?'

The nervous relief was infectious and Cato laughed. 'Well, if this is all the thanks we get, next time I won't bother.'

'You bloody better.'

Cato wiped his blade on the cloak of one of the fallen pirates and sheathed his sword, then reached out a hand and grasped his friend by the arm. 'Well met, in any case. Now we have to go.'

Macro frowned. 'Go?'

'Get off this ship.'

'But we've just won the bugger back.'

'She's sinking. All three of them are. Let's go.' Without waiting for Macro to reply, Cato turned to the rest of the marines and filled his lungs. 'Back to the *Spartan*, lads! Quick as you can!'

A few feet away Cato saw one of the men rifling the body of a richly dressed pirate and he angrily strode over and kicked the man away. 'No time for that. Optios! Get your men moving!'

The marines withdrew towards where the ram of the pirate ship was buried in the side of the *Trident*. They scrambled back across the gap, helping injured comrades as best they could, but only a few men could cross at once and Cato stared about him in frustration, slapping his fist against his thigh. Macro shook his head, and looked at his friend with a wry smile. 'Now what are you fretting at?'

A deep groan filled the air and Cato felt the deck shudder beneath his boots, causing him to stumble. He recovered, and nodded towards the ship that the *Trident* had succeeded in ramming. 'There! That's what I was afraid of.'

The decks of the ship were already awash and a moment later the sea closed over the side rails as she began to sink, dragging the prow of the *Trident* down with her. The timbers of the Roman bireme protested at the huge strain placed on the fabric of the vessel, and the marines, sensing the end was near, scrambled for the deck of the other pirate vessel. But even as they swarmed over the narrow gap, there was a loud crash from forward, and just behind the *Trident*'s bow strake the deck shattered as if a giant fist had smashed up from beneath the surface of the sea. At once water surged over the ruined bows, the deck lurched down at a sharp angle, and the marines still aboard scrambled for a handhold. Cato dropped his shield and threw himself towards the side rail, grabbing on to it with all his strength. There were still wounded men on the deck and now their groans of agony became cries of terror at the dreadful fate swirling up the slanted deck towards them.

For a moment Cato was gripped by the same icy horror. Then he saw Macro, holding on to the rail a few feet away. His friend winked. 'Time we disembarked, I think.'

Only a handful of marines were left alongside the two centurions and they leaped across the gap towards the outstretched arms of their comrades and were hauled to safety. As Cato and Macro waited for the last of their men to quit the *Trident* there was a sudden cry of alarm from the deck of the pirate ship. Cato looked round and saw that she was sinking quickly, dragged down by the combined weight of the first two ships. The foredeck lurched down, almost level with the surface of the sea. Cato felt water closing around his thighs as a wave swept across the deck of the bireme.

'Oh, shit,' Cato muttered. 'We're not going to make it.'

CHAPTER TWENTY

'Don't just bloody stand there!' Macro yelled. 'Jump!'

Cato stared as his friend clambered up on to the side rail, braced himself, as he rose up on his feet, tottering unsteadily. Then Macro launched himself across the gap and thudded against the bow of the pirate ship. His hands grasped the rail and immediately a couple of marines grabbed his arms and hauled him on to the foredeck. The sea had reached Cato's waist and he knew the *Trident* was moments away from sinking.

'Sir!' a voice called out behind him.

Cato glanced over his shoulder and saw a young marine clutching the rail further down the deck with one hand. His other shoulder had been shattered by a deep wound and the arm hung uselessly by a few raw tendons. He stared at Cato, and there was no mistaking the plea in his expression. But it was already too late to do anything. As Cato watched, the sea swept over the *Trident* and the young marine disappeared in a crimson swirl. Cato was seized by a will to live. He scrambled up on to the ship's rail and leaped across to the pirate vessel, only a few feet above the surface of the sea. The impact drove the breath from his body. His fingers scrambled for purchase on the ship's side before a hand clamped on to his wrist and a powerful arm hoisted him up the side, over the rail and dumped him on the deck.

Macro's chest was heaving as he looked down at Cato. 'No pissing about next time. When I say jump, you jump.'

'I thought I was supposed to ask, how high?'

Macro stared at him. 'There's a time and a place for smart remarks, lad. This ain't it. Come on.' He grabbed Cato by the arm and hauled him to his feet.

Over the side Cato could see the distorted outline of the *Trident* disappearing beneath the sea's surface. For a moment there was a deep groaning and grinding as the *Trident* hung on to the ram of the pirate vessel, and the deck shuddered under Cato's feet. Then, with a jarring crash, the side of the bireme gave way. The deck thrust up beneath the Romans, sending several sprawling, and the *Trident* fell away into the dark depths of the ocean. A handful of men floundered amid the flotsam, screaming for help. Macro pulled his friend away and the two centurions followed the marines over to the end of the boarding ramp where the men were anxiously pushing forward to reach the safety of the *Spartan*'s deck. Even released from the burden of the *Trident*, the pirate vessel was rapidly succumbing to the water rushing in through the hole driven into her side and her motion on the sea felt leaden. Water gleamed only a short distance beneath the gratings on the maindeck.

The ship suddenly lurched as the sea surged over the stern. With a gurgling hiss water poured across the left beam, slanting the deck over even further. Macro grabbed for the base of the foremast with his spare hand.

'She'll capsize,' Cato realised. 'Quick! Over the side.'

Macro stared at him. 'Over the—'

'It's our only chance.' Cato braced one foot against the base of the mast and hurriedly unstrapped the belt around his waist. Then, grunting with the effort, he wrenched his scale armour over his head and threw it on to the deck, where it slid down the slope and splashed into the water. 'You too!'

As Macro ditched his weapons and armour, Cato clung on to the foremast. The other marines had all returned to the deck of the *Spartan* and were hauling the tackle to raise the crow from the pirate ship's deck and swing it back aboard the trireme.

'There!' Macro threw down his chain-mail vest. 'I'll go first. Then you follow and we go straight over the side before this thing rolls over on us.'

The timbers of the vessel began to creak and groan alarmingly as the angle of the deck increased. Macro slid down into the water along the side rail. He landed with a splash and immediately turned and looked back at Cato, arms raised to cushion his friend's landing. Cato nodded, swallowed nervously, and let go. He shot down the sloping deck and crashed into Macro. Then both of them waded on to the side rail, took a breath and leaped into the ocean swell. The sea closed over Cato's head and at once his ears were filled with the dull roaring of his grunts as he struggled to make for the surface. He was aware of a dim shape close by, and a hand gripped his arm and pulled him up, towards the shimmering light.

Macro and Cato broke the surface of the sea and gasped for air. A short distance ahead of them was the weathered side of the *Spartan*, seeming to be as tall as a building from water level. The sound of rushing water from behind them was deafening and, sensing a shadow fall upon him, Cato glanced round and looked up at the glistening dark hull of the pirate vessel as it began to roll over.

'Swim!' he spluttered. 'Swim for it!'

The two centurions struck out towards the trireme, kicking clumsy strokes with their booted feet. The roar of cascading water pounded in their ears and for a moment Cato felt a current drawing him back, before he kicked free of it, struggling to keep up with Macro. Then, with a crash of spray, the pirate vessel capsized just behind them, sending out a wave that picked them up and carried them several feet towards the trireme before it subsided. Cato glanced back and saw the glistening hull rising above the sea, dark and barnacle-encrusted like a rock. Macro spat out a mouthful of salt water and shook the drenched locks of hair away from his forehead.

'Shit! That was close.'

'Too close,' Cato muttered, still kicking his feet to keep his head as far above the surface as possible and spitting out a mouthful of seawater. 'Ergh! This stuff's strictly for the fish.'

He raised an arm and waved it towards the faces lining the side rail of the trireme. 'A rope! Get a rope down here, now!'

With legs and arms working furiously against the burden of their heavy wool tunics, Macro and Cato just managed to stay afloat. Then a rope snaked over the side of the trireme and splashed into the sea a short distance away. Macro stretched an arm towards it, his fingers brushed against the coarse hemp, and closed tightly round the rope.

'Pull gently!' he shouted up to the trireme and the rope steadily tightened and then began to draw them in. Already a boarding net had been lowered over the side and two sailors had scrambled down and held out an arm each towards the two officers thrashing through the swell.

'What are you bloody waiting for?' Macro shouted. 'Get in here and give us a hand!'

The sailors hesitated a moment then let go of the net and

plunged towards Macro and Cato as they struggled towards the boarding net.

Moments later the two centurions were slumped down on the deck, gasping for breath as water pooled around them. Albinus was standing to one side, shaking his head in mock disapproval.

Cato swept the straggling hair from his brow and looked about at the ships scattered all around the *Spartan*, some still locked in battle. Just over half the biremes were still afloat, or seemed to remain in Roman hands. One of the pirate ships, struck by incendiaries, was ablaze from end to end, and black smoke billowed over her side in a dense swirling cloud. Another pirate ship was settling in the waves, about to sink. All the other enemy vessels were hurriedly disengaging and weaving a course between the battered wrecks and the survivors of the Roman fleet as they made for open sea. The reason for their flight was clear enough: the prefect, with the rest of the heavy warships, was bearing down on the heart of the battle. A safe distance behind and off to one side followed the trireme of Telemachus, skirting round the main strength of the Roman fleet as he made for the small force of pirate ships that had wrought havoc amongst the overloaded Roman biremes.

Cato rubbed his brow. 'Thank the gods, it's over.'

'It's not over,' Albinus replied quietly. 'Not by a long way. They're just regrouping. Then they'll be hanging around the fleet, waiting for the chance for a quick strike, like mountain wolves around sheep. If we don't make land before dusk then they'll come in under cover of dark and pick off the weaker ships right under our noses.'

The lookout called down, 'Signal from the flagship, sir!'

Albinus tipped his head up to face the man, squinting into the bright sky. 'Well?'

'All ships to form up on the *Horus*.'

With the large warships wallowing over the swell, the smaller ships rowed in towards the protection of the quinquireme. The trierarch of the *Horus* stood on the foredeck, raised a speaking trumpet to his lips and began bellowing a string of orders. These were relayed from ship to ship and when every vessel had raised a pennant to acknowledge the orders the *Horus* gave the execution signal. With the flagship in the lead, the other triremes formed a thinly stretched diamond shape across the sea. Packed into the middle of the diamond were the smaller vessels, most showing signs of the battle they had just survived: damaged rigging, torn sails and some with livid streaks of red trailing down from their scuppers.

Once the fleet had formed up it began to crawl across the sea, making for the coast of Illyricum, still out of sight over the horizon. The men at the oars had been exhausted by the battle manoeuvres and the ships raised their sails, while their trierarchs prayed that the northerly breeze would hold.

The pirates wasted no time in pursuing their humbled foe, and their dark triangular sails hovered on the flanks of the Roman fleet, waiting for their chance to strike, just as Albinus had foreseen. Every so often, one of the pirate ships would suddenly alter course and steer for an opening between the triremes, trying to penetrate the defensive screen. This time the advantage lay with the Romans, whose vigilance paid off as the triremes moved to close down any gap the pirates had hoped to exploit.

As the day wore on the sky cleared to a serene and unblemished blue, and the breeze slowly moderated as the two fleets crept across the sea. The pirates managed to break through twice. The first time two of their nimble ships succeeded in swooping round the heavy triremes and attacking either side of a heavily damaged bireme straggling a quarter of a mile behind the others. The ship was boarded, its crew put to the sword, a quick search made for any portable loot, and then it was fired. The pirate vessels darted away, steering clear of the trireme that had turned to try to save its stricken comrade. Worse still, in going to the aid of the straggler, the trireme left a gap for a handful of other pirate ships to slip in and ram another Roman ship before they too were forced to retreat. But the damage had been done and the Romans could do nothing more than take on the crews and as much of the supplies as it was safe to load, and leave the rest to go down with the ship.

From the deck of the *Spartan*, Cato and Macro watched with the rest of the crew as the long drama was played out over the gentle swell. Despite the dreadful losses they had suffered at the hands of the pirates, Cato found himself admiring the way Telemachus had executed his trap. His intelligence had been perfect, allowing the pirates to catch Vitellius and his fleet at their most vulnerable, and Cato was almost certain that treachery had been involved. What else could explain such confident handling of their ships when the pirates would normally have been thoroughly outclassed as well as outnumbered by the imperial navy? They knew they had the upper hand in manoeuvrability long before they had closed with the Roman fleet. And even now, they were looking for every chance to press home their attack, not content to wait until night when the triremes would be blind to the dark shapes sweeping through the Roman ships.

His admiration for Telemachus quickly wore off as Cato pondered on the consequences of this disastrous encounter. Hundreds of men must have been lost, along with much of the supplies and equipment that Prefect Vitellius needed to launch his campaign once they landed on the coast of Illyricum. It was possible that the losses were already so serious that the operation might have to be called off.

As soon as the thought entered his head, Cato dismissed it. He knew Vitellius well enough to realise that the prefect could not countenance such a setback to his reputation. Senior officers had been exiled, or even executed, for lesser failures. There was no choice for Vitellius. He had to go on with his campaign, even if the odds were now stacked firmly against him. The prefect would lead his men to victory, or to defeat and death. Those were the only possible fates open to all of them now, and as Cato silently watched the fire consuming the distant bireme he was filled with a heavy and deadening sense of foreboding.

His dark mood deepened as the afternoon dragged on, and when the lookout finally gave the cry that land had been sighted, Cato knew that a safe landfall would merely mark the beginning of a yet more dangerous phase of Vitellius' campaign.

CHAPTER TWENTY-ONE

Vitellius thrust his finger out. 'What was the meaning of that little stunt you pulled, Centurion Cato?'

'Sir?' Cato stood in front of the prefect's desk in the headquarters tent. Around him the other senior officers sat on stools and watched the confrontation warily.

'Don't play dumb with me, boy. Back there in the battle, when you took half my triremes out of the line.'

'Sir, we had to move to save our lighter ships. The enemy was cutting them to pieces.'

'Maybe, but you cost us the chance of trapping Telemachus and ending this operation at a stroke.'

'We can't be sure he was ever aboard that trireme, sir. After all, he was just using it as bait to lure our best ships away from the rest of the fleet.'

'That's just speculation, Centurion. Has it crossed your mind that the attack on the biremes might have been a ruse to lure ships away from protecting my flagship? You could have been risking my life.'

Cato shrugged. 'Warfare is risky for us all, sir. In any case, the *Horus* and the ships that remained with you would have been able to handle any attack. In my judgement the greatest threat was to our biremes.'

Vitellius glared at him. 'In your judgement? This isn't a debating society, Centurion Cato. It's the imperial navy. You obey orders from superior officers – you don't create your own orders.'

'Begging your pardon, sir, I was using my initiative. And you did not issue any countermanding order. If those triremes hadn't gone to the aid of the other ships it's certain that our losses would have been far higher,' Cato paused to add heavy emphasis to his last words, 'than they already are.'

Vitellius clamped his lips together in a thin line, and as he glanced round the tent he noticed Macro and most of the other officers nodding in agreement with Cato.

The confrontation was interrupted by a challenge from a guard posted outside the tent. Then the flaps rustled as a clerk ducked inside, clutching a bundle of slates under his arm. He straightened his back, marched up to the prefect and saluted.

'The butcher's bill, sir.' The clerk handed a slate to Vitellius as the prefect waved Cato away. While Vitellius scanned the notes on the slate, Cato and the other officers sat in silence. They were exhausted. Even after the surviving ships had reached the bay late in the afternoon there had been no time for rest. The shore curved round for a mile or so in either direction before the beach gave way to a tumble of rocks that rose into headlands. Beyond the beach the land was covered with scrub and stunted trees for half a mile before it rose steeply into a range of forested hills that stretched up and down the coast as far as the eye could see. Not far off lay a long-abandoned settlement, little more than piles of stones now.

While the triremes anchored a short distance from the shore the smaller ships had beached and immediately began unloading their supplies and equipment. The bulk of the marines, under Centurion Macro, had been assigned the back-breaking task of constructing a fortified camp around the beachhead. Unlike the men who served in the legions, the marines had had limited training in preparing fortifications and Macro drove them on with increasing exasperation and bad temper. They laboured well beyond sunset and finally completed a makeshift defensive ditch and rampart by the flickering blaze of torchlight. Beyond the sweating marines a thin screen of pickets stood in the darkness, anxiously staring into the shadows for any sign that the pirates might renew their onslaught by land.

As soon as the triremes had been anchored fore and aft in a line parallel to the shore, Vitellius had given the order for additional artillery to be mounted on the decks and trained out to sea. Any pirate ship that attempted to attack the Roman fleet now would have to brave the fire of scores of catapults. Heavy losses would be inflicted long before the pirates could close with the triremes. So Telemachus held his ships back and kept watch on the Roman fleet until nightfall. Then, as the last rays of the setting sun glimmered on the horizon, the pirate fleet turned away from the shore and steered slowly up the coast, leaving their battered foe to count the cost of the day's action.

Prefect Vitellius lowered the slate and stared at his desk. The numbed expression on the aristocrat's heavy features revealed his despair. Cato almost felt pity for the man, before he recalled that the disastrous naval encounter was entirely of the prefect's own making. The lighter ships of the fleet should never have been so encumbered with men and equipment, much of which now lay at the bottom of the sea. If they had only used a convoy of transports to carry the supplies and equipment needed to launch the campaign against the pirates then the enemy would have been beaten off easily. It would have taken longer to make the crossing with transports, but that would have been a tiny price to pay as things had turned out.

As he pondered uselessly on what might have been, Cato realised that Vitellius was not wholly at fault. The perfect timing of the pirates' attack was more than a coincidence. Even if the fleet had been spotted by a pirate ship as it left Ravenna there would not have been enough time for word to have got back to Telemachus so that he could assemble a fleet and intercept the Romans at their most vulnerable. Telemachus must have been forewarned.

Vitellius sighed, and stood up. 'It's not good news, as I'm sure you're already aware. We lost eight of the biremes, two more are badly damaged, as is one of the triremes. She was holed and will need to be repaired at a dockyard. We also lost most of our artillery and siege tools. Much of the food was stored aboard the triremes, so we won't starve to death.' He smiled weakly, but none of his officers responded, and the smile died as the prefect continued, leaving the most painful news to last.

'Nearly eight hundred men were lost with their ships, another sixty killed aboard those vessels that survived, and a further eighty-three wounded . . .'

Cato looked round at the other officers and noted their mostly hostile expressions. The human cost had been terrible indeed, and many of these men had lost comrades they had known for years. But the cost to Vitellius was even higher, Cato reminded himself. This was a bitter defeat and there was no disguising it in the report he must send back to Rome. But the time it would take for the report to be sent, read through, a response considered and a messenger sent back to the prefect, would give him as much as a month to retrieve the situation.

'It's a bloody disaster,' a voice muttered.

'Who said that?'

No one moved. No one replied. For a moment all was still, until Minucius stood up.

'It was me, sir. Just saying what all the lads here are thinking. The pirates have given us a good kicking, and the word's out that we were betrayed.'

'Betrayed?' Vitellius raised an eyebrow. If the men were looking for a traitor he might turn this to his advantage.

'Someone sold us out, sir. Told 'em where to find us.'

There was a low chorus of angry grumbling and Minucius was emboldened as he continued, 'We should find the bastard. Make him pay for it, nice and slow, like.'

The officers nodded and a few offered chilling suggestions for the fate of the traitor once he was discovered. Vitellius moved closer to the fire so that all could clearly see him by its glow. He raised his hands to quieten them down.

'All right! You have my word. When we find the man, he's yours to deal with as you wish, on one condition.'

Most of the officers looked at him suspiciously; then Minucius cleared his throat. 'What's that then, sir?'

'You give me your word that his death will be as painful as possible.'

The officers laughed with relief, and Minucius nodded solemnly as the noise died away. Then there was an awkward silence as they waited for Vitellius to continue addressing them.

Macro coughed. 'So what happens now, sir?'

'We carry on with the plan,' Vitellius replied firmly. 'We still have enough ships to take on the pirates.'

'No, sir.' Heads turned towards a trierarch at the rear of the tent. Albinus stood up so that he could be clearly seen and heard. 'We need more ships. More biremes.'

'And why's that?' Vitellius replied coolly. 'From what I saw today those ships are worse than useless.'

Albinus shook his head. 'That's not fair, sir. The men on those ships fought the best battle they could today. It's not their fault their ships were no match for the pirates. If we hadn't changed course and gone to help them, I doubt whether any of the biremes would have survived.'

Cato took a sharp intake of breath and looked round at the other officers. Albinus' criticism of his commander could scarcely have been more open, and the centurions and trierarchs looked to Vitellius to see how he would respond.

For a moment he just glared at Albinus, then finally he nodded slowly and replied, 'Your point is well made, but quite academic, as things stand, Albinus. I still wish to know why we need more biremes. Our main force, the triremes, are more or less intact. Once we throw them in against the pirates it'll all be over quickly enough.'

'Yes, sir. Provided the pirates are prepared to sit there and wait for the triremes to come for them . . .'

'So?' The impatience in the prefect's voice was apparent to all. 'What are you saying?'

'You've served in the legions, sir.'

'What of it?'

'Then you know the tactics well enough. The lighter forces are there to find and pin the enemy down so the main strength can close in and destroy them. At least that's how it works at sea. I assume you do the same thing in the army.'

'Of course we bloody do!' Macro snapped. 'We're not bloody fools, you know. At least the lads in the legion can build a proper fucking camp!' Macro waved an arm towards the dark outline of the rampart stretching round them. 'Not this bloody shambles—'

'Thank you, Centurion,' Vitellius cut in. 'That's enough.'

Macro's mouth was still open, ready to deliver the rest of his diatribe, but he clamped it shut and nodded.

'Very well, then,' Vitellius continued. 'So we need biremes.'

'No, sir. We need *more* biremes. We need to match their numbers, at least. I counted a dozen of the bastards, and all of them were well-handled. They've got good crews, and good trierarchs to command them. Frankly, they're better than us, sir. That's why we need more ships. We need some kind of advantage if we're going to stand a chance against them the next time it comes to a fight,' Albinus concluded firmly.

'Well, there aren't any more biremes,' Vitellius snapped. 'I can't just magic them out of thin air, can I?'

'There's the six you left at Ravenna,' Albinus said flatly.

Cato stood up, cleared his throat and added, 'There's another thousand marines we could use as well, sir.'

'No!' Vitellius slapped his hand against his thigh. 'I will not leave Ravenna defenceless. Rome would have my head if anything happened.'

'Rome may well do that already, sir,' Cato spoke quietly, 'once they get word of what happened today. If we're to continue operations against the pirates, we'll need every ship, every man we can draw on.'

Vitellius stepped towards him. 'And if they do attack Ravenna?'

'We have our orders, sir.' Cato laid heavy stress on the first word. 'The operation must take priority.'

'And Ravenna?' The prefect responded quietly.

'Ravenna will have to take its chances, sir.'

'I see. Is that your advice? Willing to put that down in writing?'

Cato clenched his teeth to prevent himself letting slip any acid words of contempt for his superior. Then he swallowed and replied, 'That's my advice, sir. Given our orders. But the decision is yours. Goes with the rank.'

'I see.' Vitellius dropped his gaze and stood silently in thought. The other officers were also silent, as they waited for his decision.

The prefect knew he was in a wretched position. He had lost a quarter of his force, as well as a good quantity of his equipment. What had begun as an overwhelming demonstration of force directed at crushing the growing pirate threat, had turned into a near disaster that threatened to destabilise the entire region. If he called off the operation then it would be seen as an unambiguous defeat, and the Emperor was not renowned for his toleration of defeated commanders. Vitellius feared that his career, maybe even his life, was in danger. He frowned. His career was all that gave meaning to his life. Without the promise of power and wealth he might as well be dead. So there was no possibility of calling off the operation. That much was certain. The campaign must continue.

The question was, did he have enough men and material to ensure success? He had been defeated, but if the pirates were found and destroyed, and the scrolls recovered, then the initial setback could be quietly glossed over. Indeed, if Vitellius could pin the blame for the defeat on some traitor then he might escape censure for the defeat altogether. As long as he was ultimately victorious. But did he have the forces to do it? He was not sure. Certainly Albinus did not think so, and the expressions on the faces of the other trierarchs as they had listened to their comrade indicated that they too felt that more biremes were required. They must know their business, Vitellius reflected. With the remainder of the fleet and the marines he had left in Ravenna he would just about replace the men and ships lost earlier that day. But that would leave the port and the naval base virtually defenceless. He would have to ensure that the pirates were put under enough pressure that they would not be able to mount a raid on Ravenna. If the unthinkable happened and they did slip through and sack the port, then Emperor Claudius would show him no mercy.

Then he recalled what Cato had said, the firm reminder that maybe there were even greater issues at stake: the scrolls that Narcissus had ordered them to retrieve, at any cost.

At any cost . . .

Damn the man for not putting those orders in writing. Then at least Vitellius could have claimed that the terrible risks he ran in deploying all his men and ships against the pirates were risks demanded by the terms of his orders. But Narcissus had been too clever for that, as usual. There would be no evidence to lay against him should Vitellius try to bring such a charge. Just as there would be no acceptable excuse for failing to recover the scrolls.

As he thought through his options one clear course of action emerged as the most effective strategy for the prefect to pursue, and he fixed on it with a growing sense of despair, reluctant to make the final commitment by giving the necessary orders. He looked up at his officers and his heart sank as he saw them watching him, waiting for him to speak, to set out his plan of action. Once he began there must be no turning back. He cleared his throat, and the officers stared at him intently.

'We must carry on with the operation. If we fail to take the fight to the pirates now, then who knows how powerful they may become. They could strangle our trade, if they wished. We cannot afford to let that happen, gentlemen. I accept Trierarch Albinus' argument that we need to have sufficient force to face the enemy on acceptable terms. To this end I will send an officer back to Ravenna to bring up our reserve forces and equipment . . .'

He glanced round, and his eyes fell on Cato, warming his thin frame close by the fire. It might be wise to keep that one as distanced from the real project of this operation as possible, the prefect considered. Vitellius needed to claim all the credit available for retrieving the scrolls. Besides, there might be other opportunities to exploit in this situation, and he didn't want another agent of Narcissus looking over his shoulder. There was Centurion Macro as well, of course, but Vitellius did not consider the older officer as much of a threat. Macro was too guileless for his own good. It might be as well to keep the two separated. Cato would be the one to return to Ravenna, then.

'Centurion Cato!'

Cato stiffened his back. 'Yes, sir.'

'At first light, you and Albinus will take the *Spartan* back to Ravenna. Her complement of marines will remain here to give you more space on board for the return trip. You'll bring back the rest of the fleet, with the marines and replacement supplies. I'll have my clerk draft your authority to act in my name.'

'Yes, sir.'

'Gentlemen! That is all. Centurion Macro is taking the first watch. The rest of you can turn in until your watch is called. Dismissed!'

As the officers rose stiffly around the fire and trudged off towards the campfires of their units, Cato remained behind. He nodded towards Macro and the latter reluctantly joined his friend as they approached the prefect.

'What do you want?' Vitellius snapped. 'Make it quick. I'm tired.'

Macro nodded. 'I expect every man in the fleet is tired, sir.'

Vitellius ignored him, focusing on Cato alone. 'What do you want?'

'Why are you sending me back for reinforcements? Surely I'd be more use to you here, sir? Given our orders from Narcissus.'

'I have to write a dispatch to the Imperial Secretary,' Vitellius explained flatly. 'I have to report on what's happened. Narcissus will want to know the situation. I need you to make sure it reaches Ravenna and gets sent on to Rome.'

'Why me?'

'You I can trust. Those others,' Vitellius gestured towards the officers dispersing into the night, 'might not be so loyal to the Emperor. I have to be sure that the message gets through to Narcissus. That's why it has to be you. As for Macro here, well, I need all my best officers ready for anything that bastard Telemachus decides to throw at us.'

Cato stared at the prefect with cold, bitter eyes. Then he saluted.

'May I go now, sir?'

'Of course,' Vitellius did not return the salute, but nodded in the direction of the tent lines of Cato's century. 'You're not needed at the moment. Get some sleep. I'll have the report ready for you before first light, when the *Spartan* sets sail.' He turned to Macro. 'You'd better join your men on watch.'

As the two centurions picked their way through the camp, Cato glanced over his shoulder to make sure they were out of earshot.

'While I'm gone, watch yourself.'

Macro frowned. 'What do you mean?'

'I'm not sure. I don't trust him.'

'What's new? No man in his right mind would trust that bastard. What do you think he's up to?'

Cato shook his head. 'I don't know. He's splitting us up, for some reason. All we can be sure of is it's nothing to do with getting this message through. So just watch yourself, you hear?'

Macro nodded. 'You sound just like my mother!'

Cato glanced at him. 'While I'm in Ravenna, want me to look in on your mother for you?'

As soon as he had said it Cato wished he had kept his foolish mouth shut. Memories of his calamitous encounter at the Dancing Dolphin flooded back.

'No. Leave it,' Macro said quietly. 'Don't mention her again.'

They walked in silence for a moment, then Cato changed the subject. 'We'd better find this traitor soon. Before he gets another chance to sell us out.'

Macro nodded. 'But he could be anyone.'

'He could be,' Cato agreed. 'But then again, he'd have to have some way of getting in touch with the pirates. That narrows things down.'

Macro smiled. He could almost hear Cato thinking. 'Anyone in mind?'

'I'm not sure. Not yet. But I have an idea where to start looking.'

CHAPTER TWENTY-TWO

'Your orders.' Prefect Vitellius held out a sealed parchment to Cato as they stood on the shore. A boat was waiting to take Cato out to the *Spartan*, lying at anchor a short distance out to sea. The trireme was barely more than an outline as the first light of the new day filtered over the mountain peaks. 'I've empowered you to act in my name when you get to Ravenna. Don't hesitate to take what we need. If any of the locals try to hinder you, you must act ruthlessly. Extreme circumstances call for extreme actions, understand?'

'Yes, sir.'

'Good.' Vitellius lowered his voice as he held out a small sealed package to Cato. 'This is the report. Make sure it's sent on to Rome as soon as you land.'

Cato took the package and tucked it into his haversack.

'Right, then. That's all, I think.' Vitellius nodded to himself. 'I'll see you in a few days, with the reinforcements. You're to rejoin us at the earliest possible opportunity. I'll hold you accountable for any unwarranted delay.'

Cato returned his look with cold disdain. 'I understand, sir.'

'Just as long as you do, Centurion. It would be a shame to have to end our long-standing antipathy. But I'm sure I'd find fresh enemies before long.'

A thin smile flickered across Cato's lips. 'I don't doubt it, sir.'

Vitellius stared at him for a moment and then turned away and strode off. Macro approached Cato as soon as the prefect had disappeared amongst the tents. He extended his hand and the two officers clasped each other on the forearm.

'Safe journey,' Macro grinned. 'With our recent experiences of life at sea, you'll need all the luck you can get.'

'Don't I know it.' Cato smiled back. 'Macro, if we ever live through this mess you have my permission to kick my lights out if I ever so much as look at a ship with a fond expression.'

'You can count on it.'

Cato smiled. In a world determined by the whim of the fates it was reassuring to know that he could rely on Macro's steadiness. Cato patted his friend on the shoulder and turned towards the waiting boat. He clambered over the transom and the sailors ran the boat out into the gentle surf that rolled and hissed up the shingle. Once through the surf they climbed aboard, took up their oars and rowed Cato out towards the looming hulk of the *Spartan*. Cato turned his head back for one last glimpse of his friend and saw Macro lift his hand, and turn away, marching back amongst the tents crowded between the beach and the dark line of the rampart.

As the sun rose over the mountains the trireme cleared the bay and set her elegant bows into the open waters beyond. The sky was overcast and the sea was a steely grey with a heavy swell. A stiff breeze was blowing off the coast and the crew had sheeted the mainsail in tightly at an angle across the deck to make the most of the favourable wind.

As he stood on the aft deck Cato noted that there was a tenseness amongst the sailors, and they gazed round at the horizon as if expecting a host of pirate ships to come tearing down on them the moment they ventured beyond the safety of the rest of the Roman fleet and clawed their way out to sea. He turned and paced slowly over to Albinus. The trierarch looked as anxious as his men and Cato tried to affect the same fearless calm he had seen so often in Macro.

'Reckon they're still out there?'

Albinus nodded. 'Bound to be. They'll have left a few at sea to keep an eye on us.'

'Any danger?'

Albinus looked at him. 'At sea, there's always a danger. From them, from the Gods and from the elements.'

Cato smiled faintly. 'I meant the enemy.'

'I know you did. But with this heavy sea we should make better going of it than they will.' Albinus glanced up at the grey clouds overhead. 'I'd be more concerned about the weather. Looks like we're in for a bit of a blow.'

'Bit of a blow?' Cato raised an eyebrow. 'Sounds like some kind of nautical euphemism, if ever I heard one.'

It was Albinus' turn to smile. 'All right, then. We're in for a storm. High winds, heavy seas. Bloody horrible all round.'

'I think I preferred "bit of a blow" after all.' Cato glanced over his shoulder at the coastline of Illyricum, and saw that the entrance to the bay had already disappeared over the horizon and only the serrated line of mountains was still in sight.

'Sail ho!'

All across the deck, heads tilted up to the masthead, noted the direction of the lookout's arm and then turned towards the direction he indicated.

'Two . . . no, three sails.'

Albinus cupped his hands and shouted up, 'What's their heading?'

After a short pause the lookout made his reply, with a weary fatalism that was evident to all on deck. 'Closing to intercept us, sir! I can make 'em out more clearly now. It's them pirates again.'

'Very well. Call down the moment they make any course changes!'

Trierarch Albinus dropped his hands to his side, and clenched them tightly before he thrust them behind his back where they would not betray his state of mind to anyone but Cato and the steersman.

'Three of them,' Cato mused. 'Enough to take us on?'

'More than enough, if they're handled well. They've got the wind gauge, and they'll try and close in on us at an angle.'

'Can't we outrun them?'

Albinus pursed his lips as he calculated the relative speeds of his ship and those of the pirates. 'Not unless the weather worsens. Otherwise they'll catch us before noon. They've the edge in terms of speed and numbers. But they'll have to board us. It's too dangerous to try and ram anyone in these conditions. Besides, the *Spartan*'s a tough ship. She's got firm sides; made from well-seasoned wood.' The trierarch nodded to himself with pride. 'They'll not hole us.'

There was a degree of certainty in his voice that went beyond mere bravado, and Cato was slightly reassured. He crossed back to the other side of the deck and, with the rest of the crew, kept an eye out for the first sign of the pirates' sails on the horizon.

Less than an hour later he saw them, three tiny dark triangles, pitching in and out of sight as the trireme rose up on the crest of each wave, then disappearing as the warship surged down into the trough.

Albinus kept an anxious watch on the enemy's progress, and as soon as they had closed enough that their sails were always in view he called out to his crew, 'Hands aloft! Shake out the last two reefs!'

Some of the crew glanced at him doubtfully before they threw themselves on to the rigging and scrambled up towards the peak where the main yard hung across the deck. They quickly inched themselves out along its length and bent over to work the reefing knots loose. The sail, already taut as a drum, wrenched the heavy leather from their grip with a rippling crack and then, as the loosened sail flapped in the wind, the crew hauled in the sheets and tied them off on the deck cleats. Under the additional pressure the trireme heeled further over to windward and Cato gripped the rail as he glanced down into the foaming sea racing past a scant few feet below the side of the ship, almost submerging the oar ports. The increase in speed was immediately apparent and as Cato watched the pirates' sails for a short while he was sure that the *Spartan* was slowly drawing ahead of them. He moved up the canted deck towards the trierarch, blinking away the salty spray that stung his face as the bows crashed through a wave.

'Isn't this a bit risky?'

Albinus patted the side rail. 'She can take it. Unless the wind gets any stronger. Then we'll have to take those reefs back in, if we don't want to lose the mast.'

'Oh.' Cato looked forward and saw that every rope was taut and vibrating under the strain of the mainsail, every scrap of it exposed to the northerly wind. Then he glanced back at the pirate ships and slapped a hand down on the side rail with a cry of triumph.

'We're drawing ahead of them!'

Albinus nodded. 'Yes. But two can play at that game. Look!'

He pointed towards the pirate ships and Cato could see tiny figures swarming aloft to take the reefs out of their sails. Shortly afterwards the enemy was slowly gaining ground on them once again.

Cato turned to Albinus. 'What now?'

'We'll have to make a run for it. Head down wind and hope that we've got the more weatherly ship.'

He turned to the steersman. 'Take her before the wind.'

'Aye, sir.'

As the trireme's bow started to swing away from the pirates Albinus shouted orders to his crew and the mainsail sheets were cast off until the wind came from directly behind the ship. Then they strained to haul the sheets in tight and cleat them home. Sailing downwind, the wind passing over the decks moderated and Cato felt a wash of pure exhilaration as the trireme coursed down one wave and climbed the next. For the first time he could sense something of the attraction that the sea held for men like Albinus and his crew. Then he glanced aft and saw that the pirate ships had changed course and were now directly behind the *Spartan*, barely a mile off. Cato's hand unconsciously went for the pommel of his sword.

'How much longer before they catch us up?'

Albinus squinted at their pursuers for a moment. 'Four hours, if we're lucky. Before nightfall, at any rate.'

As the chase continued across the white-capped expanse of grey sea the wind steadily increased in strength and the rigging of the trireme fairly hummed under the strain. Albinus went forward and rested his hand on the mainsheets, and anxiously stared up at the taut seams of the sail. Yet when he returned to the aft deck and glanced at the pirates it was clear that they were steadily closing, and that there was no chance of taking in a reef. Behind the pirates a grey film had closed in over the horizon and the sky above it was a filthy dark grey.

'What's that?' Cato pointed. 'A storm?'

'Squall, more likely. Rain and wind, that's all. Still . . .' The trierarch's expression suddenly tightened in firm concentration. He gauged the distance between the *Spartan* and the pirates before fixing his eyes beyond the three vessels, staring into the fast-approaching gloom. Then he turned and grinned at Cato. 'We might be in luck. As soon as that squall closes round us, I'll alter course. We might lose our friends, or at least gain enough distance to see us into the night, and try and lose them then.'

The veil of rain swept across the sea towards the pirates, suddenly swallowing them up and hiding them from the sight of those aboard the trireme. The crew stood to the mainsheets and braces, ready to move swiftly as soon as the trierarch gave the command. Just before the grey haze was upon them Cato sensed a freshening of the wind and it veered wildly, causing the mainsail to flap and boom for a moment before the wind direction steadied with a low keening moan through the rigging. The rain struck with almost no warning, and glinting shafts thundered down on the deck and exploded in a shimmering carpet of spray about the crew's feet. Cato hunched down inside his cape, holding the hood over his head with his spare hand as he clutched the side rail.

'Loose sheets!' Albinus roared out close by, his voice straining to be heard above the sudden din of the squall. 'Steersman! Bring her about!'

The trireme lurched round, heading for the Italian coast

once more. The mainsail flapped and thundered like some vast bird.

'Hands aloft! Take in a reef!'

Cato watched anxiously as the sailors climbed the rigging, and inched their way along the yardarm. Below them the deck rolled from side to side, threatening to pitch the sailors into the raging sea. When all the men were in position along the yard the trierarch shouted an order and they began to draw the sail in, until the first reefing tie was within reach. They hauled the ties in and hurriedly fastened them around the yard before making their way back to the mast and clambering down the rigging, chests heaving with the exertion and excitement of the moment.

'Well done, lads! Now sheet her home and let's get as far from those bastards as we can!'

With the wind across her aft quarter the trireme pitched and rolled at a sickening angle as she clawed her way through the squall. Cato's stomach began to churn. He lurched towards the side rail.

'Not that side!' Albinus yelled, thrusting an arm out towards the far side of the ship. 'Downwind!'

Cato pivoted round, clamped a hand over his mouth and half ran, half slid, down to the left-hand side of the ship and vomited over the rail. There seemed to be no end of it, and for an age he stood, hunched over the side rail, gripping the rough wooden surface as tightly as he could, racked by bouts of sickness that wrenched his body right down to the very pit of his stomach. All the time the rain lashed down, drenching his cloak and the tunic beneath, finally fetching up cold and clammy against his shivering skin.

After a while, he noticed that the air about him seemed brighter, and the torrential pounding of the rain on his shoulders began to subside. Cato raised his head and glanced round, just as the grey shroud of the squall began to pass, and then it was gone, just as suddenly as it had fallen upon them. The hiss of the rain subsided and then it was beyond earshot as the squall raced away to the south. After the savage intensity of the howling wind and rain, it seemed unnaturally quiet as the trireme surged across the rolling sea. A shaft of sunlight pierced the overcast, falling across the patch of sea the *Spartan* was traversing, and the water dripping from the rigging gleamed like diamonds. Cato wiped the acrid spittle from the corner of his mouth and turned towards Albinus.

'Did we do it? Did we lose them?'

Albinus shrugged. 'Can't say just yet. Wait a moment.'

Both men went over to the sternpost and stared intently as the squall receded. There was no sign of the pirate ships, and after a moment the trierarch breathed a deep sigh of relief and nodded his satisfaction. He glanced at Cato with a nervous smile. 'Looks like we—'

'Deck there. Enemy sail in sight!'

The trierarch and the centurion stared aft, just as three glistening sails emerged from the grey haze at the rear of the squall, less than a mile off. Cato's sickness subsided as a current of despair welled up inside him.

'Shit!' Albinus pounded the sternpost with a clenched fist. 'The bastards second-guessed us. Whoever's in command of that lot is a clever little sod and no mistake.'

'We'd better get ready for them,' Cato suggested, still feeling too sick to assume direct command of the ship. 'You'd better give the necessary orders. I'll be better in a moment.'

Albinus nodded, and turned back to his crew, bellowing out orders for the men to arm themselves and prepare to repel boarders. Cato continued to watch the enemy as they closed on the *Spartan*, sails close-hauled and straining at every seam. The pirate ships seemed to be closing faster than ever, and Cato realised that they had not taken in any reefs. For an instant he cursed Albinus' timidity, and wondered why the trierarch had not immediately ordered his men to get aloft again to shake out the reef in the *Spartan*'s broad mainsail.

Albinus rejoined him, staring anxiously as the enemy clawed ever closer to their prey. Already the foredecks of the smaller ships were packed with men, their armour and weapons glinting in the sunlight that spread across the sea as the clouds dispersed. The pirates sailed in close formation, and only when they were within extreme catapult range did their plan of attack become apparent. Two of the ships began to ease upwind, to close in on the trireme's right side, while the third dropped a little to windward, to take her from the left. The defenders would have to split their strength to face both attacks.

'All hands! Stand to!' Albinus bellowed to the crewmen gathered on the deck. They scrambled for their weapons and snatched up shields and helmets from the lockers behind the foredeck. The section leaders formed their men up on either side of the trireme and Cato knew that there were too few of them to hold the enemy off. If they had been trained and armed as well as the marines then they might have stood a chance. But they were sailors first, and warriors a poor second. Their desperation to survive would be their only advantage in the coming fight.

Stepping back from the rail, Cato reached for the clasp around his neck and wrenched it free from his sodden cloak, which thudded to the deck. Then he shouted an order to the nearest sailor to fetch his helmet and shield from the trireme's cabin. He turned to Albinus.

'If anything happens to me, and the *Spartan* wins through,

make sure these dispatches reach Rome.' He slapped the wet haversack at his side. 'If it looks like the ship's lost I'll take care of them. Either way, they must not fall into enemy hands.'

'I understand. Let's just make sure it doesn't come to that.'

Cato smiled. 'You can be sure I'll take as many of them with me as I can.'

'We all will.' Albinus nodded towards his men. 'They know there'll be no mercy.'

'Good.'

There was nothing more to say, and the trierarch and the centurion stood side by side as the pirate vessels closed in, the shouts and taunts of the men in the bows of the pursuing ships carrying clearly across the waves. The sailor returned with Cato's helmet and shield. With an eye to the approaching enemy, Cato calmly tied the straps of the helmet and took the shield, shifting his grip until it was most comfortable.

'All right then, let's make sure they don't forget the men of the *Spartan* in a hurry.'

Even as the words faded on his lips there was a distant splintering crack. Cato looked towards the leading ship, just as its mast shuddered for an instant, and then pitched to windward in a graceful arc, sail and rigging leaping to one side as if plucked by a giant invisible hand. The tangled mess of timber, rope and canvas pitched into the sea, immediately dragging the bows round, directly into the path of the ship surging across the waves behind the leader. It was too late to alter course and the second ship rammed the leader at full speed with a jarring crash that threw the men on both ships to the deck.

Albinus roared with laughter and slapped Cato on the

back. 'Did you ever see such a sight? Stupid bastards! Oh! Look there!'

The mast of the second ship wavered a moment and then slid backwards and crashed down on to the men scattered across its deck, eliciting a fresh chorus of cries and screams.

Albinus' face was awash with delight at his enemy's misfortune. 'That'll show 'em.'

Cato was only just recovering from the stunning reversal of fortune. 'What happened?'

'What always happens when you have too much sail in too much wind. Snapped their mast clean off!'

The third ship held its course for a moment longer before its trierarch realised that he could not hope to tackle the trireme alone. He hauled his wind and turned the vessel to go to the aid of his comrades. Albinus rubbed his hands with unrestrained joy.

'Time to finish them off, I think!'

'No.'

Albinus turned to Cato with a confused expression. 'Sorry. What was that?'

'Leave them.'

'Leave them? But they're at our mercy. We just have to turn and run them down. The last one'll run for it the moment he sees us go about.' There was a pleading expression in his eyes that Cato could well understand. After the torment of the previous day the chance to exact a crushing revenge would be sweet indeed. Albinus leaned closer and lowered his voice. 'There'd be no risk, Centurion. I swear . . . I'd bet my life on it.'

'No. We can't chance it. Our orders are to get back to Ravenna and get reinforcements. I'll not take any unnecessary risks. Our comrades are counting on us.' Cato could see that the trierarch was not convinced and he tried another line of thought. 'Look, supposing we did turn on them and somehow they managed to get men aboard the *Spartan*. There's more of them than us. And if we're lost what becomes of Vitellius and the others?'

Albinus looked from Cato to the pirate ships, already falling behind, and a look of bitter frustration crossed his features. For an instant Cato was sure that he would have to pull rank on the man. He tensed himself up and drew a deep breath. But before he could speak Albinus turned away from the pirates and called out to his crew.

'Stand down! Stand down!'

The cries of jubilation and excitement on the main deck died away, and at once a low grumble of discontent rippled through the sailors as they turned to face their trierarch.

'Stand down! Return weapons to lockers and get back to your sailing stations! Now! Section officers! Get your men moving!'

With a chorus of shouts and rough handling the junior officers dispersed the men, and the off-duty watch was dismissed below, leaving their comrades to stay on deck ready to respond to any new orders.

Albinus turned to Cato. 'There. Happy now?'

Cato stilled his tongue and stared back in silence, until the other man's gaze faltered, and turned away, over the stern, across the sea to the distant pirate ships slowly rising and falling on the swell.

'Albinus,' Cato said quietly, 'we have our orders. Our duty is to carry them out as immediately as we can.'

'I know that, damn you. It's just that I wanted to see those scum suffer.'

'You will. Not now, but soon enough. Savour that thought.'

Albinus gave a brief nod and then turned away and strode

down the length of his ship in silence, glowering at anyone who dared to cross his path. Cato let out a low sigh of relief, grateful that the man had seen reason in the end. But there would be no restraining him next time, and then the Gods better show some mercy to the pirates, because Albinus would spare them none in his desire to make them pay for what they had done to his comrades.

A sudden gust of wind caused Cato to tremble uncontrollably as it cut through his soaked clothing and chilled his flesh to the bone. Then, a dreadful thought struck him and he thrust a hand behind his back and wrenched the haversack round to the front. It was dark with sea water, and his freezing fingers struggled with the straps before at last he could open the flap and peer inside. The scroll with his orders was still in its leather holder and would be dry enough. But the package carrying the report from Vitellius was sodden. As Cato went to lift it out of the haversack, the seal fell off and the wrapping opened a little. Inside he could see the first of the waxed slates that comprised the reports.

For a moment he was still, as the first temptation to do what he knew he should not flickered across his mind. It would be easy enough. He could wait until they reached Ravenna. Then, as the remaining biremes were loaded with men and supplies, Cato could take the opportunity to read the prefect's report, and then reseal it before sending it on to Narcissus back in Rome. It would be a simple thing, and then he would know what Vitellius was up to. Maybe there would be something in the text about the scrolls; something to explain why they were worth the lives of so many men. For a moment some voice inside him reminded Cato that it would be a breach of trust for him to read the report. If it was ever discovered that he had pried into an official imperial dispatch there would be dangerous consequences.

Then he recalled that he was dealing with Vitellius, after all.

'Bollocks,' Cato muttered to himself, as he refastened the flap. He decided to read the report the moment he reached Ravenna.

CHAPTER TWENTY-THREE

The people of Ravenna were angry. A crowd had gathered at the gate to the naval base and men were hurling abuse at the sentries in the tower above the entrance. The gates themselves had been closed and a locking bar lowered into the brackets. There was no point in taking any chances with the mob, Cato decided. They may not like the situation but there was nothing he could do about it, given his orders. Inside the base the marine centurions and the trierarchs of the remaining biremes were working their men at a feverish pace to complete the loading of food and equipment.

Cato had resolved to return to Illyricum as soon as he could, despite the pleas of the town council. A deputation had been sent to him to demand an explanation for stripping the town of its defenders. Their spokesman, a wasted figure of a man, had been full of the usual haughty arrogance of provincial officials. Cato had listened to Rufius Pollo as he expressed the council's outrage, then Cato apologised politely and said he was bound by his orders.

As word spread through the port all the opinionated idlers who hung around the wine shops staggered down to the harbour front to shout colourful insults at the men behind the closed gate. They were joined by children, keen to see what all the fuss was about, and before night fell on the day that the *Spartan* had sailed into port, the wide thoroughfare between the quay and the warehouses was filled with enraged townspeople.

'Want me to send a century out to disperse them?' asked Centurion Metellus, standing beside Cato as they peered over the battlements at the mob.

Cato considered the offer for a moment and then shook his head. 'No need for that. They'll disperse soon enough, once they realise they're wasting their time. No point in provoking any more bad feeling than we already have.'

'Fair enough, sir.' Metellus tried to hide his disappointment. 'Still, we'll need to teach them a lesson one day. Can't let that rabble think they can get away with it. They've been mouthing off at us ever since those pirates first came on the scene.'

'Someone else will have to teach them a lesson,' Cato said wearily. 'But not now. Not us. We're too busy.'

Metellus shrugged. 'If you say so, sir.'

'I do.' Cato turned to his subordinate. 'Make sure none of your men does anything to provoke those people. They're here to guard the gate. That's all. Understand?'

'Yes, sir.'

'I'll be in my quarters. If there's any change in the situation send word to me at once.'

'Yes, sir.' They exchanged a salute and Cato turned away and descended the narrow staircase to the street behind the gate. As he crossed the parade ground he glanced out over the naval harbour. Four biremes were moored bow to stern along the dock, with two more anchored a short way out, waiting for their turn to be loaded. A continuous flow of men moved between the ships and the storehouses, driven on by the harsh shouts of their officers. At this pace the ships would be loaded before nightfall, ready to leave at first light the following day. The northerly wind had reduced to a steady breeze, and if it held then Cato and the reinforcements would reach Vitellius five days after the *Spartan* had set out from Illyricum.

There were a few things Cato would have to see to first. His thoughts went back to the prefect's report, spread out on a table in a locked room at the headquarters building. As soon as he had given his orders to the officers in charge of the garrison, Cato had retreated to Vitellius' study and opened the unsealed package, taking care to preserve both the linen wrapper and the seal. The message on the tablets had not been damaged by the water, and Cato arranged them in order before he tried to read the report. Unfortunately it made no sense. There were words all right, but they were comprised of meaningless arrangements of letters. A code then. Understandable, given that the message might have fallen into enemy hands before it reached Ravenna.

As soon as Cato realised he was looking at a coded message he recalled that the agents at the imperial palace preferred to use an Augustan code: the transposition of letters in the alphabet according to an agreed key. Simple, but effective enough to deter those who lacked the intelligence to work out the key. Cato had spent most of the morning experimenting with single value transpositions, with no luck. So the code had to be made up of alternating values, and by mid-afternoon he had discovered the values; four, two and five. With a hastily written copy of the alphabet Cato had already decoded all but the last tablet.

The prefect's report began with a shrewd anticipation of the council leader's protest to Rome. Vitellius explained that he had been obliged to strip the port of its garrison in order to guarantee a swift and overwhelming defeat of the pirates. He provided a brief description of the sea battle, claiming to have driven off the pirates with substantial losses on both sides. Cato had smiled bitterly as he read that part. Vitellius went on to outline his current strength and intentions. That was as far as Cato had got before Metellus had called him to the main gate to see the growing mob gathering outside. Apart from the blatant misrepresentation of the disastrous first encounter with the pirates, and a rather optimistic schedule for future operations, there was nothing remotely sinister in the report so far. And, infuriatingly, no detail about the scrolls for which so much blood had already been shed.

Now, Cato was eager to return and complete the decoding, before he had to risk a trip into the port to deal with the other pressing matter. He entered the headquarters building and hurried upstairs to the prefect's suite of offices. Only a handful of clerks were still at their desks, drafting inventories of the supplies being loaded on to the biremes. Cato strode through them, groping for the key in his purse. He fitted it to the lock, turned the key, opened the door and entered. He glanced at the nearest clerk.

'I'm not to be disturbed. Not unless there's an emergency.'

'Yes, sir.'

Cato closed the door and sat down in the prefect's finely carved chair. There was still some watered wine in the cup he had poured earlier and Cato took a quick sip before taking up his stylus and starting work on the final tablet. Each letter in the report corresponded to another letter further down the alphabet and as Cato decoded he made a copy of the message on a blank tablet he had taken from the prefect's stationery locker. The gist of the message was becoming quite clear, and Cato felt a chilling sense of fear, which gradually gave way to a desire for revenge. When he reached the end he set his stylus down and read through his copy.

* * *

In conclusion, our forces have achieved a qualified success so far, in no small part due to the diligence with which I have carried out the planning, preparation and execution of the operation. It is therefore, with great regret, that I have to report that an early resolution of the pirate threat and possible recovery of the Sybilline scrolls was compromised by the actions of Centurion Cato during the naval engagement mentioned above.

At a critical point of the battle, as the enemy flagship was in full retreat and being pursued by the *Horus* and the trireme squadron, Centurion Cato ordered his ship to break off the pursuit and turn on the lighter enemy vessels engaging our bireme force. A charitable explanation of his action might be that the centurion had gone to aid some of our ships who were in some slight difficulties at the time. However, it is possible that Centurion Cato's desire for personal glory overrode his obedience to orders. It is also possible that he deliberately chose to close with an enemy of less impressive force than the enemy's flagship.

In any event, his ship broke formation, and a number of the other triremes followed his lead. This left me with insufficient forces to close with the pirate commander and I was obliged to break off the pursuit.

As a consequence of Centurion Cato's recklessness, the operation will take considerably longer than I had anticipated. I therefore request your permission to have the centurion removed from my command and returned to Rome for disciplinary proceedings. Given the sensitive nature of the mission you asked me, and Centurions Cato and Macro, to complete, I cannot proceed with any certainty of success while encumbered with a man who has neither the experience nor the courage required for the job. It pains me to report to you in these terms, Narcissus, since I know you have some regard for the abilities of the individual in question. Nevertheless, with the stakes being as high as they are I am sure you will understand my grave concerns and give your assent, as speedily as possible, for the removal of this burden, one way or another.

Vitellius

Cato set the tablet down and drew a deep breath. The report was as good as a death warrant and he felt a moment of icy fear gnawing at his guts as his mind raced to grasp the full implications of Vitellius' closing remarks. His first response was bitter hatred for the prefect. The conclusion of the report went beyond injustice. It was pure self-serving dishonesty, designed to shift the blame for the sea battle fiasco on to Cato. The prefect meant to kill him. That much was evident. If a suitable opportunity arose he might not even be prepared to wait for the permission of the Imperial Secretary.

Cato poured himself another cup of wine and didn't water it down this time. Before he could make plans to deal with this new danger, he needed to understand why the prefect wanted him dead. Presumably it had something to do with the scrolls. The Sybilline scrolls . . . Not *the* Sybilline scrolls, surely?

Whatever they turned out to be, the Imperial Secretary thought these scrolls were vital enough to risk a large force of men and ships for. And now it seemed that Vitellius considered them important enough to want Cato dead and out of the way, so that he could take them for himself.

Cato realised that he must find some way out of the danger he faced. He might write his own report and send it on to Rome with that of Vitellius. He could explain the truth behind the débâcle of the naval engagement. He might also express his doubts about how far the prefect could be trusted to recover the scrolls for Narcissus. But even as these thoughts raced through Cato's mind, he knew that it would be pointless to attempt to tell the truth. Vitellius was a favourite of Emperor Claudius, ever since he had been given credit for saving the Emperor from the blade of an assassin during the imperial visit to the army in Britain. He was also one of Narcissus' most trusted agents. The word of a lowly centurion would carry little weight against that of an aristocrat. Indeed, it was more than likely that Cato's accusations would be interpreted as malicious at best, and sinister and suspicious at worst. That would be how Vitellius would misrepresent the charges against him and Cato would quietly disappear from the scene. Another anonymous corpse dragged from the Tiber, flung into a common grave and covered with lime.

Cato drained the cup of wine, and stared again at the prefect's report. As he did so a smile slowly formed on his face. Very well, if he dare not accompany Vitellius' lies with his own account, then he would alter the prefect's report so that it condemned Vitellius by itself. Leaning forward over the desk, Cato reached for some fresh slates and began to rewrite the report.

A while later, as dusk began to gather about the port, he sat back and admired his work. Let Vitellius dig himself out of that one, he mused. Cato tied the wax tablets together through holes in the wooden frames and carefully wrapped them in the linen packaging. Then he erased the report on the original slates with firm sweeps of the reverse end of his stylus. Lastly, he heated some fresh wax and dripped it on to the package before pressing the original seal of the fleet prefect into the wax and letting it set. He inspected the results carefully, and smiled in satisfaction as he rose from the desk.

Before he left the office, Cato was momentarily tempted to leave his uncoded version of the report out on the desk for the prefect to discover upon his return. There was huge satisfaction at the thought of Vitellius knowing that he had been bested by the man he had sought to destroy. Cato toyed with the idea, then dismissed it with a sense of regret. He picked up the stylus, heated the broad end over the flame of an oil lamp and erased his work, destroying any trace of the decoded message. Vitellius would know soon enough that his plot had been frustrated. Let him suffer the uncertainty of knowing how it had been achieved.

Cato unlocked the door and stepped into the large office outside.

'You!' He motioned to one of the clerks still at his desk. 'Come here!'

'Yes, sir.'

'Take this dispatch to the courier station. It's to be sent to Rome at once.'

'Yes, sir.'

'Better have the rider leave by the shore gate. No sense in having him chance the mob. See to it.'

The clerk saluted, then hurried from the office clutching the dispatch in both hands. Cato had to fight to restrain the nervous thrill building up within. The anticipation of Vitellius' realisation that he had been set up was extremely gratifying. Only the gods could save his career and reputation now.

CHAPTER TWENTY-FOUR

Cato's good humour stayed with him as he quitted the naval base by a small side entrance after night had fallen. It was cold and a light wind brought a fine drizzle with it as it gusted through the streets. Cato pulled the hood of the cloak over his head and hunched his shoulders beneath the wool folds. Barely a hundred angry and drunk townspeople were left of the mob outside the main gate, but there was no sense in risking his life by trying to pass through them into the backstreets of Ravenna. Cato had stripped off his uniform and donned a simple tunic and boat cloak with cheap sandals; the typical garb worn by the sailors who thronged the streets of the port. He skirted round the harbour front and made his way into the winding network of thoroughfares and narrow passages in the most run-down quarter of the port.

The street on which the Dancing Dolphin stood was far quieter than the last time Cato had been there. The marines and the navy had been the main source of custom for the myriad bars and brothels of the area. Unoccupied prostitutes sat in their curtained alcoves with sullen expressions, which brightened into laboured seductive looks as they caught sight of Cato approaching down the side of the street. He refused to meet their eyes, or respond to their explicit sexual entreaties, as he strode past, head down.

There was only a handful of customers in the Dancing Dolphin when Cato entered. He kept his hood up for a moment as he glanced round. The only face he recognised was that of the barman leaning on the counter as he waited to serve a customer. He looked at Cato hopefully, and the centurion worked his way through the haphazard arrangement of tables and benches towards the counter. The barman gave him a thin, unconvincing smile of welcome.

'Evening. What can I get you?'

'Mulsum.'

'Right.' The barman dipped a ladle into a steaming jar and filled a bronze cup, sliding it across the bar to Cato. 'That's three asses.'

Cato plucked the small coins out of his purse and slapped them down on the counter. Despite the price, the drink was only just palatable and Cato could feel the sediment in his mouth as he gulped down the first warm mouthful.

The barman returned the ladle to the jar. 'Anything else?'

'Yes.' Cato took another sip. 'Portia. I need to speak to her. Let her know I'm here.'

'And you are?'

'Centurion Cato. She knows me.'

The barman stood back from the counter and weighed Cato up. He clearly decided that the customer was of little account, and shook his head. 'You can't see her. She's not here.'

'All right, sunshine. Where is she, then?'

The look of dull preoccupation that crossed the barman's face as he tried to make up an excuse was eloquent enough for Cato.

'Uh, she's, uh, gone to the wine wholesaler.'

'I see. And he only opens at night, I suppose?'

'Er, yes . . . no. He's doing it as a special favour.'

'Really?' Cato smiled mirthlessly, then leaned closer. 'Look, mate, she's on the premises. There's no point in denying it. Just go and tell her that Cato – Macro's friend – is here and needs to speak to her urgently. Now go. Before I have to make you.'

Cato felt his heart quicken as he stared at the barman, trying to act the part of a man who would not take 'no' for an answer. The barman stared back at him, slowly kneading his hands together in a soiled cloth. At length he pursed his lips and snorted with contempt.

'I said she's not here. Now, I think you'd better drink up and leave, before I throw you out.'

Cato flipped his cloak open to reveal the pommel of his sword, and casually drew the blade. 'I think you'd better go and look for her.'

The barman's eyes fixed on the gleaming swordpoint and he nodded quickly. 'I remember now. She's doing the accounts. I'll tell her you're here.'

Cato nodded. 'Thank you.'

Cato kept his sword up, and the barman backed carefully along the wall behind the counter until he was out of reach, and then hurried through the small doorway into the passage beyond. Once the man was gone Cato sheathed the blade and looked round the wine shop at the other customers. A few faces had turned towards him out of curiosity, but most continued talking in low undertones with their friends, or just stared ahead in a drunken stupor. He turned back to his mulsum and raised the cup. Then he recalled the gritty sediment and set it back down on the counter with a grimace.

'And what is wrong with that?'

Cato was momentarily startled by the voice and looked round sharply, before attempting to recover his composure.

Portia was standing inside the door frame, in the shadows, and he heard her chuckle.

'My man told me we had a heavy at the bar. Made no mention of a boy.'

'Not a boy,' Cato replied through clenched teeth. 'A centurion.'

'Touchy young fellow, aren't you?' She stepped into the dull light of the bar and Cato saw the amused smile she was not even trying to suppress. He felt himself blushing as Portia approached and stood the other side of the counter. 'I thought you were in Illyricum, sticking it to those pirates.' The bitter irony of the last words hung in the air like an accusation.

'I was. But the prefect needed someone to come back for reinforcements.'

'So I heard. I assume things aren't going well for our side. Now it seems you're leaving us open to attack.'

Cato said nothing, but glanced down to try to hide the guilt he was feeling.

'What can I do for you, Centurion? Is this about that idiot son of mine?'

Cato nodded. 'That. And another matter.'

She raised her plucked eyebrows. 'Sounds ominous . . . Any news of my man?'

'Minucius? He's safe.' Cato recalled the flimsy rampart that had been erected around the remains of the fleet. 'At least he was when I left him.'

'Safe,' Portia repeated softly, then brushed her hand over her hair, tied back in a simple ponytail. 'Good. I'll make an offering for them tomorrow.'

'Them?' Cato smiled.

'Yes, why not? Even that fool friend of yours could do with a little help from the gods.'

There was an awkward silence before Cato summed up the nerve to say what he wanted. 'You know, I think a little reconciliation might be in order.'

'Then you'd better tell *him* that,' Portia replied coldly. 'Last time I saw my son, he seemed content to beat my husband-to-be into a pulp and destroy my livelihood.'

Cato shot a glance round at the dingy wine shop and Portia sensed his disdain at once.

'You might not think it's much, but it's been my bread and butter for years. Minucius and I have sunk every spare sestertian into this place. If we hadn't come into a little money recently I'd never have forgiven Macro for the damage he caused the other night. As it is, I'm selling up. Soon as Minucius gets back we're leaving Ravenna.'

'Leaving?'

'Cato, I don't mean to end my days serving behind a bar. Minucius and I intend to find a small estate and retire quietly.'

Cato raised his eyebrows. 'Must be making a tidy profit from this place.'

Portia snorted. 'I wish. No. The money comes from Minucius. His uncle died some months ago. Seems the man was wise enough not to have children,' she added with feeling. 'He left it all to his only nephew.' She flashed a bitter smile. 'Makes a bit of a mockery of all the years I've put into this place, wouldn't you say?'

Cato shrugged. 'Better late than never. The same applies to making things up with Macro.'

'Aren't you forgetting something? I left him and his father. Just dumped them and ran off with another man. Can you imagine how much that would hurt a boy that age? Even though I had my reasons, I could never forgive myself for doing that. I've often imagined what he must have gone through – tormented myself with it. And all the time I've been sure that however bad it made me feel, it was far worse for him, if not for that idle drunk of a husband. You can be sure that Macro will never forgive me.'

'He might,' Cato replied, 'if you give him a chance.'

Portia frowned, and then patted his hand. 'Look, you seem like a nice boy, Cato. But this really doesn't concern you.'

'Macro's my friend. It concerns me.'

'Have it your own way, then . . .' They stared at each other in silence for a moment, before Portia's gaze wavered. 'All right, tell him that I will speak with him when this business with the pirates is over. He can have one last chance to grow up. If he can't bring himself to behave like an adult I'll wash my hands of him. After all, I've got a future with Minucius. I really don't need to dredge up the past.'

'Fair enough.' Cato nodded. 'I'll tell him.'

'Now, if that's all . . . No, wait. You mentioned another matter.'

'Yes.'

'Well?'

'You recall that night we came here?'

Portia arched her eyebrows. 'What do you think?'

Cato glanced down to hide his shame. 'There was a man with us. A merchant. Anobarbus.'

'I remember him. Nice-looking man.'

'Have you seen him since then?'

'Not for a few days after the fight. Then he turned up again. He's been in here two or three times. Made a beeline for any men from the fleet.' Portia smiled at the memory. 'Very flash with his money. Bought a round for everyone on the last occasion.'

'Really?' Cato raised an eyebrow. 'Do you know where I can find Anobarbus? I need to have a word with him.'

Portia shook her head. 'Sorry. No idea . . . But you might ask that man over there.' She gestured towards a man slumped across a table to one side of the door, head cradled on crossed arms.

'Him?'

'He's one of the gangmasters down at the warehouses. Contracts porters for all the shipowners and merchants in the port. If anyone knows where your man is staying, it'll be Laecus there.'

CHAPTER TWENTY-FIVE

'Laecus?' Cato stood over the man, his nose wrinkling at the stench of wine and sweat. A cloak was bundled on to the bench beside Laecus and the gangmaster wore a sleeveless tunic of soft leather stained and worn through years of hard work down at the harbour. Laecus didn't stir, and Cato leaned forward and shook the man's shoulder; a mass of muscle and tattoos. 'Laecus . . .'

The gangmaster grumbled softly and his eyes flickered for a moment before his lips puffed out in a slow belch. Cato winced as the stale fumes of wine and garlic wafted up to him. 'Nice.'

He took a firm grip on the man's shoulder and shook him firmly. 'Laecus! Wake up, man!'

'Gerroff.' Laecus flapped a hand at Cato, waving him away. 'Leave me be, you bastard. Can' you see I'm fucken 'sleep?'

'No, you're not.' Cato shook him again, more forcefully. 'I have to speak to you. Sit up!' He looked back towards the counter. 'A pitcher of water over here!'

While he waited for the barman to return, Cato let go of Laecus and the gangmaster slid back into his stupor, mumbling incoherently as the centurion wrinkled his nose. The barman emerged from the back room and crossed over to Cato with a pitcher and two cups. He set them down on the table beside Laecus.

'Shall I pour, sir?'

'Yes, all of it.'

The barman glanced at the cups and frowned.

'Not in the cups, you bloody fool! On him! Empty all of it on him.'

The barman slowly grinned. 'Oh! I get it.'

He gripped the jug carefully, took aim and upended it, releasing a torrent over the gangmaster's head. As soon as the pitcher was empty the barman backed away, hurrying out of range. Laecus jerked up, spluttering in confusion and anger.

'What the fuck . . .?' His eyes glanced round and fixed on Cato. 'Here! What are you—'

'Quiet!' Cato snapped. 'Just sit still and answer my questions.'

'Sit still?' He laughed. 'No. I'm going to take your head off, you little gobshite!'

Laecus lurched round, sweeping a huge arm across the top of the table and sending the cups flying across the room and to shatter against the wall. But before he could rise from the bench Cato had stepped back and, with a weary sigh of resignation, drew his sword again.

'Easy, there! Sit down.'

Laecus paused for a moment, eyes narrowing as he took in the sword and then the young man standing behind the blade. With the water dripping from the straggling locks plastered on to his scalp, Laecus swiftly sobered up enough to know he was at a disadvantage. He dropped back on to the bench and leaned away from Cato, resting his back against the cracked plaster on the wall.

'All right,' Cato nodded. 'Now that I have your attention, I need to ask you some questions. Does the name Anobarbus mean anything to you?'

'Anobarbus?' The gangmaster raised a fist and rubbed

his chin as he considered the question. 'Never heard of him.'

'Try harder,' Cato growled. 'An older bloke. Bit thin. Trades in art and sculpture.'

'I might know him,' Laecus said slowly. 'What's in it for me?'

'Not being held for questioning down at the navy base.' Cato gave him a thin smile. 'It'd be better for you to freely answer my questions here, rather than let my men knock the answers out of you. Now then, do you know of this man?'

'All right. Let me think . . . This Anobarbus, arrived in the port a few days back?'

'Sounds like the man I'm looking for. Done any work for him?'

'No.'

'You know anyone who has?'

'No.'

'Laecus, you're going to have to do better than this if you don't want a few painful hours alone with my men. Do I make myself clear?' Cato stared into his eyes, and the other man glanced down.

'Clear enough, sir. Yes, I know him. It's my business to know him and any other traders and merchants who pass through the port. Soon as I heard there was a new man in Ravenna I went to see him.'

A sudden thought struck Cato. When the merchant had entered the port he had been part of a military convoy and had not paid the toll, or had to register his name and business. 'How did you hear about him?'

'Easy enough. Anobarbus has been in and out of town on business a few times since he first arrived. I have a boy who waits by the town gate. He makes enquiries about any visitor who might be of interest to me. Usual details: name, trade and lodgings.'

'I see.'

'Anyway, Anobarbus seemed like a good prospect, so I went and visited the address my boy gave me for his lodgings.'

'What do you know of Anobarbus' business?'

Laecus shrugged and rubbed his bleary eyes. 'Not sure, exactly. He claims to deal in statues, urns, pots, furniture. Good-quality stuff. So he said.'

'You've seen any of this merchandise?'

'A few pieces. He rented space in my cousin's warehouse to store the stuff. Local purchases from local towns. Nothing spectacular, you understand.' Laecus flashed a grin. 'This is the arse-end of Italy. Too far away and too dull for the taste of your millionaires back in Rome. Antiques are different. Their agents have been out here for years scouring the place for old bits and bobs. They've pretty much cleared the area out and have moved on to Greece and Asia looking for stuff to ship back to their clients.'

Cato scratched his chin. 'So why's Anobarbus still here?'

Laecus looked at him in surprise. 'Same reason every other merchant is laid up in town. Them pirates. As it happens he's waiting for his ship to come in, loaded with statues from Greece.'

'This ship have a name?'

Laecus nodded. 'The *Priapus*. Tough old bird. Slow but sturdy.'

'You know her?'

'Yes. The captain's a cousin of mine. She was expected to return a month ago.'

'Think the pirates might have taken her?'

'Maybe. But Cassius is a safe enough pair of hands. If I

know him, he's holed up in a port and drinking himself stupid while the weather improves and hoping that you lot get your arses together and sort them pirates out.'

Cato's expression stiffened at the jibe. Then he nodded at the empty wine jug on the far side of the table. 'I see. You and your family drink while my men die. That's how it is, eh?'

Laecus looked at him, warily noting the cold expression in Cato's eyes. 'No disrespect, sir, but that's what you get paid for.'

That was true enough, Cato reflected, and the man was within his rights to imply that the fleet was falling down on the job. He shrugged the thought aside and refocused. So Anobarbus had some proof that he was what he had claimed to be. Still, it might be a useful cover for a man who was in the area on another purpose. Cato looked up at the gangmaster.

'As far as you know, has Anobarbus visited Ravenna before?'

'Maybe.' Laecus ran a hand through his cropped hair. 'I wouldn't know. We get so many people passing through.'

'Do you know where he's staying?'

Laecus nodded. 'Nice digs, he's got himself. House guest of Rufius Pollo, one of the council members.'

'I know him,' Cato smiled thinly. 'We met earlier. Seems that our friend Anobarbus has some useful local connections. Where does this Rufius Pollo live?'

Laecus waved a hand vaguely. 'Over by the pump house.'

'Right. You can take me there. Up you get.'

Laecus turned his eyes to Cato and shook his head. 'Not till I'm done with my drinking.'

Cato nodded at the empty wine jug. 'You've done with that, already. Come on. Up!'

Laecus didn't move. He stared back at Cato for a moment, then sniffed. 'All right. What's it worth?'

'Another jug, and the satisfaction of knowing that you have provided loyal service to the Emperor,' Cato smiled, then jerked his thumb towards the door. 'Let's go.'

It was close to midnight when they reached the council leader's house. The town had quietened down and they had met only a handful of people hurrying through the dark maze of Ravenna's streets. By the time they reached the more affluent quarter centred on the pump house where the water pressure was high enough to run fountains, the narrow passages had opened out into wider thoroughfares. Almost at once the two men bumped into a patrol of the watch, but once Cato revealed his identity and rank, the watch let them pass and tramped on down the middle of the street, hobnails echoing off the high walls and giving ample warning to any criminals in their path to make a run for it.

The house of Rufius Pollo had the usual understated exterior of an affluent Roman townhouse. Blank plastered walls stretched out each side of a heavily studded wood door. The faint sound of voices drifted over the wall, and just audible between the muffled chatter and trills of laughter, the gentle notes of a flute.

'There you go.' Laecus muttered. 'Now let's have the money. Price of a jar of wine, you said.' He did a quick calculation, then doubled the result and held out a hand. 'Six sestertians should do.'

Cato brushed the hand to one side. 'Not until after we've finished our business.'

He strode up to the door and rapped the iron knocker twice. Almost at once the watchman's inspection slot rattled open and a pair of eyes scrutinised them from the interior.

'What's your business at this time of night?' Before Cato could respond the man glanced over their clothes and continued in the same breath. 'Better make yourselves scarce, before I call the watch down on you.'

'Better not,' Cato replied. 'You'd only embarrass your master. Tell Rufius Pollo that the acting commander of the naval base wants to see him.'

The doorkeeper cast his eyes over Cato once again, more searchingly this time. 'Acting commander? Acting drummer boy, more like. Be off with you!'

Cato slammed his fist against the side of the inspection slot, making the doorkeeper jump. 'I am Centurion Gaius Licinius Cato, senior officer present at the fleet of Ravenna. I demand to see Rufius Pollo, in the name of the Emperor! Now!'

The doorkeeper stared back at him for a moment, before grumbling. 'Wait there.' He closed the inspection slot and left Cato and Laecus staring at the door. Cato felt embarrassed at the slight to his authority and at first he refused to turn and meet the gaze of the gangmaster, fearing that the man would not hide his amusement at Cato's display of hubris. Instead Cato turned away and looked up at the sky. Most of the clouds had cleared and the pitch-black depths of the heavens were scattered with the glitter of tiny stars.

'Should be good weather tomorrow,' Cato said casually. 'A calm day for the crossing.'

'Maybe.' Laecus spat into the gutter. 'Maybe not. Weather changes at the drop of a hat in this season.'

'Really?' Cato glanced at his companion. 'That's a comforting thought the night before a voyage.'

The gangmaster started scratching his backside absent-mindedly. 'Wouldn't go back to sea, even for good money.

Well, maybe for really good money . . . The sea's a whimsy bastard.'

Cato raised his eyebrows. 'Colourful. I take it you once had something to do with the sea. Some trade? A sailor perhaps.'

'A sailor, all right.' Laecus stared up at the stars and shuddered.

'Why did you give it up?'

'Too fond of life. That is to say, too fond of drinking to give up life. The sea's no place for a man. It ain't natural. Leave it to the fish, and the demons that live under the surface.'

Cato stared at him, and saw a deep-rooted fear in the man's face for the first time that evening.

Laecus coughed to clear his throat and tried to sound calm. 'Demons, yes. And pirates. This lot have been the worst. Picking off ships, killing the crews, or taking them for slaves, and then vanishing. And every time the navy has tried to track them down they've failed. Like they knew when and where the fleet was going to appear. Must be some kind of magic involved.'

'Or just good intelligence,' Cato suggested.

With a sharp rattle of a drawn bolt the door was unlocked and swung silently inwards on well-oiled hinges. The entrance hall was dark, but bright lights burned at the end of a long, high-ceilinged corridor that opened out into a garden courtyard. The doorkeeper waved them inside and locked the door behind them.

'This way please, sir. The master will see you at his table.'

Cato paused. 'At his table? There's no need for that. He can be discreet if he wants. I don't mean to disturb his entertainment.'

'But you have already, sir.' The doorkeeper bowed his head. 'Now, if you please?'

'Very well. Laecus, you wait here. Doorkeeper!'

The doorkeeper turned round again, fighting to keep an irritated expression off his face. 'Yes, sir?' He responded testily.

'Bring this man a jug of wine.'

The doorkeeper's eyebrows rose in surprise at the temerity of such an order and then he smiled obsequiously. 'I'll see what refreshment can be arranged for your man, once I've taken care of you, sir.'

'Thank you.'

The doorkeeper turned away, paused an instant to glance back in case there was anything else, and then led Cato down the corridor. They strode past walls hung with rich tapestries that deadened the sounds of their footsteps. Neat busts of what Cato assumed were members of the family peered out from shallow niches at regular intervals.

They emerged from the corridor into a large peristyled garden, replete with statues and topiary, wavering slowly under the glow of hundreds of lamps hanging from the trellises that stretched across the garden. It was early spring and a large number of braziers glowed amongst the party-goers, adding their smoke to the thin greasy eddies rolling off the tiny flames of the lamps. A large dining room looked out over the garden and many more tables extended from the seating area. Richly dressed guests were draped over the benches. The meal was over and the last of the plates and serving dishes were being collected by household slaves who neither spoke nor dared to meet the eyes of the guests in their effort to remain invisible. Many of the guests had left their tables and wandered about the garden talking in the loud, thoughtless manner of those who had drunk too much and relaxed their guard without thinking. A small group of musicians stood to one side of the tables, and were setting down their instruments as Cato passed by.

He glanced around at the guests, looking for Anobarbus, but the merchant was nowhere in sight.

'Centurion!'

Cato looked towards the head of the table and saw Rufius Pollo rising up into a sitting position, arm raised to gain Cato's attention. 'Over here! Come and join me.'

Squeezing through a group of excited teenagers, Cato made his way towards the host of the party and nodded his greeting. Pollo patted the vacant seat to his left and beckoned to one of his slaves at the same time.

Cato sat down on the edge of the dining couch. 'Nice house you have here, Rufius Pollo.'

Pollo smiled modestly. 'Oh, I'm sure it's as nothing compared to the houses of Rome.'

'Nothing?' Cato shook his head. 'It would compare most favourably, I assure you.'

'You're very kind,' Pollo replied civilly. 'I'm afraid you've missed the banquet, but I'll have my man see if there's anything left you can have.'

Cato waved a hand. 'Most kind. But no thank you. I've already eaten.'

'You're sure? Very well then.' Pollo clicked his fingers and thrust a long bony finger at the slave and waved him away. At once the slave dipped his head, backed away two steps and turned to scurry off.

'What's the big occasion?' Cato asked.

'Big occasion?' Pollo chuckled mirthlessly. 'Why, Centurion, in a way I suppose we're celebrating – if that could possibly be the word – your decision to leave us at the mercy of the pirates. One last feast to use up my best stores before my family and I leave Ravenna and head for the shelter of our estate inland. Far inland.'

'Don't you think that's a little alarmist?' Cato asked quietly.

'You think so?' Pollo laughed. 'Do you know how many such gatherings are taking place tonight? By this time tomorrow, I'd be surprised if more than a third of the households in this quarter of the port will still be here. Who can blame them? Not one marine will remain to stand between them and the pirates when they come.'

'If they come.'

'When they come,' Pollo repeated firmly. 'How could they resist?'

'And you won't be alone. I'm leaving a century of marines in the naval base.'

'To protect the base,' Pollo responded shrewdly. 'Not us. In fact, I imagine you're leaving them behind to protect the base from us . . .'

Cato ignored the jibe, and continued speaking calmly. 'None the less, they will remain and if we're lucky they might just fool Telemachus and his pirates into believing that Ravenna is adequately defended.'

'I doubt it'll take him long to see through that sham.'

'Really?' Cato watched Rufius Pollo closely. 'What makes you think that? Why should Telemachus suspect?'

'Come now, Centurion. I'm old. I'm not a fool. Someone's been feeding information to the pirates about almost every move the fleet has made. That's no secret . . .' He looked down at the ground and shook his head, before glancing back at Cato with a forced smile. 'Anyway, I'm failing in my duty as a host. How may I help you?'

For a moment Cato stared back at Pollo, wondering how much the man really knew about the pirates' source of information. Pollo would hardly dare to drop open hints to a man with hundreds of marines at his command. Except

Cato was alone and the marines might as well be in another province at that instant. He suddenly felt vulnerable, even here, amid scores of guests, and he looked round quickly and saw that a handful of Pollo's companions were watching them closely.

Pollo smiled at the centurion's discomfort. 'As I said, is there anything I can do for you, before you leave my house?'

'Who said I was leaving?'

'Trust me. You will be, very shortly.'

'All right. Tell me one thing. I'm looking for someone. A friend. I was told he was staying here, as your guest.'

'Well,' Rufius Pollo stretched out his arms, 'as you can see, I have more guests than you can wave a stick at, although some of these miscreants do actually have homes to go to. What is your friend's name?'

'Anobarbus.'

Pollo's eyes betrayed a flicker of surprise at the name, then he composed his features and tipped his head slightly to one side. He stared intently at the centurion for a moment and then lowered his voice as he leaned forward to speak to Cato. 'A friend, you say? If I was to ask you what the blind man seeks, what would you reply?'

Cato frowned. He hadn't the slightest idea about the merchant's family, and was surprised at the strangeness of the question. He shook his head.

'I've no idea. Blind man? What do you mean?'

'It's nothing.' Pollo's gaze flickered to one side, and he gestured towards the hall that led to the entrance. 'Anobarbus was here. He left early in the evening. Long before you arrived.'

'Where did he go?'

'I don't know.'

'I see.' Cato paused before he continued. 'Might I ask you

to explain how he came to be a guest in your house?'

'Simple enough. We have friends in common back in Rome. They told him to look me up when he arrived in Ravenna.'

'What friends?'

'Just friends.' Pollo smiled. 'Tell me, Centurion, do you suspect Anobarbus of some crime?'

'Did I say that?'

'No. But I find it strange that you are conducting enquiries at this time of night. Why do you want to find Anobarbus? *Do* you suspect him of some crime? Some treachery?'

Cato paused before replying. 'I only want to eliminate him from my list of suspects.'

Pollo flinched. 'You have a list?'

'I can't disclose official information.'

'I see . . .' Pollo leaned back, keeping his eyes fixed on Cato. He affected a yawn. 'Now, I'm afraid you really must go. You've quite exhausted my hospitality. My men will show you out.'

'No need.' Cato stood and backed off a few paces. 'I know the way. I bid you good night, Rufius Pollo. Until we meet again.'

'We won't.' Pollo shook his head, and waved towards a pair of burly-looking slaves lurking at the back of the dining room, and discreetly pointed at the centurion. Cato turned away and walked quickly towards the corridor. He glanced back and saw that the slaves were doing their best to keep up as they pushed through the guests crowding the dining room. As soon as he was clear of them Cato ran down the corridor, ignoring the surprised expressions of the guests who turned towards the sound of running feet on the tessellated floor.

'Laecus!' he called out. 'Get up! We're leaving.'

Ahead of him the vague mass of the gangmaster emerged from the shadows, a small jug of wine in one hand.

'What's up, sir?'

'Get the door open!'

Cato threw himself forward and by the time Laecus had caught the sense of urgency the centurion thudded into the door beside him, fingers groping for the thick iron bolt that secured it. Behind them sandled feet padded down the corridor. With a grating rasp they worked the bolt and heaved the door inwards.

'Come on!' Cato shouted, shoving Laecus into the street. 'Run!'

They scrambled down the steep steps on to the broad tufa stone paving and started back towards the heart of Ravenna. They were only a short distance down the street when Pollo's men burst out of the house, dagger blades glinting in the wan glow of the light from within.

One of them pointed. 'There!'

'What the hell's happening?' Laecus grunted as he ran beside Cato. The centurion said nothing but gritted his teeth and darted towards the opening of a narrow alley, quickly praying that it wouldn't turn out to be a dead end. The alley was as black as a Parthian's heart, and rubbish had been left in long neglected piles, threatening to trip them up as Cato and Laecus stumbled headlong, desperately trying to gain some ground on their pursuers. They took a turning to the right and ran on, then took another turn, to the left this time, into an even tighter alley that reeked of excrement and rotting vegetation. A short way down the alley Cato could just make out the opening to a small yard and pulled the gangmaster in with him, crouching down behind a small cart.

As they squatted down, lungs straining for breath and ears filled with the pounding of blood, Cato drew his sword and stared through the opening to the yard and into the blackness of the alley beyond. All was still and there was no sign of Pollo's men.

Laecus tugged Cato's tunic. 'Would you mind telling me what the fuck is going on here?'

'Wish I knew,' Cato whispered. 'Keep quiet!'

They waited, but the streets were silent. Once a voice called out, some distance off, and there came a muffled reply, then nothing. Cato waited until he had recovered his breath and his heart beat steadily once again. Even though his body was still, his mind raced as he struggled to deal with the evening's events. His earlier suspicions about Anobarbus seemed to have more weight to them now. But what was the merchant's relationship with Rufius Pollo? The latter clearly feared that Cato was on to him somehow, and wanted the centurion silenced. Were they both selling information to the pirates? Cato frowned. It didn't seem to make much sense. But if Pollo was not dealing with the pirates, and nor was his friend Anobarbus, then who were they working for?

CHAPTER TWENTY-SIX

Cato left Laecus a short distance from the inn, handing him a handful of bronze coins as they parted.

'Get yourself some more wine and go home,' Cato smiled. 'You deserve it.'

'Deserve it? I bloody need it after all that sneaking around. Besides, I might just drink enough to make me forget this stench.' He pulled out a bit of his tunic and gave it a hesitant sniff. 'There's no way the wife's going to let me back in the house in this state.'

Cato patted him on the back and set off towards the naval base, keeping to the side of the streets and watching for any sign that he was being followed. As he warily made his way through Ravenna, Cato tried to concentrate on the crosscurrents of conspiracy that seemed to have caught him up. His suspicions about Anobarbus' involvement with the pirates clearly had some basis, and it made some sense. Taking payment for feeding information to the pirates was bound to be a lucrative sideline for any merchant. But how was Anobarbus linked to Rufius Pollo? He was not simply a house-guest. That was certain. Why else send men after Cato? Had the intention been to warn him off, or to take care of him permanently? It was easy enough for Cato to visualise: a swift stabbing in a filthy side street to curtail his investigations. That implied that Pollo was colluding with

Anobarbus. But it made no sense. What could Pollo possibly gain from having the pirates ravage the commerce that fed Ravenna and was the source of Pollo's wealth? Furthermore, Pollo was clearly determined to quit the port in the face of possible pirate raids. He had far more to lose from helping Telemachus than to gain. So if Anobarbus and Pollo were not working for Telemachus then who were they working for? The Liberators?

Cato paused at a street corner to rub his eyes. He had only been able to snatch a few hours' sleep over the last few days and his head ached terribly. Worse still, his mind felt clouded by fatigue and it was difficult to keep focusing on the confused situation. When he opened his eyes again and stared towards the sea, he noticed the first faint band of dawn fringing the clutter of roof tiles on the surrounding buildings. The sky was clear overhead, with the prospect of good sailing weather. The small flotilla of biremes at the naval base would be preparing to set sail within the hour and Cato pushed himself away from the wall and hurried on.

By the time he reached the naval base the sun had already risen over the horizon and dazzling golden light pierced the windows of the prefect's office and cast their outline on the far wall. Squinting, Cato gazed down on the naval harbour. All of the biremes rode at anchor, their decks covered with the bundled shapes of sleeping men. Only the *Spartan* remained moored alongside the quay, gangway down, waiting for Cato to come aboard and take command. There was a last matter to attend to first.

After quickly returning to his quarters to change back into uniform, Cato made for headquarters. Entering the administration section he pointed to the nearest clerk.

'In here, Postumus. Bring a slate.'

'Yes, sir. Begging your pardon, sir?'

'What is it?'

'Some of the officers have been asking for you all night.'

'What did you tell them?'

'Nothing, sir. Just what you said. You were in your quarters and not to be disturbed for any reason.'

'Good. That's all they need to know. Now let's get on with it.'

Once the clerk had settled on a stool beside the prefect's desk Cato dictated his orders.

'One: issue a warrant for the arrest and detention of the merchant known as Anobarbus. He might be found at the house of Rufius Pollo. Have the house watched just in case. Once Anobarbus is taken, he is to be held in isolation pending the return of the prefect and the fleet from Illyricum. He is not to be visited by anyone, nor is he to be permitted to communicate with anyone.

'Two: Rufius Pollo is to be kept under observation. I want to know who visits his house, where he goes, who he talks to. Have the information kept up to date and ready for me to read on my return.'

Cato looked up and saw the surprised expression on the face of the clerk. 'Problem?'

The clerk pursed his lips. 'Well, sir. Rufius Pollo? He's the richest, most powerful man in Ravenna. And he's got influence back in Rome. If he finds out we're spying on him . . .'

'Well, make sure he doesn't find out. Use the best men. Even a town this size must have a good network of informers.'

'Yes, sir.'

Cato searched the clerk's expression for any hint of guile. Perhaps the conspiracies that seemed to flourish in this port stretched as far as the naval base. Then Cato was angry with himself. He was starting to see enemies in every corner. Then again, maybe he should. That would be safest, but he must leave the base within the hour and ensure that steps were being taken to trap the traitors while the fleet was away dealing with the pirates. He had to trust to the loyalty of the Emperor's servants. There was no one else.

He leaned towards the clerk and indicated the slate resting on the man's lap. 'Someone in this port is betraying us to the pirates; telling them about our every movement. It's already cost us a number of ships and hundreds of men. I want them found and dealt with. If I find out that they've been warned off, then I'll make sure that those responsible will pay with their lives. Understand? This is to be kept secret. Tell only those men you need to use, and tell them only what they need to know. I'm leaving this in your hands, Postumus. Make sure you don't fail me.'

'Yes, sir. Is there anything else?'

'No . . .'

Postumus nodded. 'Very well, sir. Can I ask what authority I can act on if your orders cause any conflict with the officer you're leaving in command here?'

'Wait.' Cato pulled a blank wax tablet over and hurriedly wrote a note to cover the clerk's instructions. When he had finished Cato saw the prefect's seal box sitting at the edge of the desk. He pulled it over, lifted the teak lid and took out the seal of the commander of the Ravenna fleet. He pressed the seal firmly into the wax, checked the imprint was sound and slid the tablet across the table to Postumus. 'There. Until Vitellius returns you have the final say in this matter. You're only to use this if the centurion gives any orders likely to compromise your investigations.'

'I understand, sir.'

Cato saluted and the clerk turned away and left the office. For a moment Cato stared at the desk, torn between two duties. More than anything he wanted to find those who had betrayed their countrymen to the pirates. There was nothing more despicable, to his mind, than men who were prepared to put individual greed before the greater good of the Empire and its people. Their base treachery would cost them their lives. But there was nothing else he could do about that now. Hundreds of miles away in Illyricum his comrades were waiting for badly needed reinforcements to tip the balance against Telemachus and his pirates. Even now, they might already have been attacked again, perhaps even defeated and wiped out. Cato clenched his fists at the thought. That was foolish. Worse, it was a moment of puerile panic. The pirates had had the advantage in the first encounter, thanks to treachery. Next time the Roman warships would be unencumbered by provisions and equipment, and there would be more of them. The pirates were not likely to survive a second head-on engagement. Even Vitellius couldn't make a mess of that.

Cato tried to recall as much of the meeting with Telemachus as he could. The man was cool and collected, a realist, ruthless. He would not be duped into a battle he could not win. It was far more likely that he would adopt a strategy of attrition: pouncing on isolated Roman foragers and patrol vessels, wearing the Romans down until their campaign had to be abandoned, or until they were reduced to a weak enough condition for the pirates to risk a final, devastating attack. Between the thirsty ambition of Vitellius and the cunning and guile of Telemachus things looked bleak for the men of the Ravenna fleet.

Cato thumped his fist down in frustration as he rose from

his chair. He strode out of his office and left the headquarters building. Across the parade ground, beside the wharf, the *Spartan* stood ready to sail. The marine guard at the head of the gangway stiffened to attention and grounded his spear as the centurion approached.

As soon as his boots clumped down on to the deck Cato called out to the trierarch. 'Get underway immediately!'

Cato made his way aft and stood by the oarsman as the sailors shipped the gangway and cast off the mooring lines. Several men raised a stout post and thrust the bows out from the wharf, then worked their way down the length of the vessel, easing her out, until there was a sufficient gap to allow the crew to slip the long oars out from her sides. As the pausarius beat a slow rhythm the oars steadily swept through the water, churning the surface as the *Spartan* began to glide forward, out into the naval harbour towards the rest of the flotilla. Seeing this, the trierarchs of the biremes bellowed out orders to raise anchors and get underway, taking up station behind the *Spartan*.

The flotilla emerged into the main harbour and a few early risers stood and watched from the wharf and the decks of the merchant vessels crowded into the safety of the harbour defences. From the stern of the trireme Cato gazed out over the sprawl of warehouses and the red-tiled roofs of the town beyond. Already the distance made the buildings look like toys.

With the sun now well clear of the horizon, the *Spartan* turned into the open sea, directly into the dazzling orb. Her bows lifted to the increase in the swell of the sea and Cato sensed a faint breeze on his cheek. As soon as the warships were clear of the land the trierarch gave the order to ship oars and raise the mainsail.

Cato's eyes closed for a moment, blinked open, closed

again, and then he surrendered to the warm, comforting desire for rest. There was a sudden whirling sensation and he opened his eyes just in time to stop himself from falling on to the deck.

'You all right, sir?'

Cato glanced round at the helmsman. 'I'm fine. Just tired. Think I'll sit down for a moment.'

He lowered himself to the deck and braced his back against the side of the vessel. An hour's rest. That's all. Just an hour, Cato told himself firmly. Moments later his head dipped forward until his chin rested on the folds of his cloak. He breathed heavily and regularly, completely oblivious to the rise and fall of the deck and the bustle of the crew as they settled the *Spartan* down for the day's sailing.

The oarsman glanced down at him, smiled and shook his head, before concentrating on keeping his vessel on course for distant Illyricum.

CHAPTER TWENTY-SEVEN

'They've been kept busy.' Albinus nodded towards the shore and Cato followed his gaze and saw that the beachhead's defences had been much expanded and improved in the few days that he had been absent. A large fort rose up a short distance from the beach with high ramparts surrounded by a triple defence ditch. Two stockade walls extended down to the sea to protect the fleet, most of which had been beached, though a handful of vessels rode at anchor. A lookout station had been erected on the nearest headland and, as Cato watched, a signal flag was fluttering from the watchtower, to be answered by a distant flash of colour from the fort. At once there was a flurry of activity aboard the ships anchored off shore. Cato squinted to catch the detail and saw tiny figures forming up on the fore and aft decks, the sun twinkling on polished armour and weapons. Moments later the oars were unshipped and the triremes began to edge away from the shore towards the *Spartan*, and the column of smaller biremes sailing in tight formation behind her.

Albinus turned towards Cato and smiled. 'Seems like they're taking no chances with us.'

Cato nodded. 'Good thing too. The fleet's had more than enough surprises. I think the prefect's finally learning.'

Albinus glanced at the centurion. 'You've served with him before, then?'

'In Germany, then in Britain. He was the resident broad-striper amongst the tribunes.'

'I see. How did he perform?'

Cato paused a moment to consider the issue. He recalled the time he had fought alongside Tribune Vitellius, defending a small German village against a horde of barbarian warriors who had managed to lure a cohort of the Second Legion into a cleverly worked ambush. Vitellius had shown his courage in the desperate hours that followed. The trouble was, ever since, he had proved to be a venal traitor who had not one shred of compassion for any man or woman who dared bar his route to power. Already a number of corpses lay strewn in the wake of the young aristocrat. He was a dangerous man to most, and downright lethal to those who posed any threat to him. For Albinus' sake Cato dare not tell him the whole truth. He coughed and looked towards the shore as he answered. 'He performed well enough. He's got the balls for the job. Just don't cross his path.'

Cato sensed Albinus staring at him, waiting for more, but the centurion kept his silence and in the end Albinus turned away, and muttered quietly, 'Fair enough, Centurion. I understand. Don't worry about me. I'll keep my distance.'

'See that you do.'

There was a shout from the mast-top. 'Fort's signalling, sir!'

The two officers glanced towards the small fort on the headland and saw a green pennant flicker out to one side in the wind as it rose up the signal mast.

'It's a challenge,' Albinus explained. Then he cupped a hand to his mouth and shouted an order forward to the mainmast. 'Make the recognition signal and get our colours up!'

A pair of sailors took a bundle of red material from a side locker and hurried to the ratlines, before attaching the toggles at the end of the pennants to a sheet. Then the pennant was quickly hauled up to the top of the mast where it whipped out with a dull crackle in the afternoon breeze. There was a short pause, then the pennant flying over the fortlet dipped down and vanished. The ships in the bay eased up on their oars, turned round and headed back to their anchorage. Then, almost at once, another pennant rose up above the fort and Albinus stiffened beside Cato, and then turned round to scan the horizon.

'What is it?' Cato asked anxiously.

'The fort's sighted a sail.'

'A sail?' Cato raised a hand to shade his eyes and looked north along the coast. He saw it almost at once: a tiny dark triangle, almost invisible against the distant coastline. He raised his other arm and pointed. 'There! See it?'

Albinus followed the direction indicated and screwed up his eyes as he tried to make out the details. 'No . . . I . . . Wait a moment. Yes, I see it. A galley, I think.' He paused to look at Cato, eyebrows raised. 'Damn, you've fine eyes. I'd never have seen it. I'm getting old.' He turned back towards the distant sail. 'Must be a pirate, keeping watch on the fleet. Well, now they'll know we've made good our losses. Telemachus won't be risking another sea battle, I'm thinking.'

Cato nodded. 'Not if he's half as crafty as he seems. From now on, it's going to be a contest of strength over guile.'

Albinus scratched his chin. 'The question is, whose strength and whose guile?'

The sky had turned a dull pasty blue as the squadron of reinforcements rowed slowly towards the beach. On deck the sailors were busy dragging up a stout cable and thick wooden stake from below deck to tether the trireme securely to the shore. The marines, and all spare hands, clustered in front of the aft deck to help raise the bows of the trireme as they approached the shore. There was a splash from behind as an anchor was dropped over the stern. The cable rasped out through the aft hawse as the vessel crept towards the shingle where tiny waves crashed and foamed up the gentle slope, before rushing back towards the next wave. Further up the beach a figure watched the ships glide in. The red cloak and gleaming breastplate revealed him to be the prefect, surveying the new arrivals. Cato stared at the prefect with a bitter expression as he recalled the contents of Vitellius' report. Then his lips flickered into a smile as he thought of the message he had replaced the report with. By now it was well on the way to Rome. There was a gentle shudder through the timbers beneath Cato's boots as the bows had grounded. The vessel lifted for an instant, then settled with a more solid jarring sensation and those standing on deck lurched forward as the trireme stopped moving.

'Cease rowing!' Albinus bellowed. 'Ship oars, and get the gangways down!'

On either side, the rest of the small squadron drew up to the shore and beached themselves on the shingle. Sturdy ramps were manoeuvred out through the hinged openings to one side of the prow of each vessel, before dropping down on to the shore. As soon as the way was clear, Cato marched down the gangway and crunched up the shingle towards the prefect, waiting amongst the tussocks of grass that grew beyond the high-water mark. After nearly two days at sea, the ground seemed to pitch and dip beneath him and he tried to walk as steadily as he could. Ahead of him, Prefect Vitellius took a step forward and Cato saluted him.

'Centurion Cato! Here at last. I was starting to wonder what had happened to you!'

Even though the prefect was smiling, there was no mistaking the implied rebuke and Cato clenched his teeth angrily before he could make himself reply in a cordial enough manner.

'We came as soon as we could, sir. Ask my trierarch.'

'There's no need for that!' Vitellius clapped him on the shoulder. 'We're glad to see you. I can use the men.' He lowered his voice. 'Truth is, I need them badly. The way things are going I'm not sure if we're hunting the pirates, or they're hunting us.'

'It can't be that bad, sir.'

Vitellius chuckled bitterly. 'You don't think so? Well, right now I'll take whatever good spirits I can get . . .' The prefect paused to stare out to sea. 'Bloody bastard pirates. As Jupiter is my judge, I'll make them pay for daring to defy Rome.'

'Yes, sir.'

'Come. We need to talk. In my tent.'

The prefect turned and walked back towards the gate of the fortified camp, and Cato followed. Inside the camp the rows of tents stretched out each side of the main thoroughfare. Most were the usual goatskin, but a number of them were made from linen and heavily stained and worn leather, and Cato realised that they were cut from old sails to make good those lost. Men were sitting in front of their tents, and they jumped up to salute as the two officers passed by. Cato saw the tense and worn expressions in their faces and wondered what had happened in his absence.

As they reached the tents of the fleet's headquarters, erected on a slight mound in the heart of the camp, a light breeze lifted the flaps and Cato savoured its coolness. Then the smell hit him: the sharp acrid smell of burned fat, hanging across the camp even in the faint breeze blowing offshore. Vitellius glanced round as they entered the largest of the tents, and caught Cato's puzzled expression.

'It's the funeral pyres. We cremated the dead a few days ago.'

Cato glanced up at the prefect and noted, to his surprise, that Vitellius seemed to have been moved by the fate of his men. Or was it simply the inconvenience their deaths had caused him?

The prefect grimaced. 'It was quite a sight. And there'll be more. We lost another eight men in the night. One of them didn't stop screaming right until the end. Between that and the raids we've not had much rest.'

'Raids, sir?'

'Oh, yes,' Vitellius smiled wearily. 'Our friends have kept up the pressure. Three days back they landed some men further up the coast. They've been picking off our sentries and foraging parties with slingshot. Every time I send out a detachment to chase them down, they turn and run for the hills. In fact, your friend Macro's out hunting for them right now. I didn't even have to ask him to volunteer.'

'I can imagine, sir.'

'At the same time they've tried a few cutting-out expeditions: sending in a few small boats at night to try and snatch one of the triremes.' Vitellius gestured vaguely towards the sky as he slumped down on a couch; one of the luxuries he had brought with him from Ravenna. 'We've been lucky with the moonlight the last few days, and seen them in time to drive them off. But the next few nights are going to be darker. And then . . .' He shook his head.

Cato felt the dead weight of exhaustion and despair settle on his shoulders. The prefect had done nothing to take the fight to the pirates then. He had just sat inside the fortifications and passed the initiative to Telemachus.

'What about your plan, sir?'

'Plan?'

'To patrol the coast. Find their base.'

'That's in hand. I sent six of the triremes up the coast the day after we landed. They didn't find anything. The coast here is a mass of small islands and inlets. You could hide the Misene fleet in these waters for years without anyone discovering a single ship. It's hopeless.'

Cato kept silent and regarded the prefect closely. Vitellius was clearly at his wits' end. With the defeat at sea, and now the operation stalled on land, the situation must look bleak indeed to the ambitious aristocrat. Behind everything else that was going on lay the retrieval of the scrolls. Cato was wholly aware that his future and that of Vitellius depended on finding the scrolls and making sure that they were safely delivered into the hands of Narcissus. But whereas the prefect might suffer a fall from grace if they failed to find the scrolls, the consequences for Cato, and Macro, would be far more deadly. The prefect had to be persuaded, or provoked, into going on the attack.

Besides, Cato reasoned with himself, the stakes were high for others as well. The men under Vitellius' command needed a victory. The enemy must not be allowed to whittle them down. If the worst happened and the Ravenna fleet was defeated, then the whole of the Adriatic could be pillaged by the pirates, and it would take months to gather another fleet strong enough to defeat them. Thousands more lives would be lost, scores of ports and settlements sacked and few merchant vessels would dare to leave port. Trade, the lifeblood of the Roman economy, would be choked off; strangled just as effectively as Cato would be at the hands of one of the executioners of the Praetorian Guard. Cato winced at the unpleasant thought. Very well then, his fate was linked directly to that of Rome. For that reason he must convince Vitellius to act swiftly. For everyone's sake.

He coughed, clearing his throat.

Vitellius looked up, raising an eyebrow. 'Yes?'

'Sir, it's the scrolls. We have to get them.'

'Tell me something I don't know, Centurion.'

'Well, we can't get them if we just wait here, sir. We . . . you have to do something. We can't just let them bottle us up in this camp and bide their time. Right now, we must outnumber them. We have more men, more ships—'

'For now,' Vitellius cut in bitterly. 'But it'll be dark tonight, and every night until the next moon. You can be sure they'll be coming back for another attempt on our ships.'

There was a sudden thrill of activity in Cato's mind. Ideas rushed to the front of his consciousness, and possibilities and the consequences of possibilities flowed in a torrent of thoughts. Very soon, he had the outline of a plan – a small plan, to be sure – but one that would wrest the initiative back from the pirates, and mark the first step in setting the men of the Ravenna fleet back on the offensive. Cato looked across to the prefect, his eyes bright with an excitement he found impossible to repress.

'Well then, sir,' Cato smiled, 'let 'em come. In fact, let's make sure they come. Let's offer them some bait they can't refuse.'

CHAPTER TWENTY-EIGHT

'This was not a good idea,' Macro growled as he squinted into the darkness. Over the side of the ship they could hear the waves breaking gently on the shingle some distance away. The black mass of the arms of the small bay they had chosen for the ambush stretched out around them. Away from the land, the sky and sea blurred together into a forbidding gloom.

'Can hardly see a bloody thing,' Macro continued.

'That's the whole idea,' Cato replied patiently. 'It'll work in our favour. Trust me.'

Cato could just make out the weary look on his friend's face as they sat on the deck. All around them marines were sitting in strict silence against the sides of the bireme, weapons close to hand. Linen side screens had been erected around the deck to give the ship the profile of a merchant vessel. After six days' cruising along the coast the disguise had finally lured some overeager pirates. From a distance, or in the dark, the bireme would pass for something far more innocent, and tempting, as it quietly wallowed in the gentle swell.

The only signs of life were up on the beach – a handful of campfires, around which huddled the sailors from the bireme. Two men stood sentry, dimly visible on the fringes of the light cast by the fire – the same light that would silhouette the bireme from the sea. That was what Cato was counting on. Somewhere, out to sea, stood the three ships that had shadowed the bireme during the afternoon. They had been cautious enough, hovering on the horizon, no doubt suspicious of such easy-looking prey. The bireme had played its part well enough, affecting some slovenly watch-keeping before turning away from the threat at the last moment, going cumbersomely about and fleeing from the pirates as dusk fell.

The pirates too were playing their own game, having moved away as if they had given up the chase and were sailing back up the coast. Shortly before they were out of sight Cato gave the order for the bireme to head into land, steering towards the bay he had reconnoitred the day before and decided at once that it would be suitable for his trap. A concealed battery of catapults stood close to the shore at the base of each low headland, ready to sweep the surface of the sea between them when the time came to spring the ambush. Two more biremes were anchored in the shadows of a small cliff, ready to slip their cables and row into action. If the pirates took the bait there would be little chance of escape.

As Cato reflected on the details of his plan, he was suddenly struck by a terrible sense of doubt. Supposing the pirates had given up the chase, as they had seemed to, and were even now bedded down and peacefully sleeping many miles away up the coast? Come the morning the marines and sailors who had spent an uncomfortable night under arms, nerves strained in the long wait for the appearance of the enemy, would be bitter and angry and would curse the young centurion and take him for a fool. On top of their recent defeat and the pirate raids of the previous nights it could only further damage their morale.

If this ambush failed Cato had no doubt that the prefect would not be willing to try anything else and Telemachus would have his victory over the Roman navy. A dangerous precedent would have been set for any other pirates lurking around the fringes of the Mediterranean. The Emperor would show no mercy to those he held responsible for such a state of affairs . . .

Macro stirred beside him, and peered over the side, glancing out to sea. He sniffed irritably and slumped back down beside Cato.

'I'm telling you, they aren't coming,' he said softly. 'We must have been waiting for at least six hours already. We're wasting our time.'

'Patience,' Cato hissed back. 'They'll come.'

'How can you be so sure?'

'They're pirates, aren't they?'

'Pretty bloody smart pirates,' Macro responded bitterly. 'They've had the drop on us from the moment this campaign started. What makes you think they'll fall for it?'

'Think about it. They've been snapping up prizes for months. The result is that more and more merchants have been afraid to come out of port. It's the pirates' very success that has been starving them of prey for the last month or so. I'd bet that we're the first merchant ship they've seen for a long time. They won't be able to resist the temptation. I'd bet my life on it.'

Macro grunted. 'You are betting your life on it. Mine too.'

Cato shrugged. 'Then you'd best pray that I'm right.'

'And if they don't come?'

Cato didn't reply, but just sat quite still, head cocked slightly to one side.

Macro nudged him. 'Well?'

'Quiet . . .' Cato tensed and stared out to sea, his body motionless.

'What is it?'

'I'm not sure . . . Over there, look.' Cato pointed towards the black mass of the nearest of the headlands and Macro followed the direction of his finger and strained his eyes to make out any detail.

'Can't see anything.'

'No?'

Macro shook his head.

'Me neither,' Cato admitted with a soft chuckle.

'Very fucking funny. I just hope you find it as funny when the Emperor has us thrown to . . .' Macro glanced out to sea and nudged Cato. 'Looks like you were right after all.'

Cato snapped his head round and saw the enemy vessel at once, as if it had simply materialised from the gloom. The pirates had unstepped the mast to lower the profile and the slender oars were muffled as they slowly propelled the ship into the bay no more than half a mile away.

'Pass the word!' Macro prodded the nearest marine with his boot. 'Enemy in sight. Make ready but no one moves until the signal is given. Go.'

The marine shuffled off in the darkness to spread the word and the two centurions turned back to stare at the approaching pirate vessel. Cato grasped Macro's arm. 'There . . . to one side. The other two. Looks like we'll make a clean sweep of it.'

'Got to catch them first.'

'Yes . . .'

As they watched, the enemy vessels crept forward across the bay, gaining definition as each thrust of the oars brought them closer. Soon they could hear the soft splash and rush of the pirates' oars and could make out the white surge of water along the bows. Above the prow of each vessel a dense mass of dark shapes crowded the fore deck, still and silent as they closed on their prey. Macro slowly drew his sword and clenched his hairy fist around the handle. He looked at Cato.

'Not yet,' Cato whispered. He looked past Macro to where the nearest marine grasped a boarding grapple, with a length of rope dipping down to coil resting on the deck. He caught the man's eye and waved his hand down. The marine hurriedly lowered his head.

The enemy came on and Cato's mind raced at the prospect of the imminent struggle. His heart pounded with excitement and his mouth was quite dry. In a moment it would all begin and chaos would rage over the deck that surrounded him. Three centuries of marines crouched motionless behind the linen superstructure and Cato could sense their tension, determination to kill, and fear. Nearly two hundred and fifty of them, each with a white band tied about his head for identification. But how many pirates were aboard those ships gliding down towards them? A hundred on each, Cato guessed. It would be a closely fought battle before the other two biremes could join the struggle. But once they did, then the fate of the pirates would surely be sealed.

Above the soft lapping of the water along the hulls Cato could now hear the first quiet words of command, and the excitement in the voice was unmistakable. Cato smiled. The pirates must think that their approach had not been detected and they were about to pounce on the merchant ship without the alarm even being raised. With a jarring thud the bow of the lead pirate ship ground into the side of the bireme and scraped along the beam. The other ships glided towards the stern and across the bow, ready to add their crews to the boarding party.

Cato snatched a lungful of air and jumped to his feet. 'NOW!'

With a deep-throated roar the marines rose up from the shadows and tore down the linen screens that had disguised their warship. Those who had been equipped with boarding grapples swung them up and out and they sailed through the darkness, thudding down on to the decks of the enemy vessels. At once the lines were pulled tight, the barbs lodging in the timbers of the pirate ships, and they were drawn in towards the bireme. At the stern a flame crackled into life as a marine set a lamp to the oil-drenched beacon prepared earlier. The wavering glow lit up the marines swarming across the deck, as well as the shocked and surprised faces of the pirates aboard the vessel held fast to the stern of the bireme. Moments later more flames flared up in the distance to acknowledge the signal and the trap was complete.

For a moment the pirates were silent, then their leaders roared out orders and with a great cheer they clambered up on to the rails of their vessels and threw themselves at the Romans.

'GET 'EM!' Macro roared close by, and the marines pressed forward to meet the enemy. For a moment the two sides were distinct and separate and then there was only chaos as the deck of the bireme was covered in a mass of bodies hacking and slashing at each other with swords, daggers, clubs and axes. In the pale light of the beacon only the white headbands of the marines could distinguish one side from the other. Around Cato a thin line of marines dissolved as the pirates jumped in amongst them and threw themselves into the attack.

'Look out!' a voice cried in Cato's ear as five or six dark

forms flew through the air and crashed down on the Romans. Cato snatched up his small round buckler and thrust it towards the nearest enemy. The pirate sprawled across the centurion, carrying them both down on to the deck, the impact driving the air from Cato's lungs in an explosive gasp of pain. He felt smothered, and the stench of the man's hot breath was in his face as Cato dropped his buckler and clawed over the pirate's shoulder, searching for his throat, clamping his fingers down on the windpipe. The man reared up, choking with agony as he tore himself free of Cato's grasp. Then there was an explosive grunt as Cato slammed the tip of his sword into the man's side, just below the ribcage. The pirate wrenched himself free, toppling away from Cato and a warm gush of blood splashed down on to Cato's arm. He thrust himself up and crouched low on the deck, glancing madly about as the fight raged on every side. Above the clatter of weapons and the groans and cries of the men locked in conflict, Cato heard Macro yelling out to his men at the top of his voice.

'Get them! Kill them all! Kill 'em!'

Cato grabbed the buckler from the deck and pushed his way into the mêlée, thrusting himself between two marines hacking away at the heaving crowd of pirates who had forced their way on to the deck of the Roman ship. Directly in front of Cato a huge man landed on the deck with a thud. He wore a linen cuirass and brandished a heavy curved blade, which he swung back over his head the moment he saw the Roman officer in front of him.

'No you don't!' Cato shouted, sweeping his buckler up to meet the blow and thrusting his sword forward. The blade caught the man in the chest, making him stagger back a pace, but the point only cracked the surface of the cuirass, and made a shallow cut into the muscle beyond before it fetched up against a bone. Even so, it robbed the blow that hissed down at Cato of much of its force and the sword glanced off the buckler with a dull ring and struck the deck. A searing pain shot up Cato's left arm and his fingers went numb, nervelessly releasing their grip on the handle of the buckler, which fell away. Cato snatched back his blade, altered the angle and thrust the point up into the soft flesh under the pirate's chin, and punched it into the man's skull. The pirate toppled backwards and Cato wrenched the blade back with a wet crunch.

He straightened up, glancing round, but it was impossible to tell how the fight was going. The writhing mass of marines and pirates was too confused for Cato to work out which side had the upper hand. Over the heads of his men he could see the growing flicker from the beacon on one of the biremes rowing towards the fight. Then he was aware of another enemy rushing forwards, swinging an axe as he pressed in towards Cato, teeth locked in a wild grimace of hatred and rage in the dim glare of the flares of light from the aft deck.

A sudden surge of men closed in on Cato, pressing into his flesh, and to his horror he found that his sword arm was pinned to his side. The pirate snarled with glee and then swept his axe round, slicing through the night air at Cato's neck. Cato lashed out with his boots and slipped down towards the deck. Above him the axe swished overhead and crunched through the spine of the man standing next to Cato. On his hands and knees Cato felt the warm drizzle of blood splattering down across his shoulders. As dark bodies drove him on to his side a new terror gripped him: that he might be crushed to death on the deck. Shielding his head as best as he could with his numb left arm, Cato held his sword close, ready to thrust, and tried to regain his feet. But a fresh surge knocked him down, and at once a booted foot stamped down on his chest.

'Get off!' Cato shouted. 'Get off me!'

A face glanced down in shock and at once the boot was removed. 'Sorry, sir.'

Before Cato could reply the broad tip of a spear plunged into the man's throat and carried him back, out of sight. Cato knew that if he did not get off the deck soon he would be dead. He drew a deep breath and powered himself up, lashing out with sword and fist at anybody in his way, regardless of whether it was pirate or marine. Then he was up again, feet braced apart and sword ready. The press of the mêlée had passed him by and now the focus of the fight was moving aft, behind the mast. He stepped aside as a handful of marines swept past and threw themselves into the struggling mass. Breathing heavily, Cato took a moment to glance round and saw that one of the biremes was only moments away. Her marines were crowded above the prow, ready to join the battle and decide the outcome. Cato turned and saw the other bireme slightly further away, oars surging through the sea as she hurried towards the fight.

But already one of the pirate trierarchs had realised the terrible danger he and his men were facing. Beyond the stern of Cato's bireme, he could see one of the pirate ships lurching away, then snag on one of the grappling lines. A distant shout sent one of the pirates running to the side rail and he parted the line under a flurry of axe blows.

'Shit . . .' Cato muttered. The ship would escape unless someone was alerted to its trierarch's intentions. Only the furthest bireme could intercept in time, but the mêlée on the deck stood between Cato and the stern, from where he could attract their attention and shout his warning. He sheathed his sword, hurried to the side of the bireme and threw his legs over the rail, scrabbling for purchase on the planking with the toes of his boots. Then he began to work his way aft, the dark glimmer of the sea a short distance below. Beyond the rail the scrape of weapons and curses and cries of the battle continued and Cato kept his head low as he shuffled awkwardly along the side of the bireme. Then the rail began to curve up towards the steering oars and the sweeping fan of the sternpost. Gritting his teeth, Cato strained his arms and pulled himself up, but as soon as his head rose above the rail a thin pirate smiled toothlessly and leaned towards him, dagger drawn back to slash Cato across the throat. Just as Cato was preparing to throw himself backward into the sea a burly arm wrapped itself round the pirate's neck, yanking him off his feet. The man grunted and then his whole body spasmed, before it toppled to one side and Macro plucked his blade from beneath the pirate's shoulder.

Macro's eyebrows rose as he caught sight of his friend. 'Centurion Cato, leaving so soon?'

'Shut up and give me a hand.'

As soon as Cato was aboard he saw that the fight on the bireme's deck was going the Romans' way. The pirates had been forced amidships and were fighting back to back around the mast, urged on by an ornately dressed man whose heavy gold rings glimmered in the light of the beacon. Cato nodded his satisfaction and then indicated the pirate vessel pulling away into the darkness. 'Bastard's trying to give us the slip.'

'Can't be having that,' Macro grinned as Cato turned towards the bireme that had still not managed to join the fight. He cupped a hand to his mouth and shouted across the water. 'Alter course! Stop them getting away!' He thrust his arm out towards the fleeing pirate ship. 'Get after them!'

There was a moment's delay before the bows of the bireme slowly swung away and with a surge of oars she swept narrowly past the grappled ships and went after the surviving pirate ship. The two vessels made for the entrance to the bay where glittering torches now marked the positions of the hidden batteries. The clatter of ratchets carried across the waters as the artillery crews wound back the torsion arms and prepared to fire at the oncoming ships. Cato and Macro could hardly make them out as they blended with the dark sea as the pirates desperately made for the open sea, pursued by the Roman warship. Moments later a glittering streak of fire arced up from the nearest headland towards the middle of the bay, silhouetting the hull of one of the ships before the flaming bolt struck the sea and was instantly extinguished.

'They'll have his range soon enough,' Macro commented, just as three more bolts arced into the night sky. Moments later the sharp cracks of their released torsion arms carried across the bay. The battery on the other side began to join the barrage and scored a hit with their first attempt, sending a shower of sparks springing into the air as the flaming bolt lodged in the pirate ship's deck. A distant cheer echoed off the cliff rising up from the shore, and the barrage continued.

Macro nudged Cato. 'I've just had a nasty thought.'

'Me too,' Cato muttered bitterly. 'I should have realised the danger.'

The two centurions fell silent as the fiery barrage arced over its glittering reflection in the sea, and shortly afterwards the bireme took its first hit. As they watched, the Roman ship was struck two more times.

'Shit!' Cato pounded his fist on the wooden rail. 'I should have known!'

A small fire had started on the pirate ship and as distant

figures struggled to douse the flames the trierarch of the bireme quickly turned his vessel about and headed back into the bay at full speed as the excited crews on the catapult concentrated their fire on the lead vessel. Before the bireme could get out of range a final shot caught in the furled sail and set it alight. Meanwhile another fire had flared up on the pirate ship and as the flames spread, the men at the oars fled from their benches and began to dive over the side, abandoning the vessel to a raging inferno that lit up the entrance to the bay in a brilliant but terrible glare of red and orange. Closer inshore the crew of the bireme were struggling to extinguish their own fire with a chain of sailors passing water up to men sitting astride the spar, who desperately attempted to quench the flames.

Cato thumped the rail again, consumed with frustration and self-reproach, until Macro slapped a kindly hand on his shoulder.

'There's nothing we can do about that. Besides, we've done well enough tonight. Now it's time to finish up here.' Macro nodded down towards the knot of enemy hemmed in around the mast.

A fresh wave of marines from the other bireme was swarming over the bows and chasing down and slaughtering the few pirates still alive at the prow.

The two centurions picked their way over the tangle of bodies and descended the steps to the main deck. Macro sheathed his sword and roughly pushed aside a handful of marines at the edge of the mêlée.

'Pull back!' he bellowed. 'Pull back! Give 'em some space!'

The order was relayed through the marines by the junior officers, and the marines gradually broke away from the pirates, warily stepping backwards across the deck, made slippery by the blood. The men took care where they placed their feet to avoid tripping over the bodies sprawled beneath them. A space opened up around the handful of bloodied men clustered on the main deck. They glared their defiance at the marines and kept their weapons raised and ready to use. An uncanny silence filled the air as the fighting ended and men on both sides waited expectantly. Cato and Macro pushed their way through the marines until they emerged a few paces away from the surviving pirates. Cato sought out the leader he had seen earlier and pointed towards him.

'Tell your men to surrender!'

The pirate leader stared back and then sneered his defiance. Something about him was familiar and Cato frowned, trying to place the man. Before he could make the connection the man brandished his curved sword.

'No surrender, Roman!' he screamed in Greek. 'We'll not die like dogs on your crosses!'

Cato raised his hand to try to calm the man down, and replied in the same tongue. 'I give my word you'll not be executed. Slaves you will be, but at least your lives will be spared.'

'Never!' the pirate leader shrieked. But even as he spat his defiance at the centurion there was a dull clatter as one of his men threw down his sword and bowed his head. His comrades glanced from him to their leader and then another weapon thudded down on to the deck. An instant later, only the pirates' leader still held his weapon and he stared from side to side in frustration.

Cato held out his hand. 'Give it up, man. You've lost the fight. No sense in losing your life.'

The young man gritted his teeth and for a moment Cato was certain he was determined to go down fighting. Then his resolve crumbled and the sword fell from his trembling fingers as he stared hatefully at the Romans. And then Cato remembered exactly where he had seen him before. On the deck of Telemachus' trireme. Even now he recalled how close this man had been to the leader of the pirates.

'Ajax,' Cato muttered.

CHAPTER TWENTY-NINE

'But I gave my word,' Cato protested, and glanced round at Macro for support. The older centurion gave a slight shrug.

'You gave your word,' Vitellius repeated with a faint smile, as he glanced past Cato towards the prisoners, chained together in a small circle as they stood on the beach. A squad of marines stood in a loose circle around them, keeping guard. Vitellius shook his head. 'What makes you think that we should honour any promise given to those murdering pirate scum.'

'It was the condition for their surrender. I agreed terms with their captain, Ajax.'

'Well, more fool him. Have the leader separated from the others. If he's one of Telemachus' top men, as you seem to think, then we might be able to squeeze some useful information out of him. Bring this Ajax to headquarters and we'll go to work on him. But the rest will be crucified. Do our men good to see them nailed up.' He glanced round and pointed up at the headland. 'Up there. Where the enemy can see them, and our own men can enjoy the view.'

'Sir, I must protest.'

'Fine. You've made your protest. Now do me the kindness of allowing me to arrange for their execution.'

Cato's mouth opened, closed and opened again as he shook his head. 'This isn't right . . .'

Prefect Vitellius nodded. 'I agree. It isn't right, it's war. And this discussion is over. Now see to it that your ships are beached and the men given an extra ration of wine. They deserve it. Make sure they understand it's on my instructions. I'll want reports from both of you by the end of the day. You can do that after we've questioned the prisoner.' He gave a curt wave of the hand. 'Dismissed.'

Cato and Macro saluted, turned stiffly away and crunched down the shingle slope to the shoreline.

'Thanks for your support,' Cato muttered.

Macro shrugged. 'Sorry, but I'm with the prefect on this one. They're pirates. They should have known that they could expect no mercy from us.' Macro frowned at him. 'Don't go all soft on me, Cato. Those bastards down there had it coming to them the moment they decided to take us on. Besides, if the position was reversed, if we were their prisoners, do you really think they'd show us any mercy?'

Cato refused to meet his friend's gaze and glanced down at his boots. 'No. But that's what gives our side the moral authority. That's what makes fighting for Rome worth the while.'

'Moral authority?' Macro stopped dead and stared at Cato for an instant before he exploded with laughter. 'Fuck me, lad, you really do come up with them, don't you?'

Cato looked back, scowling over his shoulder. 'Let's just get on with it, shall we? After all, we're just obeying orders.'

'Surely!' Macro slapped his friend heartily on the back. 'Sometimes, I tell you, orders are a positive pleasure to carry out . . .'

Cato glared at him and Macro laughed again. 'Only joking. Come on.'

A crowd of marines from the fortified camp had gathered by the shore to examine the pirates and jeered loudly as a few amongst them lobbed pebbles at the prisoners. Even as the two centurions approached Cato saw Ajax reel as a stone gashed his forehead.

'Hey!' Macro roared out, making the nearest marines jump. 'Stop that! We need that one in good condition!'

The men drew aside as Macro and Cato approached the prisoners. In addition to the injuries they had received two nights earlier, several now had cuts from the stones that had been thrown at them. Normally the marines might have been a little more careful with captives who could realise a decent price in a slave auction, but since these men were pirates there was little chance that they would be spared, and therefore they could be freely abused by their captors.

Macro beckoned to the optio in command of the guards. 'The prefect's arranging a little display for this lot. Take them to the master carpenter's workshop. Except for him.' Macro pointed to the pirates' leader. 'He's coming with us. Cut him loose from the others.'

'Yes, sir.' The optio saluted.

The prisoners were jostled into a rough column while their young leader was taken to one side, under the eye of a marine who kept a firm hand on his shoulder while the other rested on the pommel of his sword. Ajax watched in sullen silence as his men were led into the camp, chains jingling as the shingle crunched under their bare feet.

Meanwhile, the two centurions strode down to the biremes beached in the shallows where Cato gave orders for repairs to the fire-damaged bireme while Macro organised the unloading of the wounded, and passed on the news of the prefect's extra issue of wine. The last order raised a good-humoured cheer and the men eagerly set to work to finish their duties and clean their kit, all the while looking forward to the prospect of getting out of their skins on the cheap, but potent, wine procured for the navy.

Cato watched them for a moment with a growing feeling of contempt. More than a few grateful toasts would be made to Vitellius that evening for the extra ration of wine. The same Vitellius who had only days before led them into a disastrous sea-battle that had cost the lives of hundreds of their comrades. Were their memories so short? Then again, the successful ambush of the pirates had won them back a large measure of confidence, and the improvement in their spirit had been evident to Cato as the crews of three biremes, their two prizes and the prisoners had made their way back down the coast to join the rest of the fleet. Now Vitellius was trying to buy himself back into their affections, and Cato had no doubt that he would succeed the instant these men sank into the warm intoxicating embrace of the prefect's gift.

Cato turned towards the prisoner and looked him over closely once again. He was sure of it. This was the same man he had seen aboard the pirate flagship, alongside Telemachus . . . The pirate chief referred to him as a lieutenant. But as Cato struggled to recall the moment in as much detail as possible he was dimly aware that there had to be more to it than that. Ajax was no mere underling. He was one of the pirate chief's senior men. And now he had fallen into Roman hands. Small wonder that Vitellius had been so pleased with the result. At last they had some kind of advantage over their elusive foe.

Ajax turned his head, scanning the ships and the men around him with a keen intelligence, then he met Cato's eyes and glanced down, bowing his head and letting his shoulders sag into a very convincing aspect of dejection.

Cato smiled. The man was good, and was going to play up to his captors for all he was worth.

As soon as Macro was satisfied that all was in order he strolled over to Cato. 'Ready? Then let's take this little beauty back to headquarters for a chat.' He strode over and raising his vine cane Macro prodded Ajax in the small of his back. 'Come on, let's be having you!'

The prisoner lurched forward with a rattle of chains and threw his head back to spit at Macro, who immediately slapped him hard across the face with the back of his hand.

'Now, now. Show some manners!'

Macro pointed up the beach with his cane, indicating the entrance to the camp and the three of them set off.

Vitellius was awaiting their arrival in his tent. Standing to one side of the tent were two hard-looking men who, Cato realised, must be interrogators. Like most of the specialists in the Roman military, these men would be thoroughly versed in their art and, from the look of them, Cato suspected that they would have had plenty of opportunities to put that training into practice.

As the two centurions and their prisoner entered the tent Vitellius nodded to a sturdy wooden chair with a high back in the middle of an area that had been cleared of any other furniture. Even the rugs that normally covered the ground had been neatly rolled up and placed to the side to avoid getting stained. Macro guided the prisoner over to the chair.

'Wait there.'

At once the two interrogators moved in and tore the soiled clothes off the prisoner, throwing them to one side until he stood naked before them. One of the interrogators firmly pushed him down into the chair and then produced some leather straps, and the two of them tied Ajax's wrists and ankles to the chair.

'Right then.' Vitellius slowly walked round the prisoner and then stopped directly in front of him. 'I think we'll have this one flayed alive.'

Ajax glanced up with a terrified expression and Vitellius grinned. 'So! We understand Latin. That should make things a little easier.' The prefect stopped smiling and fixed his attention on the prisoner.

'Listen to me. There are some questions I want answers to. I want to know where your fleet is based. I want to know how many ships you have, how they're defended and how many men you have. Lastly I want to know where the scrolls are. If what Centurion Cato tells me about you is correct, and you are one of Telemachus' top men then you'll know exactly what I'm talking about. Those are the questions. You've got the answers. If you tell me now you'll save yourself a lot of pain and suffering. If you try to hold anything back, these men,' he nodded at the interrogators, 'will go to work on you. They know how to inflict agonies you couldn't begin to imagine. All you need to know is that you will talk. One way or another.'

Ajax sneered. 'You're not doing such a bad job of talking yourself, Roman.'

Vitellius smiled. 'Ah! Such courage in the face of adversity. I'm almost impressed. Let's begin, shall we? I'm keen to see how well you cope.'

The prefect stepped aside. 'Gentlemen, he's all yours.'

There was no preamble. No attempt to try to put the frighteners on the pirate by laying before him the instruments of their trade and letting his imagination go to work. The interrogator with the heaviest build simply stepped up to the chair and slammed his fist into Ajax's face, shattering his nose with a dull crunch. The young man's head cracked against the chair back. There was a moment of stunned silence before he cried out in pain, then Ajax realised what he had done and clamped his mouth shut and opened his eyes wide and glared defiantly back at the interrogator as blood gushed over his lips and dripped on to his chest. The next blow came in from the side, on his cheek, with a soft thud.

Cato and Macro stood to one side, watching in silence as the interrogator went about his work; landing a steady sequence of blows to head and ribs. Although Cato felt sickened by the display of violence he told himself that it was necessary. Ajax had the information that would save him and Macro, and redeem Vitellius, and put an end to the pirates' menacing of the seaways. What was this young man's suffering when measured against all the other factors? And yet Cato felt a wave of disgust wash over him and he wanted no part of this. But he could not leave. Everyone would know that he hadn't the stomach for it, and if word of that spread round the camp he would be a laughing stock. He must affect a cold detachment from the torture being carried out in front of him. Of course, it was easier in the resolution than the act, and when a thick gout of blood splattered on his cheek, Cato felt bile rise in his throat and he swallowed nervously.

After a while Vitellius stepped in and waved the interrogator to one side. It was warm in the tent, and the man's skin glistened as he took a step back from the pirate sagging in the chair.

'That'll do to start with, thank you, Trebius.' Vitellius flashed a smile at the interrogator. 'We don't want to damage him too much at this stage.'

The interrogator was taken aback. 'I know what I'm doing, sir. He'll be able to talk for a while yet.'

Vitellius raised his hands. 'Forgive me. I didn't mean to

cause any offence. But before we continue . . . is there anything you want to tell me, young Ajax?'

The pirate was breathing heavily and at first it seemed that he hadn't heard the prefect. Then his head lolled to one side. He opened his eyes and spat out some blood.

'I'll make you pay for this, Roman . . . I'll make you suffer . . . And, if you kill me, then my . . .' Ajax glanced up anxiously for an instant, before his face twisted into a mask of bitter hatred once again. 'He'll make you pay.'

Macro glanced at Cato and spoke softly. 'He?'

Cato shrugged. 'Telemachus, maybe.'

Stepping closer to the prisoner, Vitellius bent forward and said gently, 'Who'll make me pay? Your friend, the pirate chief? You really think so?'

'You're going to die, Roman.'

Vitellius gave a light laugh. 'Friend, we're all going to die. Some just get to die sooner than others. The timing is all that matters in life. Now, you know the questions. I want the answers.'

'Fuck you!' Ajax jerked his head up and spat in the prefect's face.

Vitellius instinctively recoiled, then wiped the bloody spittle off his cheek with the back of his hand. He smiled. 'No, fuck you, you pirate scum.' He nodded at the interrogator. 'Back to work, Trebius. Make it really hurt this time.'

'Yes, sir.' The interrogator turned to his assistant. 'Pass us the cutters . . .'

Ajax held out for the rest of the afternoon and even Macro was moved to admiration by the young man's courage. Ajax had screamed when the interrogator cut off his little finger, and then gouged out several chunks of flesh, but not once had he begged for it to end, or answered the questions

Vitellius put to him. Cato felt more and more sick as the torture dragged out, through one hour, then the next. Just when he felt he must object and try to put an end to this pointless mutilation, the pirate finally gave in, sobbing in terror and agony, as he blurted out a name.

'Vectis terra . . .' he whispered.

'What's that?' Vitellius leaned closer, straining his ears to catch the word. 'Speak up!'

'Vectis terra . . . my father's at Vectis terra.'

There was a sudden stillness in the tent as the Romans exchanged a look of surprise. Cato shook his head, angry with himself for missing the now obvious connection between Telemachus and Ajax. Of course their features were similar. And why would so young a man be so highly placed amongst the pirates, unless he had a blood connection with their leader?

Vitellius was the first to speak. 'Now *that* is interesting. So you are his son.'

Ajax did not respond, but hung his head down and refused to meet the gaze of his captors.

'Well then!' Vitellius could not restrain his delight at the discovery. 'I'm sure you will be of even greater use to us now, Ajax. I wonder . . . I wonder just how far your father would go for your safe return.'

Ajax spat blood on to the floor. 'I'd rather die!'

'Of course you would. But would he rather you died? That's the question.' Vitellius crossed to the side of the tent, unravelled a map and ran a finger up the dark lines that marked the coastline until he found the place. 'Vectis terra, you say . . . Hmm, I don't think so. That's too far off the trade routes. Your ships would have to sail for days before they reached their hunting grounds.' He turned round and chuckled. 'Nice try, young Ajax.

I knew you'd lie first time. Now we'll have the truth, if you please.'

The prisoner hung his head in despair as the prefect crossed back to him.

'Come now, Ajax. We will make you tell us the truth in the end, however long it takes. The only question you must ask yourself is how much pain you want to endure before you give us the truth. If you cooperate with us, then I give you my word you will live. If you persist in this foolish and pointless attempt to resist, then there will be torment, heaped upon torment, until you do tell us the truth. Then there will only be death.'

Vitellius reached down and lifted the pirate's chin. 'So you see, young man, the only sensible thing to do is accept that you will tell us what we need to know. Now, or later, it doesn't matter which. But you will tell us . . . Trebius!'

'Yes, sir!'

'Are you ready?'

'Yes, sir.'

'Back to work then.'

Ajax stared in horror at the interrogator. Then he clenched his eyes tightly shut for a moment and whispered, 'Petrapylae . . .'

Vitellius smiled and patted him on the head. 'Good lad.'

The prefect returned to the map and began to scan it closely. After a while he straightened up and turned back to his prisoner with an angry expression. 'There's no such place. Now tell me the truth, or—'

Cato stepped between them. 'Sir, the chart's one of ours.'

Vitellius glared at him 'So?'

'His first tongue is Greek. Petrapylae – the Gates of Rock, or something like that. Can I see the chart, sir?'

Vitellius waved a hand. 'Be my guest.'

Cato flattened out the map and glanced up the coast from their present position. Then he tapped his finger on the parchment. 'Here. This looks like it. The Gates of Stone.'

'Let me see that!' Vitellius hurried over, looked at the point Cato indicated, and nodded as a smile formed on his lips. 'That must be it.'

'Makes sense, sir. It's off the trade routes. There's an abandoned Greek colony there; mountains on all sides. The entrance looks narrow enough to defend well.' He shrugged. 'Of course there's plenty of other equally possible sites on this stretch of coast.'

Vitellius looked over his shoulder. 'Supposing he's lying?'

'Then we keep him alive until we've reconnoitred the area, sir. If he's trying to mislead us we can always interrogate him again.'

'True. But there's one more thing.' Vitellius went back over to Ajax. 'The scrolls. Are they kept there?'

There was a pause, then Ajax nodded. Vitellius stared at the prisoner for a moment before turning his gaze towards Cato and Macro. 'You believe him?'

Macro shrugged. 'Seems like the most obvious place to keep 'em, sir. We're having a hard enough time finding their ships, and Telemachus will want them somewhere he can keep an eye on them and protect them. If they're as valuable as people think.'

'Valuable?' Vitellius sniffed. 'They're more than that, Centurion. In fact, they're invaluable.'

Before either of the centurions could probe any further, the tent flap lifted and one of the prefect's bodyguards thrust his head into the tent. His eyebrows rose slightly at the sight of the battered prisoner.

'What is it?' Vitellius snapped.

'Begging your pardon, sir, but there's a boat heading in from the sea.'

'A boat? What kind of boat?'

'Looks like some kind of yacht sir. She's small but she's fast.'

'Heading this way, you say?'

'Yes, sir. Straight for us.'

Vitellius looked at Ajax for a moment before making a decision. 'He'll keep. Cato, Macro, pass the word to the senior duty officer. He's to have two centuries stand to. And alert the artillery batteries. I want them ready to fire, if necessary, the moment the boat's in range. I'll join you shortly.'

They saluted and ducked out of the tent. Vitellius turned to the interrogator. 'Right then, just a few last questions . . .'

Outside the headquarters tent Cato and Macro had a clear view down the slope leading to the rampart and the beach beyond. The sun was brassy and bright and they had to shade their eyes and squint as they stared out to sea. Far out, little more than a vague silhouette, they could see the boat, lateen sail out to one side as it ran before the wind. They strode down to the shore and relayed the prefect's order before turning their attention back to the approaching boat.

'Now who the hell's that?' asked Macro.

Cato shrugged. 'No idea.'

'Whoever it is seems to be in a tearing hurry to get here. Imperial courier, or something?' Macro wondered aloud.

As they watched Cato felt the blood chill in his veins as he recalled the dispatch he had sent to Rome. There was a crunch of shingle and Cato suddenly sensed the eyes of the prefect falling on him and made himself stand quite still and resist the temptation to turn towards Vitellius. Instead he concentrated on the new arrival, until his eye was drawn to a distant movement on the promontory above the bay. A line of crosses stood dark against the western sky. On each one hung a tiny figure. Even as he watched, the last cross was raised into place, a man writhing on its wooden arms.

Cato suppressed a shudder of fear. If Vitellius discovered that Cato had opened his dispatch, then there was a good chance that he would find himself sharing the fate of the pirates nailed to the crosses hanging above the bay.

CHAPTER THIRTY

The small ship held its course and sailed into the bay as the sun dipped down towards the horizon. From the shore Cato could make out a cluster of figures on the deck. The slanted light illuminated red cloaks and glinted off polished armour.

Macro grunted beside him. 'Looks like top brass. Wonder what they're doing here.'

They both turned towards Prefect Vitellius, standing a short distance away as he squinted at the approaching ship with an anxious expression. Macro leaned closer to his friend.

'Has this got anything to do with that report he sent back to Rome, do you suppose?'

Cato tried to sound genuine as he replied, 'I really have no idea. We'll have to wait and see.'

Macro looked at him curiously for a moment. Then glanced round to make sure he would not be overheard, before he spoke softly. 'Cato, do you know something about this?'

'About what?'

'Don't get cute with me, lad. I know you.'

For a moment Cato was tempted by the need to unburden his anxiety. But he would not put Macro in any more danger than he was already in. He owed the man that much at least.

'I'm sorry. There's nothing to tell you.'

Macro looked at his young friend intently, and wasn't convinced. 'Nothing you're willing to tell me, you mean. Well, be a bloody obstinate fool and keep it to yourself then. You always do . . .' The veteran patted Cato gently on the arm. 'Just be careful, eh?'

Macro moved closer to the shore and stared at the boat, which had lowered its sail. Two long sweeps were thrust out from each beam and the crew rowed the remaining distance towards the shore. At the last moment the oars rose up and the crew shifted them round to punt the bows up on to the beach. A small wave carried the craft on to the shingle where it grounded with a scraping crunch. The men at the rear of the boat advanced along the deck and clambered over the bows to dry land. There were six of them, mostly young staff officers; no doubt aristocrats working their way through their first military apprenticeships. A short distance behind them was an older man, dressed in a simple tunic and thick military cloak. Cato and Macro recognised him instantly and looked at each other in surprise.

'Vespasian?' Macro shook his head. 'What the hell is he doing here?'

Cato had no idea. He was as surprised as his friend to see their old commander again. The last time had been months before, when they had accompanied the legate on their return from Britain. Cato and Macro turned to glance at Vitellius. Two years earlier the prefect had served as a tribune under Vespasian and there had been intense and bitter rivalry between them.

Vitellius took a sharp breath and waved a hand at the officers around him. 'Follow me!'

The party from the fleet strode down the beach towards

the new arrivals while Vespasian and his tribunes drew themselves up and waited a few paces above the waterline.

'Sir!' Vitellius called out, and forced a smile. 'What brings you here?'

Vespasian appeared to be equally cordial as he extended his hand and the two officers clasped arms. 'The Imperial Secretary sent me. I'll introduce my staff officers later. But first we need to talk. Narcissus wants to know how the operation is proceeding.'

Vitellius frowned. 'But I sent him a report. He must have received it several days ago. Unless . . .' He glanced round at Cato.

'The report arrived safely,' said Vespasian. 'Narcissus thanks you for it, but in view of the, er, complexity of the situation he wanted to send someone to assess the progress you're making first-hand. Since we have served together before, Narcissus gave me the job.' Vespasian smiled. 'So here I am, reluctantly.'

'I see.'

'On the way in I noticed that you've met with some success at least.' Vespasian turned and indicated the promontory.

'That? My men set a trap for the pirates. We took three of their ships and a few prisoners, including a man close to their leader, Telemachus. I was questioning him when I had word of your approach. The rest I had executed to serve as a warning to the pirates and to encourage our own men.'

'A warning to the pirates?' Vespasian mused. 'Then they must be close at hand.'

'They keep us under observation,' Vitellius admitted warily.

'Really? Well, let's not waste any time,' Vespasian continued in a lighter tone. 'It's been a long and uncomfortable journey. My tribunes and I could do with some refreshment.'

'Of course.' Vitellius turned round to one of his staff officers. 'Run back to my quarters. I want a tent prepared. Food and wine for all senior officers and our guests as soon as possible. Go.'

As the man ran off Vespasian cast his eye over the fortifications lining the beach, and the fleet anchored in the bay or beached on the shingle. 'You've made a good job of the fortifications. Looks like an excellent base from which to conduct operations.'

Vitellius bowed his head graciously.

'Mind if my staff and I have a look round before we take advantage of your hospitality? It'll give your men a chance to make the proper arrangements.' Vespasian smiled.

'Of course, I'd be happy to—'

Vespasian raised a hand to interrupt the prefect. 'I've imposed enough on you already.' Vespasian glanced round at Vitellius' officers before he singled Cato out. 'Centurion Cato! Good to see you again. Would you be kind enough to act as our guide?'

'I'd be honoured, sir.'

'Thank you. Prefect Vitellius, we'll join you in a short while.'

'I'll look forward to it, sir.'

Without a further word Vespasian moved off along the beach, Cato at his side, while his staff officers kept a short distance behind. Vitellius watched them closely for a moment, smiling as he relished the harsh punishment that would shortly be inflicted on Centurion Cato. The report he had sent back to Rome had been completely unambiguous in pointing out Cato's dereliction of duty. Vespasian would surely be carrying a warrant for the young officer's death. But while the removal of Centurion Cato was a satisfying prospect, it was deeply worrying that Narcissus had sent Vespasian to assess his progress. Clearly the carefully worded description of the early stages of the campaign had not succeeded in pulling the wool over the Imperial Secretary's eyes. Vespasian would have to be handled carefully if the true scale of the disaster was to be concealed from Narcissus. Vitellius turned round and beckoned to Macro.

'Sir?'

'Get back to the prisoner. Clean him up and take him somewhere safe and secure and out of earshot of Vespasian.'

'Yes, sir.'

Vitellius stared in silence at the retreating backs of Vespasian and his party for a moment longer, then he turned away and strode into the camp.

As soon as he had finished inspecting the shore defences Vespasian dismissed his staff officers and ordered Cato to take him around the outside of the ramparts. When they were a safe distance from the palisade Vespasian turned to the centurion and spoke bluntly.

'All right then, time to dispense with the pleasantries. The Imperial Secretary hit the ceiling when he read the prefect's report. An imperial fleet almost defeated by a bunch of pirates. Hundreds of lives lost and valuable equipment sent to the bottom of the sea. And when I passed through Ravenna, the place was on the verge of anarchy. I had to send to Arminium for a cohort of auxiliaries just to keep the lid on the situation. When news of that gets back to the palace Vitellius had better make sure his affairs are in order and his will is written.'

'It's that serious, sir?'

'The prefect might survive if we can defeat these pirates

quickly, and find those scrolls. At least his report had the virtue of being honest and not trying to cover up for the mess he's made of things. That might just save him.'

Cato winced. There seemed to be no end to Vitellius' good fortune. You could drop him off the Tarpeian Rock and he would land on his feet.

'Centurion, I need to know exactly what the situation is here,' Vespasian continued. 'Prefect Vitellius is supposed to be on a punitive mission, taking the offensive right to the door of the pirates' lair. Instead, I feel as if I've just arrived in a bloody besieged city. How the hell did it get to this? Speak plainly. I suspect I don't have to worry about you covering up for this particular superior officer, given your past experience of Vitellius.'

Cato returned his superior's knowing smile and quickly marshalled his thoughts as they slowly walked along the perimeter of the defences.

'We've lost a quarter of our strength in total, including wounded. Many of the ships are damaged and since Vitellius has kept on the defensive it hasn't helped the morale of the men.' Cato paused and pointed towards the treeline on a hill no more than a mile distant. 'Worse still, the enemy have got troops out there, harassing our foraging parties and having the odd shot at sentries during the night. The pirates have faster ships and better crews and they've eluded every attempt to chase them down.' Cato gestured towards the distant crosses on the headland. 'That's the only success we've had since the start of the campaign, sir.'

'What happened?'

'We set a trap in a cove further up the coast. They took the bait and paid the price.'

Vespasian looked at him shrewdly. 'Whose idea was that? Yours?'

'I was there,' Cato replied. 'It was simple enough.'

'Maybe. But you did it, while the prefect sat on his arse in the camp. That's the point.'

'Well, someone had to do something, sir.'

'Don't be such a fool,' Vespasian said sharply. 'Don't apologise, Cato. As far as I can see, you're about the only one who has done anything useful here. Is there anything else I should know?'

'Well, sir, it's possible we may have discovered where the pirates are operating from.'

Vespasian stopped and stared at him. 'You tell me that now?'

'One of the prisoners we took the other night was the son of Telemachus. The prefect had an interrogator go to work on him earlier this afternoon. He gave us a location.'

'Do you think he's telling the truth?'

Cato shrugged. 'I don't know, sir. He's got some guts. He might be lying to us to buy time for his father and their men. On the other hand, the interrogator was doing a pretty good job of breaking him down.'

Vespasian regarded the centurion closely. 'Did he mention anything about the scrolls?'

Cato felt his pulse quicken and decided at that instant to chance his arm. He fought to keep his voice calm. 'Scrolls, sir? The Sybilline scrolls?'

Vespasian was silent for a moment before he replied, 'So you know? I was told that only the prefect had been informed.'

Cato thought quickly. 'The Imperial Secretary told us about them when he briefed us for this mission.'

'Us? You mean Centurion Macro knows about them as well?'

'Yes, sir.' There had been no time to think of anything

else to say and Cato prayed that he had not placed his friend in any peril.

'I see . . . You'd best be careful, both of you. Knowledge of the scrolls is a dangerous thing.'

'But, sir, it's not as if no one knows about them, nor what they contain. The priests in the temple of Jupiter have been consulting them for hundreds of years.'

'The first three books, yes. But imagine how much happier they'll be if they get their hands on the other three, and see the full picture.' Vespasian turned to look out to sea, towards Italy and Rome. He sounded wistful when he spoke. 'I imagine that quite a few people would give anything to possess the missing scrolls . . .'

Cato's mind was still racing to deal with the implications of what Vespasian had just told him. The other three Sybilline scrolls? It was impossible. They had been destroyed, burned by the Oracle. Or were supposed to have been. But if they existed, they would be a potent weapon for any ambitious man in Rome with an eye to exploiting the superstitions of the mob. Any man like Vitellius, or . . . A cold sensation trickled down Cato's spine as he regarded Vespasian. At that moment, the senator turned back to the centurion and for a moment Cato thought he detected a hint of pity in Vespasian's face. Then the senator's expression hardened.

'Well, Narcissus must have had his reasons for telling you. In any case, you'll understand their importance. And why they cannot be permitted to fall into any else's hands, least of all the enemies of the Emperor.'

Cato nodded.

'Very well.' Vespasian looked round at the hills nearby, at the shadows in the treeline of the wood that sprawled up the slopes. Then he turned and looked at the camp, fixing his eyes on a sentry glancing nervously over the palisade as he patrolled along the rampart. Vespasian shook his head. 'I've seen enough. It's time to act.'

Vitellius looked at the senator in shock. 'You can't be serious.'

'I am,' Vespasian replied firmly. 'By the authority vested in me by Emperor Claudius and the Senate and People of Rome, I hereby relieve you of command and assume your rank and authority as prefect of the fleet of Ravenna.'

There was a stunned silence in the tent as the assembled officers watched the confrontation. For a moment Vitellius did not respond, as if in a trance. Then he shook his head and stiffened his back. 'No. You don't have the authority to do that.'

'Yes I do.' Vespasian turned to one of his tribunes and clicked his fingers. 'Decius, the authorisation, please.'

The tribune reached a hand under his breastplate and extracted a folded sheet of papyrus. He handed it to Vespasian who, after he had carefully opened the document, offered it to Vitellius.

'Read it.'

Vitellius stared at the document for a moment, as if it was poisonous. Then he reached out and took it. Vespasian's authority was confirmed by Emperor Claudius himself and written in an unusually terse manner. Nevertheless it was clear enough concerning the all-embracing power conferred on the new commander of the Ravenna fleet. Vitellius folded the document and handed it back.

'Congratulations, sir,' he said in a tone laden with bitterness. 'The fleet is yours to command . . . Might I ask what is to become of me?'

Vespasian had anticipated the question and had his reply ready. Under the terms of his authority Vespasian could have Vitellius arrested and condemned for incompetence. He could even have him executed if he wished. But in either case there would be difficult questions to answer when he returned to Rome. Even though the Emperor's favourite had made a disastrous mess of the campaign, Claudius was still fond of him. Fond enough to exact a revenge on the man responsible for destroying his protégé. And if Vitellius lived, he was sure to smooth-talk himself back into favour, and pose a danger to Vespasian in the future.

Vespasian had little choice. Vitellius had to stay with the fleet for the rest of the campaign, where Vespasian could keep an eye on him. Besides, with a bit of luck, and a judicious allocation of duties, Vitellius might well be killed and then Vespasian's problem would be solved.

He stared at Vitellius for a long time, as if weighing up the man's fate, before he responded.

'You stay here. Given the losses suffered as a result of your decisions, I'll need every man who can hold a sword. For now, I'll keep you on my staff. But you'll go into the line the moment the fighting starts.'

Vitellius bowed his head.

Vespasian looked round the tent at the other officers, many of whom were still astonished by the extraordinary event unfolding before them. 'No other man will be held culpable for the failure of the fleet thus far. You will all continue in your current posts. Bear in mind, though, that back in Rome there is considerable displeasure with your performance. You have a chance, gentlemen, to set the record straight; to win back your honour and the honour of the fleet. I advise you to think on that. From tomorrow we take the fight to the pirates.'

A murmur of approval rippled through the officers. Then Vespasian nodded towards Macro and Cato. 'There are some here who have served under me before. They know that I drive my men hard. But they also know that I am fair. Serve me, as they have served me, and we will win. We will kill or capture every last pirate and destroy their ships and their base. And when it's all over there will be booty for all of us that survive. But if you fail me, in any way, you can expect no mercy. Gentlemen, do we have an understanding?'

The officers nodded, and some muttered in affirmation.

'Very well. The party's over. Get back to your units and get ready to move. We're breaking camp tomorrow and heading up the coast. There'll be no questions at this time, gentlemen. You're dismissed . . . Centurions Macro and Cato stay where you are. I've got a little job for you.'

As the other officers filed through the tent flaps Macro leaned closer to his friend and whispered, 'Any idea what that's about?'

'No.'

'Great. Just great.' Macro shook his head. 'I'll bet good money that it's the shit end of the stick for us once again.'

CHAPTER THIRTY-ONE

Two nights later the yacht that Vespasian had commandeered landed the two centurions ten miles down the coast from the area known as the Gates of Stone. Cato and Macro wore grey tunics, and carried their swords and rations for three days. The instructions from the new prefect of the Ravenna fleet were clear enough. They were to reconnoitre the area and try to locate the base of the pirates. If, indeed, it was there. Ajax had been promised new torments if it turned out he was lying. Cato and Macro were not to attempt any heroics and must ensure that they were not seen by the enemy. The yacht would wait for them in a secluded bay a few miles closer to the Gates of Stone.

While the two centurions scouted the area the main force under Vespasian was slowly advancing up the coast behind them. The warships had been readied for imminent battle. Any equipment that Vespasian had decided was not essential for the operation was left at the beachhead. Five of the biremes, damaged in the fight with Telemachus, were burned on the shore to deny them any use to the pirates. One bireme was sent back to Ravenna with those men who were too badly wounded to be of any use for the rest of the campaign.

The fleet made occasional sightings of sails far out to the horizon, but the enemy was content to simply keep them under observation and not risk battle. Vespasian was mindful of the possibility that the pirates might have spies within his force as well as back in Ravenna and made sure that the watch was doubled on the walls of the camp each night. The sentries were ordered to keep watch both outside and inside the camp in case anyone attempted to communicate with the pirates. At present there would be little to report which the pirates could not see for themselves, but when the decisive moment of the campaign came Vespasian would need to move swiftly and surprise the enemy. They must not receive an advance warning.

Vespasian knew that he was taking a risk that the pirate base might not be where Ajax claimed it was, but the location seemed logical. Down towards Risinium, the coastline was well settled and offered few places to conceal a pirate fleet. In the other direction, the coastline became a maze of islands and deep bays flanked by forbidding mountains. That's where Telemachus and his pirates would be holed up. Far enough from the trade routes to remain invisible to passing ships, yet close enough to venture out and continue the raids that had caused Rome so much embarrassment over recent months. If Ajax's information was accurate the campaign should be settled in a matter of days. If the information was false then Vespasian would make sure that his next round of interrogation and torture produced the right result, no matter how much time and agony it took.

After a night in the open, and a day clambering along narrow twisting goat tracks, keeping an eye out for any signs of habitation, Macro and Cato found a small cave near the top of a mountain to shelter for the second night. The entrance was narrow and concealed from distant view by a finger of rock that rose close by the entrance. Indeed, they would have missed it entirely had the track they were following not passed right by the entrance. Inside, the cave had a dogleg into a recess which was just big enough for the two men to set a small fire and lay down beside it. They put down their packs and slumped on the ground to catch their breath. At length, Macro shook his head wearily.

'Why us? Why'd he pick us? Has to be someone else's turn by now.'

'You heard him,' Cato replied. 'We're the best men for the job.'

'And you believed him?' Macro sniffed. 'Remind me to sell you a used cart when we get back to Rome.'

'The legate might have meant it,' Cato replied stiffly. 'He's counted on us in the past and we haven't let him down.'

'Hang on.' Macro sat up. 'Far as I recall, you've volunteered the both of us, or he's ordered us to go. So either we're plain mugs, or he thinks we're expendable. Either way, it's not the direction I want my career to take – whatever's left of it.'

Cato gave him a wan smile. 'Come now, you're telling me that you're not enjoying this?'

'What? No sleep for two days, twenty miles of mountain hiking, I'm cold and hungry and maybe only a few miles away from the lair of hundreds of bloodthirsty pirates. What's not to enjoy?'

'That's my Macro!'

'Oh, piss off . . . You just enjoy making yourself a home of this damp little hole. Me? I'm going to have a bloody fire.'

While Macro gathered some wood from the scrub growing on the moutainside and prepared a fire, Cato got the goatskin map, a pen and a small pot of ink from his haversack and spread it out on the cave floor. By the fading light of the cave opening he began to add detail to the sketchy outline of the area that the clerk had copied on to the goatskin from one of the staff maps. Working carefully, Cato marked in the hill range they had travelled across that day, together with the paths they had followed, and then began to examine the vital section of the map they would complete the next day. After climbing to the summit of the mountain above them, he and Macro would examine the entrance to the bay and then descend the slope on the far side of the mountain and rejoin the fleet.

Behind him, at the back of the cave, Macro was striking a flint over his tinder box. Sparks flashed down on to the charred linen inside. After a few attempts the material took some of the sparks and began to glow. Macro blew over it softly and then transferred the tiny flame to the kindling and continued blowing until it caught light and a crackling sound filled the cave as Macro built the small fire up.

'There!' He leaned back with a smile. 'Soon be warm in here.'

'Nice job.' Cato made himself smile back. He felt guilty for the genuine friendship that Macro shared with him. By implicating Macro in Cato's supposed knowledge of the Sybilline scrolls he had placed his friend in danger. For the sake of Macro, and for the sake of their friendship he owed it to the older man to tell him the truth. He must be made aware of the content of the scrolls, and their significance.

'Macro . . .'

The other man looked up from his fire. 'Hmm?'

'There's something I have to tell you. About those scrolls Narcissus is after.'

'Oh.' Macro caught the awkward tone in his friend's voice. 'What about them?'

'I'm not sure where to start. I . . .'

'Just spit it out, man. You can worry about the details and niceties later.'

'All right . . .'

Macro shook his head. 'For fuck's sake, Cato, get on with it. Anyone would think you were asking for my hand in marriage.'

Cato laughed. 'Well, I was wondering about that. Watching you bent over that fire made me realise what a good wife you'd make.'

Macro wagged a finger at him. 'Careful, lad. Never take a joke too far.'

'Right, sorry . . .'

Macro stared at him a moment, then sighed. 'The scrolls?'

'Oh, yes, of course.' Cato shuffled into a comfortable position and hugged his knees, facing the fire. 'I found out what they are. You've heard of the three Sybilline scrolls?'

Macro rolled his eyes, and responded with forced patience. 'Yes. I think I've heard of them.'

'And the story behind them?'

Macro looked doubtful now. 'They were given to King Tarquin by the Oracle of Cumae. Weren't they? A long time ago.'

Cato nodded. 'About five hundred years back. But the Oracle didn't give them to him, she sold them to him. For a fortune. She only sold him three of the books.'

'There were more?'

'Oh, yes. Six in all. Six books that that were supposed to prophesy the entire future of Rome and her people. Quite a prize. So she came to Rome and offered them to Tarquin for a price that would have beggared him. Naturally he refused. So she went away and burned one of the books and came back the next day with five and demanded the same price. He refused again, so she burned another and returned to demand the same price. He refused one last time and she destroyed a third book. When she came before him again he was desperate and paid what she was asking. And that's what we have in the Temple of Jupiter today. Our priests go to consult them whenever there's a crisis of some kind and try to work out what will happen. Not easy when you only have half the information in front of you.'

'I see,' Macro looked into the wavering glow of his fire. 'So what have these scrolls we're after got to do with the Sybilline scrolls?'

Cato leaned forward slightly. 'Don't you see? They *are* the Sybilline scrolls.'

'What, are you saying the ones in the temple of Jupiter are fakes?'

'No. No. Listen. Think about it. The Oracle knew these scrolls were priceless. So why on earth would she destroy them?'

'Like you said. To get some leverage on negotiations with King Tarquin.'

'Which she did,' Cato admitted. 'But wouldn't the smart move have been to put the scrolls somewhere safe and only say that she had burned them? Later on, along comes a new king, with a new fortune, and the Oracle, or her successor, reveals the existence of the remaining scrolls. By that time the people in Rome would have discovered that the first three books were almost useless on their own. They would be prepared to pay almost anything to possess the last three books to complete the prophecy.'

'So why didn't she try to sell the books at a later date?'

'I don't know. Maybe she felt the time wasn't right. Maybe she was waiting for Rome to be rich enough to afford the price she wanted. Perhaps she was too good at keeping a secret and died before she could tell her successor about the books and where they were hidden. I don't know. I'm only guessing. There are stories told of men who claimed to have seen them. I even heard that they fell into the hands of Mark Antony, just before the battle of Actium. He might have beaten Augustus, but for some reason Antony's nerve failed at the last moment and he abandoned his fleet to its destruction. The story goes that he read the Sybilline scrolls on the eve of the battle and that they foretold his defeat.'

Macro stared at him. 'Do you think it's true?'

Cato chuckled. 'How can anyone know? His fleet lost because he cut and ran. If he fled because of some prophecy then he's an even bigger fool than historians take him for. Our destiny is not written in the stars. We make it as we will. The rest is just a story.'

'It might have been true,' Macro persisted. 'There are more things in the heavens and the earth than can be found in all those books you read, Cato.'

'Maybe.' Cato shrugged. 'Or maybe Antony was as poor at commanding a fleet as he was at selecting a lover.'

Macro shrugged and stared sullenly into the fire, and Cato feared he had gone too far in undermining the superstitions that Macro held dear to his heart. He decided to change tack and cleared his throat. 'It's clear enough what's happened since then.'

'Oh?'

'Someone discovered the scrolls and recognised them for what they are. They struck a deal with the Emperor – or Narcissus, more likely. He sent out an agent with the gold to pay for the scrolls and the agent duly headed back to Rome bearing the scrolls that would complete the Sybilline prophecies. At last the rulers of Rome would know what the future holds for the Empire and could make their plans accordingly. Assuming there's any substance to the prophecies.'

'What if they're wrong?' Macro asked.

Cato shrugged. 'It doesn't matter. All Narcissus has to do is let on that he has all the scrolls, and most of his enemies won't dare to act against him for fear that he already knows their intentions. That's quite a useful political tool. Almost a treasure in its own right . . . Only, the scrolls never made it back to Rome. A short distance from Ravenna, the ship on which Narcissus' agent was travelling was attacked and captured by Telemachus and his pirates. When it dawned on Telemachus what he had got his hands on he knew he could demand a vast ransom for the scrolls. Better still, if other parties were made aware of the scrolls' existence he could sell them to the highest bidder. The Emperor and Narcissus won't be the only ones after the scrolls. There'll be others. Like our friends, the Liberators. So Telemachus played one off against the other and forced the price up. Only he got too greedy and Narcissus decided that he must get the scrolls back at any cost. So he sent us out, and the Ravenna fleet, with orders to stop at nothing until the pirate menace is eliminated.'

'And the scrolls are recovered.' Macro nodded. 'So this whole thing is about the scrolls?'

'Not quite. They'd have to deal with Telemachus and his men at some point. But a campaign against the pirate threat would be a good enough cover for the real operation to retrieve the scrolls. The only difficulty is that the Imperial Secretary would have to keep that side of things a secret, for fear of alerting his rivals not only to the existence of the scrolls, but also their whereabouts.'

'I see. But if it's such a big secret, how do you know about it?'

Cato flushed. 'I read Vitellius' report. The one he sent back to Rome.'

Macro looked horrified. 'You did what?'

'Well, there was a storm. The seal got wet and broke. I didn't trust him, so I read the report . . .'

Macro stared at him wide-eyed. This was a breach of protocol of the most severe nature. A legionary could be executed on the spot for many lesser offences. He swallowed nervously. 'So go on then. What did it say?'

'Knowing our friend Vitellius you won't be surprised that he lied through his teeth about that sea battle and the shit situation he left us in. He tried to blame me for the losses we suffered.'

'You?'

'Why not? He needed to shift the blame off his shoulders. And with me out of the way, then there'd be only you and him in the know about those scrolls. If anything happened to you, he'd be able to make up any story he liked and keep the scrolls for himself.'

'Why do that?'

'So he could sell them on. Or, better still, use them to advance his own interests. You know how ambitious he is.'

'I know that all right,' Macro replied with feeling. 'The bastard.'

'Anyway,' Cato smiled, 'I made a few alterations to the report before I sent it off to Rome.'

Macro was astonished, and felt sick over what Cato had just told him. 'You altered it?'

'I had to.' Cato shrugged. 'I was dead if I didn't. So I just changed it so it told the truth.'

Macro glanced up sharply. 'That's why they sent Vespasian here.'

Cato nodded.

'Fuck, Cato. You really do take some chances. If this ever gets out they'll break every bone in your body.'

'At least . . .' Cato looked at his friend in embarrassment. 'Look, I'm really sorry about this. Sorry that I've got you involved.'

'What do you mean?'

'I sort of tricked Vespasian into telling me about the scrolls. I saw the reference to the Sybilline scrolls in Vitellius' report and made out that I knew the full story when I was briefing Vespasian about the situation here. He swallowed it, and before I knew what I was saying I said that you knew about the scrolls as well.'

Macro frowned and shook his head. 'So? So what?'

'Until this is all over, anyone who knows about the scrolls is going to be in great danger. The stakes are too high to risk having any loose ends.'

'I see.' Macro nodded. 'Thanks, mate. Thanks a lot. Much as I like you, Cato, and think that you've turned out to be a damn fine soldier, there are times when I really do wish that I'd never met you. Fifteen years, I'd served, before you turned up. Sure I'd been in some bad scrapes, but in the last two years you've nearly got me killed more times than I can care to think about. Now this . . .'

'Sorry.'

'Stop apologising. It's too late to do anything about it now.' Macro scrunched his haversack up into a tight bundle and lay down beside the fire, back towards Cato. He was silent for a moment before he muttered, 'Just promise me, one thing.'

'Yes?'

'If we get out of this mess, no more adventures.'

'Well, I'll do my best.'

'Huh . . .'

* * *

In the morning, they rose with the first light of day glimmering off the walls of the cave. Macro stretched his stiff limbs and coughed as the cold air swept into his lungs. Cato kept quiet, still a little shamed by his confession of the previous evening. They packed their provisions back into the haversacks, put on their boots and emerged from the cave. The sky was leaden and a cold wind blew up the side of the mountain, clammy with the threat of rain.

'Which way?' asked Macro.

'Straight up. We should have a view of their anchorage and base from the peak of the mountain.'

'If the information's accurate,' Macro said gloomily. 'Chances are, it won't be.'

'We'll know soon enough.' Cato thrust his haversack behind his back and started along the track that wound up the rock-strewn slope. A moment late, mouthing a foul curse, Macro set off after him.

As they rose higher, a mist closed in. Then they seemed to be up into the base of the clouds themselves and a chilly drizzle pattered around them. Slowly, the ground began to level out and tussocks of windblown grass struggled to get a purchase amid the boulders and gravel.

'Nice,' said Macro. 'But I'm sure the view is worth it.'

'View?' Cato glanced round. 'Don't count on it.'

Macro shook his head. 'Thought you were the one who had mastered irony?'

Cato smiled. 'Sorry.'

'There you go again . . .'

They found some shelter from the wind and rain under a rocky overhang and sat down, huddled inside their military cloaks, chewing on some of the dried beef from their haversacks. The hours passed and still the sky remained grey and foreboding. Then late in the afternoon, Cato estimated, the clouds thinned and a faint glow of sunlight bloomed across the mountain top. The rain stopped, and patches of clear blue sky broke through the clouds. Below them, the mountainside slowly became visible until there was even a hint of sea far below where its foot dipped into the bay. At last the bright breeze blew away the last of the cloud cover and the two centurions had a fine view of the other half of the Gates of Stone – the mountain on the far side of the opening to the bay. From there the ridge swept far inland and circled round and finally climbed up to the mountaintop where Cato and Macro were sitting. Below them the waters of the bay glittered serenely and out at sea tiny whitecaps danced across the tops of the waves.

'All right, I admit it,' said Macro. 'The view was worth it.'

'Yes,' Cato replied. 'Especially when you consider that aspect.'

He raised his hand and pointed at the mountain opposite. At its base a small spur of rock curved out into the bay. At the end, overlooking the bay was a small fortified village, while in the calm waters below were the tiny slivers of galleys, anchored in two neat rows.

CHAPTER THIRTY-TWO

'That's it!' Macro thumped one fist into the other. 'Has to be those bloody pirates!'

Cato squinted down into the bay, scanning the ships. Two were definitely triremes, and the liburnian rigs of most of the others were the same as the ships that had attacked the Ravenna fleet, like the two ships they had captured several nights ago. He nodded.

'It's them all right.' He reached behind him for his haversack, dragged it round and undid the straps. Macro glanced down in surprise.

'I don't think this is the best time for a snack. The sooner we get back and report this to Vespasian the better.'

Cato shook his head as he took out the map and his stylus set. 'Not until I've mapped it.'

'All right,' Macro conceded. 'But do it quickly.'

Cato did a fair approximation of the bay with its causeway and fortifications and the layout of the ships, and then packed away his equipment.

'Let's go.'

The summit of the mountain was only a short distance above them and the two men bent forward and climbed up the track, feeling far more cheerful than they had for what seemed a long time. If all went well, the Ravenna fleet would sail into the bay and crush the pirates within a few days. Then they could return to Rome in triumph and Narcissus would lift the charges against them and, who knew, maybe reward them into the bargain. Life was starting to feel good again and Macro was tempted to sing. He began by humming a marching song that had been popular among the legions in Britain shortly before he and Cato had been forced to leave the island. Macro took a breath and began to sing.

> 'Oh, when I was a young lad,
> A brave soldier I wanted to be,
> To travel the world, fight the foe
> And screw every—'

Cato grabbed his arm and hissed, 'Quiet!'

Macro wrenched his arm free and turned angrily on his companion. 'What the hell do you think you're doing?'

'Shhh!' Cato glared at him desperately. 'Listen!'

They crouched down on the track and Macro tilted his head and strained his ears. Almost at once he heard the faint sound of talking not very far away, from the crest of the mountain. The centurions both looked up, their eyes following the track, which disappeared round a boulder no more than fifteen paces away. Someone called out in a strange tongue, then again, as if waiting for a reply. They heard boots scrabbling on loose stones and then the voice called out again, nearer this time.

'Shit!' Macro whispered. 'Must have heard me.'

'He's not raised the alarm yet.' Cato thought quickly, glancing around the surrounding slope. But there was little cover. In any case, the man had heard them, and from the tone of his voice, did not expect to find any enemy lurking down the track. Cato pointed towards the boulder.

'Up there! Quick!'

They moved as swiftly and quietly as they could up the track, and had almost reached the weathered mass of the boulder when a man strode round it and stopped dead no more than five paces away. He was dark-featured and wrapped in a thick cloak over which he had belted his sword, a heavy falcata. The pirate stared at them, mouth gaping, but no sound issuing from it. For an instant all three were still. Cato reacted first, throwing his pack down and snatching at his sword as he threw himself at the pirate. With a gasp of terror the man's hand dropped to his weapon, but his scrabbling fingers merely fumbled at the pommel. Cato slammed into him, left hand clawing for the pirate's throat as the tip of his sword punched through the man's cloak and into his stomach with all the force Cato could throw behind it. The pirate doubled over the blade with an explosive groan and tumbled back on to the stony path, Cato crashing down heavily on top of him. The impact drove the remaining breath from his lungs so that the only sound that came from his lips was a rattling gasp for air. Even as he knew he was doomed, the pirate threw his hands towards his attacker's face, scratching at Cato's eyes, stubby cracked nails gouging at the flesh on the Roman's cheeks.

Cato was close enough to smell the reek of onions and wine on the pirate's breath, but he ignored the stench and thrust harder with his sword arm, aiming up into the ribcage, probing for the man's heart to end his struggles swiftly. The pirate suddenly flailed with his arms and legs and drew his knees up hard in a last desperate spasm, catching Cato in the groin. Then his body tensed for a moment, before slowly growing limp.

As Macro scrambled up, Cato released his grip on his sword and rolled to one side clutching a hand to his balls as a wave of nausea swept up through his guts.

'Oh . . . shit,' he managed to gasp before he threw his head to one side and retched. 'Ohhherrrr.'

Macro checked that the pirate was dead and then turned to his friend and grinned. 'Tough luck!'

Before he could laugh at Cato writhing on the ground, hands clutched between his legs, they both heard a voice calling out. Then another man spoke.

'There's more of them!' Macro hissed to Cato. 'Stay here!'

Macro unclasped his cloak and let it drop to the ground as he unsheathed his sword and crept up to the boulder. Balancing carefully, Macro crouched low and peered around the boulder. The track wound across a rock-strewn plateau to a small shelter, above a cliff that overlooked the bay on one side, and seaward approaches on the other. The pirates' lookout station was constructed of stone and weatherproofed with sods of earth packed into the gaps between the stones. A small eddy of smoke rose from the turf roof and a man was standing by the entrance, nonchalantly stretching his neck and shoulders. He rolled his head and then glanced down the track, calling out impatiently. He reached for a spear and began to walk in Macro's direction.

Macro carefully eased himself back behind the boulder. 'One more coming this way. At least another one in the shelter. Keep quiet. I'll take him.'

'Keep quiet?' Cato gasped and gritted his teeth as another wave of nausea swept through his guts.

Macro crouched low, holding his sword by his side, ready to spring out and attack the moment the other pirate came round the boulder. His heart beat madly in his chest and he tried to still his breathing as footsteps crunched on the path just a short distance away. The footsteps ceased and the man called out again, this time his words edged with unmistakable concern. He came forward again, more cautiously. Macro glanced down and realised that the pirate would see the body of the first man at any moment. He reacted instinctively. Drawing a sharp breath he scrambled out from behind the rock and ten feet away from him he saw the pirate, levelling his spear.

'Shit!' Macro hissed, pausing only an instant before he charged forward. The pirate, still momentarily stunned, reacted at the last moment and, grasping the spear firmly in both hands, he thrust it at the Roman. Macro swept his sword arm out, knocked the spear head to one side and charged on, aiming for the man's throat. But his sleeve caught on the end of the spear and yanked him back. Macro tumbled backwards, the impact driving the breath from his lungs.

With a triumphant grin the pirate plucked his spear from Macro's sleeve and stepped towards the Roman, prodding the tip of the spear into his chest. Macro felt the hard iron tip cut into his flesh and winced. The man shouted at him, nodding towards the sword in Macro's outstretched hand. The centurion understood at once and let the blade fall from his fingers.

'All right! All right, I give up.'

The pirate, keeping his eyes on his prisoner, turned his head back slightly and opened his mouth to call out towards the shelter. But before he could say anything, there was a dark blur and a thud as a rock the size of a man's fist struck the pirate a glancing blow on the side of his forehead. With a grunt he reeled back, raising one hand from the spear shaft. At once Macro rolled away, and snatched up his sword. He scrambled round and hacked at the back of the pirate's knee, slicing through tendons and shattering bones. The man dropped heavily. His skull cracked on a rock and he went limp, blood rippling from a deep tear in his scalp. Macro looked up and saw Cato leaning against the boulder.

'Nice shot, lad.'

Cato waved a hand in acknowledgement and slumped down again with a grimace. Macro glanced at the pirate and ran on towards the shelter, fifty feet away. The stones crunched loudly under his iron-nailed boots, but the element of surprise was lost now; only speed mattered. Before he reached the shelter an arm swept back the leather doorflap and a turbaned head emerged from the entrance. A dark-skinned face with yellow eyes turned towards Macro and just had time to register a look of shock and fear before Macro launched himself at the man with a loud roar. They tumbled back into the shelter, falling on to a small pot steaming over a cooking fire. The man gave a shriek as his back was scalded by the contents of the pot and scorched by the fire. The thick air of the shelter was at once tainted with the smell of porridge and the acrid stench of burned hair. Macro's sword had lodged in the man's hip, and he released the grip, and pinned the pirate down, one hand clenched around his throat and the other grasping one of the man's wrists. He continued to scream, even as Macro tightened his grip around the man's throat, crushing the windpipe. For a moment the man bucked and writhed desperately until, after what seemed an age, his strength failed and he lost consciousness. Macro held him down a while longer, to make quite sure he was finished, and then rolled to one side breathing heavily.

A shadow fell across the entrance to the shelter as Cato leaned against the rough wood of the door frame. He looked down at the body smothering the fire and his face wrinkled with distaste.

'You didn't have to cook him . . .' Cato glanced at his friend. 'You all right?'

'Fine. Just fine.' Macro pulled himself up and squatted over the body as he grasped the handle of his sword with both hands and tore it free. He wiped it on the worn tunic of the pirate and returned it to its sheath, before brushing past Cato into the fresh air and away from the smell of smouldering flesh and burned hair.

'How about you?' Macro nodded down at Cato's crotch.

'I'll live, but I'm not so sure any putative heirs will.'

Macro smiled. 'And there's me always telling 'em how you've got balls of iron.'

'Thanks for your concern.' Cato sat down, looked round the small lookout station and thought for a moment. 'We've got a problem.'

'We have?' Macro nodded at the dead pirate inside the shelter. 'Not any more. I think we got them all.'

'That's just it. What happens if the pirates discover we've killed these men? Think about it. They'll know we've been here, and that means we've discovered where their base is.'

Macro nodded, grasping the implications of the new situation at once. 'They'll run for it. And we're back to square one. With a bloody pissed-off Prefect Vespasian into the bargain. But surely, if we can get back to the fleet in time, we can still trap them in the bay before they discover we've taken out their lookout station.'

Cato shook his head. 'They're going to find out long before then.'

'Why?'

'That first man. I got the impression he was expecting someone when he heard you singing. Makes sense. There's no food up here. The lookouts would need to have food sent up to them. And if he was expecting someone, you can be sure they'll be here soon enough, see the bodies and raise the alarm at once. Probably from right here, which means Telemachus will have plenty of time to escape long before we even get back to Vespasian.'

'Shit,' muttered Macro. 'So what do we do? Wait for the supplies to turn up and take care of them as well?'

'No. We can't delay getting word back to the fleet.'

'Great!' Macro slapped his thigh in frustration. 'So what do we do?'

'Only thing we can do,' Cato replied. 'You go back to the fleet and tell them everything. Take my map, that'll make it clearer. I'll stay here and wait for the supplies to turn up.'

'That's madness,' Macro protested. 'You've no idea how many men there'll be.'

'Can't be more than one or two,' said Cato. 'That's all they'll need to lead the supply mules up the track.'

'And what if they bring up men to relieve this lot?' Macro shook his head. 'You wouldn't stand a chance. Not meaning to cause any offence or anything, Cato, but you're no champion gladiator.'

'No offence taken,' Cato said grudgingly. 'We'd just better hope they don't change their lookouts too frequently.'

Macro looked at him in silence for a moment, trying to think of any further arguments he could use to dissuade his friend, but Cato was right. They simply could not risk the enemy being aware that their secret lair had been discovered. If only they had not blundered on this lookout post. If only he hadn't started singing, Macro reproached himself bitterly. They might have seen the lookout post in time to skirt round it and continue their journey back to the fleet with the enemy being none the wiser. He looked at Cato.

'I'll stay. You get back to the fleet. It's my fault we had to kill them.'

'No.' Cato shook his head. 'We had to silence them. Otherwise they'd have warned the pirates of the fleet's approach. We were lucky to have found them. Don't blame yourself.'

Macro shrugged, still unable to entirely shift the burden of guilt.

'You go.' Cato insisted. 'Vespasian must be told the pirates are here. The message has to get through, and you're the best bet. I'll do my bit here.'

'I see. And how will you get back to the fleet once you've dealt with the men bringing the supplies?'

'I'll stay up here until the fleet arrives. If we do surprise them I'll make my way down and you can tell them to send a boat for me. If I'm badly outnumbered here, I'll run for it. After I've set this place on fire. That'll be the signal to our side that the pirates have discovered we're on to them. I'll not take any pointless risks, Macro,' Cato tried to reassure his friend. 'Sooner a live centurion than a dead hero.'

Macro laughed. 'The wisest thing you've ever said, Cato. All right then, I'll go.'

'Right now would be good.'

'What? No rest? And me just having come out of a fight?'

'Just go, Macro.' Cato took the map from inside his tunic and held it out to his friend. 'Here.'

Macro leaned over and took the map. 'I'll see you later, Cato.'

'Remember, don't stop for anything. Be careful. No more singing.'

'What's wrong with my singing?' Macro grinned, then turned away and marched across the top of the plateau. Cato watched him, until the path dipped down the far side of the mountain and his friend disappeared from view. He was alone, except for the spirits of the three men whose bodies lay on the mountain top with him. Around the silent and still lookout post, a cold damp breeze blew mournfully.

CHAPTER THIRTY-THREE

Cato waited until the pain in his groin had subsided enough for him to move around easily. Now that Macro was gone, the first doubts about the wisdom of the course of action he had insisted on occurred to him. If three men came up the path he would be at a disadvantage. He could count on disabling one pirate when he surprised them. That would leave a straight fight with one man, which he should be able to handle. But two men? He had seen enough fights to know that almost any two men, with their wits about them, could defeat a man on his own. Provided they took their time and divided his attention. Cato made a decision. If he was faced by more than two men he would set fire to the lookout post and run for it.

The thought of fire drew him back to the present. The pirate slowly roasting on top of the fire was beginning to smell terrible. Cato took a breath of cool air and then plunged into the shelter. The interior was filled with smoke and the stench of burning hair and seared flesh was quite sickening. Cato gritted his teeth and bent over to grab the ankles of the pirate, pulled the man off the cooking fire and dragged him outside. Before Cato could spring any surprise on the enemy he must dispose of the lookouts' bodies. A latrine ditch lay fifty feet from the shelter and Cato dragged the corpse over to the ditch and, nose wrinkling with disgust at the stench of raw human waste, he rolled the body into the ditch. When he returned to the man he had hit with the rock Cato realised the pirate was still alive, but only just.

For a moment he debated whether to finish him off. The man was dead one way or another: he could expect no mercy from Vespasian if the Roman fleet won the day. The injury to his head looked severe enough to kill him eventually, and yet Cato could not find the resolution within himself to end the pirate's suffering. If it had been a fight Cato would have no compunction about killing his man, and doing it quickly and efficiently with no sentiment. The prospect of killing a helpless man, however, disturbed him. It was irrational to have such perverse scruples, he reasoned with himself as he lifted the man under his shoulders and started dragging him towards the latrine ditch. The pirate groaned feebly as Cato hauled him across the rocky plateau and dumped him on top of his comrade.

Cato turned away quickly and made his way back to the first man, the one he had killed on the path. As he moved the body he saw that the ground was soaked with blood, and there was more splattered across the side of the boulder. Once the body had joined the others Cato cut some strips from a cloak laying outside the shelter and found a water skin before he returned to the path beside the boulder. He worked quickly, dowsing the stains and rubbing them away with the rags, expecting the enemy to arrive any moment. At last he was satisfied that he had done enough to hide the evidence of the fight. The water was already soaking into the path and would soon disappear. In any case, Cato told himself, the pirates would not be expecting any trouble up on the isolated mountain top. The threat they would be guarding against was from the direction of the sea. The mountains that ringed the bay had been hard enough going for Cato and Macro, travelling as lightly as possible. There was little chance that a heavily armed force of soldiers would be able to scale the steep slopes undetected.

Having taken care of the bodies and washed the blood away, Cato took the chance to examine the lookout station more closely. Not far from the shelter the plateau narrowed and dropped away in a precipitous cliff. From its tip it was possible to look far along the coast on either side. The pirates had constructed a crude signal station with a mast, beside which sat a small chest. Cato lifted the lid and saw bundles of brightly coloured material. All quite useless, of course, without any idea of what each pennant signified. Beside the mast sat a peculiar-looking device mounted on a small post. Two highly polished metal plates were fixed at angles to each other and Cato surmised that it might be some kind of heliograph.

He returned to the shelter, picked up the lookouts' spears then went back to the boulder to keep watch down the track that sloped away for nearly a quarter of a mile before disappearing over a small spur thrusting out from the side of the mountain. He set the spears down behind the boulder and eased himself into a position overlooking the track. He would see them coming in plenty of time. He settled down to wait, leaning up against the boulder as the sun rose into the sky and began to bathe the world in its warm glow. The light breeze slowly drove the clouds before it, clearing them away down the coast and revealing for the first time the full distance that could be observed from the top of the mountain.

For a while Cato revelled in the sense of Olympian detachment he felt as he gazed down on the bay at the foot of the mountain rising up opposite his position. Tiny figures swarmed around three ships drawn up on the beach. They had been rolled on to one side and wedged so that an expanse of their underside was clearly exposed. Smoke coiled up from fires twinkling further up the beach and Cato guessed that the pirates must be applying a fresh layer of tar to the bottom of the ships. His gaze slowly travelled along the thin strip of land that linked the beach to the citadel at the end. That was the only viable approach to the citadel since on the other three sides it was protected by sheer rocky cliffs. The landward side was defended by a solid-looking masonry wall with a gatehouse, from which a timber bridge projected across a defence ditch. Behind the wall, a jumble of whitewashed houses climbed up to the highest point of the rocky spur, where a small tower nestled above the sea, twinkling at the foot of the cliff. The pirates must have seized the citadel, or perhaps it had been abandoned long ago. In any case, Telemachus had chosen an excellent location for his base of operations, in every respect save that there was no alternative route out of the bay should an enemy block its entrance. Hence the need for a lookout station with such commanding views of the approaches to the pirate base, Cato realised. The pirates would need plenty of warning if they were to make a clean escape from the bay.

Gazing out to sea Cato caught sight of the tiny triangle of a sail several miles away; some merchant ship no doubt keeping a wary eye out for pirates, blissfully ignorant that they were sailing right by the hidden pirate lair. He was suddenly aware that had he and Macro not intervened, the lookouts would already be signalling the presence of the merchant ship and thereby sealing her fate. He smiled at the thought that there was one prize Telemachus and his pirates were never going to seize.

As the sun climbed to its zenith it grew so warm that Cato discarded his cloak and set it down beside the boulder as he kept watch. Then, shortly before noon, he heard a voice cry out. He drew his sword and tensed up, but quickly realised the sound had not come from down the slope, but from the other direction, towards the lookouts' shelter. Cato turned round and scanned the plateau. Almost at once he saw a dark shape rise up from the ground and his heart leaped in his chest. There was another cry, a plaintive mixture of pain and a call for help. Then Cato realised that it was the wounded man, sitting up in the latrine ditch.

'Shit!' Cato hissed through clenched teeth. He should have killed him earlier. Now he would have to, before the man recovered enough to become a danger, or called out to warn his comrades. But he just watched in horrified fascination as the man tried to climb out of the ditch, lost his grip and slipped back down, out of sight with a cry of pain and frustration. A moment later his head rose over the rim and he tried to pull himself out of the ditch again.

A distant braying caught Cato's ears and he tore his gaze away from the latrine ditch and stared down the slope. At first he could see nothing. Then a man appeared on the track where it crossed the spur. He was leading a mule with two large baskets slung either side. Another mule appeared behind him, then three men carrying spears. Cato felt a sick feeling of dread wreath its way round his stomach as he watched the men slowly climb up the track. There were too many of them. He eased himself back behind the boulder and was about to make for the shelter to set it ablaze when he stopped and looked at the base of the rock more closely, struck by a sudden inspiration. Placing the palms of his hands against the rough surface of the boulder he braced his legs and pushed steadily. For an instant nothing happened, had been broken by the boulder. The stricken animal was on its side, front legs thrashing on the loose surface, while its back legs lay crushed and inert. Behind the second mule the bottom half of one of the pirates protruded from beneath the boulder, his head and upper torso flattened to a pulp. Beside him sat one of his companions, staring in shock at a broken leg, the sharp white splinter of bone thrusting through the torn and bloody flesh of his shin.

The third pirate was unharmed, but momentarily frozen in horror as he stared at his companions. But he saw Cato the instant the Roman stumbled round the edge of the boulder, spear grasped tightly, drawn back and ready to thrust. The pirate hesistated for no more than an instant efore he turned and sprinted back down the track, rambling as he struggled to retain his balance.

'Bastard!' Cato cursed him, and jumped over the injured ate as he chased the fleeing man. Cato knew the pirate st not be allowed to escape at any cost, and he threw self down the slope. The pirate did not have much of a , but Cato realised that he would never catch the man e burdened with the spear. He slithered to a stop, hing heavily, drew back the spear, sighted along its h and threw it with all his strength. It flew in a low tory straight for the man's back and even as he turned d to glance at his pursuer, the iron head slammed into ehind his left shoulder blade, piercing flesh and bone it tore through his heart and ripped out through the f his chest. The impact threw him forward and s and he cartwheeled down the path before falling nert heap on the side of the mountain.

leaned forward, resting his hands on his knees as t his breath. Then he strode down to the body to t the man was dead. Sightless eyes stared up at the

then he felt it shift a little and small pebbles from around its base rattled down the path.

There was another cry from the man in the latrine, louder now. If Cato didn't silence him the men on the track would hear him long before they reached the plateau. Cato took a last glance down the slope to gauge their pace and then turned to run back towards the shelter. He ran on to the latrine and slowed to a walk a few steps from the edge of the trench. The sun had heated the mixture of ordure, urine and blood to a ripe odour and Cato felt his stomach tighten. The wounded man was still crying out as Cato leaned cautiously over the trench.

'Quiet!' he said harshly in Greek.

The man looked up at him with wide, terrified eyes. Then he opened his mouth and screamed out.

'Shut up!' Cato hissed at him. He jabbed a finger at the man and then pressed it to his lips. 'Shhhh! Be a good pirate and keep your bloody mouth shut!'

The man continued screaming and Cato drew his finger across his throat. 'Shut up, or else! Understand?'

Cato glanced back at the boulder in desperation. The man was going to get him killed if he continued making this racket. Then Cato realised. It was him or the man. Simple as that. Cato drew his sword and stood over the latrine for a moment.

'Sorry. But you wouldn't listen.'

At the last moment the man raised both hands, clenched together in a begging motion. He shut his eyes and turned his face away from Cato as the glinting blade slashed down into his throat. Cato straightened up as blood gushed out. The man writhed and spluttered for a moment. Cato waited until he was sure the man was quite dead and would pose no further danger, then he turned away. He ran back to the shelter, sheathed his sword and took a firm hold of one of the doorposts, pulling it towards him. It shifted a little and Cato pushed it the other way, then pulled it back. He strained his muscles to work it free and finally it erupted from the ground and he tumbled back as the roof of the shelter fell in. Snatching up the stout post, Cato raced back to the boulder, heart pounding from his exertions.

When he reached the boulder he glanced back down the slope and was shocked to see the enemy no more than fifty paces from the place where he had killed the first of the lookouts. Cato crouched down and shoved the doorpost under the base of the boulder, ramming it home as far as he could, before he dragged a large rock into place beneath the post to act as a fulcrum. Then he crept to the side of the boulder and peered cautiously around the edge until he could see the track. Already the scraping clop of the mules carried easily to his ears and then he could hear the voices of the pirates, breathless, but still bantering in the easy humorous tone of men who had no thought of imminent danger.

They climbed steadily towards the plateau and Cato wondered one last time if he was being a fool, and whether he should run for it even now. After all, the pirates had had a long weary climb up from the foot of the mountain and would be too tired to continue the pursuit for long. If Cato moved now, and doubled quietly round them he could still make his way along the edge of the plateau without being detected and follow Macro's trail down the far slope. Then he forced himself to take a grip on his fears. It was only natural that, in this moment just before a fight, his racing mind would fall victim to doubts. He must remember how much was riding on what happened in the next few moments. If he failed, these men would raise the alarm that

would allow the pirates to escape and find another base from which to prey upon merchant shipping. Many more lives would be lost. Worst of all, Narcissus would redouble his efforts to find and seize the precious scrolls, no matter how many sailors and marines it cost. Cato must not ru
from the fight. Moreover, he must not fail.

The man leading the mules stepped into view and C
eased himself back and grasped the end of the doorp
both hands. He leaned his weight on the end of the pc
waited as the mules passed the boulder.

As their driver stepped on to the plateau he cau
of Cato over the rim of the boulder and his mouth
open in surprise. An explosive grunt ripped thro
clenched teeth as he thrust his weight down on
the doorpost. For an instant the boulder waver
stones to gravel beneath its mass, then it e
gathered momentum and toppled down on t
sharp scream was abruptly cut short as the
stone crushed a pirate with a deep thud.
stopped the boulder from falling any furth
and it slammed to the ground, sending up
pebbles and dust.

Cato snatched up one of the spears a
mule-driver. The man carried no w
hands up, screaming at Cato in Latin

'No! Spare me! Spare me!'

Cato paused, taking in the thic
the man's wrists. Then he pointed a
'Get down and don't move, if yo

The man dropped the leash of
on to the path. The mule paid r
simply stared at the boulder v
nostrils. A short distance bel

sky and there was no movement to indicate any sign of life. As Cato turned back up the slope there was a piercing cry as the wounded pirate tried to defend himself from the mule-driver. The latter had picked up a heavy stone and even as Cato watched he slammed it down on the pirate's head. The man grunted and collapsed on the track. Leaning over him the mule-driver swung the rock down again and again, until it came up stained red, and dripping blood and brains.

Cato drew his sword and approached the mule-driver cautiously, speaking quietly. 'I think you got him all right.'

He nodded at the pulverised tangle of hair and skull beneath the mule-driver, and the man glanced down before he returned his gaze to Cato, eyes wide with horror and fear.

'Stay back!'

Cato stopped, and after a moment he sheathed his sword. 'There. You see, I mean you no harm.' He raised his hands. 'See?'

The mule-driver stared at him, his thin chest heaving, then he lowered his arms and tossed the bloody rock to one side and slumped down beside the man he had killed. But still he watched Cato warily.

'Who are you?'

'Centurion Cato. I'm with the Ravenna fleet. We're here to deal with the pirates.'

The mule-driver stared at Cato in silence, and then his shoulders heaved up and huge choking sobs racked his bony chest as he slumped forwards, cradling his head in his hands. Cato crept closer, tentatively reached out and gently squeezed the mule-driver's shoulder.

'It's over. You're free of them now.'

The man nodded, or he might have been shuddering.

Cato could not tell and he tried to find some more words to comfort the mule-driver. 'You're free. You're not their slave any more.'

'Slave!' The man shook Cato's hand from his shoulder and turned round with a wild expression of rage and bitterness. 'Slave! I'm not a slave. I'm a Roman . . . a Roman!'

Cato stepped back. 'I'm sorry. I didn't know . . . What's your name?'

'My name?' The man stiffened his back and stared at Cato with as much haughty disdain as he could summon up in his pitiful state. 'My name is Caius Caelius Secundus.'

CHAPTER THIRTY-FOUR

Night had fallen by the time the yacht reached the fleet and moored alongside Vespasian's flagship. The fleet was anchored in a bay a short distance down the coast from the looming mass of the mountain where the pirates had established their lookout station. The fleet lay close to the shore in complete darkness since Vespasian had forbidden the lighting of any fires or lamps. The troops on the beach had erected a marching camp for the night and were huddled in their tents, eating their rations cold. Macro waited for the crew to secure the yacht to the trireme with their boathooks, then he clambered up the rungs of the quinquireme's side ladder on to the deck and was immediately escorted to the aft cabin by a junior tribune.

The new prefect was sitting at a small table and eating a bowl of barley gruel by the wan light of a single oil lamp that could be permitted in his cabin. He looked up as someone knocked on the door and hurriedly swallowed before answering.

'Come!'

The tribune swung the door open and ducked his head under the low lintel. 'Centurion Macro's returned, sir.'

'Show him in.'

The tribune stepped to one side and ushered the centurion into Vespasian's presence. Macro stood stiffly to attention.

'At ease. Where's Centurion Cato?'

'He's keeping the enemy under observation, sir.'

Vespasian leaned across the table, eyes glinting with eager anticipation. 'You found them, then?'

'Yes, sir. Their fleet and their base. Not ten miles from here. I'll show you on the map, sir.'

Vespasian cleared the bowl and cup from his table as Macro wrestled Cato's map from beneath his cloak and tunic. He laid it on the desk and carefully unfolded it, then both men leaned over it for a closer look in the weak light. Macro indicated the peak of the mountain he and Cato had climbed that morning.

'The enemy have a lookout station up here, sir. We came across it by accident this morning and had to kill the men stationed there.'

Vespasian glanced sidelong at the centurion. 'How many of them?'

'Just three, sir.'

'Just three.' Vespasian smiled. 'You make it sound so easy.'

'We had the drop on them, sir. When surprise is on your side it makes life a lot easier.'

'True enough. Please continue.'

'Yes, sir.' Macro moved his finger across the map to the bay at the foot of the mountain opposite the lookout station. 'That's where they are, sir. We counted twenty-three ships: two triremes, eight biremes, nine liburnians and four smaller vessels.'

Vespasian pursed his lips. 'That's quite a fleet they've built up. This Telemachus must be something of an inspiring leader.'

Macro nodded. 'We found that out the hard way, sir.'

'Yes . . . What else did you see?'

'They've got a fortified citadel on this spit of rock here,

sir. Steep cliffs on three sides and a pretty substantial wall and ditch facing the mainland.'

'Nothing we can't deal with,' Vespasian decided. 'The priority is taking and destroying their ships. Afterwards we can deal with their citadel in good time.'

Macro looked at the prefect. 'I imagine that's where Telemachus will be keeping the scrolls, sir. We'll have to be careful there. Can't risk a fire, sir.'

'You have a point.' Vespasian nodded. 'There'll be no incendiaries used in any bombardment and I'll give the marines strict orders not to set fire to anything when we break into the defences.'

'Can you trust them, sir? They're marines, after all, not legionaries. There's not the same discipline.'

'Then it's up to us legionaries to set them an example, right, Centurion?'

'Yes, sir.'

Macro smiled. Vespasian was a cool one. That kind of comment from almost any other member of the senatorial class would have been taken as a glib piece of rhetoric to win over the common soldiery. But, somehow, Macro felt that this man meant it. Vespasian had the common touch, all right. He had experienced the life and the trials of his men, as far as his senior rank allowed. That's why the Second Legion Augusta had fought so hard for him in the British campaign and had carved out quite a reputation for itself in the process. Macro realised that this was the source of his own sense of loyalty to Vespasian. He was a man to follow.

Vespasian was looking thoughtfully at the map and as he stroked his broad forehead Macro realised the commander was exhausted. More than any man in the fleet. One of the many burdens of high rank, he supposed. As Vespasian examined the map Macro found that he was reminded of Cato, whose endless mental activity seemed to be shared by the prefect of the Ravenna fleet. For a moment Macro envied both men the capacity for such elaborate thinking. It was a talent you either had, or hadn't, and Macro fully accepted that he was not gifted in that manner. For him, soldiering was a far more direct and immediate experience, and he liked it that way, even as he knew that it meant that he was unlikely to rise much beyond his present rank. The alternative, the endless deliberation of Cato and his like, struck Macro as being more of a curse than a blessing.

Vespasian tapped the map. 'Well, we've got them, provided we close the trap swiftly. There's only one problem – the approach to this bay. Thanks to you and Centurion Cato we can get close without them knowing it, but the moment the fleet appears round the side of this mountain they're bound to see us. They'll have a good hour to make sail and prepare their defences. We need to find a way of getting closer before they're aware of the danger.'

Macro cleared his throat. 'A night attack, sir?'

'No.' Vespasian shook his head. 'Out of the question. It would be hard enough to coordinate in open waters. We'd lose ships on the rocks. The fleet would reach them piecemeal and they'd organise a defence long before we could close on them in sufficient strength to have a realistic chance of victory. It has to be by daylight. By land, perhaps. If we put a force ashore on the other side of the mountain, they could climb across during the night and attack the moment the fleet comes into sight.' Vespasian looked up in excitement. 'That might do it.'

'Beg your pardon, sir, but it won't work.'

'Oh?' Vespasian frowned. 'Why not?'

'It's these mountains, sir. Cato and I just about managed

to cope with them. Those marines are good lads, but they're not great marchers and that kind of terrain will kill them, sir. Even if they did get over the mountain, they'd take far too long and be too tired for much fighting when they reached the enemy.' He met his superior's eyes and saw that Vespasian looked irritated by his assessment of the terrain. 'Sorry, sir. That's how I see it.'

'All right, then,' Vespasian responded grudgingly. 'We have to come up with something else . . . something to get us in close before they realise they're under attack . . . some kind of Trojan horse.'

Macro puffed out his cheeks and Vespasian chuckled at the gesture. 'You have a problem with Greek mythology, Centurion?'

'Not as long as it stays in the books, sir.'

'Don't like books, I take it?'

'No, sir. I get enough stories from the other ranks as it is.'

'Well, perhaps you should read a little more, Centurion. Nothing like it for broadening the mind, and inspiring the imagination.'

Macro shrugged. 'If you say so, sir. But I don't think there's really enough time to knock up a wooden horse. Besides, there's the transportation problem. Something big enough to hide a decent-sized force in is going to be an absolute bugger to get on board a ship. Even one this size.'

Vespasian watched him in amusement as Macro explained his misgivings. When the centurion had finished Vespasian couldn't help smiling.

'What have I said, sir?' Macro looked offended. 'I just don't think it will work, sir. However good an idea it might seem,' he added quickly. 'Besides, that's the kind of low crafty trick that only the Greeks would use.'

'Sometimes, even the Greeks did the right thing,

Centurion . . . But, no. You're quite right. It wouldn't work. We'll have to try something else.'

Macro nodded happily, glad that his commander had seen reason. This was the unfortunate side of the creative intelligence of men such as Vespasian and Cato, Macro reflected. Once in a while their imaginations rushed way ahead of their reasoning and needed to be reined in by a fatherly word of restraint, from more worldly heads.

Vespasian took a last look at the map and gave a faint nod, before he met Macro's gaze again, this time with a mischievous twinkle in his eyes. 'Very well. Not a Trojan horse. A Trojan whale, then.'

Macro winced. What on earth was Vespasian thinking of now?

'Those two pirate vessels you and Centurion Cato captured a few nights back . . .'

'What about them, sir?'

'I think it's time we put them to good use.'

CHAPTER THIRTY-FIVE

Caius Caelius Secundus woke shortly after sunset and looked round anxiously before memory of the Roman centurion's rescue flooded back to him in a wave of images and emotions. Just above him was what remained of the roof of the shelter. He reached over and picked up a cloak that had been left for him by the bedding and wrapped it around his thin shoulders. With a grunt Secundus rose and, bending low, he moved over to the entrance of the shelter. He paused a moment before cautiously pushing the leather tent flap to one side and peering out. A short distance away a faint glow radiated up from the fire pit on to the face of Centurion Cato. They had spoken briefly after the ambush, when Cato had led him across the plateau to the shelter. Secundus had been exhausted from his long climb up the mountain, and emotionally overcome by his sudden release from captivity. The rage that had burned in his heart at the months of indignity and suffering had exploded in a moment of fury when he had crushed the pirate's head and afterwards he felt numb and spent as Cato had tried to make him comfortable and let him rest.

Now the young officer glanced up as he became aware that he was being watched, and smiled at Secundus.

'Feeling better?'

'Much.' Secundus emerged from the shelter and

straightened up. A faint aroma of stewing meat wafted into his nostrils and immediately he was reminded of how hungry he was; how hungry he had been throughout his captivity. Secundus walked stiffly over to the fireplace and sat down opposite his rescuer. Between them, hanging from a small tripod was a battered iron pot filled almost to the brim with a thick bubbling liquid. 'Smells good. What is it?'

'Barley and mule,' Cato replied. 'Thought I might as well make the most of the one that got caught under the rock. The other one bolted.'

There was a moment's silence in which Secundus looked round at the night sky and saw that it was quite clear. Away to the horizon there was a broad band of watery orange that quickly faded to a dark blue and then an inky black by the time it reached the opposite horizon. Some of the brightest stars were already out, scattered across the heavens like distant specks of silver. High up on the mountain top the air was cold, and Secundus pulled the cloak tighter about him and shuffled closer to the edge of the fire pit. He looked across at the centurion.

'I haven't thanked you yet, young man.'

Cato winced momentarily at the reference to his age before he tilted his head in acknowledgement. 'You're welcome.'

There was another pause, before Secundus asked, 'So what were you doing up here? It's a strange place to find a centurion, all on his own.'

Cato sensed the suspicion in the other man's tone and smiled to himself. He would feel the same way about such a fortuitous rescue by another Roman. 'We're on a reconnaissance mission.'

'We?'

'My friend and I. Another centurion serving with the

Ravenna fleet. We had information that the pirates were somewhere in this area. We were sent in to check. Right now, Macro should be making his report. Then the prefect will head here with his full force and destroy the pirates.'

'You seem very sure of victory.'

Cato grinned. 'I'm just very sure about Prefect Vespasian. He doesn't like to waste any time when he's got an enemy lined up for a good kicking.'

'Why did you remain here?'

'Had to,' Cato replied simply. 'Once we stumbled on the lookout station we had to put it out of operation and make sure it couldn't warn Telemachus of the fleet's approach. Once our ships arrive we'll go down the mountain and join them.'

'I see.'

Cato looked at him. 'Now, if you don't mind, there's some questions I'd like to ask you.'

'I'd be delighted,' Secundus replied, and gestured towards the steaming pot. 'Over a meal.'

'Of course. I'm sorry.' Cato picked up his mess tin and leaned over the fire pit to ladle some stew into the tin. He handed it across to Secundus and sat down as the other man raised the tin to his lips.

'Careful!' Cato warned him. 'It's bloody hot. Give it a moment to cool down. You can use this.' He tossed the man his spoon.

'Thanks.' Secundus cradled the mess tin in the folds of his cloak. 'Ask away.'

'Firstly, you're Narcissus' agent, aren't you?'

Secundus looked up sharply. 'What makes you say that?'

'Narcissus briefed us about what had happened to you. That's the reason why Macro and I were given this assignment in the first place. We were sent out with Prefect Vitellius to crush the pirates and rescue you.'

'I thought you said Vespasian was the prefect.'

'He is now. Vitellius made an utter balls-up of the opening stages of the campaign and Narcissus replaced him as soon as he got word.' He cleared his throat. 'In addition to defeating the pirates we were also tasked with retrieving the scrolls.'

Secundus tensed up for an instant, and then he raised a spoon of stew to his lips and blew across the surface to cool it down. He did not look up when he stopped blowing. 'Scrolls? What scrolls would they be?'

'The ones you were carrying back to Rome.'

'I was carrying quite a few messages back to Rome at the time of my capture.'

'Maybe.' Cato shrugged. 'But I think you'd remember the scrolls I'm talking about. The Sybilline scrolls.'

Secundus stared at him. 'You know about them? Who else knows?'

'Macro, Vitellius, and now Vespasian, of course. Officially, that's the list of the people in the know.' Cato told the lie comfortably enough. 'We've been told to get the scrolls back at any cost. And you, of course.'

Secundus couldn't help smiling. 'But, according to Narcissus, the scrolls are the priority. My rescue was a supplementary goal. Am I right?'

'You know Narcissus.'

'Well enough . . . It seems that you've got *your* priorities the wrong way round, Centurion Cato. You've freed me, but the scrolls are still down there with Telemachus. I understand he wants to ransom them.'

'If only it was that simple. It's not so much a ransom as an auction.'

Secundus carefully sipped the soup off the spoon and smiled contentedly before he returned his thoughts to the wider political situation. 'I imagine that if there's anyone else who wants to get their hands on the scrolls, the Liberators would have to be top of the list.'

'That's my thinking,' Cato agreed. 'But let's face it; anyone with the right money and the right connections would have more than a passing interest in possessing the scrolls. It's not every day that the entire future of the Empire is laid out right in front of your eyes.'

'That's why it has to be Narcissus who gets them.'

'He's hardly a neutral power in this situation.'

'No. But he's a safe pair of hands, and because he only serves the Emperor, there's little risk of him using the knowledge to further his own ends. In every other respect I'd trust him about as far as I could spit a brick. He's a bastard all right, but at least he's our bastard.' Secundus paused to sip another spoon of stew. 'But we're getting ahead of ourselves. Telemachus still has the scrolls.'

'Do you know where he's keeping them?'

Secundus nodded. 'I think so. When I was first captured he kept me in a cell in the citadel. I was tortured for the first few days while they tried to get every scrap of information they could out of me concerning those bloody scrolls. First they beat me, then dragged me up to his private quarters where he'd question me. Him and that son of his. Young Ajax has a cruel streak a mile wide.'

Cato smiled. 'You might like to know he's been on the receiving end. We took him and two of their ships the other day.'

'Good for you, Centurion. Little bastard deserves it, after what he did to me . . . Anyway, that's where I saw them – the scrolls. On his desk. Telemachus had them out a few times when they were torturing me. The scrolls are kept in a small casket.' Secundus paused to fix the image in his mind. 'It's black, decorated with gold and onyx cameos. The last time I was questioned was over a month ago. That's the last time I saw the scrolls. I assume Telemachus is still keeping them safe in his quarters. There's something else you should know. I think Telemachus has a spy in the fleet. He once told me to give up any hope of being rescued. He boasted that he knew every detail about the Ravenna fleet. More than enough to ensure its defeat.'

'They gave us a hiding,' Cato confirmed. 'We lost several ships and hundreds of men. You're right about the spy. The pirates knew exactly where to intercept the fleet, and how vulnerable our lighter ships would be under their load of supplies and equipment. If we ever find out who the spy is I don't think any power on earth is going to stop the men from tearing him to pieces.'

'They said they had beaten the Ravenna fleet. I didn't believe them at the time.' Secundus shook his head sadly at the unlikely prospect of the reversal of arms. Like all Romans he was raised to believe in Roman invincibility. For Cato, at the sharp end of imperial policy, the successful defence of the Empire's borders by the widely spread legions and fleets seemed nothing short of a miracle.

Secundus continued quietly. 'Seems that Telemachus is as good as he thinks he is after all.'

Cato shook his head. 'He's had his run of luck. His time's up, or will be very soon. You'll see. Now tell me, what happened after the questioning was done with?'

Secundus gestured to his wasted body with his spare hand. 'I was sent down to the stables to look after the mules. Since then, it's been endless mucking out, and trips up to this place every three days. Rowing a bloody great boat across the bay, and then a bastard of a climb up this mountain.'

'How long before you and the others are missed?'

'We're expected back by nightfall today.'

'That's fine,' Cato replied. 'I'm surprised they didn't keep you somewhere nice and secure. You might have escaped.'

'I was always watched.'

'Fair enough. You must have seen enough of this base to provide some useful information once you were ransomed.'

Secundus looked up at Cato. 'What makes you think they were ever going to let me go? Besides, one of the guards told me that they were going to quit the bay soon, and find another lair, next to some new hunting grounds.'

'Did Telemachus ever mention the Liberators?'

'He said there were other parties interested in the scrolls.'

'Did he ever mention the name of their agent?'

'No. But I think I saw him once.' Secundus' brow crinkled as he recalled the details. 'I was loading the provision boat when a ship came in and landed a Roman. They took him under guard. Straight to the citadel. I never knew his name.'

'Then what did he look like?'

'Mid-thirties, maybe forty. Medium build . . . Nothing outstanding about him. Except the scar.'

'Scar? What about it?'

'He had a livid red mark on his cheek, like a burn . . . Sorry, that's all I can remember.'

'It's enough. If I could produce this man again, would you recognise him?'

'With that scar, I should think so.'

'If I'm right, his name is Anobarbus. That mean anything to you?'

'No. Sorry.' Secundus lowered his head and smelled the stew in the mess tin. 'I can't tell you how good this is.'

'There's plenty there, help yourself. But don't overdo it. It wouldn't go well with Narcissus if I saved you from torture and slavery only to kill you with kindness.'

Secundus laughed, drew a breath at the wrong moment and started choking on the stew, which dribbled from his nose as his body was racked by a fit of coughing. Cato sprang up in alarm and hurried round to deliver a hefty whack to the other man's bony back. He raised his hand to repeat the blow, but Secundus ducked away from him.

'Stop! I'm all right! I'm all right. No need for that.' He coughed a few times and then looked up at Cato with a chuckle. 'Sorry about that, but I haven't had a laugh for months. I haven't dared to. Thanks.' He smiled. 'You've made me feel much better. Almost human again. Thank you, Centurion Cato.'

For a moment the sense of relief was almost too much to bear and Secundus' eyes glimmered with tears. He cuffed them away quickly, set the mess tin down and rose to his feet.

'I'll sleep now.'

'You do that.' Cato smiled. 'I think tomorrow might just be a very long day.'

Cato rose with the dawn, waking suddenly into full consciousness from a deep sleep. He had been a soldier long enough to make the transition easily and at once. He threw back the pirate's sleeping blanket he had taken from the shelter and was on his feet an instant later, stretching his arms and shoulders. The sound of snoring came from the shelter and Cato decided to let the imperial agent sleep on for a while yet. The man needed time to rest and recover from his long ordeal at the hands of the pirates.

Cato made his way over to the signal station on the edge of the cliff, sat down and leaned against the signal mast. The horizon was clear, and there was no sign of any shipping along the coast. Before the pirates had established themselves in this area there would have been scores of sails in view. Cato turned and looked down towards the bay on the opposite shore. A thin haze of smoke eddied over the pirates' citadel and a few tiny dots moved along the shore by the ships. A peaceful enough scene, for the moment. All that would change once Vespasian arrived.

Cato stared down on the world for a while. The view was awe-inspiring and he quickly became lost in a peculiar serenity. Far below him, men were preparing for a new day of work on the beached pirate ships. Somewhere out there the men of the Ravenna fleet might be preparing themselves to fight a bitter battle with the unsuspecting pirates. Yet from up here, all these details seemed quite puny and inconsequential in the face of the mountains stretching out on either side, and an ocean that swept out to the horizon, unconfined by any sign of distant land. How peaceful it looked.

Then a small detail at the periphery of his vision stirred him back into full consciousness of his situation. Far below, on the blue sheen of the sea, five vessels were crawling across the sea half a mile off the rocky shore at the base of the mountain. They must have been visible for some time Cato realised, angry with himself for not spotting them sooner. Five galleys, he realised as he made out the twin lines of splashes that punctuated their progress. He watched them keenly as they turned towards the long inlet and headed straight at the far mountain and the pirate base beyond. As they drew closer he strained his eyes and saw that the two vessels at the head and tail of the small convoy were liburnians. In between them were three biremes. Cato frowned. What could this mean? Where was the Ravenna fleet?

Just then, as the lead liburnian emerged from the shadows into the sunlit expanse of ocean there was a dazzling flash from its fore deck. As Cato turned to look at the vessel directly the flash came again. Then another. There was a brief pause before there were three more flashes. A signal, Cato realised. The pirates were flashing a signal to the lookout station. He was seized by panic as it dawned on him that they were expecting a reply, or for the signal to be relayed. Cato stood up, trying to think. Then he turned and ran back to the shelter, shouting at the top of his voice.

'Secundus! Secundus! Get out here, man! Hurry!'

A moment later the leather curtain was wrenched aside and Secundus tumbled out of the shelter, rubbing his eyes. As soon as he saw the tense expression in the face of the centurion rushing towards him he straightened up. 'What's up? What's happening?'

'Pirate ships approaching the bay!' Cato pointed to the cliff edge. 'They're signalling us. You have to help me. Come quick!'

He beckoned and turned back to the signal station. When Secundus had caught up with him, breathing hoarsely, Cato saw that the ship was still flashing its signal. He turned to the imperial agent. 'Come on, you've been with them for long enough to know the drill! What does the signal mean?'

Secundus frowned.

'Quickly man. There must be some kind of recognition signal. Something they used to show that they were friends and all was well . . . Tell me! We have to make the pirates in the bay think they are safe for as long as possible. Someone's going to see those ships any moment. Unless we relay the right signal they're going to know something's wrong up here and raise the alarm. Come on, tell me. What should I do?'

'I'm thinking.' Secundus shut his eyes and thought back to his time down in the pirate base. 'Yes! Yes, I remember. The black pennant! Raise the black pennant!'

Cato looked at him. 'Black? Are you certain? Not the heliograph?'

'No – that was for communicating with the citadel. They used flags for signalling to approaching ships. They flew the black pennant whenever their ships came back from a raid.'

Cato snatched up the bundle of dark linen from the locker and fixed the toggles to the loops of twine on the mast halyard. As soon as the pennant was securely attached he hauled it up the mast and fastened the halyard securely about the wooden cleat. Overhead the light morning breeze rippled the ten-foot length of material out against the blue sky.

Cato turned to Secundus. 'I hope you're right.'

Secundus swallowed nervously. 'We'll know soon enough. One way or another.'

CHAPTER THIRTY-SIX

'What's that?' Macro pointed up at the mountain. Beside him, on the foredeck of the liburnian, one of the seamen shaded his eyes and squinted for an instant before he replied.

'A pennant, I think, sir.'

'What colour?' Macro snapped. 'Quickly, man!'

'I . . . I can't quite make it out, sir. Seems dark. Might be blue . . . or black.'

Macro turned round and cupped a hand to his mouth. 'Get the prisoner up here!'

As the word was passed for Ajax to be brought up on to the deck, Decimus came forward and joined Macro. None of the men on deck wore the uniform or carried the equipment of the imperial navy. Instead they were kitted out from the clothes and weapons taken from the two captured liburnians. Decimus sported a fine silk turban and bright yellow tunic. Macro, true to his nature, had gone for a dour brown cloak and leather breeches, and he shook his head at the extravagant costume of the ship's trierarch as Decimus climbed up on to the small foredeck. Both men stared up at the tiny shadow flickering against the light of the sun rising behind the mountain.

'He saw our signal then,' said Decimus.

'Someone did,' Macro replied quietly. 'There's no way of knowing if it's Cato up there or someone else.'

'What do you think?'

Macro scratched his stubbly chin. 'I'm not sure. If it's Cato, then how could he know the correct response? He might have had to run for it after all. That means the lookout post is back in their hands.'

There was a commotion behind them and the two officers turned to see Ajax being unceremoniously bundled out of the hatch on to the deck. Two marines wrenched him on to his feet and dragged him forward. Below the coaming of the hatch Macro could see the glint of armour from the marines packed below decks and out of sight. As the deck of the liburnian pitched up on the crest of a wave and then swooped down the far side Macro realised how uncomfortable it must be for the marines. But there was nothing he could do about it. They must remain out of sight until the very last moment if the prefect's plan was going to succeed.

The marines pulled Ajax up in front of the two officers, pinning his arms behind his back. He looked at them defiantly and Macro shook his head and sighed. 'Good try, sunshine, but it won't work with me. I saw them break you. So drop the act.'

'Fuck you, Roman!' Ajax tried to spit in Macro's face, but his mouth was so dry with fear that he just made a sharp blowing sound.

'Nice manners,' said Decimus, raising his fist. 'Think I should teach him some new ones?'

The young man's eyes flashed anxiously to the trierarch and Macro let him suffer a moment's anxiety before he shook his head.

'No. Leave him. He can catch up on his suffering a little later. Right now I need him in good condition.'

'Shame,' Decimus muttered as he turned back towards the inlet opening up in front of them, and stretching back into the mountains. They had memorised the location of the bay from Cato's map and Decimus scanned the base of the most distant mountain for first sight of the citadel.

'Relax,' said Macro. 'We won't be able to see it for some time yet.'

He turned to the prisoner and pointed up towards the lookout station. 'See there? That pennant. We made the signal you told us about, and they've come back with that. What does it mean?'

Ajax glanced up, staring hard. He swallowed nervously before he turned his eyes back to Macro, and smiled. 'It's too late, Roman. That's the black pennant. It's a warning. They know you're coming. My father will be gone long before you reach the bay.'

Macro did not reply. He did not react at all, but just stared at the young pirate and tried to decide if the man was telling him the truth. To one side he was aware that Decimus was shifting uneasily.

'He's right. It is black. Or as good as . . . Macro?'

'Quiet.'

'It's black. They're on to us.'

'So he says . . .'

'I'll give the order to turn about.'

It was at that moment that Macro saw the swiftest look of triumph and relief flash across the prisoner's face and he knew that Ajax was lying to him.

'Hold your course, Decimus.'

'But you heard him.'

'Hold your course. That's an order. He's lying. The signal must mean we've fooled them.'

Decimus opened his mouth to protest, but years of hard

discipline bore fruit and he saluted instead. 'Hold our course, yes, sir . . .'

Macro turned to the two marines. 'Take the prisoner below. Try not to damage him on the way down, eh?'

'Sorry, sir. Couldn't help it. He's a bit frisky, like, sir.'

Macro made an exaggerated show of looking the prisoner over. 'Well, he's tied up and a little the worse for wear. I should think he wouldn't present too much of a challenge, even to a couple of marines.'

The two marines coloured, and then quickly, but carefully, marched their charge away.

Decimus nodded towards the signal station. 'Does that mean it's not Cato up there?'

Macro shrugged. 'I don't think it can be, unless he's managed to capture one of the pirates and forced them to reveal the signals system. I think that's expecting a bit much of him.' Macro smiled grimly. 'Even Cato has to duck a fight once in a while. I just hope he got away safely.'

'He seemed a resourceful enough lad,' Decimus agreed.

'Sometimes that's not enough. Sometimes you need a generous helping of luck and Cato's used up more luck than any man has a right to expect . . . We'll know, soon.'

Macro shifted his attention to the mountain on the other side of the inlet, no more than six or seven miles away. The five ships under his command would reach the bay well before noon. Shortly afterwards the Ravenna fleet would appear from down the coastline, in full view of the lookout station, and make for the bay at top speed. At that point he and his small command must strike with devastating speed and impact, and keep the pirates busy until Vespasian could bring the rest of the fleet up. If the prefect was delayed, or the pirates recovered quickly enough to mount a determined resistance, things could go very badly for Macro and his small force of marines and seamen.

The sun climbed into a clear morning sky, the breeze strengthened and Decimus asked for permission to raise the sails.

'The wind's favourable. We can make the bay on this course without having to put a tack in.'

Macro glanced down at the oarsmen straining at their benches. 'If we keep the men at the oars and raise the sails we should get there a lot more quickly.'

'Too quickly,' Decimus cautioned him. 'We can't risk pulling too far ahead of the fleet, sir.'

'The sooner we reach the bay, the greater the chance we have of taking them by surprise. You know that as well as I do, Decimus.'

'That's true, sir. But if we exhaust the men at the oars they'll not fight so well. We'll have a hard enough job as it is, without tiring the men beforehand. I'm sorry, I know how keen you are to get stuck into them, but that's how it is.'

Macro nodded reluctantly. 'All right then. Signal the ships to set sail and ship oars. Just pray that they don't see us coming in time to take any precautions against our little ruse. If they do, then we're as good as dead.'

As Macro stood at the prow of the liburnian he stared at the slowly approaching headland and willed his vessel over the intervening waves. Even with his limited imagination Macro could readily visualise some pirate fishing or swimming off the point, away from the fouled waters of the anchorage. Glancing up the pirate would see the five sails making for the inlet and immediately pass word of his sighting on to Telemachus. The pirates would be cautious with a Roman fleet looking out for them. They'd be formed up and armed and the crews on their ships would have the vessels prepared for action. As soon as they saw through the ruse the Romans would be massacred and the waters of the bay would be stained red with their blood.

Macro tried to dispel the horrific images playing out in his mind. Vespasian's gambit stood every chance of succeeding. The pirates had sent the very same liburnians out to seize shipping several days earlier. They would be expecting them to return, and would be overjoyed by the apparent evidence of their success. Better still, if Macro had been correct in his judgement about the black pennant, the pirates would be satisfied that the correct recognition signal had been given and all was well. The odds were on the side of Rome, but Macro still felt the need to beseech the aid of the gods as well. He prayed silently to Mars and Fortuna, and promised them each a votive spear if he came through the coming fight alive, and the Ravenna fleet triumphed.

They were no more than a mile from the headland when he saw two figures watching the approaching vessels from the cliff top above the headland. As the ships approached Macro waited for them to turn and run, but they remained standing, gazing at the five ships. As the vessels closed to within half a mile one of the watchers raised an arm and waved a greeting. Macro swallowed nervously and waved back, suspecting some kind of test. But still there was no sign of alarm, and the ships began to pass round the headland. Far behind them, Macro knew, the signal was being given for the rest of the fleet to get under way and race towards the bay as fast as wind and oar could carry Vespasian's warships.

A thin haze of smoke hung in the air beyond the end of the cliff and then the rocky promontory, on which the pirates' citadel sat, began to ease into view around the cliff face. On the deck around him, Macro sensed the tension run through the crew like a skewer and he turned to them with an angry growl.

'Take it easy, blast you. As far as they know, we're all good friends. So smile and wave at them for all you're worth. Understand?'

The disguised sailors and marines on deck nodded at him uneasily and continued about their duties, or lined the side and stared as the bay opened up before them. At first sight the expanse of water seemed filled with enemy ships. Then Macro counted them, and saw that there were only the same number as he and Cato had marked on the map two days ago. There was barely any swell on the surface of the sea and the reflections of the pirate galleys glimmered unevenly under the dark hulls, only a few hundred feet away now. Curious faces appeared along the sides of the nearest vessels and most waved in celebration at the sight of the captured biremes sailing between the two liburnians. Beyond the enemy vessels the citadel loomed above the bay and Macro could make out the frames of several catapults mounted along the wall, and on a handful of platforms overlooking the anchorage. But there was no tell-tale trickle of oily smoke that indicated incendiary missiles being prepared. So far, so good, Macro comforted himself. He turned aft, caught Decimus' eyes and nodded.

'Lower sails!' Decimus called out in Greek. 'Unship oars!'

One by one the other four vessels followed suit and turned slowly in towards the anchorage pirate ships. While the sailors unhurriedly furled the sail and attached the ties, the stroke was kept nice and slow to allay the pirates' suspicions, and make it seem that the new arrivals were simply making their final approach. To encourage the deceit, Decimus gave the order for the deck crew to prepare the anchor cable as the liburnian glided into the bay. In the gloom below the open deck hatch Macro saw anxious faces peering up into the sunlight, ready to surge up and into battle. Not just yet, Macro cautioned himself. He must give the order at the very last possible moment and get as close to the enemy ships as he could before they dropped the disguise.

Decimus had orders to make for a trireme first, and whispered softly to the steersman to steer close to, but not at, the pirate flagship. Over the side, the regular movement of the oar blades swept up, forward and down into the calm waters of the bay, churning up the refuse and sewage that floated on the surface.

'Ajax!'

The shout made Macro jump and he looked up to see a smiling face on the aft deck of the trireme. The man called out again, in some unintelligible tongue that might have been Greek as far as Macro could tell. He made himself smile and open his arms in an expansive gesture of friendly greeting, even as his heart pounded against his chest. The man repeated what he said just a moment before and Macro laughed heartily, causing the pirate to frown in confusion. He looked from Macro to the other men on the deck, who avoided his eye, and then he straightened up, staring intently at the deck of the liburnian – at the hatch leading into the hold. Macro turned away from the trireme, cupped his hands and drew a deep breath.

'NOW!'

CHAPTER THIRTY-SEVEN

Before the sound of his voice even echoed off the face of the cliff, orders were being screamed out across the decks of all five ships. As the marines swarmed from the holds, the crew snatched up grappling hooks and the oarsmen steered towards their target ships. Macro indicated one of the triremes and Decimus nodded and passed on the order to the steersman. On each beam the long oars swept forwards, down, were hauled back and swept forward again as the galleys picked up speed over the rapidly narrowing stretch of water that separated them from the pirate ships. At first there was no immediate reaction from the other side as the pirates stared in uncomprehending surprise, then horror, at the ships heading straight for them. The marines had been ordered to keep silent as the ships closed in and an eerie quiet hung over the bay.

Then, after what seemed a long pause, the pirates began to respond to the attack. Their officers shouted out orders and men scrambled across the decks to find their weapons. Over on the beach, where the three vessels were still being caulked, the enemy were slower to react and watched in silence as the Roman vessels swept into the attack. Then from the citadel came the long flat blast of a horn, sounding the alarm, and only then did the pirates fully realise what was happening. But it was already far too late for those vessels closest to Macro's small squadron.

At the last moment the steersman thrust hard against his giant paddles and the port-side oars stopped dead in the water, causing the liburnian to swing round and fetch up against the side of the trireme with a jarring thud that trembled through every timber of the smaller ship.

'Grappling lines away!' Decimus yelled from aft, and the three pointed iron hooks sailed up and over on to the deck of the trireme. The seamen quickly pulled the lines tight and cleated them before snatching up their lighter weapons and swarming up the ropes on to the enemy vessel. The marines, more heavily armed, hurriedly raised boarding ladders and clambered up after their comrades. Macro pushed his way through the packed ranks to the nearest ladder and climbed up. He grasped the side rail of the trireme and swung himself on to its deck. He landed heavily, legs braced, and snatched out his sword from under his cloak.

The fight for the trireme was already decided. Only a skeleton crew was aboard, as Vespasian had foreseen. The rest must be ashore, billeted in the citadel or amongst the shelters stretching up the slope beyond the beach. Three bodies lay sprawled on the deck. A fourth man was slumped against the mast, coughing up jets of blood. Two men were trying to surrender just beyond the mast, but the marines cut them down without mercy and charged down the gangway leading below the deck. The orders had been made clear to every man of the assault party: no prisoners were to be taken. They could not afford to waste men to guard them, and any time taken to deal with prisoners would kill the impetus of the attack.

Some of the pirates who had managed to escape the first wave of Romans had run to the far side and were diving into the sea. They swam for the shore as fast as possible while Macro's men threw anything at them that came to hand: belaying pins, pots and jars and even the pirates' own weapons, abandoned in their terrified bid to escape their attackers.

Macro left his men to it and ran aft to the steering deck, taking the small staircase in a single bound. He ran to the rail and looked over the water to see how his small squadron was doing. The closest bireme had nearly seized its prey, and beyond, across the decks of the other ships, the fight was well underway. He thumped his fist down in satisfaction at the success of the start of the attack. But he must keep up the momentum. Leaning over the side he spotted Decimus and waved his sword to attract the trierarch's attention.

'Make ready to move! Get the crew back aboard. I'll deal with the marines!'

Decimus saluted and shouted orders to his men at once. Macro ran back on to the main deck.

'First two sections, with me! The rest of you, back to the ship.'

Due to the frantic excitement burning through their veins it took a moment before the first men responded to Macro's order and made their way back to the boarding ladders. As the first boarders returned on deck from the hold, Macro grabbed their optio by the arm.

'Take some men. Get back below and get some fires started. Make 'em good. Then get back to our ship.'

'Yes, sir.'

'We can't wait for you.' Macro nodded to a small boat tied on to the deck. 'You'll have to take that. Go!'

He turned away, clambered over the side and climbed down to the liburnian. The deck was filled with excited, grinning marines flushed with the thrill of their easy victory.

Macro made his way over to Decimus as the grappling hooks were retrieved and the boarding ladders taken down.

Decimus grinned at him. 'One down, just twenty or so to go.'

'Piece of piss,' Macro laughed. He turned and pointed to a bireme, inshore of the vessel they had just taken. 'That one's next. Get us alongside as fast you can.'

The men at the oars pushed the liburnian away from the side of the trireme before they got the vessel under way again. As they left the large warship in their wake Macro saw a thin wisp of smoke drift up from the deck, before it thickened into a swirling cloak of smutty grey as the flames began to take hold. Ahead of them the crew of the bireme were making what preparations they could to repel boarders. While the brief assault on the trireme had been taking place these pirates had time to arm themselves and take up position along the side of their ship. Several were armed with bows, and javelins had been snatched up and hastily leaned against the side, ready for use. As before, only a fraction of the crew were aboard but Macro counted nearly twenty of them. Enough to put up a spirited defence.

Macro cleared his throat to address the marines. 'This one's going to be a proper fight, lads. But it's the same routine as before. Go in quick, go in hard, and take no prisoners.'

Most of the men raised a cheer, but the veterans amongst them were already appraising the challenge ahead and weighing up their chances of success as the liburnian surged towards the enemy ship. When they were within fifty paces, Macro heard an order shouted from the deck of the pirate ship and several javelins darted out across the sea.

Macro just had time to shout a warning. 'Shields up!'

Then the heavy iron tips of the weapons thudded down

on to the deck or punched through shields with a loud crack. There was a cry of pain as one man went down, the shaft of a javelin having passed through his stomach, pinning him to the side rail.

'Get that out of him and get him below! The rest of you, keep your bloody shields up! Decimus! Get some of your men to start hitting 'em back!'

As the distance between the two ships closed, there was just enough time to exchange a few more volleys, and then Decimus gave the order to back-water and as the men at the oars killed the forward speed of the liburnian, the ships met bow to bow with a jarring blow that knocked most men off their feet in a tangle of limbs and equipment, as curses and cries of pain and anger cut through the air.

Macro scrambled up, shouting, 'Get those grappling lines up! Go! Go!'

Once again the iron hooks thudded down on the enemy ship and were pulled taut. The first marine began to scramble up the side of the bireme. But before he reached the deck a pirate rose up behind the rail wielding a large axe in both hands. The heavy blade swept through the air and split the marine's helmet and skull right down to his shoulders. The body spasmed, and dropped into the narrow slit of water between the two vessels. As the other marines hesitated beside him, Macro snatched up a javelin, sighted it and threw it across at the axeman. The heavy tip struck him squarely in the breast and he staggered back out of sight.

'What are you waiting for?' Macro bellowed at the marines. 'Want me to do everything for you?'

With a snarl of rage Macro grabbed hold of a rope, hauled himself up and jumped on to the deck of the bireme, ready to take apart the first pirate he saw. He was the first

Roman to board the vessel, and at once four of the pirates turned on him, swords raised. Behind their blades their eyes were pitiless. At his feet lay the bloodstained axe of the man he had killed. Macro snatched it up in both hands and whirled it round his head.

'Come on then,' he sneered. 'Who thinks he's hard enough?'

Behind him the rope juddered as the next Roman climbed up. One of the pirates shouted at his comrades and threw himself at Macro. The axe sliced down, through the man's arm just above the wrist and the sword, with hand still attached, thudded to the deck. Macro kicked the screaming pirate to the side and charged at his companions. The first carried a small shield, which he desperately threw up to deflect Macro's blow, but the impact hurled him to one side and he flew back across the deck, stunned. As Macro swung the axe back for the next blow, one of the pirates turned and ran off to find a safer foe, while the last timed his attack perfectly and slashed at Macro's chest with a curved, thin blade that cut through the cloak, tunic and sliced across the flesh beneath. Macro felt a pain as if someone had lashed the side of his chest with a red-hot iron.

'Fuck!' he cursed through tightly clenched teeth, and recoiled back against the side of the ship. The pirate grinned and jumped forward, sword angling up at Macro's throat, but before the blade could strike, a javelin thrust knocked it to one side and the first marine up the rope behind Macro jumped down on to the deck and slammed his fist into the pirate's face, knocking him down. The man reversed the javelin and thrust the spiked end into the pirate's heart, ripped it free and looked for his next enemy.

As more marines climbed aboard and fanned out, Macro

glanced down at his injury and saw blood seeping through the tattered fabric of his tunic. He swore again and dropped the axe, then threw his cloak down and carefully felt his way through the torn material of the tunic. Nearly a foot of his chest had been laid open and he winced as his fingers lifted a flap of skin.

'That's not good,' he muttered, and pulled the tunic over his head. The wound was clean enough, but bleeding heavily. Drawing his sword, Macro cut a broad strip from the ruined tunic and tied a rough dressing around his chest, tight enough to help stem the bleeding but not too tight that it might restrict his breathing. More marines piled on board and began to fight their way aft. But the pirates were mounting a tough defence, Macro noticed, staying together and fighting with a grim determination to save their ship. Even when the marines began to outnumber them and force them aft, they fell back slowly, making their foes fight for every inch of the deck. Three marines had been cut down, and even as Macro watched, two more fell to the deck, one slashed through his hamstrings, the other thudding down with a broad-bladed dagger thrust into his eye.

'Go on, lads!' Macro called out to his men. 'Go get 'em!'

Before long, the weight of numbers decided the issue. The marines lowered their shields and bodily thrust the pirates back, cutting them down the instant they stumbled, or came within range of a short sword. Pools of blood stained the deck and made the going slippery for the marines' boots. One by one the pirates fell until only a handful were left to defend the aft deck. As they fought on desperately, Macro called over a squad of marines and sent them below to light fires. Almost at once there was a loud clamour from the hold and, clutching his arm tightly to his side, Macro ducked his head into the gangway.

'What's happening down there?'

One of the marines dashed back, squinting up into the sunlight. 'Some prisoners, sir. Locked into the bilges.'

'Then get 'em out, man! Break the locks and get 'em out.'

'Yes, sir.' The marine dashed back into the shadows and the sounds of timber being hacked and chopped rose up to the main deck. As the last of the pirates was cut down on the fore deck, Macro heard a commotion from the main hatch. A handful of terribly ragged and filthy men scrambled on to the deck, desperately shading their eyes from the glare of the sun as they glanced round to take stock of the battle raging around them. Macro pointed to the side.

'Off the ship!' he shouted. 'Get on board the liburnian. We're firing this one! Move yourselves!'

At the sound of flames crackling and the sight of smoke curling up from below, seaman, marines and prisoners hurriedly quit the bireme and made for the safety of the other ship. As Macro waited for his turn on the rope he looked round at the bay once again. Four ships were ablaze. The trireme Macro had boarded shortly before was engulfed in flames and the heat from the inferno beat across the sea so that even at this distance Macro felt its sting. Elsewhere the marines were fighting for control on four more vessels. On the fringes of the battle one of the pirate ships was trying to get underway, its small crew struggling to drive it forward with only a handful of the oars manned.

Ashore, the beach was swarming with men dragging small boats down to the water. Some had already been launched and were making for the nearest vessels still in the hands of the pirates. On the citadel the artillery crews were hurriedly aiming their catapults and bringing up ammunition. A thin haze of smoke rose from fires heating oil for the incendiaries.

In a moment, Macro realised, they would be attempting a few ranging shots. They were welcome to try, he smiled. With the fusion raging across the surface of the bay they were as likely to hit one of their own vessels as a Roman ship.

Nevertheless, a moment later a dull crack carried across the water and as Macro looked up he saw a flaming arc rise from the direction of the citadel. It came on, seemingly aimed right at the centurion, before it reached the peak of its trajectory and the roaring sound of the flames could be clearly heard above all the sounds of the battle. At the last moment it dipped and hit the sea with a loud splash and brief hiss of steam not twenty feet from the side of the bireme.

'Bloody hell!' one of the marines muttered. 'If that's only his first attempt, we're dead.'

'Lucky shot,' Macro said with forced calmness. 'Next one will miss us by a mile.'

The marine wasn't convinced. 'Well, I ain't staying here to find out, sir.'

Macro laughed. 'Me neither. Let's get off this ship sharpish.'

Once everyone was back on board the liburnian Decimus gave the order to shove off and Macro indicated the nearest of the Roman ships, locked in a fight with the crew of another bireme. 'Over there. Get us on to the other side and we'll finish them off.'

'Yes, sir.' Decimus glanced down at the crude dressing tied round the centurion's chest. 'You all right there?'

'Does it bloody look like I'm all right?' Macro snapped. 'Send me a medical orderly and carry out your orders!'

While the trierarch returned to his position by the oarsman, Macro eased himself down against the side of the ship. He felt a bit faint and for an instant saw cobweb-like shadows on the periphery of his vision. He balled a hand into a fist and thumped the deck. He was damned if he was going to let an injury stop him from leading his men in this fight. Not now. Not already. Not before Vespasian arrived and completed the victory over these pirate scum.

While the galley pulled towards the two biremes the medic peeled off Macro's crude dressing, hurriedly cleaned the wound and applied a fresh linen dressing. As the man worked Macro watched the artillery crews up on the citadel try a few more shots, but they did not have the range of any Roman ship now that his liburnian was beyond reach. But as the catapults ceased their brief barrage, the boats from the shore began to move in amongst the ships. Someone with a wise head had ordered them to give a wide berth to any ships fighting it out. Instead, they made for the undamaged vessels still at anchor and swarmed aboard to ready their ships for battle. Once they were underway and their decks packed with armed men thirsting for revenge, Macro's five ships would be outnumbered two to one. He had to do something to improve the odds.

Macro swung towards the nearest marine optio and beckoned to him. 'I want some bows brought up for your men. Get a fire lit, and use fire arrows on any pirate ship that comes in range.'

The optio saluted, lowered his shield and ran off to carry out Macro's orders. The centurion was already giving orders to another group of marines to launch volleys of javelins at the small boats packed with pirates that were making for the ships that had not yet been engaged. Neither action would cause much damage. The fire arrows would be extinguished easily enough and the javelins might cause a few casualties, but it would at least distract the enemy and win Macro and his men a little more time.

The liburnian glided alongside the bireme and once again the marines hurried into action, with a rousing yell that caused the pirates to recoil for a precious instant before battle was joined. But already, Macro noticed, there were noticeably fewer of them and those still able to fight looked weary from their exertions. While the outnumbered pirates were swept from the bireme's deck, Macro called for his armour and the medic helped him into his scaled vest and attached the harness over the top. Macro jammed his skullcap on his head and pulled on and fastened his helmet, feeling more content at once with the familiar weight of his equipment.

'Don't put too much strain on that injury, sir,' the medic advised. 'You'll need to rest it, or the bleeding will start again.'

'I'll take a few days off sick then, shall I?' Macro looked at the man irritably, before he turned to the nearest boarding line and climbed stiffly on to the enemy deck. It was immediately apparent that the fight for this ship had been hard and bloody. Bodies were strewn across the deck, and many of them were marines, Macro noted anxiously. But at least the ship was in Roman hands. Macro sought out the commander of the other Roman ship and saw Centurion Minucius wiping his blade on the tunic of a dead pirate. Minucius had been chosen for the mission since he was an old hand; tough and reliable. Macro had been content for him to come, despite their personal differences.

'Minucius! Over here.'

The centurion hurried towards Macro and gestured at the carnage littering the deck. 'Looks like they've finally got the stomach for a decent fight.'

Macro nodded. The initial shock of the attack had worn off and the pirates were quickly recovering. Now they had a clear idea of the size of Macro's assault force, it would not be long before they moved on to the attack. Already, one of the pirate ships that had escaped the attention of the raiders had slipped its anchor cable and was back-watering the oars on her starboard side to swing the bows round to face the confused mêlée of warships at the other end of the anchorage. Soon it would be joined by several others whose decks were already swarming with men.

Minucius followed the direction of Macro's gaze, then glanced round at the headland. But the sea was calm and clear and there was no sign of the rest of the fleet.

'Don't get your hopes up,' Macro said quietly. 'They won't be here for at least another hour.'

'I know.' Minucius gave him a thin smile. 'The question is, will *we* still be here in an hour?'

CHAPTER THIRTY-EIGHT

'How's our side doing?' asked Secundus, breathing heavily.

They had started their descent of the mountain as soon as the five ships had begun their attack on the pirate fleet. The surprise at the turn of events lasted only a brief moment before Cato realised what was happening. The centurion and the imperial agent now scrambled down the steep track as fast as they could. The loose gravel and stones made the going difficult and dangerous, and they had to proceed at a pace that was making Cato boil with impatience and anxiety as he helped the older man. Every mile they had to stop for a brief rest. Each time Cato looked across the bay to watch the battle unfolding in the distance. No sound carried to them as the tiny figures struggled to and fro aboard the ships, like ants scurrying across children's toys.

'Cato, how are we doing?' Secundus asked again.

Cato was leaning against a rock, both hands shading his eyes as he stared towards the bay. 'It's hard to make it out from here. There's several ships on fire. One seems to have cut its cable and is drifting towards the cliffs. Some ships are alongside each other, and I can see some fighting. But I can't tell who has the upper hand. I can't even tell which side is ours any more.'

Secundus shook his head. 'What the hell is your prefect

playing at, sending in five ships against the pirates? That's a suicide mission.'

'I don't think so,' Cato countered. 'That's not Vespasian's style. This has to be some kind of opening move.'

'Opening move?' Secundus looked at Cato with raised eyebrows, then gave a bitter laugh. 'I don't think those men are going to be around long enough for your prefect's winning move. Assuming there is one.'

Cato shrugged. 'Just trust the man. He hasn't let us down yet. Let's move.'

'There's always a first time,' Secundus grumbled as he struggled back to his feet. They started down the path again. At this rate, Cato calculated quickly, they would not make it down to the shore until sunset. Once night fell they would have to stop, since he dare not risk continuing along the treacherous path in the darkness. By then the battle might have been decided. If it went badly for the Roman fleet then there would be no point in continuing in that direction, and the only route to safety would be back up the path.

'Cato? What happens when we reach the foot of the mountain?'

'Assuming our fleet's won the day, we take your boat and row across to join them.'

'And if they lose?'

'They won't. Now save your breath, and keep going.'

They continued down the path in silence, save for the heavy breathing of Secundus and the faint squawking cries of gulls below them. They passed some stunted trees and a short distance ahead of them the track led into the shadows of a dense forest of pine trees. Cato stopped.

'You know this path well?'

'Too well,' Secundus grimaced. 'I've been up and down it more times than I care to remember these last two months.'

'How far do the trees go down?'

'All the way to the shoreline.'

'No breaks? Nowhere we can keep an eye on what's happening across the bay?'

Secundus thought for a moment and then shook his head.

'Shit . . .' Cato bit his lip. The last thing he wanted was to climb all the way to the bottom of the mountain in complete ignorance of how the battle was proceeding. But there was no helping it. That was the lie of the land and they would have to start descending through the trees in the hope that the pirates were being defeated. But as Cato scanned the shore opposite he saw that the fighting had contracted into the curve of the bay, and the galleys and small boats were all converging on the tight knot of vessels locked in battle. That could only mean one thing. The Romans were losing, and losing badly. Unless something happened quickly they would certainly be overwhelmed by the pirates.

'What's that?' Secundus asked, and raised his finger to point out to sea. 'A warship?'

Cato glanced round to where the mass of the mountain tumbled steeply into the sea below. The sleek prow of a trireme was rowing into sight. Almost at once other vessels began to emerge on either side. All of them had sails raised to assist the rowers, and as Cato and Secundus watched the Ravenna fleet hoved into sight and bore down on the pirate lair at the fastest speed they could manage.

Cato turned to the imperial agent with a smile. 'There. I told you Vespasian had something planned.'

'True,' Secundus smiled contritely. 'But, if you ask me, I think he's cut things just a little too fine.'

Cato turned and saw that the man had a point. It would take the fleet nearly an hour to round the headland and enter the bay. From the way things seemed to be going, the survivors of the first five ships could not hold out that long.

From the tower on the fore deck of his flagship, Vespasian had a clear view across the stretch of sea dividing the two mountains. Above the distant headland a thick pall of smoke billowed into the sky. Behind him the pausarius' drum beat a steady rhythm and each lusty stroke of the oars caused a tiny lurch in the deck beneath his boots. The breeze that filled the sail came in over the stern beam and could not have been more perfect for his purpose as it drove the fleet on. Yet the prefect was more anxious than he had ever been in his entire life. His men were fighting and dying just a few miles ahead, and he must relieve them as swiftly as possible. And it was not just the lives of his men that weighed on his mind. If this plan failed the pirates would escape, free to prey on shipping in the Adriatic, Telemachus would still be holding the scrolls to ransom and Vespasian would be disgraced.

'Looks like Centurion Macro's creating his usual havoc,' Vitellius laughed as he joined his commander in the tower. 'Let's hope your plan is working, sir.'

'It's working,' Vespasian said firmly.

'That's good,' Vitellius nodded. 'Because if, for any reason, it isn't going as we . . . as *you* had hoped, well, I'd hate to think of the consequences . . . sir.'

Vespasian clamped his mouth shut, biting down on his anger, and tried not to rise to the bait. Vitellius, however, was enjoying the moment and decided to twist the knife as far as he could.

'Of course, it was a risky plan,' he mused. 'But in war, I suppose risks are unavoidable. I wonder if the people back in Rome will appreciate the need to take such chances. I can only hope they understand your reasoning as well as I do, sir.'

Vespasian raised a hand. 'I think that will do, Tribune. You've made your feelings quite clear.'

'I think not,' Vitellius replied quietly enough so that only Vespasian might hear. 'I don't know how you did it, but I'll make you regret taking my command away from me. One day. You'll see. So forgive me if I don't wish your plan well.'

Vespasian looked at the man with open disgust and contempt. 'By the gods! . . . You'd really like it if this worked out badly.'

'Of course I would.'

'And those men over there? Do their lives mean nothing to you?'

Vitellius shrugged. 'What are a thousand Romans to me? What do they matter? They are merely the chaff of history. Only those who make history will ever be remembered, my dear Vespasian. Which do you think you are? Chaff or a man of destiny?' He looked at the prefect searchingly and suddenly pointed at him. 'There! I knew it. So please, spare me the moralising about the lives of those men. This is about you, and your place in history. Do yourself the courtesy of seeing your motives for what they are . . . sir.'

Vitellius took a step away before Vespasian could reply. He stiffened his back and saluted, and gave the prefect a sly smile before he turned to descend from the tower. Vespasian watched him stroll back down the deck, and the prefect's heart seethed with hatred for the man. One day there would be a reckoning between them, and only one would live to see the dawn of the morrow. But even as Vespasian made that resolution, and turned back to the smoke rising above the headland, he felt a horrible doubt settle on his heart. Vitellius had been right about his ambition. And out of gratitude for that knowledge Vespasian decided to appoint the tribune leader of the first assault party to go ashore.

'Get the catapult trained round on that one!' Macro shouted to the squad of marines up in the tower. The centurion thrust his arm out to indicate the bireme circling round their flank. The ship was already beginning to turn towards them. Fortunately, Telemachus had obviously ordered his men to board and capture the ships in Roman hands rather than ram and sink them. But, Macro reflected briefly, that was a small mercy that did not make him feel particularly thankful, given the overwhelming advantage the enemy had in numbers as they closed in on his shrinking command.

Only three of his vessels remained, grappled round the second pirate trireme as they fended off the attackers coming at them from all quarters. One of the liburnians had earlier been boarded by three vessels at once and the sailors and marines had been quickly overwhelmed and slaughtered. The other ship had caught fire when the brazier its crew had been using to light fire arrows had been overturned when the ship collided with its next victim. The flames had spread, engulfing both vessels, and the seamen and marines had been forced to jump into the sea and swim for the other Roman ships. Unfortunately there were plenty of small craft in the water and their pirate crews immediately rowed into the area and ruthlessly hunted down the Romans splashing in the water. One by one they were clubbed to death or dispatched with spears.

The crew of the catapult heaved the weapon round to line up with the prow of the oncoming pirate ship, then the optio made a slight adjustment to the elevation, jumped to one side and wrenched the launch lever back. The torsion arms swept forward with a loud crack and the two-foot iron-tipped bolt shot out in a shallow arc. There was a brief pause as Macro and the crew followed the bolt, then it disappeared amongst the men crowding the prow of the pirate ship in a flurry of limbs and smashed armour. The crew thrust their fists into the air and cheered.

'Well done!' Macro beamed at them. 'Now, don't bloody stand there! You've got the range. Give it to 'em!'

The crew threw themselves to work on the tackle, and the ratchet clanked steadily as Macro made his way aft to see how the fight was going at the other end of the trireme. The deck was stained with sticky splashes of drying blood and medics were tending to the Roman wounded lying in the sparse shelter each side of the ship. Macro wondered if there was any point in having them treated. If the pirates won the day the Roman wounded would be massacred without a shred of mercy. In which case the ten or so men who were caring for them would be better used in the defence of the surviving vessels. Then, as Macro passed a man who was clutching his hands across his stomach, trying to hold his guts in, the centurion relented. Most of these men were dying. The least he owed them was the chance of some comfort before they passed into the shadows. He stepped round the pile of bodies heaped about the mast, and climbed up on to the stern deck.

Centurion Minucius was there with a party of men armed with bows taken from the pirates' armoury. They were concentrating their efforts on three small boats that had approached the stern of the adjacent bireme. Macro took a quick glance over the side and saw that two of the boats were filled with bodies, covered by feathered shafts. Most of the men in the third boat were already down and a handful crouched close to each other, taking shelter behind small round shields.

'Very good,' Macro nodded, and turned to see a cluster of pirates around the end of a boarding ramp that had been lowered from their ship on to the bireme. At the other end of the ramp the marines were desperately fighting to prevent the leading pirates from stepping down on to the deck. It took only a few men to create a sufficient space for the rest to be fed into a swift rush of bodies that would sweep in amongst the defenders. Macro indicated the threat. 'Minucius! See if you can break that lot up.'

'Yes, sir. Over there, lads! That group by the ramp. Let 'em have it!'

Bowstrings sang as a steady shower of arrows began to fall on the heads of the densely packed ranks and, as Macro had hoped, they immediately forgot about boarding the enemy ship and looked to their own protection instead, ducking for cover behind the side rail, or under their shields.

Another threat averted, Macro nodded. But he was just buying no more than a fraction of the time he needed before the fleet arrived. He wondered what had driven him to volunteer for this. Vespasian had asked for someone to lead the assault and he had been the first man on his feet. That it would be a risky venture went without saying, but Macro had no idea that it might be suicidal. Such thoughts rarely entered his head. He went where the fight was and made the best job he could of it. So far he had survived. But all good things must come to an end, he thought, and maybe this was his time.

Certainly the situation was not promising. The Romans were boxed into the curve of the bay, with no hope of fighting their way out through the dozen remaining pirate galleys that ringed them. Even so, Macro had half his men left, lining the sides of the four ships grappled together, and so far they were holding their own. They had the advantage in that they were defending and did not have to run the risks of trying to board an enemy vessel. That stage of the operation was well and truly over.

Macro looked round the bay with a measure of satisfaction. The other trireme was slowly settling into the sea; just the upper works were visible, and flames still licked up from the charred remains of the furled sail drooping from the mast. Around the bay, another six ships were well ablaze. The pirates had managed to board two other vessels that had been fired, and put the flames out, but enough damage had already been done to their rigging that it would take several days to repair. Half the pirate fleet had been destroyed or put out of action, and the ships and men that were left had spent themselves in a bid to crush Macro's force. When Vespasian arrived, he would overwhelm them easily. The prefect's plan had worked well enough, even allowing for the sacrifice of Macro and his advance force.

Macro had already given orders that if the enemy looked like seizing any of his ships, the crews were to set them ablaze before retiring to the next friendly vessel. Of course, he smiled grimly, when the defences of the last vessel were breached, and the fire was set, it was every man for himself and over the side. If that looked like happening, he would make sure that the medics put the injured beyond the reach of the pirates, and the flames.

'Sir! Centurion Macro, sir!'

Macro heard the call through the enraged shouting of fighting men and the clatter and scrape of weapons and screaming of the wounded, and turned towards the sound. At the front of the trireme he saw the optio in charge of the catapult waving an arm to attract his attention.

'What is it?' Macro called back. But his throat was dry and the words came out in a croak. He spat and cleared his throat and tried again, with cupped hands. 'What?'

'There, sir! Look there!' The optio pointed at the headland. From the aft deck, Macro could see nothing but open sea. But already the pirates approaching the fight were also turning on their decks to face the open sea, and after a moment of silence Macro heard cries of anger and despair carry across the water towards him. He frowned and looked seaward again, confusion turning to hope and joy as it dawned on him what they must have seen.

Just then the prow of a warship thrust past the headland. A long deck emerged behind it with oars churning up the sea alongside. Then came the mast with a full red sail billowing out at an angle. There, painted in the middle of the sail, was the faded silhouette of an eagle.

CHAPTER THIRTY-NINE

As the vista of the bay unravelled before the trireme, Vespasian's heart glowed with satisfaction. Macro and his men had done a fine job. Most of the pirate fleet was damaged or destroyed. The rest were clustered about a small tangle of ships where the fighting was still continuing and the prefect realised that some, at least, of the men he sent ahead had survived. He drew a deep breath and smiled as the burden of guilt that he felt over sacrificing Macro and his men was lifted. Already the pirates were disengaging from Macro's ships and turning to meet the new threat. But as more and more Roman warships came round the headland the will to resist crumbled away. There was no time to organise a defence against the Ravenna fleet, and the pirates watched in growing horror as the imperial galleys closed in on them. Most of the pirate crews, seeing the overwhelming strength of the enemy, turned for the shore and fled. A few of the pirate commanders recovered their wits quickly enough to make a break for it, ordering their tired crews to the oars in a desperate bid to clear the bay before the trap was closed. Vespasian pointed them out to one of his junior tribunes.

'Signal the second bireme squadron to go after them. I don't want a single ship to escape.'

'Yes, sir.'

While six biremes peeled away to cut the pirates off, the rest of the fleet swung round to face the shore and continued under oars as the sails were furled. A ragged cheer drifted across to them from the survivors of Macro's force, and some of Vespasian's men answered their greeting. But most of them gazed fixedly forward at the approaching beach, steeling themselves for the coming assault. The pirates who had remained ashore were fresh and ready for action. Their leaders were hurriedly forming them up to attack the Romans as they landed.

The shallows between the two sides were filled with fleeing figures, and few of them had the strength of spirit to regroup with their more defiant comrades. Most ran through the gaps in the ranks and disappeared into the sprawl of huts above the beach, heading for the shelter of the trees that covered the hillside beyond. Others made their way along the causeway, running for the safety of the citadel, anxiously glancing to the side to watch the Romans as they headed for the drawbridge that led across the defence ditch and into the heavily fortified gateway. On the walls above, some of their comrades waved them on, but most stood still and watched the drama in the bay, knowing full well the scale of the disaster that was unfolding before their eyes.

Around the flagship the catapults of the Ravenna fleet cracked as they loosed shots at any enemy ships that showed any sign of attempting resistance. Vespasian had left the fleet's lighter vessels the task of taking control of the ships still in the anchorage. Meanwhile, the rest surged towards the shore.

'Marines aft!' came an order from the flagship's stern, instantly echoed across the decks of the other Roman ships. They had trained for such a landing many times and quickly packed the space just in front of the aft deck, shifting the centre of balance in each vessel so that the prow was raised ready for beaching. The sailors and marines braced their legs apart to absorb the shock. The bay shelved evenly so the flagship only shuddered a little as the keel met the sand and its momentum drove it a short distance further before lurching to a halt.

'Marines forward! Lower the gangways!'

Vespasian glanced down from the tower as the marines trotted past. He saw Vitellius amongst them and gave him a brief wave.

'Good luck, Tribune! I'm counting on you to lead the assault.'

Vitellius glared back, saluted stiffly and pushed his way forward to where the sailors were swinging the gangways out over the gentle surf each side of the prow. As soon as the crew released the tackle the ends of the gangways splashed down.

'Move! Move yourselves!' the centurion commanding the trireme's marines bawled out, and the first men swung on to the wooden ramps and charged down the steep incline into the waist-deep water, holding their shields up to stop them getting soaked and unmanageable. The rest followed in a steady stream of men, into the sea and surging forward to emerge, dripping, on the sand. Vitellius braced himself when his turn came and ran down the gangway, almost losing his balance, until he collided with the marine ahead of him. The man tumbled headfirst into the sea and Vitellius quickly waded round him towards the shore, leaving the marine to rise up, drenched, and angry.

More ships beached either side of the flagship, disgorging their marines, and their centurions hurriedly formed their men into ranks as they arrived on the beach. A short distance beyond them the pirates were shouting their war cries with a rising intensity. Men clattered their weapons against their shields and individuals thrust forward towards the Romans, screaming insults and gesturing defiantly. From the distant battlements of the citadel came the sound of a powerful horn, splitting the air with a deep resonant note that carried clearly across the bay and echoed off the slopes of the mountain above. A great cheer rose up from the pirate ranks and they rolled forward unevenly, gathering pace and then charged down the sand towards the Roman line. The archers and catapults on the Roman ships had time for just one volley. Then the marines hurled their javelins forward, snatched out their swords and presented their shields to the enemy. Scores of the pirates were struck down by missiles and tumbled over in fine sprays of sand. Their comrades swerved round them or jumped over, sparing them no more than a glance as they charged the Roman line.

The loose sand robbed the charge of much of its impetus and the two sides came together in a string of individual duels and small skirmishes along the shoreline. Vespasian watched the fight with an initial stab of doubt and uncertainty, such as he always felt when his men first came into contact and there was no telling who had the advantage. But it was soon clear that the pirates were outclassed and outnumbered by the marines and they were slowly driven back up the beach and across the shingle beyond, leaving a bloody flotsam of dead and injured in their wake. As the battleline reached the huts, the rearmost pirates began to turn and run away, some discarding their shields and weapons as they went. Their leaders tried to head them off and drive them back into line with blows from the flats of their swords, and when that didn't work, cutting their men down as a warning to the others. However, the moment the enemy was thrust back amongst the huts, any cohesion that was left in their ranks was shattered and the rout became general as they streamed away up into the shelter of the wooded slopes. The marines broke ranks and went after them, running the slower pirates down and killing them mercilessly. Once they tired of the pursuit and had had their fill of killing, the marines began to take prisoners and small groups of pirates were escorted back to the beach and placed under guard.

Only a handful of the enemy, out to the flank nearest the citadel, managed to form up and retreat to safety along the causeway, pursued all the way by the marines. A bireme from the second squadron attempted to get close to the causeway to bring its catapult to bear on the enemy as they edged back towards the citadel, but immediately came under bombardment from the artillery sited along the wall. When the first incendiary struck the bows in a brilliant explosion of flame and sparks, the trierarch hurriedly backed his ship out of range. As Vespasian watched, arrows and slingshot from the ramparts began to strike the marines down, but such was the heat of their excitement that they continued pursuing the pirates right up to the defensive ditch before they realised the danger and began to back off, shields raised as they retreated along the causeway. The last of the pirates ran across the drawbridge into the citadel, the gates were closed and a moment later the drawbridge slowly began to rise until it was almost vertical in front of the gate.

The battle was over then, Vespasian decided. After mopping up the pirates still scattered about the bay, only the siege of the citadel remained. Telemachus and what was left of his men were bottled up on the rock behind that wall.

They had lost every one of their ships so there was no way they could escape, and there would be no ally to attempt to relieve them. Their defeat was as certain as night follows day. Only one issue remained in doubt: the secret purpose for which all this blood had been shed; the recovery of the scrolls. That, Vespasian decided, was going to be tricky. If they were still in Telemachus' possession he would surely try to use them to strike some kind of a deal. That was something Vespasian could not easily permit. The Ravenna fleet would not stand for any arrangement that let the pirates off the hook. The threat of mutiny – almost the worst fate that a commander could contemplate – would be very real.

The sounds of fighting had diminished, to be succeeded by the pitiful cries of the injured and occasional clatter of weapons from some isolated duel as the last of the pirates with any fight left in them defiantly sold their lives.

Vespasian descended from the tower on the foredeck of the *Horus* feeling content, but drained by the strain of the days since he had taken command of the fleet. Soon it would be over, and if all went well, he would return to Rome in triumph and present Narcissus with the scrolls.

When the last of the pirates had been cleared from the bay the Roman fleet began to unload their equipment and supplies. Some prisoners were immediately set to work digging a ditch and raising a rampart across the end of the causeway to contain their comrades in the citadel. Others were constructing a palisade around the Roman beachhead.

Vespasian, satisfied that disembarkation was proceeding in an orderly fashion, took a small boat across the bay to where Macro's ships floated amidst a tangle of fallen rigging and were surrounded by floating wreckage and bodies. Streaks of blood ran from the scuppers down the side of each galley. Scattered across the hulls, wedged into the timber, were arrow shafts and heavy bolts. As the prefect's boat approached, picking its way through the debris of battle, the exhausted survivors appeared along the sides of the ships and someone raised a ragged cheer for the commander. When his boat drew alongside one of the biremes, Vespasian clambered up the wooden rungs of the side ladder and on to the deck. He was immediately struck by the evidence of the desperate fight these men had put up while waiting for the rest of the fleet to arrive. Bodies lay heaped about the mast, and the decks were smeared with dried blood and discarded weapons and equipment. Overhead the main spar hung at an almost vertical angle, the severed starboard shrouds swaying lazily.

'Where's Centurion Macro?' he asked the nearest marine.

The man gestured across the deck to where the trireme loomed over the other vessels. 'There, sir.'

Vespasian crossed over and climbed the boarding ladder to the larger vessel. It too bore the scars of the recent fighting and, as Macro's last line of defence, was where all the injured had been carried. They lay or sat in long rows to each side of the deck and several marines were busy erecting awnings to shelter them from the sun. Some of the wounded saluted the prefect as he passed by. Descending the steps from the aft deck, Macro marched towards him with a broad smile. The centurion was heavily bandaged around his chest and there was a red-brown crust where blood had seeped through the dressing.

'Good to see you, Centurion.'

'You too, sir.' Macro saluted. 'Though you had us worried for a bit.'

'Worried?' Vespasian looked round at the scarred hull and tattered rigging. He could well imagine the desperation of the men who had held out here while the fleet raced towards the bay. He turned back to Macro and smiled. 'Surely you didn't doubt me, Centurion? I'd hoped after the years we have served together you'd have a little more faith.'

'Oh, I knew you'd come, sir. I just wasn't convinced I'd still be around when you got here.'

'Well, you are. I hope you've been looking after young Ajax.'

Macro nodded at the main hatch. 'He's down below, sir. Had him moved there after we took this trireme, since it was the safest place. Centurion Minucius is guarding him.'

'Very good.' Vespasian nodded at the bandage around Macro's chest. 'Not too serious, I hope.'

'Had worse, sir.'

'I don't doubt it. I'm afraid there won't be much time to recover from that. We've still got one last nut to crack, and I'll need your services.'

'I'm up for it, sir.' Macro stiffened. 'I won't let you down.'

Vespasian laughed and raised his voice as he continued. 'If the empire had just ten legions with officers like you, and men like these marines here, nothing would ever stand in our way.'

It was easy to say, and pretty cheap as rhetoric went, but Vespasian knew military minds well enough to know that praise from above was priceless, and enjoyed a currency that would carry these men through to the end of the campaign. It was also easy to say because it was true, he reflected. But the time for praise was over for the moment. There was work to be done, and his expression hardened into its customary professional veneer.

'If these ships are sound I want them beached. The injured can stay aboard. Order a roll call, and send it on to my staff as soon as possible. Then you and your men can draw rations and rest until tomorrow. Is that clear?'

'Yes, sir.'

'Right. One last thing. I'll need our prisoner. Have him brought to me once the ships are beached. I'll see you at the evening briefing.' Vespasian turned to go.

'Sir?'

Vespasian paused and looked back. 'What is it?'

'Cato, sir. We should send someone to look for him.'

Vespasian nodded. 'Once the camp is ready. Tomorrow, first thing, I'll send a squad up the mountain to find him.'

'Thank you, sir.'

By late afternoon the Ravenna fleet had completed the unloading of equipment and supplies. The marines and their prisoners were finishing the construction of the defences for the camp, running up from the beachhead to include the containment fortifications across the causeway. The components of four large onagers had been carried up to within range of the citadel wall and the engineers were already assembling the weapons. From the fall of the shot of the pirates' artillery pieces earlier in the day the engineers had a good idea of the reach of the enemy weapons and worked a safe distance outside it. Foraging parties had already been sent out to find rocks suitable for ammunition and the pile was steadily growing in size on the ground levelled for the onagers.

Vespasian's impatience was such that as soon as the first siege-weapon was assembled, he ordered that it be rolled forward and commence bombarding the gatehouse. The chief engineer selected five rocks of almost equal proportions and gave the order for the onager to be prepared. With six men heaving on the stout lever the ratchet steadily clanked until the throwing arm came to rest on the loading cradle. Two men heaved one of the rocks into the cup and stood back. The chief engineer made a final sighting, raised his arm to signal that he was going to loose the first shot, and when his men were clear, he dropped his arm. The release lever was thrown and with a creak from the sinews of the torsion cords the arm slammed forwards against the retaining bar, hurling the rock towards the citadel. Vespasian and his staff officers followed its trajectory until the rock fell beyond the wall and out of sight. The dull sound of the impact came to their ears as a thin haze of dust rose above the gatehouse.

'Down two!' the chief engineer called out as his crew began levering the throwing arm back. They counted two less clanks of the ratchet and loaded another rock. As the second shot arced towards the wall, it was noticeably harder to follow in the gathering dusk. The rock impacted a few feet below the battlements of the gatehouse and a small shower of masonry fell into the defence ditch as the onager crew gave a cheer.

'Well aimed!' Vespasian called out to the chief engineer. 'Use up the last three of your rocks. Then have the other weapons erected. I want that wall down by tomorrow morning.'

The chief engineer pursed his lips. 'It ain't going to be easy, sir. We'll be shooting blind. Chances are most will go wide of the target. Be a waste of ammunition, sir.'

Vespasian smiled patiently. 'I didn't ask if it was going to be easy; I just asked for it to be done. Please see to it.'

The chief engineer saluted and turned back to his men. 'Come on! You heard the prefect. Let's get 'em set up.'

Vespasian turned to one of his staff officers. 'Have Centurion Minucius bring his prisoner up. I want two sections of marines for an escort, right away.'

The tribune saluted and trotted off, leaving Vespasian staring at the citadel while three more rocks pounded the walls of the gatehouse. As he watched the prefect pondered his next move. Vespasian suspected that what he was about to do was futile. But it had to be tried, to save time and lives. If Telemachus had a weakness then a father's love and pride in his son might just be it.

A short time later a small party advanced along the causeway. A tribune went on ahead with a trumpeter, who gave a regular two-note blast on his instrument to alert the defenders to their approach. Curious faces lined the battlements and Vespasian ordered the party to halt, just outside of slingshot range. He cupped his hands to his mouth and called out.

'Is Telemachus there? . . . Telemachus?'

For a moment he wondered if the leader of the pirates had been killed in the fighting. If that was the case, then this attempt to end the siege was doomed to instant failure. But even as the doubt arose Vespasian saw a tall figure appear above the gatehouse.

'I am Telemachus,' the figure cried out in Greek. 'What do you want, Roman? It's not too late for you to surrender. I may yet be merciful!'

The laughter of the defenders reached Vespasian's ears and he could not help smiling at the man's brave attempt to raise the spirits of his men. In different circumstances, the Empire could have used a man with his ability and capacity for leadership. But Telemachus had chosen piracy over service to the Empire, and he must die as a consequence. Vespasian turned towards Centurion Minucius.

'Bring Ajax forward. Make sure they get a good view of him.'

Minucius hauled his prisoner out in front of the prefect

and the escort party. He stood behind Ajax and pinned his arms back securely as he whispered in the pirate's ear. 'Don't even think of trying to make a break for it. I'd gut you before you got ten feet.'

Vespasian stepped forward and stood beside Ajax. 'Telemachus. We have your son! I offer you his life in exchange for your surrender, and the surrender of your men.'

There was silence from the citadel before Telemachus called out his reply. 'And if we surrender, Roman, what then? Crucifixion? We'd rather fight you and die here, in our homes, than die on your crosses.'

'You will die, Telemachus, one way or another. But your men will live. As slaves, but they will live – your son too – if you surrender before my men begin their assault at dawn. If you defy me, then Ajax will be crucified where I stand, and then we will take your citadel and there will be no mercy. What is your answer?'

Ajax wriggled desperately in the grip of Minucius and shouted. 'Father! Don't—'

At once Minucius punched him viciously in the kidneys. 'Shut it, you . . .'

'Roman!' Telemachus shouted. 'You touch him again, I swear I'll—'

'You'll do nothing!' Vespasian shouted back. 'Nothing but what I demand. And I demand your surrender!'

There was brief pause before the reply. 'No!'

It was as Vespasian had feared, and his heart felt heavy with the burden of all the deaths that would almost certainly result from the pirate leader's defiance. He looked up at the wall. 'Very well. I'll return at dawn with your son. I will ask for your surrender one last time. I give you my word that your men, and Ajax, will be spared.'

He thrust a finger towards Telemachus. 'Until dawn tomorrow!'

Vespasian turned away, and beckoned to Minucius to bring the prisoner with him. 'Take him back to the trireme and guard him well.'

'Yes, sir.' Minucius thrust his prisoner ahead of him.

Ajax twisted his head over his shoulder for one last despairing glance back towards his father as the party marched quickly back to the Roman lines.

As soon as they reached the safety of the marine pickets, Vespasian strode off towards his headquarters tent, followed by his tribunes. Most of his officers would already be assembled for the briefing and would be exhausted after the day's fighting. It would not be fair to keep them longer than was absolutely necessary, given that they would need to prepare for the morning's assault on the citadel. Only those officers too seriously injured would be excused attending.

That included Vitellius.

As Vespasian had hoped, the tribune had been wounded in the thick of the fighting. Unfortunately the pirate had botched his opportunity and only struck the tribune's helmet before the blade glanced off and laid open Vitellius' shoulder. The tribune had described the incident in great detail when he encountered Vespasian on the beach shortly after the prefect had stepped ashore. His shoulder had been swathed in bloodstained bandages and the man had barely been able to stay on his feet. As Vespasian approached his tent he shook his head in bitter regret that Vitellius still lived.

Vespasian swept through the flap, and the centurions and trierarchs rose wearily to their feet as he marched through them to his campaign table and took his seat.

'Thank you, gentlemen.' He waved them into their seats and looked up with a warm smile. 'Firstly, my thanks to you all for a fine performance today. I'll do what I can to make sure that our masters in Rome recognise your valour and professionalism. Especially those who served with Centurion Macro this morning. Outstanding work.' He bowed his head towards Macro, who shuffled self-consciously on his bench.

'But our work is not yet over,' Vespasian continued. 'Telemachus and some of his men still live. That is a state of affairs I am determined to resolve by the end of tomorrow.'

The officers stirred uneasily, and some glanced at each other with slight shakes of the head. Vespasian had anticipated such a reaction, and fully sympathised. They had the pirates bottled up, they weren't going anywhere, and in the normal run of events this would be the time to sit back and starve them into submission. Any assault on the citadel, even if it was successful, would be an unnecessary waste of lives. But, Vespasian reflected, these officers were not privy to the Imperial Secretary's orders that the scrolls be recovered as quickly as possible, at any cost.

He cleared his throat and looked up, meeting their gaze. 'I will offer them terms at first light. We have one useful bargaining counter – the son of Telemachus. However, I imagine that even if Telemachus would sacrifice everything to save Ajax, his subordinates will not and they'll make it quite clear to him that surrender isn't an option. So, an assault on the citadel looks like the most likely outcome, I'm afraid. We can't afford a long siege. Every day that we sit out here presents Telemachus with an opportunity to work some kind of escape. He cannot be permitted to slip through our fingers. If he does then all the comrades we have lost in the last month will have died in vain.'

He paused for a moment and the thud of an onager sounded from the direction of the causeway. Vespasian nodded in that direction. 'The bombardment will continue until dawn. I'm hoping to have breached the defences by dawn. Much of the rubble will fall into the ditch, but we'll still need to carry faggots and scaling ladders forward. I'm not pretending that it will be easy and painless, but it has to be done. The best way to save lives is to go in hard and go in fast.' He smiled. 'In case any of you are sniffing at my use of the word "we", I assure you that I will be going in with the first wave. I'll be leading a party to find and take Telemachus alive. So I'm looking forward to this as much as you are, gentlemen.'

A ripple of laughter broke the solemn mood and Vespasian took the opportunity to end the briefing at that moment. He rose from his chair. 'You'll receive your orders later on.'

He was about to dismiss them when the flap at the back of the tent was drawn aside. Vespasian looked up with a surprised expression that turned to a warm smile of greeting as two men emerged from the darkness.

'My apologies, sir,' said Centurion Cato. 'Have I missed anything?'

CHAPTER FORTY

The artillery crews continued the bombardment of the citadel through the night. Torches had been lit around the onagers' position and the men toiled ceaselessly as they ratcheted back the throwing arms, loaded the rocks and stepped back as the missiles were released with a woosh and crack, sending the rocks flying invisibly through the night to crash down on to the pirates' citadel. No lights burned on the wall to aid the aim of the Roman crews and the only evidence of the success of their efforts was the occasional distant sound of the thud of the impact and faint rumble of falling masonry. A screen of marines stood guard a hundred paces further out, in case the defenders attempted to sally out and destroy the siege weapons.

Not far behind the onagers was the fortified camp of the Ravenna fleet. Small cooking fires flickered in the darkness and the tired seamen and marines sat around them in the customary mood of quiet relief and light-heartedness of men who have survived a battle. Beyond them, along the curve of the bay, lay the dark hulls of the warships. Out to sea there were smaller craft, watching for any pirates who thought they might try to swim to safety from the citadel.

Three figures approached the beached ships along the loom of the sand. They moved purposefully towards the trireme in whose hold Ajax was being held prisoner. Two marines were standing guard at the end of the gangway leading up to the deck, and as the figures emerged from the darkness and strode towards them, one of the marines stepped forward and made the challenge.

Down in the hold, in the wan glow of an oil lamp, Centurion Minucius did not even bother to look up at the sound of the challenge. He was resting on an improvised bed of spare sailcloth laid over coiled ropes. Comfortable enough, but not so comfortable that it was possible to sleep. Which suited his purpose. He had been ordered to guard the prisoner sitting on the grating above the bilges several feet away. Ajax was chained securely to an iron ring fixed to one of the thick timber ribs of the trireme. He was not asleep, and sat brooding, nursing the hand from which the little finger had been severed during his interrogation. Minucius was watching him carefully. There would be no escape, and no suicide attempts.

Boots thudded down on to the deck and the impact of nailed soles echoed through the trireme's hold as someone marched overhead towards the main hatch. Shadows loomed against the night sky and then boots appeared on the gangway steps as a man in the uniform of an ordinary marine entered the hold. Then Minucius saw Vitellius, together with two of his bodyguards. The centurion jumped off his makeshift couch and stood stiffly to attention. Ajax's eyes glinted with open hostility from where he slumped against the side of the ship.

Vitellius waved his hand, on the unbandaged arm. 'At ease, Centurion. I've come for the prisoner.'

'The prisoner, sir?' Minucius looked surprised. 'But I've orders for him to stay here until dawn. Orders from Vespasian himself.'

'Yes, well, the prefect wants him now. For questioning.'

'In the middle of the night, sir?' Minucius' eyes narrowed with suspicion. 'I don't think so.'

He stepped back towards Ajax and grasped the handle of his sword.

Vitellius stared at him, speaking in a low, earnest tone. 'You will hand the prisoner over to me, that's an order, Centurion.'

'No, sir. He only leaves here on the prefect's say so.'

The two men stared at each other, and then Minucius glanced at the tribune's bodyguards edging out either side of him. The centurion's sword rasped from its scabbard, and he raised the point towards the tribune.

Vitellius grinned. 'There's no need for that, Centurion. All right then, you've seen through my ploy. I need the prisoner. Now, I could take him by force. But you might harm me, or one of my men, in the process. I can't afford that. I'm short-handed enough as it is. So I want to make you an offer.'

'Offer? What kind of offer?'

'To make you rich, very rich. Now, I know you could use the money. I've checked your records. You're due for discharge next year.'

'Yes. So?'

'You're a Roman citizen, so there'll be the usual gratuity. You've probably saved enough for a comfortable retirement. You'll live well enough, but there won't be any luxuries. I imagine a man like you will buy into a farm, or an inn. Why not aspire to a better life, Minucius? After twenty-five years of service you deserve it.'

The centurion stared at him. Vitellius could almost hear him thinking it through, and had to struggle to stop himself smiling. Men were so simple when it came down to it. Provide them with the right incentive and it was possible to make them do anything. For some men, it was the prospect of love, or even merely sex. For others it was riches, and Minucius was old enough to know the more lasting value of money.

Minucius watched the prefect's expression closely. 'And what do I have to do to earn this fortune?'

'Bring the prisoner with us.'

'Where are we going, sir?'

'For a little boat ride. Ajax here is going to show us a way to get into the citadel.'

'Into the citadel?' Minucius snorted. 'I should have known. Stand back!'

Vitellius went to raise both hands to placate the centurion, but the bandage on his shoulder restricted the gesture. He frowned. 'Just a moment!'

He took a pace away from Minucius, reached across his chest with his spare hand and unfastened the knot on the bloodstained banadages, then quickly removed them and stuffed them inside his tunic. A moment later the bandage from his head had also been removed and Minucius shook his head at the absence of injuries beneath the dressings.

'Well, well.'

'I needed an alibi,' Vitellius explained. 'As far as everyone is concerned, I'm recovering from injuries in my tent. That's where they think I am now.' He held out a hand to Minucius. 'The deal is this. You come with us. We get into the citadel where Ajax leads us to his father's quarters. He has something I want. It's locked away in a small box. Ajax was kind enough to tell us that his father keeps his own private fortune close by. I keep the box and its contents and you and my bodyguards here can keep whatever treasure you can carry away. We get what we want and get back here before we're missed.'

'And the prisoner?'

'Once we have what we're after, we take him back as far as the boat, then release him.'

'And how do I explain his escape?'

'He picked his lock with a nail and jumped you when your back was turned. Then he slipped over the side and swam across the bay to the citadel. You'll be discovered, alive, but dazed. My man here will make the attack on you look convincing.'

Minucius sized up the burly bodyguard standing behind Vitellius. 'I'm sure he will . . . So what happens if *you* are missed?'

'I've left a letter stating I've gone to spy on their defences,' Vitellius smiled. 'To redeem my honour, you understand. If all goes to plan I'll destroy the letter when I get back to my tent. We've taken care of the sentries. They've been bound and gagged and dropped into the anchor cable locker. Of course, if we are successful, they will have to be disposed of. That will be blamed on Ajax.'

Minucius nodded slowly. 'It seems you've thought of everything, sir.'

'I've tried to. So what do you say, Centurion?'

'It's all very interesting,' said Minucius. 'So what's in this box you're prepared to risk our lives for?'

'Nothing that would concern you. Nothing you would want. Now, do we have a deal?'

Minucius thought for a moment and shrugged. 'What choice do I have? If I say no, you'll kill me and take him anyway.'

'Of course. So do the logical thing. Believe me, it's for the best. It will be dangerous. But if we're successful you'll be the richest man in Ravenna. By a long way.'

'What's to stop you killing me once I hand the prisoner over?'

'I've far more to gain by having you work with us. Besides, what would be the point? There'll be much more treasure there than the three of you can carry off so we have nothing to gain by treachery and everything to gain by working with you.'

Minucius stared at him a moment and then thrust out his hand and grasped that of the tribune. 'You have a deal, sir.'

'Good man! Now let's get the prisoner and get going. There's no time to waste.'

Minucius undid the prisoner's chain and pulled him up. One of the bodyguards set to work with the tip of his sword, working the ring bolt loose. As soon as it dropped to the deck he reached into his belt-purse, took out a nail and laid it down beside the ring bolt.

'There,' Vitellius smiled. 'Clear evidence of our resourceful prisoner's escape. Now let's get going.'

The five men climbed the gangway up to the deck, moved towards the stern of the trireme and climbed down over the side into one of the small boats moored to the warship. Vitellius took his place in the bows, Minucius and Ajax in the stern and the two bodyguards took an oar each. Untying the mooring line, they thrust the boat out from the trireme and clumsily placed their oars into the holding pegs. One of the blades splashed down into the water.

'Quiet, you fools!' Vitellius hissed. 'Take it easy. We mustn't be seen or heard!'

Chastened, the two bodyguards went about their work carefully, gently dipping the oars in, pulling a slow stroke and then sweeping the blades of the oars back across the surface for the next stroke. The surface of the bay was calm and the boat glided across towards the dark mass of the rock upon which the citadel rested. As the boat pulled past the dark strip of the causeway their passage was punctuated by the sounds of the onagers striking their retaining bars and the more distant crunch of the impacts.

Minucius leaned closer to Ajax and whispered, 'Why are you helping them?'

'To live,' the young man whispered back. 'He promised to let me and my father escape when it's over.'

'I see.' Minucius was surprised at the young man's gullibility, but then maybe he had been so broken by his torture that he would believe almost anything with a quite pathetic conviction.

They made for the point at which the cliff face dipped slightly towards the sea below and soon the sound of waves lapping against the bottom of the cliff could be heard from the small boat.

'Stop rowing,' Vitellius called softly. 'Ajax, what now?'

'Go forward. See that rock. Go round it. Slowly.'

The boat eased forward, towards a seemingly unbroken line of rocks, one was bigger than the rest. The gentle swell swept against them in a faint wash and hiss, and for a moment Minucius was sure that the pirate deliberately intended to wreck the boat on the rocks. Then he saw what Ajax had been looking for: a narrow opening behind the larger rock that led into a small pool beyond. Vitellius' bodyguards immediately rowed hard for the opening and the boat shot through the gap into the sheltered water beyond. There was a flat slab of rock at the base of the cliff, which towered over them until, at the top, they could make out the faint loom of the whitewashed buildings that perched above the sea.

'There,' Vitellius pointed, and the boat eased forward and bumped against the rock. The tribune scrambled over the side and stepped ashore, keeping a firm grip on the mooring rope. One of his bodyguards went after him while his comrade helped Ajax and Minucius out of the boat.

'Sir, shall I tie her up?' asked one of the bodyguards.

'No. Best pull the boat up, over by the base of the cliff where it won't be seen.'

While the two men heaved the boat out of the water and dragged it across the seaweed-covered rocks, Vitellius led the others over to the foot of the cliff and at once saw the beginnings of an uneven line of hand and footholds that led up the rock face. He tested the first few and climbed up four or five feet before nodding in satisfaction and dropping back down beside the others. Vitellius turned to one of his bodyguards.

'Trebius, you first. Go up and see where this comes out. We'll follow behind . . .'

'Yes, sir.' The man's reluctance to climb a cliff in the dark was evident to all, and Vitellius leaned closer to him.

'Think of the treasure, man. Now go.'

The bodyguard started up the cliff-face, climbing steadily from hold to hold. Vitellius waited a moment and then heaved himself up. 'Me next. Then Ajax, then Minucius. If the boy tries anything funny, silence him, Centurion.'

'Yes, sir.'

Vitellius nodded to his other bodyguard. 'You take up the rear, Silus.'

They slowly ascended the cliff, taking great care. Ajax, who had climbed the cliff many times before, was much more certain of the way and would have pulled far ahead of Minucius had the centurion not grasped his ankle and reminded him of Vitellius' threat. Twice the lead man lost his way and the others had to stop while he backtracked, and Ajax whispered instructions to help him find the right holds again. But at last they emerged, one by one, into a small cutting at the top of the cliff where the ground was strewn with fallen rubble and Vitellius realised that they were standing in the ruins of a house that must have collapsed into the sea. Around them rose the pale walls of other houses, their windows shuttered against the cool night air. For a while they sat in silence, recovering their breath.

Then Vitellius whispered, 'Boots off. Tie the laces and hang 'em round your neck.'

Once they were ready he nudged their prisoner. 'Time to move. Remember, the centurion will be right behind you. You try anything, and he'll kill you before you know it. Understand?'

'Yes,' Ajax replied softly as he rose up. 'This way.'

He led them over the rubble until they came to the remains of a wall that gave out on to a narrow street beyond. They waited a moment to make sure that all was still and then climbed quietly over the crumbling masonry and crossed to the black shadow of the building opposite.

'How far?' Vitellius whispered.

'Up this way, across a small junction, up the slope to the gate.'

'You go first.'

For an instant, Vitellius thought he made out a smile on Ajax's face, but it was probably just a shadow. Then the young man crept forward, closely followed by the four Romans, as they silently made their way up a narrow cobbled street, boots bumping their breasts as their bare feet padded over the stones. Ahead a dim light glimmered, silhouetting the end of the street, and revealing the open space beyond. Ajax crept forward, but Minucius held him back firmly, then went ahead and peered slowly round the corner.

The junction opened on to a small square and in the far corner a fire burned on the cobbles. Around it huddled the sleeping forms of men wrapped in blankets. One was awake and sat with his back to the junction, staring into the flames. Keeping his eyes on the man, Minucius waved the others on and he grabbed Ajax's wrist as the young man trotted by. They ran along the front of the run-down houses facing the square. Crouching low, they moved as quickly as they could without creating any sound, until they were clear of the square and had disappeared back into the shadows of a short alley that led up to a large gateway. The doors had long since rotted and now leaned against the sides of the arch. Ahead was a small courtyard and beyond it, the squat, square mass of an old fortified watchtower. Light spilled from the edges of a shuttered window at the top of the tower and on the platform above they could hear men talking in low voices.

Minucius stopped inside the arch and pulled Ajax down while the others came up behind.

'Is this the place?' Vitellius asked softly.

Ajax nodded.

'Where are the sentries? There should be sentries at least.'

'Maybe they're down by the wall,' Minucius muttered. 'In case Vespasian tries an assault in the night.'

'So who's up there on the tower?'

'Catapult crew,' said Ajax. 'There's one mounted on top of the tower.'

Vitellius glanced up at the dim outline of the battlements, then looked carefully around the courtyard before turning back to Ajax. 'All right then, how do we get inside?'

'Follow me.' Ajax rose up, still in the centurion's grasp, and pointed with his spare hand. Vitellius pressed Minucius in the back.

'All right. Go.'

They crossed the courtyard and moved down the side of the tower until they came to a large studded door. Minucius groped across the weathered timber and his fingers closed on a large heavy iron latch. He was about to lift it when there was a sudden snort only a few paces away, and a shape stirred on the ground, before a raucous snoring rumbled in the darkness. All five of them started at the noise, and when he recovered from the shock, Vitellius pulled Trebius closer and whispered. 'Take care of him.'

There was a quiet scraping from the man's scabbard. The bodyguard leaned over the snoring sentry and, clamping a hand over the man's mouth, he thrust the tip of his dagger under the sentry's chin, through the bottom of the skull into his brain, and twisted the handle violently from side to side. The sentry's body spasmed, and jerked before going completely inert. Trebius slowly removed his hand and pulled the blade free. He wiped it on the sentry's tunic and returned the dagger to its scabbard. He bent down, lifted the body under the shoulders and dragged it round the corner before padding back to the others.

'Inside,' Vitellius commanded, and Minucius lifted the latch and slowly pushed the door back. The faint creak did not create an echo and he knew that there was only a small space beyond the door. The centurion stepped inside tentatively and slid his bare feet to and fro, until his shin brushed up against the edge of something hard. He leaned forward and felt with his hands. A step, and beyond that another.

'Stairs, here to the right of the door,' Minucius whispered. 'What now, lad?'

'Go up. My father's quarters are on the corridor to the left. The stairs continue up to the catapult platform at the far end.'

Minucius led the way on all fours, a step at a time until his fingers detected the landing. He peered round and saw a dim light under a door a few feet away. Beyond that the corridor was barely visible before the darkness swallowed it up again. The centurion crept forward to the door, lowered his head to the stone floor and squinted through the small crack running along the bottom of the door. He could see the legs of various pieces of furniture, a discarded cloak and a few chests. There was no sign of anyone. He listened a moment, but there was only the distant murmuring of voices from above.

'I think we're alone,' he whispered towards the staircase, and there was a faint shuffling as the others joined him.

'Stay back and keep hold of Ajax,' said Vitellius. 'My bodyguards will go in first . . . Right, open the door.'

The latch grated faintly and then the glimmer along the floor instantly spread up alongside the door as it opened and a moment later they were looking into Telemachus' quarters. As the bodyguards padded ahead, Vitellius and the others followed them inside and the tribune quietly shut the door behind them.

They had the room to themselves and all four Romans breathed easily as the tension subsided. The room was large and almost square, with a shuttered window in each of the external walls. The remains of a fire glowed in a hearth and lit the room in a rich orange hue. A couch covered in a fine woven rug stood in one corner. At the other end of the room was a large wooden table and behind it a huge chair that looked more like a throne. On either side of the table were stacked small chests. Vitellius looked at them eagerly and then turned to his bodyguards.

'There you go, boys! Just as he said. Come on, let's have a look.'

Trebius and Silus crossed over to the table and Vitellius lifted the lid of the topmost chest. Inside they saw the dull gleam of gold. He lowered a hand, clenched a fistful of coins and raised them up for the others to see. The bodyguards and Minucius could not help but grin at the sight. Vitellius smiled at their reaction. 'You can help yourselves, but keep it quiet. Now then,' he turned to Ajax. 'Show me the one I want.'

There was a slight hesitation as the pirate ran his eyes over the chests, then he pointed. 'That one there, under the table.'

Vitellius' eyes followed the direction indicated and he saw an ornately decorated black box. He bent down and retrieved it. His heart was beating fast as he placed the box on the table. Vitellius could hardly believe he was in the presence of the Sybilline scrolls. He ran his hands across the lid, down to the catch and slid it open. There was a keyhole – but the box was not locked. He took a deep breath and lifted the lid. Inside, in the light cast by the fire, he saw three thick scrolls, in soft leather covers, laying side by side.

'Scrolls?' Minucius said in surprise. 'Is that it? Scrolls?'

Vitellius looked up at him with a thin smile. 'Yes. Just some scrolls.'

'But I thought it was something . . . special.'

'These are special, Centurion. Some of the most important documents ever written.'

'Oh?' Minucius shook his head and chuckled. 'Well, you can have them, sir. I'll content myself with the gold.'

'You do that . . .' Vitellius turned back to the scrolls, reached a hand out and touched them reverently. Then he looked up quickly. 'Get whatever you want from those chests and let's get back to the boat.'

'And what happens to me?' Ajax asked. 'What of our deal, Roman?'

Vitellius looked at him. He needed the pirate a while longer, as insurance in case they ran into any of Telemachus' men. But once it was all over the pirate leader's son was as expendable as the rest of them. Vitellius placed a hand on the man's shoulder.

'Once we reach the boat, I'll set you free. You can return to your father's side.'

'And your promise to spare us, if the citadel falls?'

'You have my word.'

Ajax looked at the tribune suspiciously for a moment and then nodded, apparently satisfied. He made his way round the desk and sat down in his father's chair. He intertwined his fingers to form a rest for his chin as he watched Minucius and the two bodyguards start to open the treasure chests.

Vitellius picked the box up and moved over towards the fireplace. He set the box down and sat beside it. Reaching over to the woodpile, he placed two logs on the embers and stoked the fire up until there was enough light to read by. Then he opened the lid, picked up a scroll and examined the leather cover wrapped over the edge of the scroll. There was some faded text on the cover and he tilted the scroll handles to read it better. It was in Greek, as he had expected, and as the tribune silently translated the script his excitement increased to an almost unbearable pitch. His fingers trembled slightly as he slid the cover off and discarded it. The prophecies were written in fine red strokes on the best vellum he had ever seen. It was almost as soft as the skin of a baby, and he had to still a faint tremor of horror even as the comparison occurred to him. Vitellius rolled the scroll from one handle to the other, scanning the text as it foretold the future of Rome year by year. His eyes lighted on references to a disaster in the forests of Germany, the rise of a mad young prince who would make himself a god, his succession by a foolish cripple . . . Vitellius raced on, eyes scanning the scroll in feverish anticipation, until at last his hands were still and he found what he was looking for. He read the passage slowly, then again, and again to be quite sure, and he felt the fire of ambition burn in his veins as he read it out quietly.

When the last of the Claudians
By his own hand, is laid low,
Rome shall pass to one who
Bears the sign of the hunter's bow . . .

'What was that, sir?' asked one of the bodyguards.

'Nothing,' Vitellius replied quietly without turning round. 'It's nothing.'

The bodyguard looked at his master for a moment, and then shrugged before turning back to the boxes spread across the floor around the desk. Every box that he and the other two Romans had opened was filled with gold, silver and sometimes precious stones. There was enough wealth in the chests to buy any one of the finest houses in Rome and fill it with every luxury a man could imagine. Yet, as the muted sounds of astonishment and celebration carried across the room to Vitellius, he could not help but sneer at their antics in pure contempt. All the gold in the world was as nothing compared to the value of the scroll resting on his lap.

Vitellius hurriedly wound the scroll back to the start as he relished the knowledge that he was destined to be one of fate's most favoured sons. Later, when he was safe, he would read through the rest of the prophecies at his leisure. Carefully replacing the scroll in the box, he shut the lid and, with it tucked safely under his arm, the prefect rose to his feet.

'Time we were leaving.'

Minucius and the bodyguards hurriedly stuffed the last few coins and jewels into their purses and knapsacks. As the centurion turned to retrieve the prisoner from his father's chair there was a burst of shouting outside the window.

CHAPTER FORTY-ONE

For a moment the four Romans stood still as the shouting swelled in volume. Minucius was the first to break the spell and he crossed to the shuttered window, carefully slid the bolts back and eased the shutter open a fraction. Down below, the courtyard was swarming with men, some holding torches aloft. There was a grumble of wheels on cobbled stones and a moment later a narrow wagon lumbered through the gateway. The pirates made way for it as it circled the yard and stopped when it was pointing back towards the gateway. One of the torch-bearers shouted some orders and the pirates moved to the arch at the side of the gateway, threw back the doors and went inside. They reappeared shortly afterwards clutching javelins, bows and arrows, and Minucius realised that the pirates' arsenal must be under the courtyard walls. The weapons were deposited in the bed of the wagon and the pirates went back for more.

'What's happening?' Vitellius whispered.

'They're loading a wagon,' Minucius replied. 'Looks like they're getting ready to throw everything they've got at the marines when the assault goes in.'

'Damn . . .' Vitellius clenched his fist in nervous frustration. 'There's nothing for it. We'll have to wait until the courtyard's clear. Unless there's another way. Watch him!'

Minucius spun round and saw that Ajax was moving towards the door. At Vitellius' warning Trebius drew his sword and leaped towards the door, cutting Ajax off. For an instant the pirate's eyes narrowed as he calculated his chances against the bodyguard. The hesitation was long enough for Minucius to close on him from behind and kick his legs away. Ajax tumbled to the floor with a winded grunt.

'Don't try that again, sunshine,' the centurion growled. 'Don't want to have to cut your hamstrings if I can help it.'

As Ajax sat up painfully and eased himself against one of the treasure chests, Vitellius came over. 'Is there another way out of here?'

Ajax shook his head. 'Only the archway. There are cliffs on the other sides.'

'Can we climb down?'

'No. It's a sheer drop. It would be madness to attempt it in the dark.'

'Well, it won't be dark for too much longer,' said Minucius. 'As soon as it's light the prefect is going to come looking for our prisoner. Then we're well and truly in the shit.'

'Thanks for that cogent summation of our predicament,' Vitellius responded icily. The bodyguards exchanged a puzzled look, which was not lost on their tribune. 'You two weren't hired for your conversation. Now watch him, while I think.'

Vitellius returned to the window and peered cautiously through the narrow gap. Down in the courtyard the pirates continued to load the wagon. At the present rate, the vehicle would be loaded soon and the courtyard would empty, leaving Vitellius and his men enough time to get out of the citadel and return to the trireme before dawn. He stood still and waited in silence, clutching the box of scrolls to his side.

The other men in the room sat down close to Ajax and one of the bodyguards filled in time by cracking his knuckles in a rhythm that quickly irritated Minucius.

He poked the man in the chest. 'Stop that.'

'Why?'

Minucius stared at him in anger. 'You stop it, because the fucking centurion is telling you to stop it, squaddie.'

'I ain't no squaddie.' Trebius' nostrils flared. 'And you ain't no centurion. At least you won't be once this is all over.'

Vitellius turned round hurriedly. 'Quiet! You two trying to get us killed?'

Minucius nodded towards the bodyguard. 'What did he mean, "once this is all over"?'

'Nothing. Ignore him. He's just playing the fool.'

'That's not what it sounded like to me.' Minucius rose cautiously to his feet and backed off a step, hand resting on the pommel of his sword. Before he could say another word there was a shout from the courtyard and, with a crack of a whip, the wheels of the wagon ground across the cobblestones.

'They're going!' Vitellius looked out of the window. Sure enough the rear of the wagon disappeared into the shadows under the gateway. The men in the courtyard did not follow it, but leaned against the courtyard walls and waited. Some of them immediately squatted under the light of one of the torches that had been placed in a bracket on the wall and began a dice game.

'What the hell are they waiting for?' Vitellius muttered. 'Move, you bastards . . .'

But they didn't move. They just waited, and time seemed to stretch out in an endless torment of frustration and a growing sense of peril for the Romans waiting in the tower room overlooking the courtyard.

Minucius thumped his fist into the palm of his other hand. 'We've got to do something, sir. We stay here and we're as good as dead.'

'One way or another . . .' Vitellius conceded. 'Why don't they move?'

A slow rumbling of wheels announced the return of the wagon, and the men in the courtyard jumped up and approached the vehicle as soon as it entered the courtyard. The bed of the wagon was filled with wounded men, hastily bandaged, and they were unloaded and carried down into the cellars. As soon as the wounded had been moved the men in the courtyard began to load the wagon with more weapons carried up from under the watchtower. Vitellius looked up from the courtyard and felt his heart sink. A faint loom of lighter sky was defined by the inky black silhouette of the mountains on the opposite side of the bay.

'Oh, no . . .'

Minucius turned round. 'Sir? What is it?'

'We're about to run out of time. It'll be dawn soon.'

'Then we must do something, sir. Right now!'

'What do you suggest, Centurion?'

There was the briefest hesitation before Minucius continued more softly, 'The cliffs. We'll have to chance them.'

'But you heard Ajax. It's impossible.'

'We have to try it. Send one of your men out the other side to have a look.'

'There's no point. Ajax said—'

'Ajax could be lying, sir. We can't afford to trust him. At least send your man to check.'

Vitellius frowned with irritation and glanced outside. The sky was definitely lighter now. There was no time to waste. He put the scroll box on the desk and faced his men.

'Very well. I'll go and see for myself.' He hesitated at the door and looked back over his shoulder. 'Trebius, you'd better come with me in case we run into anyone.'

'Yes, sir.'

Vitellius turned to Minucius. 'Keep the prisoner quiet and stay back from the window. We won't be long. We'll knock twice to let you know it's us.'

After the door had closed behind them, Minucius waited a moment until the faint sounds of their shuffling footsteps had faded away, then he turned to the other bodyguard and smiled.

'I'm curious about those scrolls. Aren't you?'

Silus shrugged. 'I suppose.'

Minucius stood to one side of the box and scratched his chin. 'There's more to this than scrolls. Has to be. Something to do with the box, perhaps. Something else hidden in it.' He frowned as he leaned over the box and then pointed to a mark on the lid. 'What's this?'

The other man ambled over and looked where the centurion had indicated.

'I don't know. Just where it's been knocked or chipped.'

'No.' Minucius stepped aside and back to make room for the bodyguard. As Silus leaned forward, Minucius gripped his sword handle tightly. 'Look closer.'

'What? I don't see . . .' The bodyguard began to straighten up.

Minucius snatched his sword out, swung it wide and chopped viciously into the bodyguard's neck. The blow snapped his head to one side as it cut through flesh, muscle and spine. Minucius ripped his blade back and poised ready to strike again. Blood jetted out from the bodyguard's neck, and with one last look of surprise at the centurion, Silus crumpled to the floor and a pool of blood steadily widened around his head and chest. He twitched for a moment, and then his body was still.

The lad had been right, Vitellius reflected in despair, as he and Trebius crept back into the tower and quietly made their way up the stairs to Telemachus' quarters. They had edged round the base of the watchtower, peered over the edge of the cliff and heard the sea swirling round rocks far below. Even though it was still quite dark it was clear that there would be no escape in that direction. They had found only one place where the cliff seemed to tumble away in a steep slope, and Vitellius had sent Trebius down to see how far he could go. But after clambering a mere twenty feet down, the bodyguard came to a sheer drop and was forced to climb back up.

So they were trapped in the citadel, while the enemy remained in the courtyard. With the sky steadily growing lighter there was only the slimmest of chances of making it back to the fleet before Ajax was missed. It had always been a risky business, Vitellius conceded, but he was playing for high stakes and that meant being prepared to defy the odds. Only, now that he was trapped, Vitellius fervently wished he had never been made aware of the scrolls.

They reached the landing and walked softly towards the door. Vitellius raised his fist and tapped on the rough wooden surface with his knuckles. Then he lifted the latch, pushed the door back gently and entered the dimly lit chamber. Ajax was sitting at the desk once again and he looked up with a sardonic smile as the tribune entered the room, closely followed by Trebius. Wrapped in a tightening sense of despair Vitellius could not help a surge of anger at the young man's expression.

'What are you grinning at? Where's—'

There was a dull thud and Trebius gave an explosive gasp. Vitellius immediately turned and saw a look of intense surprise etched into the bodyguard's face. Both men glanced down at the bloody tip of a sword protruding a finger's length from his chest. Then Trebius convulsed as he was thrust from behind, and the blade disappeared, leaving a gaping tear in the front of his tunic. An instant later the material was drenched in dark blood. There was another convulsion, and Trebius slumped to his knees. Vitellius looked up and saw Centurion Minucius emerging from the shadow behind the door, bloodstained sword in hand. Trebius' head lolled back and to the side and he looked puzzled as his eyes fixed on Minucius. Then they glazed over and he toppled onto the floor.

Vitellius hesitated a moment too long before his hand shot to the sword hanging at his side, and Minucius stepped forward, and pointed his sword at the tribune's throat.

'Don't! Keep you fingers off that weapon.'

Ajax stood up and hurried over and Vitellius saw that he too carried a sword. There was no way he could fight his way out of the situation, and he lowered his hand to his side. He glared at Minucius.

'What is the meaning of this treachery?'

Minucius smiled. 'Come now. Someone with a mind like yours must be able to figure this out.'

'What are you talking about? What—'

'Quiet, Tribune.' Minucius kept his eyes fixed on Vitellius as he addressed his remarks to Ajax. 'Go and get some men. And send for your father.'

The pirate nodded to Minucius before he hurried from the chamber and then they heard his feet thudding quickly down the stairs.

Vitellius looked at the centurion with narrowed,

calculating eyes. 'What did Ajax promise you? Money? A way out of here? You couldn't have fallen for that?'

'I didn't,' Minucius chuckled. 'In any case, I've already had more than enough money from his father . . .'

'His father?' Vitellius frowned, then the truth hit him like a slingshot to the head. His eyes widened as he raised a finger at the centurion. 'The traitor. The one that has been plaguing the fleet's every step . . . you?'

'Me.'

'But why?'

'You said it yourself. I'm coming up for my discharge. I've been dreading it for the last few years. My savings were going to be just enough to eke out my retirement in comfort. But who wants comfort when you could have luxury? So I cut a deal with Telemachus, and have been selling him information for the last year. I've got enough stashed away to live very well. Now you've provided me with a chance for a little extra. I imagine Telemachus is going to be grateful to the man who returned his son to him. And handed him a high-ranking hostage into the bargain.'

'You bastard . . .'

Minucius laughed and shook his head. 'Tribune, don't act so indignant. Why are you here in the first place? It doesn't exactly have much to do with integrity and loyal service to the Empire. Those scrolls over there, whatever they are, you were not going to use them for the benefit of the Emperor, were you?'

'Not the present Emperor, no.' Vitellius' lips flickered into a smile. 'So what's your price, Minucius?'

'Price?'

'To get me out of here.'

'We aren't going to get out of here. It's too late. It'll be light soon and there won't be any chance of making it back to the fleet. And if we're stuck here, then the pirates are going to find us soon enough. So I decided that it was time I left your employment.'

They heard Ajax's voice shouting orders down in the courtyard and Vitellius licked his lips nervously and took a step closer to the centurion. 'Look we can make a deal.'

Minucius stepped back and raised his sword. 'Keep your distance!'

'Listen to me! I can make you rich, far richer than you can imagine.'

The heavy sound of feet pounding up the staircase made both men glance towards the door, and Minucius shook his head. 'Sorry, Tribune – no negotiations. You've just run out of time.'

The door burst open, and Ajax and several pirates swept into the room, swords drawn, ready to strike. Ajax thrust Vitellius back, steering him into the corner where he fell on to the bed. Then he barked an order and two of the pirates came over and stood guard.

Ajax turned to Minucius. 'I've sent a man for my father. He'll be here soon. In the meantime, drop your sword.'

'What?'

'Drop your sword and stand over there by the table, hands on your head where we can see them.'

'But I'm on your side. I told you.'

'We'll see. Now drop the sword.'

Minucius shook his head and Ajax stabbed a finger at him. 'Drop it! Or my men will drop you.'

Minucius' lips tightened into a bitter expression. Then he threw the sword down at Ajax's feet, brushed past one of the pirates and strode over to the desk where he turned and thrust his hands on his head.

'There! Satisfied? I don't think Telemachus is going to be, when he see's how you've treated me.'

'Leave my father to me,' Ajax said in a soft, menacing voice. 'And if you're lying then I'll see to it that you die painfully.'

There was a chuckle from the far corner of the room as Vitellius sat himself up and pressed his back into the corner of the chamber. 'Seems like you're in the shit as much as me, Centurion.'

'I don't think so, Tribune. You'll see. Soon as Telemachus gets here.'

'Quiet!' Ajax shouted. 'Both of you.'

They waited in silence, under the watchful gaze of the pirates, and outside the grey gleam of the coming dawn filtered through the open shutter. In the distance they could hear the regular crack and crash of the Roman onagers, while the sound of the wagon being loaded echoed up from the courtyard walls. By the time they heard the sound of someone climbing the stairs, the sky outside was washed with the rosy glow of the first rays of the sun. Footsteps approached along the corridor and then Telemachus strode through the open doorway, eyes glancing round the chamber and instantly fixing on Vitellius, and then Minucius. A look of surprise flashed across his face.

'Centurion? What are you doing here?'

'It couldn't be helped. Your boy was taken prisoner and the tribune there wanted to use him to get into the citadel. I was given the choice of helping him out or being killed. So I had to go along with them. Once we got here I set your son loose at the first chance and turned the tables on them.' He nodded towards the bodies of Trebius and Silus.

Telemachus gave the centurion a sceptical look and then glanced at his son with a raised eyebrow. Ajax nodded.

'I see . . . Well, you've not picked the best of times to end our little arrangement.'

'End the arrangement?' Minucius said anxiously. 'What do you mean?'

'You'd find it difficult to return to your side now without arousing any suspicions. And, as you will have noted, your fleet is about to storm this citadel. How do you think they will react if they find you here, amongst the enemy? You're no use to me as a spy now, Centurion. But, I will do you no harm. You can fight alongside my men, and perhaps win back some of the honour you have defiled by betraying your people.'

'There's no need for that!' Minucius started forward, but one of the pirates stepped menacingly towards him and the centurion raised a hand to show he meant no harm to the pirate chief. 'Telemachus, there's a boat hidden at the base of the cliff. It's big enough to hold you, your son and two or three other men, or a few valuables.' He looked meaningfully at the chests lying about the table, their treasures gleaming inside them. 'You can't see the boat from the sea, or from the top of the cliff. We can hide there, wait until dark and slip out of the bay, with some of your treasure. You can start again, somewhere else.'

Minucius sounded desperate and Telemachus looked at him with pity and disgust. 'It hasn't come to that yet. Meanwhile I'll fight your marines the moment the first one sticks his nose over whatever's left of our walls. This boat of yours will be my last resort. We'll go to it when the time comes, and take some of the loot with us.' Telemachus turned to the tribune. 'Is that what you've come for? My fortune?'

'He came for the scrolls,' Minucius interrupted, pointing at the chest on the table. 'In that box. That's all he wanted.'

'I'm sure it is,' Telemachus replied quietly as he looked at the tribune again. 'So who are you working for? I've already met the agent sent by the Liberators. So is it the Emperor? Or yourself?'

Vitellius drew himself up stiffly. 'I serve Emperor Claudius! I am his most trusted agent. If anything happens to me, you can be sure the Emperor will hunt you down and have you killed like dogs!'

'I'm sure he would pay a pretty ransom for you,' mused Telemachus.

Desperation gleamed in the tribune's face. 'Count on it!'

'Then we might have some use for you . . .' Telemachus scratched his chin for a moment and was about to speak again when a horn blared across the citadel.

Minucius turned towards the sound, straining his ears as more notes sounded. But these were more distant and lighter, and with a thrill of fear he recognised the sound. 'Those are Roman horns! They're starting the assault!'

Telemachus snapped some orders to his men. At once two of the pirates sheathed their weapons, closed in on Vitellius and began to tie him to the bed.

'What will you do to him, Father?' Ajax asked in Greek.

'I'm not sure. He might be useful.'

Ajax gripped his father's arm and continued, 'If we survive this attack, let me be the one to kill him.'

'Kill him? Kill a valuable hostage?'

'Father, he tortured me. He humiliated me. He made me tell him about those scrolls. I must have vengeance . . .' Ajax pleaded.

'Later. We must go to the walls. Come! You too, Minucius. If the Romans break into the city, we'll come back for some gold and make for this boat of yours.'

Telemachus hurried from the room. Ajax followed after him. Only Minucius remained, alone with the bodies of

Vitellius' bodyguards. He took a last look at the treasure, shook his head sadly. 'Oh, Portia . . . what the hell have I got myself into?'

Then with an angry growl Minucius snatched up his sword and set off after the pirates.

CHAPTER FORTY-TWO

'What do you mean, the prisoner's gone?' Vespasian asked.

The staff officer shook his head. 'I don't know, sir. He's not there. Nor is Centurion Minucius. Nor are the sentries.'

'All of them gone?'

'Yes, sir,' the tribune replied helplesly.

Vespasian glared at him, then exploded. 'That's impossible! What the bloody hell is going on here? Damn it! I'll see for myself.'

He burst out of the headquarters tent into the predawn gloom and strode down through the camp towards the ships drawn up on the beach. As he approached the trireme a small crowd of onlookers clustered about at the water's edge watching all the activity on deck where scores of marines and a handful of officers were searching the vessel for signs of the prisoner and the centurion tasked with guarding him.

'Out of my way!' Vespasian bellowed, and the small crowd hurriedly moved aside to make way for the prefect. He climbed halfway up the gangway and turned angrily towards them. 'Stop gawping and get back to the camp!'

Vespasian continued up the gangway and jumped down on to the deck with a thud, and the men, turning towards the sound, snapped to attention at once. Centurion Macro was standing by the forward hatch, listening to reports from his marines, and the prefect marched straight over to him.

'Well? What the hell is going on, Centurion?'

Macro saluted. 'Prisoner's escaped, sir.'

'I know. So explain yourself. He was left in your charge.'

'Yes, sir.' Macro winced. 'I gave orders for Centurion Minucius to guard the prisoner overnight. I made it clear that Ajax must be watched closely and must come to no harm. Two men were left to guard the gangway, sir. There shouldn't have been any problems.'

'But now both of them are gone.' Vespasian shook his head. 'Sterling work, Centurion.'

Macro said nothing.

'When did this mess come to your attention?'

'Just before dawn, sir. I came down here with Centurion Cato to relieve Minucius and his men and collect the prisoner. Soon as we saw that the sentries had gone I knew there was something wrong.'

'Very alert of you. So where's Cato now?'

'Down in the hold, sir. Where the prisoner was.'

'Show me.'

Macro led the way through the hatch opening and down the stairs, ducking his head under the thick timber of the coaming. The two officers squinted in the gloom and Vespasian wrinkled his nose at the stench rising from the bilges. The odour had been bad enough on deck, but down here it was overpowering and he wondered that men could work in such conditions. Ahead there was a pool of broken light beneath a deck grating, which revealed the huddled form of Cato leaning over one of the massive timbers of the trireme's ribs.

'Cato!' Macro called out. 'Prefect's here.'

Cato quickly scrambled to his feet and stood to attention,

head canted forward to avoid striking the deck above. He exchanged a salute with the prefect, then Vespasian glanced around the cramped hold.

'This is the place where the prisoner was being held?'

'Yes, sir. Over here.' Cato indicated an iron ring lying on the deck. Beside it was a large nail. 'Someone's tried to make up a bed over there.' Cato nodded to a pile of rope and canvas on the opposite side of the hold. 'That's where Centurion Minucius must have been.'

'I see. So what happened?'

Cato shrugged. 'I can't say for sure, sir.'

'All right then,' Vespasian continued patiently. 'What do you *think* happened?'

Cato squatted down and picked up the iron ring, then pointed to a place on the rib that had been gouged out and was surrounded by splinters. 'That's where he was chained up to the ring bolt, sir. He could have waited for Minucius to fall asleep and then used that nail to work the bolt loose.'

Vespasian inspected the timber and nodded. 'What do you think happened to Minucius?'

'Hard to say, sir. I've found no blood, so far.'

'The prisoner might have dropped the centurion over the side.'

Cato nodded towards Macro. 'We thought of that, sir. Same goes for the missing sentries, so I had some men swim round the hull. The water's clear enough, but they didn't find any bodies. My guess is that Ajax took Minucius with him.'

'A prisoner? Why?'

'Perhaps Ajax needed him to talk his way through any watch-boats they came across, sir.'

Vespasian stared back. 'Unlikely . . . What if Minucius went of his own accord?'

Macro stirred uneasily. 'Are you suggesting he let the prisoner go, sir? Why would he do that?'

'No,' Cato interrupted. 'Ajax escaped. How else do you explain the ring bolt? It's clear that someone had to work it free.'

Vespasian scratched his chin. 'Perhaps it's been made to look that way.'

'That's a possibility, sir,' Cato nodded. 'But do you think it's likely?'

Before Vespasian could reply there was a shout up on deck, and moments later boots thudded down the gangway of the main hatch. A marine squinted into the gloom and saluted as he caught sight of the prefect.

'Sir, we've found the sentries.'

Vespasian and the two centurions hurried after the marine as they climbed up to the deck and went forward. The marines were helping two men out of the anchor cable locker and as they approached Cato could see the bright red weals around the men's wrists and ankles as they stood unsteadily to attention.

'What happened?' Vespasian snapped at them. 'Make your report!'

The two men glanced at each other nervously before one, the older man, replied, 'We was on guard duty last night, sir. About the fifth hour we saw someone approaching. We made the challenge, but it was Tribune Vitellius, sir.

'Vitellius? Are you certain?'

'Sure as I'm standing in front of you, sir. The tribune, and two men. Think they was those two bodyguards of his, sir. Anyway, he told us he had been ordered to fetch the prisoner. So we let 'em pass.' His gaze dropped to his feet. 'That's when it happened, sir.'

'What happened?'

'His bodyguards jumped us. Laid my mate out and knocked me down. They took us on board, trussed us up and dumped us in this locker, sir.'

'I see . . . Did they give you the correct password?'

The marine looked surprised at the question. 'Well, no, sir. I recognised the tribune so I didn't see the need to.'

'Centurion Macro!'

'Sir?'

'Give these men a month of fatigues. Latrine duty. Maybe next time, they'll have the sense to stick to password protocol.'

'Yes, sir.'

'You can deal with them later. We've got bigger fish to fry. You and Cato come with me.'

They climbed down the gangway to the beach and strode towards the onagers, still lobbing rocks at the distant wall of the citadel. Even though the sun had not yet risen Cato could clearly see that the gatehouse had all but collapsed and rubble from the breach almost filled the ditch outside the wall. Already, the missiles arcing forward from the Roman lines were striking the buildings beyond the wall and tiny figures were attempting to barricade the end of the street behind the breach.

'Whatever Vitellius is up to,' Vespasian said as he strode along the shore, 'you can be sure that it has something to do with the scrolls.'

'Do you think he's gone after them, sir?' asked Cato.

'Yes. Why else take Ajax? But before we act, we have to be sure of our facts. I want you to go to his tent. You have my authority to enter and search it. Assuming he isn't there see what you can find and then report to me at the causeway. One other thing . . .'

'Sir?'

'That imperial agent you rescued, Secundus – I've spoken to him. He knows his way round the citadel well enough. Find him and bring him with you. Once we get inside the citadel we need to find our way to Telemachus' headquarters as swiftly as possible. You got all that?'

'Yes, sir.'

'Macro, I want you to pick two sections of marines for our assault group. The best you can find. Now both of you go!'

Vespasian was standing at the head of a dense column of marines when Cato came running from the direction of the camp. The onagers had completed their destruction of the gatehouse and were now concentrating on the walls each side of the breach in order to widen the gap before the assault went in. The troops chosen for the attack watched the bombardment closely, willing the walls to crumble so that the gap they had to advance through was as wide as possible. So they paid little attention to the prefect and the small party of marines gathered behind him with Macro and Secundus. The imperial agent had only limited experience of military service and wore his kit awkwardly. As he leaned on the edge of his shield Secundus rubbed the pommel of his sword in such an agitated manner that Macro had to lean over and still his arm.

'Take it easy.'

'Take it easy?' Secundus turned to him with a startled expression. 'When we're about to charge into that nest of pirates. I've seen 'em and I know what they're like.'

'I've seen them too,' Macro smiled reassuringly. 'And they die just as well as any other men. Besides, once we get inside that wall, they'll be too busy running for their lives to give us much trouble. You'll be safe enough. I guarantee it.'

Secundus looked at him. 'I'll hold you to that.'

'Fair enough,' Macro smiled, then pointed over the other man's shoulder. 'Here comes Cato.'

Cato had drawn armour and weapons from stores and had them bundled in his arms as he found the prefect and breathlessly stiffened to attention in front of Vespasian.

'Well, Centurion?'

'He's not there. But I found this.' Cato placed his equipment on the ground and reached inside his tunic and pulled out a folded piece of papyrus, with a seal over the fold. 'It's addressed to you, sir.'

Vespasian took the letter, broke the seal and scanned the message. When he finished he refolded the letter and stuffed it inside his breastplate as he spoke quietly to Cato. 'Seems that Vitellius is trying to win himself some glory. He's taken Ajax and gone into the citadel to spy on the enemy and recover the scrolls. For the Emperor, naturally.'

Macro frowned. 'He's mad. He'll never do it. Anyway, I thought he'd been injured, sir.'

'Something of a miraculous recovery, it seems.' Vespasian smiled quickly before he turned back to Cato. 'Anyone else see the letter?'

'Oh yes, sir. As soon as I said you had authorised the search of his tent his clerk handed me the letter . . . in front of witnesses.'

'Very neat.' Vespasian smiled grimly. 'It seems our old friend is attempting to cover his back once again.'

'Yes, sir.' Cato glanced at the citadel. 'But maybe this time he's gone too far.'

'No, I don't think so. Vitellius has a charmed life. I only hope that we can get to the scrolls before he does.'

'And if he gets there first, sir?'

'Then I hope we get to him before he escapes. Because if

we don't, and Vitellius finds somewhere safe to hide the scrolls, then when we return to Rome he can say anything he likes when he reports to Narcissus. And you can imagine how the Imperial Secretary is going to take it if we return empty-handed.'

'I don't have to imagine, sir. I know. I'll be a dead man.'

'In which case, we'd better get moving. Get yourself ready, Centurion.'

Cato retrieved his equipment and carried it over to where Macro was standing with the assault squad. As his friend helped him with the mail corselet Vespasian ordered the onagers to cease the bombardment. Immediately, a horn sounded the advance and the column of marines rippled forward along the causeway. Ahead of them, the pirates began to scurry out from their shelters and take up position along the remains of the wall either side of the breach. The marines approached the wall in silence, marching at a steady pace. As soon as they were close enough for slingshot the centurions gave the order to raise shields and the men lifted them up, almost to eye level, and stared anxiously at the men waiting for them on the wall.

The first missiles began to arc up from the citadel, and the steady rattle and thud of their impact slowly increased in intensity as the column tramped further down the causeway. Then there was a distinct crack and both centurions turned to look down the causeway. A dark line streaked towards the marines from one of the pirate catapults that had been quickly manouevred on to a platform behind the wall the moment the Roman bombardment had ceased. The bolt disappeared amongst the marines, a swirl of bodies marking its path through their ranks. But the column did not falter as it continued its advance towards the ruins of the gatehouse.

Vespasian came striding across to join Macro and the

others. He had shed his cloak and carried a shield, and he hefted its weight experimentally.

'Not quite as awkward as a legionary shield, I think.' He grinned. 'Ready, Centurion Cato?'

'Yes, sir. Just about.' Cato fastened his sword belt and made sure that it sat comfortably on his hips with the handle of the sword in an easy position to draw the weapon. Then he jammed on his felt skullcap, lowered the helmet on to his head and fastened the ties. He picked up his shield and drew a deep breath. 'Ready.'

Vespasian turned towards the citadel. 'Let's go then.'

CHAPTER FORTY-THREE

They set off at a slow trot, equipment jingling and nailed boots crunching underfoot. Vespasian led from the front and kept the pace steady to make sure that they were not tired when they reached the citadel. In any case, the main column of marines still had to fight their way through the breach and Vespasian's group would have to wait until the wall was cleared before they made their bid for Telemachus' quarters and the scrolls.

As they advanced along the causeway Cato looked ahead and saw that the marines had reached the ditch in front of the wall. The column stopped as the first century began to pick their way across the rubble from the gatehouse. Ahead of them, and on either side, the pirates were shooting arrows and slingshot, and hurling rocks and javelins into the packed ranks of the marines. Even as Cato watched, he saw the lead centurion struck down, his red-crested helmet dropping out of sight amid the heaving tangle of armour and limbs trying to scramble across the stone and timber debris filling the ditch. More men went down, but the survivors struggled on, desperate to pass through the hail of missiles and charge into the line of pirates waiting for them beyond.

The second century was beginning its advance up the rubble slope as Vespasian's party reached the rear of the column. Vespasian barked an order for the marines to move aside and he led his men closer to the wall. He stopped in the small gap behind the next century waiting to take its turn to advance into the breach. In front of them the second wave of marines was being mauled as badly as the first and the going was made even more difficult by the bodies sprawled across the rubble.

'Look out!' someone cried to Cato's right, and he just had time to turn and see another heavy bolt lash into the side of the column, running through a number of marines before it was spent. Cato noticed that the marines around him were grim-faced, some showing clear signs of the fear that knotted their stomachs as they waited their turn to advance. Ahead of them the men of the second century were wavering. Several had already gone to ground and crouched down under their shields, unwilling to go on. The rest had slowed down, instinctively, even though it lessened their chances of surviving, and now began to back away from the breach behind raised shields.

Vespasian took in the situation at once, and turning his head he bellowed across the ranks of the marines, 'On my order . . . general advance!'

Cato and Macro and every marine in the column tightened their grips on their sword handles and shield grips. Beside him, Cato noticed Secundus was trembling slightly, but the imperial agent had his sword ready and kept his place amongst the prefect's assault party. This was clearly his first experience of such an action. Cato could remember all too well his first time in action when, as a raw recruit, he had dashed into the heart of a hostile German village at the side of a howling Centurion Macro. He had been in many more fights since then, and yet there was the familiar tightness of his throat, the sickness in the pit of his stomach and a strange giddy euphoria in his head.

'Advance!' Vespasian bellowed out.

The column edged forward at a slow pace as the first rank edged up the slope of rubble towards the twenty-foot-wide gap in the wall. Cato, like the men around him, raised his shield at an angle above his head and picked his way forward along the gravel of the causeway. Then the gravel gave way to crushed stone and chunks of rock as he reached the scattered rubble at the edge of the ditch. Cato had to keep his eyes down as he picked his way up the slope. Above them he could hear the jeers and cries of the pirates as they pelted the column with missiles that clattered and thudded on to the attackers' shields. An arrow struck Cato's shield boss with a sharp ring and deflected to one side. All around him he could hear the grunts of the marines as they laboured up the slope, boots scrambling for purchase on the loose masonry. But the pirates were finding their targets, and men stumbled and fell with gasps and cries of pain. Together with the dead and the litter of arrow and javelin shafts, they slowed the advance of their comrades as they struggled up and forward into the breach.

'Keep going!' Vespasian yelled above the din. 'Keep going!'

'Come on, Cato!' Macro shouted, a few paces ahead. 'Stay with us.'

Cato forced himself on, sheathing his sword to save a hand for clambering over the rubble. Then the ground evened out. Raising his shield to one side he found himself squinting up at the dusty silhouettes of men on the crumbling wall, black against the pale dawn sky. At once something zipped through the air close to his head as a slingshot splintered a chunk of masonry and a fragment gashed Cato's cheek, just below the eye socket.

'Shit!' He faltered at the red-hot burning sensation, but knew at once that he must not stop, and scrambled on, over the debris and down into the citadel. Below them, through the heaving tangle of armoured bodies and shields, he could see the pirates waiting for them. The marines had passed through the deluge of missiles and now lowered their shields to the front as they scrambled and slid down the rubble towards the enemy. Beyond the ruined gatehouse was a wide street, and the pirates had blocked off the routes leading into the citadel with a crude breastwork constructed from rubble, barrels and piles of furniture. The entrances to the buildings had been sealed with stout timbers nailed across the doorways. A handful of marines already lay dead and injured in front of the barricades; the few men from the first two centuries to survive the ordeal as they passed through the breach.

'Re-form lines!' the prefect bellowed. At once, the centurions and the optios relayed the orders and the marines moved into place, forming tight ranks with shields to the front, and javelins held ready.

'Those men on the wall!' Vespasian pointed up to the pirates crammed on to the ramparts either side of the breach. 'Take them down!'

The marines inside the citadel turned on the pirates above them, drew back their javelin arms and unleashed a volley of iron-tipped shafts. The pirates had been tightly packed together, and there was no time to turn and flee. Scores went down, pierced by the javelins, and they tumbled from the walls. With the danger from above lifted the column of marines poured forwards through the breach. Before they could pile into the ranks of the men already inside, Vespasian shouted the order to advance and the marines moved steadily towards the enemy sheltering behind their barricade. Those marines who still had javelins now hurled them into the dense ranks of the pirates packed into the streets beyond the barricades, then drew their swords and gripped them firmly, ready to strike.

Cato and Macro were standing to one side, with the rest of the prefect's assault squad and Vespasian forced his way through the advancing marines to rejoin them.

'Secundus! Which way?'

The imperial agent glanced round the square and pointed towards a narrow thoroughfare to the right-hand side of the square. 'There.'

Vespasian nodded. 'Right! Macro, Cato, take some men and clear that barricade.'

The two centurions trotted over to the century of marines that had just entered the citadel. Their optio, a weathered-looking veteran, was busy dressing their line, as if he was on a parade ground, and shouting abuse at a hapless youngster. 'You are a fucking disgrace! Get that chin-strap tied before I throw you to the bloody pirates!'

'Optio!' Macro called out.

The officer turned and straightened to attention, barely stirring as an arrow loosed from behind one of the barricades whipped close overhead. 'Yes, sir!'

'I need four sections, right now. Form them up in front of that barricade over there.'

'Yes, sir!' The optio turned away and shouted out a string of orders to the nearest group of men scrambling through the breach. Macro and Cato looked towards the barricade, shields raised, and inspected the enemy defences.

'How are we going to do this?' asked Cato.

'Same as ever, straight through the centre and roll right over them.'

'Ah, the master of tactics speaks.'

'Got a better idea, smart-arse?'

'No . . .'

With a loud clatter of nailed boots on cobbles the optio brought up his men and formed them into a tight block, shields raised and ready to go into action. Beyond them Cato could see the rest of the marines piling into the enemy barricades; a heaving mass of armoured men and weapons, while stones and lumps of wood flew overhead in both directions as the rearmost ranks of pirates and marines exchanged missiles.

Macro waited until the formation was still, and then waved his sword arm aloft to get their attention above the din of battle echoing off the buildings in the square.

'We need to clear that barricade. Go in hard! When they break go after them. No prisoners. Once that's done, you're free to help yourselves to the loot!'

The marines raised a cheer for that and then braced themselves for the next order.

'Forward!' Macro yelled, and he and Cato slipped into the front rank as the small formation tramped towards the barricade.

The pirates watched them come on with a mix of expressions. Cato noted that some men looked cold and contemptuous, some were wild-eyed and shouting and spitting with pent-up rage. A few looked just as terrified as he felt.

'Shields up!' Macro shouted, and Cato just had time to raise his when a hail of stones cracked and rattled off the shields in the front rank. But they could do little harm against the wide curved surfaces of the marines' shields, and the formation did not even slow down under the barrage. Macro called them to a halt as they reached the barricade and the stones gave way to thrusts from spears and slashes from the heavy curved blades of the pirates' swords.

'Cato! Give me a hand here.'

Macro pointed down at the base of the barricade. There was a large tool chest. A heavy brass handle protruded from the front of the chest and Macro sheathed his sword and grasped it. Cato too put his sword away and joined his friend.

'Ready?' Macro glanced at him. 'One . . . two . . . heave!'

They pulled with all their strength and the wood grated on the cobbles as it began to shift.

'Come on!' Macro growled through clenched teeth. 'Pull!'

The handle suddenly sprang from the face of the wooden chest, nearly sending the two centurions sprawling on their backs. Macro recovered his balance and swore as he saw, round the edge of his shield, that a large section on the front of the chest had come away with the handle. He clenched his fist in momentary frustration and was about to look for another handhold to try, when there was a groan of protest and the lid gave way, collapsing into the chest and bringing down a section of the makeshift barricade with it.

'That's it!' Macro shouted in triumph. 'Now clear it away and let's get at those bastards!'

The pirates desperately aimed blows at the Romans, but with little effect as the second rank of marines leaned forward to cover their comrades with their shields, Macro and Cato pulled away pieces of the barricade and thrust them towards the side where marines threw the wreckage back into the square. In short order, the barricade was little more than a ruin between the two sides and Macro straightened up.

'Advance!' he shouted, ripping his sword from his scabbard and stepping up on to the meal bags piled behind the chest. Cato drew his weapon and clambered up beside his friend. In front of them was a sea of hostile faces and shimmering blades. Cato threw his weight behind his shield and jumped to one side, right on top of some of the waiting enemy. He landed on a short, thick-set man stripped to the waist, his skin gleaming with oil that mixed with his sweat to create a foul musty smell that filled Cato's nostrils for an instant before the pirate collapsed under the impact and Cato thrust his sword into the man's stomach. Before the pirates could respond, more marines piled through the gap and jumped down amongst the pirates, smashing their shields into the enemies' faces and thrusting at any exposed flesh that came within reach of their short swords. Even though the pirates tried desperately to hold their ground they were no match for the weight and momentum of the heavily armed marines. Step by step they were driven back from the barricade and up the narrow street beyond. Cato found himself alongside Macro again and the veteran flashed him a grin.

'This is more like it! Fighting on solid ground again!'

'Look out!' Cato shouted as one of the pirates dropped down and aimed to swipe his sword at Macro's shins beneath his shield.

Macro dropped the shield and the blade rang as it struck the metal trim. Then the shield flew up and out as Macro slammed it into the pirate's face, knocking the man cold. He slumped on to the ground and the marine to Macro's left finished him off with a shattering cut to the skull that burst the pirate's head like a watermelon.

As more of the pirates were hacked down, their comrades began to edge away from the fight. Then those at the rear began to turn and run, dashing back into the citadel to try to find shelter amid its narrow twisting streets. The panic spread through their ranks like a plague, and moments later Macro and Cato stood side by side, breathing heavily, as they watched the last of the pirates flee.

Macro glanced round at the marines. 'Don't just stand there! Get after 'em!'

The centurions stepped aside and let the marines past. As their optio emerged through the ruined barricade Cato called him over.

'Take the rest of your men and cut behind these buildings. With a bit of luck you'll come out behind one of the other barricades, and can take 'em in the rear.'

'Yes, sir.'

As the last of the marines tramped past, Vespasian and his squad approached Macro and Cato.

'Well done. Now let's find those scrolls. Secundus!'

'Sir?' The imperial agent stepped forward and Cato saw a bloody slash running down the man's sword arm.

'Lead the way.'

Secundus swallowed and nodded. 'Yes, sir. Follow me.'

The group set off at a gentle trot, up the street towards the watchtower that loomed over the citadel. Behind them a war horn sounded, to be instantly countered by the distant horns of the marines on the causeway. They passed by the entrances to houses forced open by the marines out to loot the citadel. Cato caught a fleeting glimpse of three marines cutting down a pirate as he attempted to defend his woman and children inside a crumbling hovel. But Vespasian's men continued on as the woman started screaming in terror and her cries echoed up the street after them. At each intersection Cato glanced left and right and saw more marines breaking in doors, chasing down men, women and children as they tried to flee and hacking at those too slow to escape.

'How much further?' Vespasian asked breathlessly.

'Almost there, sir.'

They abruptly emerged into a small square and almost ran straight into a party of pirates advancing in the opposite direction. Both sides slewed to a halt, momentarily shocked into silence. Then Cato opened his mouth and roared at them as he charged forward with sword raised. The pirates took one glance at the bloodied weapon and the savage expression on the centurion's face and turned and ran, bolting for one of the side streets leading off the square.

Cato chased after them a short distance, before he stopped and leaned on the edge of his shield to catch his breath. Behind him he heard Macro roar with laughter. The rest of the party joined in and Cato picked his shield up, and returned to them, his cheeks reddening.

'What's so bloody funny?'

'Nothing!' Macro shook his head and tried to stop grinning.

'Right!' Vespasian broke in irritably. 'Enough! Let's move.'

Secundus headed across the square towards an archway, beyond which they could see the watchtower. On the platform above, the crew of a catapult had caught sight of the small group of Romans and began to train their weapon round. The marines hurried after the prefect and Macro and Cato took up the rear.

'Come on, killer!' Macro grinned as he gave his friend a light shove. 'Just leave a few for me, eh?'

As they approached the archway three figures came running out of it, one of them carrying a small box. Cato threw out his arm 'Sir! Look! Telemachus and Ajax.' Cato started as he recognised the third man. 'That's Minucius!'

'Minucius?' Vespasian raised his sword. 'Get them.'

The three men abruptly turned round and ran back through the archway, as Vespasian and the marines ran after them. But Minucius and the two pirates were not weighed down by armour and had disappeared from sight as Vespasian and the first of his men burst through the archway. Macro and Cato had just entered the courtyard beyond when the catapult on the watchtower took its shot. The bolt slammed into the masonry above the arch and dislodged a shower of debris on to Macro and Cato. They emerged, covered in grit and coughing, and ran over to the base of the tower.

Vespasian glanced round the courtyard and then turned to Secundus. 'Where could they have gone? Is there another way out of here?'

'No, sir. They have to be down in the storerooms, or they're in the watchtower.'

'Right . . .' Vespasian glanced round at his men and pointed to the entrance to the storerooms beside the archway. 'First section! Over there. Search them thoroughly!'

Six marines peeled off and scurried across the courtyard and through the entrance, clattering down the steps into the gloom. The prefect turned back to Secundus.

'How do we get into the watchtower?'

'Round the side, sir. There's a door. Then up the stairs and turn left.'

Vespasian led the others to the corner of the tower, peered round, then beckoned to his men. When they were gathered around the door he lifted the latch and threw the door back, ready to attack anyone on the other side, but the stairwell was empty and he motioned for the marines to go in and climb the stairs. Only four men of the second section were left. Before they were halfway up the stairs Cato heard the pounding of footsteps from inside the building as the crew of the catapult charged towards the marines.

He pressed through the doorway close behind Macro and Vespasian, and glancing up, he blinked at the bright light pouring through an open window at the top of the stairs. A figure flickered into view, wielding a light curved blade. It flashed in the light and there was a grunt as the first of the marines was cut down. The man immediately behind him thrust his comrade's body to one side, raised his shield, sprang up the last three steps and slammed into the pirate at the top of the stairs. The man was knocked off balance, staggered backwards towards the window frame and toppled over with a piercing scream. Before the marine could recover, a second pirate thrust a spear into his side, punching through his chain mail and into his vitals. He dropped on the landing, releasing his sword and shield, and groped for the shaft of the weapon that had mortally injured him.

Down on the stairs, Vespasian thrust the back of the man ahead of him. 'Get up there! Move! Or we're dead!'

The two marines ducked low behind their shields as they climbed to the landing and turned into the corridor. Vespasian and the others hurried up the stairs behind them, hearts pounding. As he turned the corner Cato could see a long, wide corridor that was lit by shafts of light angling in through the open shutters of the windows along the side of the tower. At the far end was another staircase, leading up to the roof. In between were several pirates, hacking and slashing at the marines' shields as they forced their way along the corridor.

'Push 'em back!' Macro shouted, and charged past the prefect and Secundus to add his weight to the marines. The plastered walls echoed and magnified the scrape of blade against blade and the thuds of blows that found only the hard surface of a shield. In the confined space the short swords of the Romans proved their worth, as the first two pirates were quickly cut down and the marines rushed over their bodies to take on the surviving pirates.

A door opened down the corridor, beyond the pirates, and Minucius stepped into the corridor. He clutched a leather bag to his chest and took one despairing look at the men fighting in the corridor before he ran for the tower staircase.

'That bastard's mine!' Macro shouted as he threw his sword arm out and caught one of the pirates in the throat. The man slipped down, a hand clamped to his neck in a futile attempt to staunch the jets of blood pumping from his severed blood vessels. But, even as he slid to the floor, he thrust his sword up deep into the groin of Secundus. With an agonised groan the Roman agent slumped down on top of the pirate, driving the blade in even deeper. He fell back against the wall open-mouthed. Vespasian made to step into the gap, but Cato held his arm back.

'No, sir! Let me!'

Before the prefect could protest, Cato pushed past, thrust his shield out and ran at the pirate immediately in front of him. There was no technique to it. He just crashed into the man, and thrust his blade out, felt the jar of the impact down his forearm, twisted the handle and wrenched it back. The pirate fell away with a grunt and went down on to the floorboards. His sword clattered at his side and he raised an arm, appealing for mercy. Behind him the remaining pirates backed away from the Romans, threw down their weapons and raised their arms.

Vespasian patted the shoulder of the last marine. 'You watch them! Macro!'

'Sir?'

'Go after Minucius.'

'My pleasure.' Macro thrust the pirates to the side, ran to the far staircase and thundered up the wooden steps and out of sight.

'Cato, with me.' Vespasian held his sword ready and approached the doorway from which Minucius had emerged moments earlier. Cato looked over the prefect's shoulder and saw a large room beyond. In the furthest corner, at the end of a large table, stood Telemachus and his son. At the feet of Ajax kneeled tribune Vitellius, his wrists bound, his head yanked to one side so that his throat was exposed to the slim curved blade in Ajax's hand.

Vespasian entered the room slowly, with Cato at his side.

'Stop there!' Telemachus called out. 'One step closer and your tribune dies.'

Cato glanced at Vespasian and saw a flicker of a smile before the prefect replied, 'I suppose you want to try and strike a bargain.'

Telemachus nodded. 'The life of your tribune for the lives of my son and me.'

'Really? I think you must be mistaking me for someone who gives a shit about the tribune.'

Telemachus frowned. 'I'm telling you, I'll not hesitate to have him killed.'

'Be my guest. He's a traitor.'

For a moment all was still, as Telemachus narrowed his eyes and tried to work out if the prefect was bluffing him. Then he placed a hand on his son's shoulder.

'Bleed him a little.'

With a glint of a smile Ajax nicked the tribune's neck and Vitellius yelped as a thin crimson trickle of blood rolled down his throat.

'Next time, he dies,' Telemachus said firmly.

Vespasian lowered his shield and leaned on the rim. 'Go on then. Kill him.'

The tribune glanced at Vespasian in horror and begged in a strangled gasp, 'For pity's sake . . .'

Vespasian gave a little shrug. 'Sorry, Tribune. Wish I could help you out. But you know the policy. No negotiating with pirates. Besides, I've not come here to save your life. I've come for the same thing you were after.'

Vitellius stared back and whispered. 'You bastard . . .'

Then Telemachus realised that the prefect was prepared to see Vitellius die. He snatched up a flask of lamp oil from the table and hurled it into the fire burning in the grate. The flask shattered amid a whirl of sparks, there was brief hiss and then the flames eagerly fed on the oil and roared up. While the others reeled back from the wave of heat that leaped across the room Telemachus grabbed a small black box, opened it, snatched up the scrolls inside and took three quick strides towards the flames, holding the scrolls out. He turned to Vespasian.

'Very well then! Our lives for these scrolls!'

Vespasian took a step forward. Telemachus leaned towards the flames. 'I can't hold these for long, Roman! The deal is our lives for the scrolls. You let us go. Your word on it now, or the scrolls burn!'

Vespasian clenched his fingers on the shield trim. 'I can't let you go.'

'Then you lose the scrolls.' Telemachus winced as the heat started to burn his hand. 'Last chance, Roman.'

Cato looked from man to man, and saw that each was fixed on his course. For an instant he could not believe that Vespasian would be so reckless. But then the realisation hit him. If the prefect let the scrolls burn, and let Vitellius be killed, it would be possible to place the blame at Vitellius' feet. He had the tribune's letter stating his plans, after all. Cato would be dead in any case, as soon as Narcissus knew that the scrolls had been destroyed. No doubt Macro would share the same fate . . .

Cato stepped forward. 'Wait.'

Telemachus and Vespasian turned towards him as Cato quickly continued, 'The scrolls in exchange for your son's life.'

'I'll make no such deal!' Vespasian said through clenched teeth.

'Sir! It's the only way you'll get the scrolls, and Telemachus . . .'

'My son . . .' Telemachus wondered aloud, then looked sidelong at Ajax, and Cato knew he had been right. That was the pirate leader's weak spot: his love for his son. Telemachus' gaze flickered back towards Vespasian.

'My son for the scrolls?'

Vespasian stared back, his expression cold and merciless. Ajax turned to his father.

'No! I will not allow it! Father, you can't do this!'

'Be quiet!' Telemachus snapped. 'Well, Roman?'

Vespasian looked at the scrolls for an instant and then nodded slowly.

'Your word, Roman! Give me your word!'

'You have my word . . .'

'Ahhh!' Telemachus let out a cry of pain as he snatched his hands back from the flames and threw the scrolls on to the floor.

'Get those!' Vespasian barked and Cato hurried forward and gathered the scrolls, and then backed away, cradling them in his arms.

Telemachus gestured to his son. 'Let the tribune go. Cut him free.'

Ajax looked at his father in numbed horror, the blade trembling in his hand. Then he looked down at Vitellius with an expression of bitter hatred. For an instant Cato was certain he was going to cut the tribune's throat . . . then he leaned forward, reached down and sawed through the ropes around Vitellius' wrists. As soon as the bonds parted Vitellius scrambled away from the pirate towards the other Romans. Once he reached a safe distance he rose stiffly to his feet, breathing heavily as he faced Vespasian.

'As long as I live,' he said softly. 'I'll not forget.'

'Nor will I.' Vespasian smiled faintly. 'A lost opportunity, to be sure.'

Cato kept his eyes from the two aristocrats. There was an extremely dangerous tension in the room and he fervently wanted to remain as unobtrusive as possible. As Cato clutched the scrolls to his chest he glanced at the two pirates. After a moment's hesitation Telemachus stepped over to his son and gently placed an arm about his shoulders. Ajax stared at him, wounded and despairing, and his eyes glistened with tears, before he dropped his knife and held his father as all the grief of defeat, all the torment he had suffered at Vitellius' hands, and the terrible sacrifice of his father finally overwhelmed him. With an animal groan, his chest heaved and he poured his sorrow into the folds of cloth on his father's shoulder.

As Macro emerged on to the roof he moved warily, glancing around the doorway before he sprang through it and quickly turned round, sword poised to strike at the first sign of danger. But there was only one other person on the roof of the watchtower. From the far corner Minucius smiled uncertainly at him.

'Macro. I'd hoped it would be you.'

'Really?' Macro kept his sword up and slowly approached the traitor.

'Oh yes! You see, there isn't much time.'

'Wrong.' Macro shook his head. 'You've run out of time, Minucius. You're dead meat.'

'Wait!' Minucius raised a hand. His fist was clenched about the cords from which hung a leather bag. 'There's a fortune in here! Precious stones, some gold. It's yours!'

'Mine?'

'If you help me escape.'

Macro laughed. 'Escape! You're mad.' He waved his spare hand out across the citadel. Marines were running down the streets, intently searching for as much of the pirates' loot as possible. 'Soon they're all going to know how you sold them out. And then you're dead the moment you show your face. There's no escape for you, Minucius.'

'You can hide me. Disguise me. Get me out of here. Do it and you'll be a rich man!'

Macro pressed his lips together for a moment, to fight the disgust he felt welling up inside him. 'There are some things a man can't be allowed to survive. Betraying your mates is one of them. Now, put the bag down and draw your sword.'

Minucius stared at him, then lowered the bag to his side. 'All right then, don't do it for the money. Do it for Portia. Do it for your mother instead. She loves me, you know? She needs me.'

'Put the bag down.'

'For her sake, Macro. Do it for her. Don't do it for me.'

'Put the bag down.'

'If anything happens to me, it'll break her heart.'

'PUT THE FUCKING BAG DOWN!' Macro didn't wait to hear any more. He crouched, turned the shoulder of his sword arm towards Minucius and closed in on the traitor.

'Wait!' Minucius cried out. 'What does this prove? We both know you're the better fighter! I don't stand a chance!'

'Then you'll die.'

Minucius dropped the bag, and slumped on to his knees, stretching his arms out towards Macro. 'For pity's sake! Think of your mother!'

Macro raised his sword, determined to kill him there and then. For a moment he stood over the wretched traitor, then he clenched his teeth and lowered the blade.

'On your feet!'

Minucius glanced up, his eyes wide and burning with hope. 'You won't regret this, Macro.'

'Get up!'

Minucius scrambled to his feet, smiling nervously. 'Bless you! I knew you were a good man. A good son. We'll never forget this, your mother and I.'

'You want to help my mother?'

'What? Yes! Of course. Of course I do. I love her.'

'All right. You love her.' Macro nodded. He leaned over to the side of the tower and glanced down. The wall fell away in a sheer drop over the cliffs below, straight down into the sea, where the waves foamed white against the rocks. There would be no chance of surviving a fall from this height. He straightened up and stared at Minucius. 'If you love her, then jump.'

'What?'

'Either way you die. I'll kill you and spare you a very public and humiliating execution. Or you can jump and I'll do my best to conceal just what a treacherous little cunt you've been.' Macro forced a smile. 'For my mother's sake, you understand.'

'You're not serious?'

'Perfectly. Now there's not much time. The others will be up here any moment to see what's happened. If you're still on the roof then I'll hand you over to them. You know what that means.'

Minucius bit his lip and clasped his hands together. 'Macro, I'm begging you.'

'Do us all a favour. Jump.'

'I-I can't. I'm afraid.'

'Tough.'

A faint shout echoed up the staircase. Then again. Cato's

voice calling out to Macro. Without taking his eyes off Minucius, Macro shouted, 'Up here!'

The sound of boots echoed in the stairwell. Macro nodded meaningfully towards the wall of the watchtower and raised his eyebrows. Minucius' face wrinkled into an agony of despair and he shook his head.

'Your choice.' Macro shrugged, stepped a few paces back and turned towards the staircase. He strode over to it as Cato came scrambling through the doorway, sword raised.

Macro raised a hand. 'Easy there! All sorted out downstairs?'

Cato nodded, catching his breath.

'Did you find the scrolls?' Macro asked.

'Yes . . . Where's Minucius?'

Macro turned round. The traitor had vanished. All that remained was the leather bag lying in a crumpled heap by the wall. Macro stared at the wall for a moment before answering.

'Minucius? He was there just now.' Macro shook his head. 'Guess the old bastard must have winged it . . .'

CHAPTER FORTY-FOUR

Six days later the fleet returned to Ravenna. At first the townspeople had been overjoyed when news that the sails had been sighted spread through the streets. Crowds rushed down to the harbour front and out on to the moles to wave their greetings as the fleet approached. Relatives of the sailors and marines massed outside the gates of the naval base, anxious to be reunited with their menfolk. As the fleet made the final approach to the harbour entrance, the sails were furled and the crews unshipped the oars and rowed the warships in, passing the dense mass of merchant shipping before they entered the naval harbour.

The wounded had been loaded on to the triremes at the head of the fleet and these, the largest vessels, manoeuvred in towards the wharf and heaved their mooring lines ashore to the men waiting to receive them at each berth. As soon as the triremes had been made fast, the gangways were lowered on to the wharf and the unloading of the wounded began. A continuous flow of stretchers laden with the injured was taken to the hospital block, and then the bloodstained stretchers were hurried back to the ships to collect more casualties. There were so many stretcher cases that the walking wounded were left to make the short march across the base to the hospital unaided.

As the scale of the losses became apparent the mood of

celebration and relief in Ravenna quickly turned to a horrified despair and a shrill wailing began amongst the relatives and friends waiting outside the gates. Once each of the triremes had disgorged its cargo of injured men, the vessel was eased away from the wharf and rowed slowly out to drop anchor in the naval harbour. Then it was the turn of the other ships to unload their exhausted marines and seamen, and these tramped across the parade ground towards their barracks, looking forward to the chance of a hot meal and a long spell of relaxation in the bathhouse. Those with families were anxious to let them know they were safe, but until their kit was cleaned and properly stowed away their officers would not permit them to leave the base.

Last ashore were the prisoners: long lines of men, women and children chained together. They were led up from the dark stinking holds of the warships and goaded down the gangplanks towards one of the warehouses that was to act as their temporary prison, there to wait for the agents from the slave dealerships who would come to inspect the goods and prepare bids for the best stock in the auction that would follow a few days later. The proceeds of the sales, together with the plunder taken from the pirates' citadel would make some of the men, mostly officers, wealthy men. Others would bank their share of the proceeds, saving towards retirement, or increasing the size of their stake in the funeral club. Many of the men were keenly looking forward to blowing a small fortune on drink and whores the moment they were given permission to leave the base.

Macro and Cato watched as the last of the prisoners was unloaded. At the end of the line of filthy men in chains was Ajax, trying to stand proud and defiant as he was led off to a hard and uncertain future. He had shown no sign of emotion as his father, and the surviving trierarchs of the pirate fleet had been crucified; nailed down through the wrists and ankles before being bound to their timber frames and hoisted up along the headland opposite the citadel. On the other side of the bay great clouds of smoke billowed up from the fires set by the marines in the ravaged ruins of the citadel.

As the Roman fleet pulled away from the bay Cato had lingered a moment at the stern rail of his ship, hearing the faint cries of agony from the men hanging from their crossbeams on the headland, and the dull roar of flames. Then he had turned away with a sick feeling in the pit of his stomach and refused to look back.

Ajax met their gaze as he stepped ashore, and hesitated for an instant, so that Cato was tempted to try to offer him some crumb of comfort. Then the marine at the tail of the desultory column thrust him forward and he stumbled after the other prisoners.

'Don't go and feel sorry for him,' Macro said gently. 'He's a pirate. He knew the score.'

'I don't feel sorry.'

Macro smiled. He knew his friend well enough to know better. 'If you say so. Just remember, if our fortunes were reversed I doubt he would have shown us any mercy.'

'I know.'

'Besides, he'll do all right. He's got the spirit to make a decent bodyguard, or gladiator perhaps. Don't you worry about him.'

'I'm not,' Cato said firmly, turning towards Macro. 'It's you I'm concerned about. Are you sure you want to go through with it? You know it's going to break her heart.'

Macro nodded. 'Vespasian's given me permission to stay here for a few days. I'll follow you to Rome when she's settled. When are you leaving?'

'The moment the prefect has handed over his command. He's just leaving orders for Decimus to hunt down Rufius Pollo and our friend Anobarbus.'

'Anobarbus?'

'Seems he and Pollo have been working for the Liberators. Anobarbus was trying to cut a deal with the pirates for the scrolls. I left orders for their arrest when I came back for the rest of the fleet. Guess they must have been warned in time to run for it. Anyway, once Vespasian has finished, we're off. The horses are already saddled.'

'And the scrolls?'

Cato smiled. 'Vespasian is carrying those himself. Seems he won't trust anyone else with them.'

'Can't blame him. Just hope he never turns his back towards Vitellius.'

'Don't worry about Vitellius,' Cato replied. 'I'll watch him closely.'

'Do that.'

They stood in silence for a moment, staring as Ajax and the others were herded towards the warehouse. Then Cato turned and thrust out his arm. 'I'll see you back in Rome. Come to the house of Vespasian. He says he'll put us up until we get a new posting.'

Macro clasped his friend's forearm. 'Has to be a better billet than that rat's nest we rented in Rome.'

They both smiled at the memory of their appalling digs.

'Good luck, Macro.'

'Safe journey, Cato.'

The young officer nodded, and then turned away, marching quickly across the parade ground towards the headquarters building. Macro stared after him for a moment and then turned towards the barracks. There were many duties he still had to carry out before he could permit himself to leave the base and make his way into Ravenna and break the news to his mother. The unpleasant task weighed on his heart like a great lead weight and he would sooner spend a year on fatigues than face his mother and tell her of Minucius' death.

It was after dark before Macro felt he had discharged his duties to the point where he could justify quitting the base for the rest of the evening. At least that was what he told himself. As he became engrossed with evermore mundane tasks, the junior officers had started giving him funny looks and even Macro had begun to realise that his apparent dedication to work looked most unusual. So he handed over the few remaining jobs to an optio, fetched his cloak, belt-purse and haversack, and set off for the port. Slipping through the small door beside the main gates he emerged into a large crowd that was straining to get close to the slates that hung from the main gates on which were recorded the names of the dead and injured. Frantic eyes searched the lists, found no name and searched again to make sure before they slipped away and gave thanks for a loved one's preservation. Others read the list with a sick feeling of inevitability before they found what they most dreaded to see and fell back in grief, sobbing and howling, or just too numbed to believe the evidence of their own eyes.

Macro gently eased a path through the crowd, desperate to get away from these distraught people, yet too overwhelmed by the sense of guilt in his own survival to affect any brusque fatalism. At length he was free of them and headed along the wharf, walking slowly as he tried to think of the best way to tell Portia that Minucius was dead. But there was no easy way. How could there be? More distressing still was the nature of Minucius' death. Macro wanted to spare her that detail at least, but he knew that such grand treachery would not be a secret for long. Even if only a handful of men in the fleet knew the full story, there were others who possessed fragments of the tale who would swap stories and so it would leak out and reach his mother's ears and add immeasurably to the burden of her grief.

He turned up the thoroughfare that led into the seedy part of Ravenna, and passed a drunken crowd of merchant sailors celebrating the defeat of the pirates. For a moment he was tempted to stop and tell them how it really was. How their freedom to renew their trade had been bought with the lives of hundreds of good men. But it was to be expected, he realised. The flip side of victory was the price it had exacted on the victors. Moreover, he smiled grimly, to stop would be yet another delay in carrying out his task.

Too soon, Macro found himself standing on the opposite side of the street to the Dancing Dolphin. He stopped and stared. He wasn't yet prepared for it. Then Macro clenched his fists irritably and strode across the stepping stones that ran across the grime and filth of the street. He drew a deep breath and stepped into the bar.

There was only a handful of customers sitting about the room, and he saw Portia at once. She stood at an angle to him, setting up the cups for the evening's customers, unaware of his entrance. Macro swallowed and crossed the room as quietly as he could, but a loose board betrayed him before he could reach the counter, and she turned to look.

Their eyes met, and each stood still and speechless for a moment. Then her face wrinkled up and she leaned on the counter for support.

'No . . . no . . . no . . .' Her fingers pressed into the

wooden surface and the knuckles went white. Macro strode the last few paces and gently took her shoulders.

'Mother, I'm so sorry.'

Her head drooped and Macro felt her thin frame shudder in his hands. He looked up and saw that the customers were watching curiously.

'Mother, come with me. Back there.'

He shuffled awkwardly round the counter, put his arm across her shoulders and helped her through the doorway to the small storeroom at the back of the bar. There, he eased her down on to the stool at the small desk where she did her accounts. For a while Portia clasped her hands to her face as her body was racked with sobs. Macro remained silent, holding her with one arm. He hesitantly raised his spare hand and then gently stroked the wispy grey hair.

After a while the crying subsided, and then a little later Portia suddenly lowered her hands, stiffened her back and pulled out a bar cloth to dab around her eyes.

'What happened?'

'He was killed in the final assault.'

'He didn't suffer?'

'No. It was quick. He wouldn't have felt anything.'

'I see.' She nodded, as if that somehow made it more acceptable. 'That's good. I wouldn't have liked him to suffer. I wouldn't . . .' Her face screwed up again and more tears were wrenched from her old frame before she managed to recover a measure of composure. 'He was a good man.'

Macro was silent, and she immediately sensed something wrong in his mood.

'What's the matter, Macro?'

'It's nothing. Shall I get you a drink?'

'A drink?' Portia eyed him shrewdly. 'That's what men say when they want to avoid a subject.'

Macro looked at her helplessly.

'What happened?' she asked quietly, but firmly. 'Tell me.'

'This isn't the time.'

'Tell me!'

Macro swallowed, tried to meet her intent gaze, and wavered. He looked down and spoke softly. 'Minucius was a traitor. He was selling information to the pirates. He'd been doing it for months.'

'No.'

'Yes. How else do you think he had come by the money for all those retirement plans of his?'

'He said he'd inherited it.' She looked confused. 'He couldn't have been a traitor. How could he be? I'd have known.'

'Are you saying you never suspected him?'

Portia glared back and slapped him hard. 'How dare you!'

Macro reached up and rubbed his cheek. His mother shook her head, trembling with rage and grief, and despair. 'Macro . . . what's to become of me?'

'I've taken care of it, Mother.' He lifted his haversack on to the desk, unfastened the ties and, reaching inside, he drew out the leather bag Minucius had carried up to the roof. 'This was his. I think you should have it now.'

Portia stared at the leather bag. 'What's in it?'

'Gold, some gems, some silver. More than enough to keep you in comfort. You can still have that small estate in the country.'

Her eyes remained fixed on the bag. 'How did you come by this?'

Macro winced. 'It was with him when he died.'

Her eyes flickered up. 'You were there?'

Macro nodded.

'So what happened?'

When her son did not immediately reply a look of horror seeped across her features. 'What did you do to him? What did you do to him?'

She grasped his arms and tried to shake him. Macro looked at her woodenly. 'I offered him a choice. Either I'd kill him, or let him kill himself. He did the best thing. He took his own life.'

Portia looked straight at her son. 'Swear you didn't do it! Swear it.'

'I promise you, Mother. I didn't kill him.'

'I hope so, for your sake.' She looked away, shrunken and despairing. 'You've no idea what you would have done.'

Macro frowned, not understanding what she meant. But Portia kept her silence for a little longer, as she stared at the floor. Macro cleared his throat.

'You know, you could come back to Rome with me. It's not far from there to Ostia . . . Father's still alive, as far as I know.'

Portia looked up at him, and suddenly burst out laughing. The sound was brittle and somehow frightening. For a moment she no longer seemed in control of herself.

'Mother? What's the matter?'

'Oh, it's priceless!' She laughed again. 'Quite priceless . . . You really want me to go back to Ostia, to that stupid, worthless, violent drunk you call a father?'

Macro shrugged. 'It's just a suggestion. I just hoped . . .' He stared at her, a terrible chill of suspicion gripping him as he dimly grasped that there was something strange about what she had just said.

'What's wrong with my father?'

'What's wrong with him?' Portia's lips trembled. 'He's dead. That's what's wrong with him. Minucius was your father.'

'No . . .'

She nodded. 'He made me pregnant and ran away. So I had to marry that oaf you called a father. But years later Minucius came back for me. By then you were old enough to look after yourself. Besides, the situation was complicated enough already.' Portia continued wearily. 'I told him I'd miscarried the baby. He never knew about you.'

They stared at each other for a moment. Macro shook his head. It wasn't true. Couldn't be. But deep inside, he knew it was. There was no reason for her to lie to him, and a flood of memories and half-understood comments flooded into his mind. He looked up and met her gaze again. She nodded slowly and stood, gently closed her thin arms around his head and held him close. Macro was too dazed to react, and simply closed his eyes tightly and clenched his fists.

'Oh, my baby . . . my boy,' Portia said softly. 'What have you done to us?'

CHAPTER FORTY-FIVE

'A fine job all round!' Narcissus smiled happily. 'Couldn't have asked for a better outcome. We've got the scrolls, the pirates have been defeated and the Liberators have gone away empty-handed. Shame that Rufius Pollo and that man Anobarbus have gone to ground. But I'm sure they'll be rooted out and dealt with before long . . . Oh! My apologies, do please take a seat. I'll send for some refreshments. I assume, after your rather wearisome journey from Ravenna, that you might like a little something to eat and drink, eh?'

Opposite the Imperial Secretary stood three dishevelled individuals. Spattered with mud and sporting several days' growth of beard, they eyed him blearily. Vespasian was the first to respond.

'Yes. That would be nice. Thanks.'

While Narcissus called for a servant and gave the orders, his guests slumped down into the seats arranged in front of the Imperial Secretary's desk. Cato, mindful of his rank, waited until Vespasian and Vitellius were seated before he joined them. As soon as Cato was in place Narcissus leaned across his desk with an excited expression.

'So then, to business. The scrolls – let's see them.'

Vespasian took the small knapsack from his side and undid the strap. Then he flipped the cover back and reached inside. He brought the scrolls out, one at a time, and placed them on top of the desk, then pushed them towards Narcissus. The Imperial Secretary gazed at them in unabashed awe. Then he glanced up at Cato. 'I assume you've worked out what these are?'

'Yes, sir.'

Vespasian stirred for a moment. 'I thought . . . Never mind.'

Narcissus had returned his gaze to the scrolls and had not noticed the prefect's brief look of surprise.

'The Sybilline prophecies,' Narcissus said quietly. 'I can hardly believe they exist, and yet here they are. It doesn't seem possible.'

'It nearly wasn't.' Vespasian scratched his chin. 'You have no idea how much blood has been shed to retrieve those scrolls.'

'Yes, I'm sure I'll read all about it in your reports.' Narcissus flashed a smile at him. 'You won't find me, or the Emperor, ungrateful for your efforts, I promise.'

'That's so reassuring.'

The comment was lost on Narcissus, whose eyes had been drawn back to the scrolls. It seemed to Cato that Narcissus hardly dared to touch them. It was quite understandable, the young centurion reflected. The scrolls had been penned by the Oracle at Cumae: the sum total of many years of reading the omens and interpreting the will of the Gods, in order to map out the future of the greatest of nations. A little humility in the presence of such revered documents was the least that could be expected.

And yet there was something else in Narcissus' expression, something that troubled Cato. It was like avarice, or ambition or both. It was clear that Narcissus recognised the power that the scrolls conferred. And there was also fear, clearly visible in the hand that stretched out, and stopped just before the tips of the fingers touched the aged leather of the scroll cases.

If there was any prophetic value in the scrolls then knowledge of events to come was a double-edged gift and Cato wondered if – had he been in Narcissus' position – his thirst to know would have won out over his fear of knowing too much; of knowing what fate had in store for the Empire. After all, what would it profit a man to be forewarned of some great calamity to befall the state, or some tragedy more immediate and personal, if he could do nothing to cheat such a destiny? Sometimes ignorance could be a blessing, thought Cato with a wry smile.

He glanced at Vespasian and Vitellius and wondered if they shared his trepidation about the contents of the scrolls. Vespasian perhaps. But it was hard to imagine that the ruthless desire for self-advancement that burned in Vitellius' heart would be able to resist the lure of the scrolls.

Vitellius sniffed. 'Go ahead,' he told the Imperial Secretary. 'They won't bite you.'

Narcissus looked at the tribune searchingly, then leaned forward and drew the scrolls back across the desk towards him. 'I'll have a look at them later, when I can give them the time they deserve.'

'Oh, I'm sure they'll make for interesting reading,' Vitellius smiled. 'Assuming the prophecies don't share our soothsayers' predilection for ambiguity and wild speculation. If you need any help . . .'

'I'll manage, thank you, Vitellius.'

Glancing at Vitellius Cato could not help feeling that it was just as well that Vespasian had taken charge of the operation to retrieve the scrolls, and had taken them into his protection the moment the scrolls had fallen back into Roman hands.

The scrolls, in their knapsack, had not left Vespasian's side for the entire journey from Ravenna to Rome. Cato had watched him as closely as possible and not once had he seen Vespasian even tamper with the straps that fastened the knapsack. Of course, it was just conceivably possible that Vespasian might have risked a quick look, one night as they slept round an open fire, or shared a dormitory of an imperial staging post. But Cato doubted it. Vespasian seemed to suffer from the usual arriviste affliction of wanting to do the right thing. If his orders clearly stated that he was to deliver the scrolls to Narcissus without reading them, then it was hard to imagine that Vespasian had even opened his knapsack to give them a curious glance. Vitellius, on the other hand, could not have been trusted with them. Cato was not fooled by his flimsy explanation for his attempt to retrieve them by himself. As ever, the scheming aristocrat had confected the story to cover his tracks. If Telemachus had not caught him, then Cato was sure that Vitellius would have kept the scrolls for himself.

'Once you have read them, what then?' asked Vespasian.

'What then?' Narcissus frowned. 'What do you mean?'

'What will happen to the scrolls? I assume you'll have them placed with the others in the temple of Jupiter.'

Narcissus laughed. 'I shall do no such thing!'

Vespasian stared at him for an instant. 'I don't understand. I thought that was the whole point – to reunite the scrolls.'

'Why should I want to do that?'

'So that they can be consulted.'

'Consulted by who?'

Vespasian laughed. 'By the Emperor. By his priests. By the senate.'

Narcissus nodded. 'Precisely. You make my point for me.'

'I'm sorry. I don't get it.'

The Imperial Secretary sat back in his chair with a smile. 'If people are given access to the scrolls then they might just use them for their own political ends.'

'As if!' Vitellius grinned.

Vespasian rounded on him irritably. 'Not all of us are like you.'

'No. But enough of us are. You have spent too much time away from Rome, Vespasian. There are any number of senators out there who harbour ambitions for high office.' His eyes twinkled with malice. 'And even if they don't, you can be sure their wives do . . .'

Vespasian looked down to hide his anxiety.

'You see my difficulty?' Narcissus leaned forwards. 'It would be a huge comfort to the Emperor if every senator was as committed to serving Rome as you are. But there are many who would sooner serve their own ends. They can not be permitted to know what fate intends for us all. Surely you can see that?'

Vespasian looked up. 'I can see that we are losing a chance to take the future in our hands. To lay it before the best minds in the Empire.'

'Ah, yes,' Narcissus added, 'but the best minds are not always the best-disposed minds, if you see what I mean? In any case, it would probably be far too dangerous to trust the future of Rome to the speculations of some half-mad mystic written down when this city was little more than a village. In fact, it really doesn't matter what these scrolls say, just as long as the right people are made aware that they do exist. Then they'll be afraid of what the scrolls *might* say. Therein lies their true value, to me and to the Emperor at least. You do understand, Vespasian?'

Vespasian nodded.

'Good!' said Narcissus. 'Then you'll also appreciate why

you must tell no one about them. Only a handful of men know of their existence right now. I'd like to keep it that way for the moment.'

Vespasian smiled. 'Naturally, you won't hesitate to use the contents of the scrolls to enhance your own standing?'

A brief expression of anger flitted across his expression before Narcissus continued. 'I serve Emperor Claudius. As do you. I will use the scrolls to make the Emperor's position more secure.'

'I'm touched by your unswerving loyalty, Narcissus. I'm sure you'll be quite selfless in the way you use what knowledge you gain from the scrolls.'

They stared at each other for a moment, before Narcissus folded his hands over the scrolls and continued speaking. 'I won't insult you by asking for your solemn vow in this matter. I just ask you to understand that the stability of the Empire depends on this secret. Do I have your agreement on this?'

'I suppose, if I did not agree, then I would be quietly disposed of?'

'Naturally. It would be as if you, and your line, had never existed.'

'Then I agree . . .'

Narcissus smiled. 'Thank you. Vitellius?'

Vitellius nodded at once.

Then Narcissus turned his gaze on Cato, and the young officer felt a chill of fear ripple down his spine. He had no delusions about his expendability in matters of state. Yet he summoned enough courage to stiffen his back and stare back at the Imperial Secretary.

'Centurion, I have watched your career with some interest. You show great promise. Of course, the fates have not always matched the appropriate reward to the services you have rendered the Emperor . . .'

That's putting it mildly, Cato thought, but he nodded modestly.

'You are here because you know about the scrolls, and I need to know that I can trust you, and your friend Macro with that knowledge. I'm sure you understand the need for secrecy, and you have nothing to gain from breathing a word about the scrolls. Indeed, you have everything to lose. Which means I will not have to arrange for both of you to be silenced. That would be a terrible waste of talent. Talent the Empire can ill afford to waste.' Narcissus stretched back in his chair and smiled at Cato.

Cato's heart beat faster as a thought struck him. 'Does that mean I am no longer under sentence of death?'

Narcissus nodded. 'I will give instructions that the sentence be rescinded the moment this meeting is over.'

'Centurion Macro's in the clear as well?'

'Yes.'

'Then we will be available for reappointment to the legions.'

'What else should I do with two such fine officers?'

It was as if a great knot had been loosened in Cato's chest and he could breathe freely again. There was an instant of indignant outrage that he should ever have been the subject of such a judgement in the first place. Then he relented and relished the sense of relief Narcissus' words had given him. The anxiety was over. The shadow of the executioner that had stalked him for months faded away and he felt the great comfort of a man who can look forward to the future again. Soon he and Macro would be back where they belonged: serving with the Eagles.

'We have an understanding then, Centurion? You will not breathe a word about the scrolls to another person as long as you live.'

'Yes, sir.' Cato nodded solemnly. 'You have my word. I'm sure I can speak for Macro as well.'

'I'm sure you can.'

There was a knock at the door, and Narcissus turned towards it. 'Come!'

The servant entered the room and bowed. 'Food and wine have been prepared for these gentlemen, sir.'

'Very well.'

The servant dipped his head and retreated from the room and Narcissus turned back to his visitors.

'There. I think that concludes our business. I'll have your reports as soon as they're ready. You can leave them with my clerk.'

He rose from his chair, and the others rose as well. Then Narcissus ushered them to the door where he clasped hands with Vespasian and bowed his head in respect. 'Once again, my profound gratitude for all that you have accomplished.'

Vespasian nodded tiredly, and left the room. Cato was standing slightly behind and to the side of Vitellius as the Imperial Secretary took his arm and made his farewell. Narcissus bowed, and Vitellius dipped his head forward in acknowledgement. As he did so Cato could not help noticing a purple birthmark on Vitellius' arm just below the hem of his tunic. It was not the mark so much as its shape that caught the centurion's eye – an almost perfect crescent just over an inch long, shaped like a hunting bow.

'Farewell for now, Vitellius,' Narcissus was saying. 'Good fortune go with you.'

Vitellius smiled back. 'Oh, I'm sure it will.'

AUTHOR'S NOTE

The imperial Roman navy has attracted far less research than the legions and there are very few pieces of evidence that have survived to give us a truly accurate view of the ships. For those readers keen to read more about the navy I suggest obtaining a brief overview from Peter Connolly's excellent *Greece and Rome at War*. Beyond that there is a hard-to-find but very worthy read in Chester Starr's *The Imperial Roman Navy*.

There are a few conscious deviations from historical fact. Firstly, I have used the more recent terms of 'port' and 'starboard' to give our Roman sailors some nautical ambience. Secondly, the moving of the Ravenna fleet's base closer to the trading port. In reality the Roman naval bases were kept at a distance from the confusion of commercial shipping. However, I didn't want to tire Macro and Cato out in any long walks into town for a drink!

In addition to the two huge naval bases at Misenum and Ravenna there were additional flotillas scattered around the frontiers of the Empire. The fleets were charged with guarding the sea lanes and providing ad hoc military forces that could be landed wherever there was an urgent need for an armed presence.

Piracy was a fact of life for the seamen and merchants of the Ancient World. Indeed, in the first century BC pirates were boldly landing on the Italian peninsula to abduct travellers on the Appian Way. This hubristic attitude reached its zenith with a raid into the harbour at Ostia, in which the pirates burned a fleet of Roman warships. The audacious act proved to be one step too far for the Roman Senate, who hurriedly empowered Pompey the Great to raise a vast fleet to rid the sea of pirates. This he did in a whirlwind campaign of three months. Thereafter, pirates were forced to operate on a far smaller scale and men like Telemachus would represent an occasional threat to the sea lanes. The action between the Ravenna fleet and the ships of Telemachus would be dwarfed by the scale of the naval actions of the Punic and civil wars.

In this respect, the historic mission of the imperial navy was an unqualified success for nearly three centuries. As Chester Starr notes, their task was 'not to fight battles but to render them impossible'.

Despite Hollywood's representations of Roman galleys being propelled by chains of slaves, the reality is more likely to have been something along the lines of the Renaissance galleys, in which the men at the oars were a mixture of slaves and free men who were paid for their duties.

Now you can buy any of these other bestselling books by **Simon Scarrow** from your bookshop or *direct from his publisher*.

FREE P&P AND UK DELIVERY
(Overseas and Ireland £3.50 per book)

Under the Eagle	£7.99
The Eagle's Conquest	£7.99
When the Eagle Hunts	£7.99
The Eagle and the Wolves	£7.99
The Eagle's Prey	£7.99
The Eagle in the Sand	£7.99
Centurion	£6.99
Young Bloods	£7.99
The Generals	£7.99

TO ORDER SIMPLY CALL THIS NUMBER

01235 400 414

or visit our website: www.headline.co.uk

Prices and availability subject to change without notice.